The Routledge Introduction to Theatre and Performance Studies

Erika Fischer-Lichte's introduction to the discipline of Theatre and Performance Studies is a strikingly authoritative and wide-ranging guide to the study of theatre in all of its forms. Its three-part structure moves from the first steps in starting to think about performance through to the diverse and interrelated concerns required of higher-level study:

Part I – Central concepts for theatre and performance research – introduces the language and key ideas that are used to discuss and think about theatre: concepts of performance; the emergence of meaning; and the theatrical event as an experience shared by actors and spectators. Part I contextualizes these concepts by tracing the history of Theatre and Performance Studies as a discipline.

Part II – Fields, theories, and methods – looks at how to analyze a performance and how to conduct theatre-historiographical research. This section is concerned with the "doing" of Theatre and Performance Studies: establishing and understanding different methodological approaches; using sources effectively; and building theoretical frameworks.

Part III – Pushing boundaries – expands on the lessons of Parts I and II in order to engage with theatre and performance in a global context. Part III introduces the concept of "interweaving performance cultures"; explores the interrelation of theatre with the other arts; and develops a transformative aesthetics of performance.

Case studies throughout the book root its theoretical discussion in theatrical practice. Focused accounts of plays, practitioners, and performances map the development of Theatre and Performance Studies as an academic discipline, and of the theatre itself as an art form. This is the most comprehensive and sophisticated introduction to the field available, written by one of its foremost scholars.

Erika Fischer-Lichte is Professor of Theatre Studies at the Freie Universität Berlin and Chair of the Institute for Advanced Studies on "Interweaving Performance Cultures" founded in 2008. Among her many publications are *Dionysus Resurrected: Performances of Euripides'* The Bacchae *in a Globalizing World* (2014), *Global Ibsen: Performing Multiple Modernities* (2010), *The Transformative Power* *of Performance: A New Aesthetics* (2008, German 2004), and *Theatre, Sacrifice, Ritual: Exploring Forms of Political Theatre* (2005).

Minou Arjomand is Assistant Professor of English at Boston University. Her research focuses on the relationship between theatre and political trials in postwar Germany and the United States.

Ramona Mosse is Lecturer in Theatre Studies at the Freie Universität Berlin and former Fellow of the Institute for Advanced Studies on "Interweaving Performance Cultures". Her work focuses on the interstices between theatre and philosophy.

The Routledge Introduction to Theatre and Performance Studies

Erika Fischer-Lichte

Edited by Minou Arjomand and Ramona Mosse
Translated by Minou Arjomand

Routledge
Taylor & Francis Group

LONDON AND NEW YORK

First published in English 2014
by Routledge
2 Park Square, Milton Park, Abingdon, Oxon OX14 4RN

and by Routledge
711 Third Avenue, New York, NY 10017

Routledge is an imprint of the Taylor & Francis Group, an informa business

Title of the original edition: *Theaterwissenschaft: Eine Einführung in die
Grundlagen des Fachs*
by Erika Fischer-Lichte

© 2009 by Narr Francke Attempto Verlag GmbH + Co. KG

English Language edition:

© 2014 Routledge

British Library Cataloguing in Publication Data
A catalogue record for this book is available from the British Library

Library of Congress Cataloging-in-Publication Data
Fischer-Lichte, Erika.
[Einführung in die Grundlagen des Fachs. English]
The Routledge introduction to theatre and performance studies / by Erika
Fischer-Lichte ; edited by Minou Arjomand and Ramona Mosse;
translated by Minou Arjomand.
pages cm.
Includes bibliographical references and index.
1. Theatre. 2. Theatre–Research. 3. Performing arts. 4. Performing arts–
Research. I. Mosse, Ramona. II. Arjomand, Minou. III. Title.
PN2037.F4813 2013
792–dc23
2013033508

ISBN: 978-0-415-50419-5 (hbk)
ISBN: 978-0-415-50420-1 (pbk)
ISBN: 978-0-203-06873-1 (ebk)

Typeset in Gill Sans
by Cenveo Publisher Services

Printed and bound by CPI Group (UK) Ltd, Croydon, CR0 4YY

Contents

Figures

Tables

Author's preface

This book offers an introduction to Theatre and Performance Studies. It proposes that Theatre and Performance Studies do not comprise two separate fields of study but exist in an intricate symbiosis. They are not rival disciplines; they build on and complement one another. In Germany, Theatre Studies from the outset was founded and theorized as Performance Studies. Both are regarded in this book as academic disciplines based on research and not as a more practically oriented actor/director/designer training. This introduction does not seek to give a collection of "recipes" that must be followed in order to successfully analyze a production, research a historical case study, or write an essay on theory. Instead, it seeks to give students the basic tools to enter the discipline—each from their unique perspective—and to develop and sharpen the research questions that most interest them. Each of the book's three sections gives students a different entry point into the discipline and trains them to formulate their position within Theatre and Performance Studies.

The first part of the book interrogates the key concepts of theatre and performance and sketches their history within the discipline. It traces how the concept of theatre has changed in different languages, cultural contexts, and historical moments. We therefore need to begin by asking what theatre means to us. What sort of events are we referring to when we talk about theatre? The answer to this question inevitably leads to the second foundational concept for the discipline—performance. Like the concept of theatre, the concept of performance has multiple meanings and connotations. In defining performance as constituted in the moment of encounter and interaction between actors and spectators, we also set up the theoretical foundation of the book. At the same time, the first section of the book explores how Theatre Studies as an academic discipline developed in the United States and Germany over the course of the twentieth century. It pays particular attention to the "performative turn" in both cultures at the turn of the nineteenth to the twentieth century and traces the development of Performance Studies as a discipline in the United States during the 1960s and 1970s. The discussions provided in the first section emphasize that neither concepts nor disciplines can be taken for granted but must be considered, and perpetually reconsidered, within changing historical contexts.

In the second part of the book, the three most important fields of Theatre and Performance Studies are introduced: performance analysis, theatre historiography, and approaches to theory, explaining methodologies connected to each of these three fields through examples of various research projects that students might undertake. Ultimately, the choice of method and theoretical approach will depend on the particular questions that interest the student. There is no universal theory or universally applicable method that fits every question. This realization is an enabling one: it positions the student and their observations, interests, and intellectual inclinations at the center.

The third section of the book turns to the possibilities of interdisciplinary exchange among scholars of Theatre and Performance Studies and other disciplines. Since Theatre and Performance Studies is concerned, most fundamentally, with the study of performances, there is no single academic department that teaches all of the skills necessary to study all genres and types of performance. To analyze sports competitions, religious services, rituals, political gatherings, demonstrations, courtroom proceedings, etc., we can employ the methods of performance analysis. In order to adequately understand these performances in their contexts, we also need the specific expertise of scholars of religion, politics, law, sociology, anthropology, etc. For researchers, the pervasiveness of performance opens up interdisciplinary collaborations across fields and disciplines. For students, the open-ended nature of theatre and performance research is both a challenge and a possibility. It encourages students to use their skills in performance analysis, theatre history, and theoretical work to interpret genres of performances that are outside the realm of theatre and performance art. At the same time, though, it demonstrates that we must be aware of the limitations of our own approaches, and that certain research projects require cooperation across disciplines.

If this introduction to Theatre and Performance Studies is able to help students to develop their own research interests and questions and to find their own way into the discipline, it has accomplished its purpose.

Berlin, April 2013
Erika Fischer-Lichte

Editors' preface

This book started out as *Theaterwissenschaft: Eine Einführung in die Grundlagen des Fachs* (to translate literally, *Theatre Studies: An Introduction to the Foundations of the Discipline*). The title as it stands now—*The Routledge Introduction to Theatre and Performance Studies*—reflects the more substantive changes required by a transposition of the work from a German to an Anglo-American context. The German *Theaterwissenschaft* conceives of Theatre and Performance Studies as a single discipline. The disciplinary roots of *Theaterwissenschaft* place performance events, as opposed to dramatic texts, at the core of their subject of study. Such focus on performance events implies an understanding of the *Theater-* in *Theaterwissenschaft* as an umbrella term for *all* the performing arts as well as some cultural performances. The new title for this English edition marks what we hope may prove a productive tension between the different conceptions of the discipline across national contexts. Our edition also significantly expands on the original by drawing on additional examples of Anglo-American theatre performances and bringing these examples into conversation with the work of German and Continental European artists.

A history of the disciplines of *Theaterwissenschaft* on the one hand, and Theatre Studies and Performance Studies on the other, are the subject of the second chapter of this book. There is also a more fundamental linguistic difference in the ways that we speak, write, and conceive of performance in German and English. In contrast to the word *perform*, the German *aufführen* is a more narrowly focused term that refers specifically to a live theatrical context and is distinct from *ausführen*, which describes the doing of a particular task; to *perform* subsumes the two and allows them to be aspects of a single concept. Initially *Aufführung* seems less versatile than *performance* (and for that reason, *performance* has entered the German vocabulary). Yet, the power of the concept of *Aufführung* lies in the underlying conviction that the encounter of performers and spectators is a fundamentally transformative act. While Anglo-American scholarship often focuses on the ideas of performance and performativity as *doing*, German theatre scholarship has placed particular emphasis on the role of the spectator and the subjective experience of a performance as material for scholarly work.

The mechanisms and structures of live performance or *Aufführung* form the core of the field of Theatre and Performance Studies as Erika Fischer-Lichte frames it here. We believe that in drawing attention to the relationship between performers and spectators as a central field of inquiry, this book will offer some fresh approaches for Anglo-American readers. We especially hope that this book's emphasis on the agency of the spectators in constituting the performance will inspire students by emphasizing the value of their subjective experience of the performance and its central place in theatre and performance analysis.

Minou Arjomand & Ramona Mosse
Boston and Berlin, January 2014

Prologue: Is everything theatre?

During the 1723 carnival, Professor of Medicine Andreas Ottomar Goelicke invited Frankfurt-on-the Oder's high society to the following presentation:

TO THE

DISSECTION

OF A FEMALE CORPSE

OF A CHILD MURDERESS

taking place this coming Saturday and the following days

from five to six o'clock in the afternoon

in

THE ANATOMICAL THEATRE

together with an introductory lecture

about

the collaboration of anatomy and surgery

we invite

with due regard and officiousness:

THE HONORABLE LORDS

AND HONORABLE BARONS

as well as

THE NOBLE AND ARISTOCRATIC

STUDENTS

OF ALL THE DEPARTMENTS

AND ALL OTHER INTERESTED

PATRONS

OF ANATOMICAL DEMONSTRATIONS

ANDREAS OTTOMAR GOELICKE

Doctor and Public Professor of Medicine as well as the circle

Lebuliensis

Physicus Ordinarius[1]

****

In his *Reminiscences* (1875), the British actor William Macready described the actress Sarah Siddons' acting in a performance of Nicholas Rowe's play *Tamerlane* at Drury Lane Theatre in 1819.

> In the last act, when, by order of the tyrant, her lover Monesis is strangled before her face, she worked herself up to such a pitch of agony, and gave such terrible reality to the few convulsive words she tried to utter, as she sank into a lifeless heap before her murderer, that the audience for a few moments remained in a hush of astonishment, as if awestruck; they then clamored for the curtain to be dropped, and insisting on the manager's appearance, received from him, in answer to their vehement inquiries, the assurance that Mrs. Siddons was alive, and recovering from the temporary indisposition that her exertions had caused. They were satisfied as regarded her, but would not suffer the performance to be resumed. As an instance of the impression this great actress made on individuals who might be supposed insensible, from familiarity, to the power of acting, Holman turned to my father, when Mrs. Siddons had fallen, and looking aghast in his face, said: "Macready, do I look as pale as you?" a strange question, but one not unintelligible, under the extraordinary excitement of the moment.

(Macready 1875: 146)

***

In his performance *Visiting Hours* (1992), Bob Flanagan—who was suffering from a terminal illness that affected the lungs and digestive system—had a sick room built in a New York gallery. Connected to oxygen tanks and surrounded by pictures of his sado-masochistic experiments, he lay in bed, welcoming visitors. As in a hospital, they came during specific visiting hours to call on the invalid. They were free to enter and exit the room, to observe the pictures or the sick person, or—depending on his state—to converse with him. Bob Flanagan died four years after the performance.

***

Angela Jansen, a woman suffering from the debilitating disease ALS (amyotrophic lateral sclerosis), was the star of Christoph Schlingensief's production *Art and Vegetables: Theatre a(L)s Sickness* (Volksbühne at Rosa-Luxemburg-Platz Berlin, 2004). Her bed was placed in the middle of the audience. ALS had left her fully paralyzed and she could only communicate through a computer that translated her blinking into sentences. During the performance the sentences that she entered into the computer would appear on large screens. Mediated by technology, she discussed topics including her struggle with her health insurance, which initially refused to pay for the computer, contending that such expensive equipment was a waste given her low life expectancy of about six months. At the beginning, the audience was unsettled by the presence of a woman who refused to hide her slow death from the gaze of others, and instead wanted to communicate about it in the public space of the theatre within a thematic frame that was at times comic. As the evening progressed, the situation became more relaxed: a certain joviality emerged, and occasionally the actions onstage were even greeted with laughter. In a sense, a new *ars moriendi*, a new art of dying, was invented in this performance.

***

These four examples, which come from the eighteenth, nineteenth, twentieth, and twenty-first centuries, share the common theme of death or dying. But what else do they have in common that qualifies them to be our first examples in an introduction to Theatre and Performance Studies?

In the first case, people are invited to an anatomical dissection in a building called the *Theatrum anatomicum*. The second example describes an actor's art of portraying the death of a dramatic character on stage. In the third case, a critically ill performance artist places himself and his sickness on view in a gallery. The final example is of a production that offers fictional action on stage, portrayed mostly by disabled, non-professional actors, while a terminally ill woman lies among the spectators and communicates with them about her illness. Taking into account the radical differences between these productions, we might ask ourselves: are they all theatre?

People who begin to study theatre usually believe that they know exactly what their subject is. But what do we really mean when we talk about theatre? What sort of events do we refer to? Can all of the above examples be understood as theatre, and thus seen as appropriate research subjects? Historians of science and medicine also study anatomical dissections, to use only one example. Likewise, art historians claim performance art as part of their field. This tension raises the question: what does the field of Theatre Studies actually encompass? To put it in another way: how can we define the concept of theatre and with it our field of study?

The first two chapters of this book are devoted to answering the following questions:

- How can we define *theatre*?
- How can we delineate the field of *Theatre and Performance Studies* from this definition of theatre?

Note

1 Invitation quoted in Bergmann (2004), 177.

Part I

Central concepts of theatre and performance research

Chapter 1

The concept of theatre

The English word "theatre," as in many other Indo-European languages (for example, German *theater*, French *théâtre*, Spanish and Italian *teatro*, and Russian *teatr*), derives from the Greek word *theatron*, which comes from *thea* ("show") or *theásthai* ("to look on"). The word *theatron* was used to describe a gathering place for celebratory, cultic, political, and athletic events. The arrangement of rows of seats and viewing platforms allowed spectators to watch the entrance of processions, dances with song and music, performances of tragedies and comedies, athletic competitions, and various acts of self-fashioning by the polis of Athens. The term was used in a general sense to denote a place for watching a wide variety of events.

In English, the term "theatre" was first used in the fourteenth century to designate an open space where people could watch spectacles of various sorts. The term referred to any open space for watching, i.e. natural as well as man-made spaces. Starting in the sixteenth century, the term "theatre" began to refer primarily to enclosed buildings, a definition that has prevailed to the present day. Around the same time as the term "theatre" came to be associated with designated, institutional performance spaces, theatre also came to be understood as *drama*; dramatic texts were studied at Oxford and Cambridge primarily for learning rhetoric and understanding classical antiquity (Carlson 1993).

The term "theatre" was introduced in German slightly later, around the end of the sixteenth and beginning of the seventeenth century. The term was initially used as in the Latin *theatrum* to mean a space where something worth seeing occurs. The concept thus included any space for demonstration and ostentation, whether a place for public execution, an anatomical dissection, or an elevated location from which one could watch the actions on a battlefield. In the second half of the eighteenth century, the usage of the term became more specific, referring to performances of drama, opera, and ballets; in other words, to institutional art-theatre. Spectacles such as circuses, variety shows, stripteases, and colonial expositions that developed in the nineteenth century fell outside the category of "theatre" proper.

The historical avant-garde movement of the twentieth century (c. 1900–35) both narrowed and expanded the concept of theatre. The avant-garde understood theatre as an autonomous art rather than a medium for bringing the art of literature to an audience. They saw theatre as fundamentally different from the other arts because of the materials it uses—namely, the human body in space. At the same time, the avant-garde sought to close the gap between art and life, and to bring theatre into reality. To do so, the avant-garde expanded the concept of theatre once more to include any kind of exhibition, demonstration, or spectacle: the performances of circus artists, clowns, and entertainers; happenings *avant la lettre* that Dadaists and Surrealists staged on streets, in cafés, churches, and parliament; May Day celebrations, demonstrations, and sports festivals organized by trade unions and political parties; World Fairs; day-to-day encounters like the one Bertolt Brecht famously describes in his "Street Scene"—all could be termed theatre.[1] The concept of theatre thus radically expanded in the first decades of the twentieth century to include a plethora of activities that previously had not been understood as theatre. The rise of Fascism and Stalinism and the advent of the Second World War, however, brought the avant-garde's expansive understanding of theatre to an end, and by mid-century, the term had returned to the more limited meaning it had had during the nineteenth century.

In the 1960s, theatre artists in Western cultures started to reflect seriously once more on the concept of theatre. Once again rejecting the established bourgeois literary theatre, practitioners such as the Polish director Jerzy Grotowski redefined theatre as that which "occurs between the audience and the actor" (Grotowski 1968). At the same time, there was an exodus from theatre buildings. Theatre began to be performed in streets and squares, parks and circus tents, store windows, former factories, bus depots, slaughterhouses, living rooms, even on the facades of sky-scrapers.

In Europe and the United States, "Free Groups" and performance ensembles came together that—partly as combined living and working communes—experimented with new forms of theatrical expression. Among other things, they propagated street theatre and looked to theatrical traditions of earlier centuries such as processions and spectacles with jugglers, acrobats, fire-eaters, fools, and clowns. They would blithely mix high and low art: classical or modern dance joined with music hall, circus, pantomime, and striptease. Individual performers created a wide range of one-man and one-woman shows. Artists, primarily coming from the visual arts or music such as Alan Kaprow, Herrmann Nitsch, Joseph Beuys, and John Cage, created new theatrical genres such as happenings, action art, and performance art.

Around the same time, both academic and popular writers showed a renewed interest in using theatre as a wide-ranging metaphor. Theatre's metaphorical power goes back to antiquity. The concept was used to designate the world (*theatrum mundi*) as well as human life (*theatrum vitae humanae*). In the seventeenth century, this metaphor became commonplace. "Theatre" and "World," or "Human Life," seemed fundamentally related, and were understood in reference to one another. Life at the European courts was increasingly staged as a theatrical performance. Whether we think of the rigid court ceremonies common in the Madrid and Vienna courts, or the French ceremonies centered around the King's *lever*—his morning rituals in which every step was prescribed—we see that the court turned into a stage and courtiers and royalty into actors. This phenomenon was particularly apparent during courtly festivals. Here, every festival space became a stage. Members of the court appeared as actors; the king or emperor played himself.

Theatre was not just used as a metaphor for life at court. Aside from its extensive use in theatre itself (for example in Shakespeare, Calderón, Gryphius, or Lohenstein), it found its way into a wide variety of tracts and treatises, including philosophical, scientific, technical, and geographical discourses. A multitude of publications flooded the European market that had the words "theatre" or "theatrum" in their titles, referring to the prevailing idea of theatre as a show place, or a place in which something worth knowing is put on view. Some examples are: *Theatrum Orbis Terrarum* (Antwerp 1570), *Theatrum Virtutis et Honoris* (Nuremberg 1606), *Theatrum Chemicum* (Argentorati 1613–61), *Theatrum Florae* (Paris 1622), *Theatrum Insectorum* (London 1634), *Theatrum Europaeum* (Frankfurt 1634–1738), *Theatrum Machinarum* (Nuremberg 1661), *Theatrum Pacis* (Nuremberg 1663–85). These books were metaphorically designated as show places, places where a subject was presented to the reflection of the reader. This usage also reveals the etymological connection between *theatron* (or *theatrum* in Latin) and *theoria*, both of which derive from *thea* ("show").

In the 1970s, there was a comparable expansion in the metaphorical use of the term "theatre." The metaphor of theatre was used more and more frequently in a variety of different cultural realms: by journalists and politicians, CEOs and trade unions, clergy and scientists. It was not only the term "theatre" that was used metaphorically, but also related terms such as the stage, masks, entrances, roles, and staging. Indeed, its usage has become ubiquitous. Take, for example, this series of headlines referring to the 2012 presidential elections in the United States: "Backstage with the Santorums," "Gingrich Pulls Back Curtain on 'Predatory' Capitalism," "The Curtain has Come Down on the Republican Party," "Mitt Romney is Ready for his Starring Role," "Obama Makes a Quiet Entrance into the 2012 Race," and so on.

Likewise, the metaphorical use of the term "theatre" is often seen in academic contexts. In the humanities, more and more studies use the concept of theatre for a range of purposes. Michel Foucault opens his "Theatrum philosophicum," Jean-François Lyotard observes "the philosophical and political stage," Jean Baudrillard ruminates on the "stage of the body." The sociologist Erving Goffman studies "the presentation of the self in everyday life" through the metaphor of "front stage" and "backstage" behavior. The anthropologist Clifford Geertz researches the "theatre-state" in Bali in the nineteenth century; the historian Hayden White illuminates "historical realism as tragedy"; Richard Sennett pursues the "shifts in roles on the stage and in the street" while the psychologist Joyce McDougall dissects the "theatre of the soul." Even the physicist Heinz von Foerster speaks of "proscenium philosophy," designating a specific view of the world, and explicitly references a specific concept of theatre. The list is endless.

Since the 1970s, theatre has turned into a key concept in the humanities and social sciences. One of the most pervasive concepts in much scholarly work over the past few decades is the term "theatricality." It is used both for a variety of performances—for example, scholars writing about ritual describe rituals as "theatrical"—and for *mise-en-scènes* beyond the theatre.[2]

In the face of this expanded concept of theatre, it is crucial for scholars and students of Theatre and Performance Studies to define our concept of theatre and thus the subject of our field. If everything is theatre, and theatre can be approached from a wide variety of disciplines with a variety of research questions and methods, it raises the question why we need a separate discipline to study theatre at all. Unless we set specific boundaries for our concept of theatre, this question is difficult to answer. And until we answer the question, it does not make much sense to talk about the sub-fields, theories, and methods of Theatre and Performance Studies.

Theatre and Performance Studies differs from disciplines such as Philosophy, History, and Philology in so far as it has not been around for centuries. In fact, it was only established as a discipline in Western universities during the twentieth century. It is therefore to be expected that a discussion of how and why Theatre and Performance Studies developed is connected to the question of why we need Theatre and Performance Studies *today*.

Further Reading

On the "Theatrum Mundi"

Eggington, W. (2003) *How the World Became a Stage: Presence, Theatricality and the Question of Modernity*, Albany: State University of New York Press.
Sennett, R. (1977) *The Fall of Public Man*, New York: Knopf.

On Theatre and Science

Schramm, H., L. Schwarte, and J. Lazardig (eds.) (2005) *Collection, Laboratory, Theatre: Scenes of Knowledge in the Seventeenth Century*, Berlin/New York: Walter de Gruyter.

On Theatricality

Davis, T. C. and T. Postlewait (ed.) (2003) *Theatricality*, Cambridge: Cambridge University Press.
Féral, J. (ed.) (2002) *Theatricality*, Madison: University of Wisconsin Press.

Fischer-Lichte, E. (ed.) (1995) "Theatricality: A Key Concept in Theatre and Cultural Studies," *Theatre Research International*, 20/2: 85–118.

Fried, M. (1980) *Absorption and Theatricality: Painting and the Beholder in the Age of Diderot*, Berkeley: University of California Press.

Puchner, M. (2002) *Stage Fright: Modernism, Anti-Theatricality, and Drama*, Baltimore: Johns Hopkins University Press.

Weber, S. (2004) *Theatricality as Medium*, New York: Fordham University Press.

Notes

1 In "The Street Scene: A Basic Model for Epic Theatre," Brecht describes the model of acting and audience reception in Epic Theatre through the everyday example of a traffic accident. A witness who has seen the accident recounts what happened to a crowd of bystanders. In his critical account of the event, the witness at times imitates the drivers who caused the accident, but the bystanders are never tricked into thinking of the witness himself as a driver as they watch and listen to him. For Brecht, this critical approach to acting and audience reception was part of a political and aesthetic rejection of what he terms "Aristotelian theatre" (reprinted in Brecht 1964: 121–129).

2 As, for example, Michael Fried famously did in relation to the particular composition of painting in his book *Absorption and Theatricality: Painting and the Beholder in the Age of Diderot* (Fried 1980).

Chapter 2

The history of the discipline

The academic discipline that comprises Theatre and Performance Studies has had a different history in different national contexts, and has often been connected to both innovations in theatre and broader political developments. The first country to develop the discipline of Theatre Studies as we think of it today was Germany. In German universities during the eighteenth and nineteenth centuries, drama was taught in literature departments as the study of a particular genre of literary text (to some extent, this is still true of the way that drama is taught in many universities around the world). In the early twentieth century, however, Theatre Studies began to develop as its own discipline.

The most important figure in creating and molding this new field was Max Herrmann (1865–1942). Herrmann argued that the new discipline of Theatre Studies should focus not on literary texts but on performance, arguing that performance was the most important element of theatre. In 1918, Herrmann articulated a difference between drama and theatre that is central to the way Theatre Studies is now conceived not only in German-speaking but also in English-speaking countries. He wrote that theatre and drama are "fundamentally opposites … drama is a literary creation of one author, while theatre is the accomplishment of the public and those serving it" (Herrmann 1918).

Rather than focusing primarily on a literary text, and asking how that text was portrayed, and if the portrayal was appropriate, Herrmann emphasized the relationship between actors and audiences. He argued that a performance was a sort of game, in which everyone present participated. He even went so far as to argue that the actual creator of performing arts is the audience, and not the writer, performers, or director. Herrmann was interested not only in how spectators thought about what they saw, but also in the process of perception and their physical reactions.

Herrmann's conception of performance and of the discipline of Theatre Studies can be connected to contemporary innovations in German theatre. Above all, Herrmann was inspired by the work of Max Reinhardt (1873–1943), whose productions turned away from the traditional proscenium stage. In productions such as *Sumurun* (1910), *Oedipus Rex* (1910), and the *Oresteia* (1911), Reinhardt collapsed the physical distance between actors and spectators. In each of these productions, actors would speak and act from among the audience. In addition to bringing the actors and audiences closer to one another, it individualized spectatorial experience: lacking a clearly controlled perspective, spectators had to decide which events to follow. In the pantomime *Sumurun*, for example, Reinhardt had a *hanamichi* (a wide catwalk, typical in Japanese Kabuki theatre) built to extend across the audience seating. Actors would perform scenes on the *hanamichi*, right in the middle of the audience, as other scenes were simultaneously performed on stage. It became impossible to see everything that was happening at any given time. Interspersing actors with spectators also ensured that spectators would see not only the actors, but the reactions of the other spectators as well. In these productions the emphasis was not on the fictive world as described in the text of the play, but rather on real bodies inhabiting real space.

While developing his concept of performance, Herrmann drew on Reinhardt's productions; Herrmann, like Reinhardt, believed that the real bodies of the actors in the real space of the theatre were as important as the fictive world displayed on stage. For both, actors were not simply symbols of dramatic figures, but also real bodies. Herrmann's interest in theatre as performance, and in the bodies of performers themselves, has been central to the way that Theatre Studies developed in German-speaking countries. Indeed, Herrmann's juxtaposition between drama and theatre is at the heart of disciplinary debates that continue to this day. Because of Herrmann's focus on the performance, Theatre Studies in Germany was founded *as* Performance Studies.

Other key figures for the development of the discipline include the Munich University professor Artur Kutscher (1878–1960), who focused on the mimic and expressive quality of performance and whose research extended to the non-literary folk and religious theatre traditions in Southern Germany and Europe. His "Kutscher-seminar" on theatre criticism drew many practical students of theatre, among them Erwin Piscator and Bertolt Brecht. Another important opponent of subsuming theatre into the field of literary studies was Carl Niessen (1890–1969), the founder of the theatre museum in Cologne. Instead he wanted to connect the new discipline to anthropology. He sought to investigate all kinds of performances from various cultures and historical periods, ranging from performances of classical drama to festivals, rituals, ceremonies, and games—what we would today call cultural performances. In some crucial aspects, Niessen anticipated the shape of the American discipline that would be called Performance Studies.

In the United States, the development of Theatre Studies as an academic discipline was equally multilayered but included a more marked debate about theory and practice. While in Germany Herrmann, Kutscher, and Niessen were arguing for a discipline based on performance rather than literature, George Pierce Baker at Harvard and later Yale University and Brander Matthews at Columbia University were making similar efforts to reform the academic curriculum. Matthews—initially trained as a lawyer—came to the stage as a theatre critic and in 1892 was appointed to the newly created chair in dramatic literature at Columbia University, the first of its kind in the United States. He emphasized that "the drama ... does not lie wholly within the boundaries of literature" (Matthews 1903: 340); instead, the physicality of the performance as well as the role of the audience raised drama to an art form in its own right, according to Matthews. His collection of theatre objects and memorabilia, now known as the Brander Matthews Collection, demonstrates that he envisioned the study of theatre as something other than the study of dramatic texts. Matthews understood theatre primarily as performance, composed of many elements beyond the dramatic text.

In 1905, George Pierce Baker took a somewhat different approach by championing playwriting in his "Workshop 47" at Harvard University, set up to allow students (among them Eugene O'Neill, Philip Barry, and Thomas Wolfe) to see their own works staged. Baker defined "a play [a]s a cooperative effort—of author, actor, producer, and even audience" (Baker 1919: 11). He subsequently led the newly instituted drama school at Yale University and directed its university theatre (1925–33), further highlighting the important interweaving of theory and practice in the field of theatre. In the 1930s, the Austrian scholar Alois Nagler also arrived at Yale to teach drama. Nagler was influenced by Herrmann's research in theatre history and sought to establish theatre research as its own historical discipline. But while Herrmann was interested in the interrelationships between the physical bodies of actors and spectators, Nagler and his students prioritized the material elements of staging such as set designs and costumes (Carlson 2008: 3). Meanwhile in the Midwest, the Carnegie Mellon University's School of Drama, founded in 1914, became the first to offer a degree-granting program in drama with an emphasis on practical training that prepared for a career in the performing arts as well as radio, and later film and television. In 1921, the Northwestern University School of Speech emerged out of the School of Oratory with a curriculum that included courses in debating, theatre, radio, and later film. Finally, the University of Iowa was the first to grant doctoral degrees in theatre in 1929. In effect, practical and academic training came to exist side by side in the United States' university system, albeit increasingly located in different departments. Theatre Studies turned increasingly toward practical training while the theory of theatre and drama remained within the domain of literature departments, a development that carried its own set of challenges and tensions (Roach 1999).

In the 1970s, a third field developed that sought to emphasize the academic research and study of performance outside of the familiar frame of drama and theatre. At New York University, Richard Schechner ushered in the new discipline of Performance Studies, which emphasized the study of performance as an interdisciplinary topic. He sought to expand the field to all forms of cultural performance, of which theatre was just one possible focus (and Western theatre an even narrower specialization). Performance Studies was designed to bring together a range of disciplines such as anthropology, sociology, and musicology. Its focus was on live embodied performance as it occurred both in art and in other social contexts. Schechner drew on new developments in the theatre, or rather on performance art as it developed in opposition to the theatre. He also was deeply influenced by ritual perfor- mance, and it was in his collaboration with the cultural anthropologist Victor Turner that Schechner was able to develop his elaborate theoretical framework for Performance Studies. Schechner's framework relies on the interdependent concepts of "social drama" and "aesthetic drama," which highlight the ubiquity of performance outside of the theatre, as well as the idea of "restored behavior" which operates not as the expression of an individual self but instead as a kind of physicalized citation of social and cultural behavior. Schechner formulated an attack on Theatre Studies and Literature Departments that split the study of performance into the three different strands Theatre Studies, Performance Studies, and Drama, now often coexisting in the field across the Anglo-American university system. Self-standing Theatre and/or Performance Studies departments have become increasingly common in all of these countries over the past decades. Of course there are also exceptions: neither Cambridge nor Oxford Uni- versity have departments in any of those fields, reflecting a long-standing prejudice against theatre, perceived as popular entertainment and unworthy of serious scholarship.

From its inception in the United States, Performance Studies was involved in larger political debates that were radically changing the face of universities (Jackson 2004). The twentieth century saw a democratization of universities. With the changing demographic of the student body—that is, the integration of women and ethnic minorities into a traditionally white male university system—a reform of the curriculum gained in importance. Students and pro- fessors demanded that universities also integrate the study of non-Western cultures and works by women and people of color. In turn, critics argued that universities were abandoning the great works of Western philosophy and lit- erature in favor of inferior works, and were undermining traditional European and American values. These debates—commonly called the Culture Wars— reached their height in the 1990s, though they continue today.

It was in this context that Richard Schechner gave a seminal keynote address at the national conference of the Association for Theatre in Higher Education (ATHE), arguing that theatre departments embrace performance, and with performance, a more open curriculum:

> Theatre departments should become "performance departments." Perfor- mance is about more than the enactment of Eurocentric drama. Perfor- mance engages intellectual, social, cultural, historical, and artistic life in a broad sense. Performance combines theory and practice. Performance studied and practiced interculturally can be at the core of a "well-rounded education." That is because performed acts, whether actual or virtual,

more than the written word, connect and negotiate the many cultural, personal, group, regional, and world systems comprising today's realities.
(Schechner 1992: 9)

These new "performance departments" would study not only "the arts," but also a range of popular entertainments, rituals, politics, and interactions between people, which Milton Singer calls "cultural performances" (Singer 1959). While Schechner linked Performance Studies to the incorporation of non-Western performances in curricula, close ties developed between Performance Studies, Feminism, and Queer Studies, based on shared interests in performance and the body. The most prominent book to connect feminism, queer studies, and performance is Judith Butler's *Gender Trouble* (1990), which introduced the idea of gender performativity, arguing that gender is not a pre-existing identity, but rather is constituted through a set of performances. As we can see, the creation of Performance Studies and arguments about the focus of the field are connected to much broader political debates about the university and society at large.

Whereas in German scholarship a focus on performance developed from the presuppositions of the field, as conceived by Herrmann, in the United States Performance Studies was introduced specifically as a rejection of Drama and Theatre departments. Despite this rupture, however, the disciplines of Theatre Studies and Performance Studies have approached each other over the years. Students and professors in Theatre departments may be less likely than their colleagues in Performance Studies to focus primarily on political performances, or to rely heavily on ethnographic methods. Still, the study of theatre as performance rather than text, an attention to the bodies of performers and spectators, and a focus on non-Western performance as well as popular culture have become a central part of many Theatre Studies programs.

This book adheres to a particular conception of the field that integrates Theatre and Performance Studies—one that is in line with the German tradition of the field going back to Max Herrmann. It understands the discipline broadly as the study of performances. In other words, we are adopting Niessen's call for an expanded definition of performance beyond Western institutionalized theatre, in order to include a range of popular entertainments, rituals, and political and communal interactions between people across a variety of cultures. Such an expanded definition demands an interdisciplinary approach to the discipline as a whole.

While Theatre and Performance Studies is a discipline concerned with performance in a wide range of contexts and cultures, the overwhelming majority of the examples that we discuss in the first and second parts of the book are taken from institutional Western theatre. This has several reasons. The art of theatre is a privileged subject for Theatre Studies because it can be used as a model that can help us to work out the fundamental aspects of performance and to develop and try out theoretical and methodological approaches to performance. Studying theatre allows us to build up our skills at understanding and analyzing performances that occur outside of institutional theatres. We can later use these skills to analyze other forms of performance as well, keeping in mind their different social and political contexts. In addition, the study of performance demands cultural and linguistic expertise. For this reason, this book focuses primarily on the theatre cultures (European and American) most familiar to us. To adequately and responsibly discuss theatre cultures elsewhere in the world one needs both a linguistic and cultural expertise that goes beyond the scope of an introductory textbook on Theatre and Performance Studies.

Since the subject of Theatre Studies is performance, our next step must be to understand what sorts of processes fit into the term performance. Max Herrmann's idea of performance was groundbreaking, but it was only sketchily articulated. The next chapter of this book will clarify the concept of performance. The question we ask here is not "What are performances?" That question implies that there is a single correct and immutable answer. Instead, our question will be: "How does the discipline define performance today?" This question has a variety of possible answers, each of which opens up new perspectives on the state and future of Theatre and Performance Studies.

Further Reading

On Theatre and Performance Studies

Bial, H. (ed.) (2004) *The Performance Studies Reader*, London/New York: Routledge.

Jackson, S. (2004) *Professing Performance: Theatre in the Academy from Philology to Performativity*, Cambridge: Cambridge University Press.

Reinelt, J. and J. Roach (2007) *Critical Theory and Performance: Revised and Enlarged Edition*, Ann Arbor: University of Michigan Press.

Schechner, R. (1985) *Between Theatre and Anthropology*, Philadelphia: University of Pennsylvania Press.

Chapter 3

The concept of performance

Our starting point for thinking about performance is Max Herrmann's definition: "a game in which everyone, actors and spectators, participates." Following Herrmann, we can define a performance as any event in which all the participants find themselves in the same place at the same time, partaking in a circumscribed set of activities. The participants can be actors or spectators, and the roles of these actors and spectators may switch, so that the same person could fulfill the part of an actor for a given period of time, and then turn into an observer. The performance is created out of the interactions of participants. By this definition the term "performance" can refer to a wide variety of events: a traditional theatre performance in a proscenium theatre in which the actors and audience are strictly separated; a "Happening" in which these roles are not so clearly demarcated; a soccer game with spectators as well as a Church mass; a wedding as well as a political convention; a funeral as well as a World's Fair. In the third section of the book, we will discuss the extent to which these various types of performances can (or should) be the subject of Theatre Studies.

In this section, we discuss four central characteristics of performance: its mediality, materiality, semioticity, and aestheticity. According to our definition, a performance is inseparable from the bodily co-presence of various groups of people who come together as actors and spectators: this is linked to the medial conditions of performance, or its *mediality*. The term "medial conditions" refers to the specific conditions of transmission that are created by the simultaneous presence of actors and spectators.

In addition, we define performance by its transience. This transience is integral to the *materiality* of performance. Unlike processes of production in which people with various functions work together to create a product—a car, a washing machine, a building, etc.—a performance does not create a product. It creates itself. It is transitory and ephemeral, even if the performance involves spaces, bodies, and objects that outlast the performance.

Next, we will explore how meaning is created in performance. Everything that is brought forth and shown as a sign—whether it is a movement, a sound, or a thing—is only present for a certain amount of time and cannot be re-read or observed multiple times, like a text or picture. How meaning is created in performances through such signs can be termed the *semiotic* dimension, or *semioticity* of performances.

Finally, there is the question of what sort of *experience* a performance enables for its participants. Taken together, bodily co-presence, transience, materiality, and semioticity enable the aesthetic experience of a performance by the participants. We will define the aesthetic experience of performance more closely and distinguish it from experiences generated in other contexts. As we begin to explore all of these facets of performance, it will become apparent that they are intrinsically interrelated; it is only for the sake of clarity that we deal with each of them separately in the sections that follow.

Bodily Co-presence

A performance exists in the moment of bodily co-presence of "actors" and "spectators." Performances therefore differ essentially from texts and artifacts. Texts and artifacts are products that exist separately from their creator(s); they are not tied to the bodily presence of their creators. These products can be encountered at different times, and often in different places. Each time a person reads a text, observes a painting, or watches a film, they may have a different experience of the same work of art. But at the same time, the materiality of the text, painting, or film remains unchanged.

In contrast, a performance has very different *medial conditions* stemming from its reliance on bodily co-presence. While some of those present—the actors—move through and act in a given space, the others—the spectators—perceive their actions and react to them. These reactions can be purely "inward," i.e. imaginative and cognitive processes. But many of these reactions are outwardly perceptible. In a theatre performance, for example, spectators can laugh, cheer, sigh, groan, sob, cry; they shuffle their feet, squirm in their chairs, they cough and sneeze, crumple cough drop wrappers; they eat and drink; they whisper or comment loudly on what's happening on stage; they yell "bravo," "da capo," applaud and stamp their feet or whistle and boo; they stand up noisily, walk out of the auditorium, and slam the doors behind them.

Both actors and spectators can perceive these reactions. They feel, hear, or see them. In turn, actors and spectators react to these perceptions. The actors' acting can become more or less intense, their voices can become louder and grating or can pull the spectators in; the actors can feel energized and add gags and other kinds of improvisation. Perceiving the reactions of fellow spectators can also change spectators' perceptions. Their degree of participation, interest, or suspense may be raised or lowered, their laughter may increase, even become convulsive, or could stop and literally stick in their throats. They might start to call each other to order, or fight with and insult each other. Whatever the actors do has an effect on the spectators, and whatever the spectators do has an effect on the actors as well as other spectators.

Performances are created out of the encounter of actors and spectators; we can term this interplay the "autopoietic feedback loop." Whatever happens before the start and after the end of the performance is fundamentally different from the performance itself. For its duration, the course a performance takes is contingent. This is the case for all performances, not only performances that are designed to incorporate audience participation, in which case the contingency of the performance is even more pronounced. That is not to say that it is common for an actor playing Othello to be prevented from performing his carefully rehearsed murder scene with Desdemona by spectators rushing onto the stage to stop him (even though this has happened!). Rather, the degree and extent of the audience's sympathy can be perceived by the actors and is itself capable of influencing the intensity of the portrayal, which again can impact audience reaction.

Without a doubt it is the actors who set crucial parameters for the performance. The foundation of a performance lies in a given staging concept or set of rules that all the cast knows and follows. Theatre performances, for example, involve a staging process—usually weeks of rehearsals in contemporary theatre—in which strategies are developed, rehearsed, and fixed in a way that determines the manner in which people, objects, and noises will appear (and disappear) on stage during the performance. Depending on the form of theatre, on the director, stage designer, and actors, the staging may also consciously create and plan situations that open space for unplanned, unstaged actions, behavior, and occurrences. But even in cases in which the actors meticulously follow a completely predetermined staging, they are incapable of completely controlling the course of the performance. The reactions of the audience can give the performance a new twist.

For this and other reasons, it is important to clearly differentiate between the concepts of "staging" and "performance." Staging refers to the strategies used in advance to fix the time, duration, and manner of the appearance of people, things, and noises in a space. Performance refers to everything that happens during the staged event—in other words, the totality of the interplay between what happens on stage and the reactions of the spectators. A performance is ultimately created by everyone present and escapes the control of any one individual. In this sense it is contingent. The concept of contingency emphasizes the involvement of all participants and their influence on the course of the performance, including the interplay between these influences. The participants are co-creators who, to different degrees and in different ways, affect the shape of a performance. The interplay of their actions and behavior constitutes the performance, while the performance constitutes them as actors and spectators. It is only when they take part in the performance that individuals turn into actors and spectators.[1]

This particular quality of performances is termed "performative." The philosopher John L. Austin coined the term in the 1950s—around the same time that theatre scholars were developing new concepts of theatre. Austin first used the term in a lecture series at Harvard University called *How to Do Things with Words* (1955). He used the term for verbal expressions that perform an action, such as "I promise," "I curse you," or "With this ring, I thee wed." Such utterances don't just say something; they perform the action of which they speak. They are self-referential in that they designate what they are doing, and constitute reality in that they create the social reality of which they speak (Austin 1963). In this sense, we should remember that the word "performance" stems from the verb "to perform," i.e. to execute an action.

Theatre reflects on its own performativity. Some contemporary productions are staged in a way that collapses or reverses the roles of actors and spectators. Productions can use a wide range of techniques to reflect on their own performativity. In the opening scene of Richard Maxwell's staging of Shakespeare's *Henry IV, Part One* (Brooklyn Academy of Music, 2003) the King began to deliver his lines when Westmoreland entered and whispered something in his ear. The two began to whisper back and forth for a considerable time, while the audience sat with the house lights still on, incapable of hearing the conversation. By abandoning the convention of the stage whisper as well as keeping the lights in the audience on, Maxwell did not allow the audience to inhabit its usual form of spectatorship. The Israeli dance company Batsheva shifted the roles of actors and spectators during their performance of *Hora* (Brooklyn Academy of Music, 2012) in a different way. All of the dancers remained on stage for the duration of the performance. When they were not performing, they would sit on a bench upstage and watch other company members perform further downstage. The spectators on stage and the spectators in the audience thus faced each other—this mirroring thematized the situation of perception. These self-reflective techniques have become more common since the late 1960s, a historical moment that is generally referred to as the "performative turn" in western cultures. Theatrical forms that play with their own performativity are often termed "postdramatic" (Lehmann 2002).

Because performances develop through the interplay of everyone involved, they enable the participants to experience themselves as subjects acting and affecting others as well as reacting to and being affected by others. As subjects they are neither fully autonomous nor entirely determined, partaking in and partially responsible for the situation in which they are engaged.

This special character of performance was frequently displayed and reflected on in the experimental theatre and performance art of the late 1960s. In the United States, companies like the Performance Group (founded by Richard Schechner in the 1960s) and the Living Theatre (founded in the late 1940s and led by Julian Beck and Judith Malina) emphasized audience participation. The Performance Group's *Dionysus in '69* and the Living Theatre's *Paradise Now!* both premiered in 1968 and foregrounded audience participation. Their work cast performance as both an aesthetic process and a space for social negotiation. In Richard Schechner's production *Commune* (The Performance Group, New York, 1970–72) about the My Lai massacre, one of the performers had to choose fifteen spectators at random to stand in a circle in the centre of the space in order to portray the villagers of My Lai. Most of the time, the chosen spectators followed these directions, although some refused. In the latter case the production prescribed that the performance would be interrupted until the reluctant spectator conceded or found someone else to take their place in the circle. The performance would not proceed for as long as the spectator remained seated, refusing participation. If the person left the room, the performance could continue. *Commune* made spectators take responsibility for the event.

The dynamic that *Commune* revealed through its rules about audience participation exists in every performance. A performance is always a social process grounded in specific rules. As long as established rules are followed, the rules do not attract much attention. But when new rules are created, or rules are broken, they can become the subject of debate. This social process becomes a political process when, as in *Commune*, a power struggle arises between actors and spectators or different factions of spectators over the course of the performance. Since the actions and behavior of each individual are co-determined by others, and can in turn co-determine the ongoing action, there is no such thing as passive participation in performance. Instead, each individual shares responsibility for the shape of the performance. Being present in a performance implies a level of consent with the performance. Those who object to the performance have to make their criticism known or leave the space. By remaining part of the performance, participants also take responsibility for it.

Above all, this shared responsibility is important to consider in the case of political performances such as political rallies and other kinds of mass spectacle. It is often assumed that rallies and spectacles are simply tools to manipulate the people who partake in the event. Yet it is naïve to assume that the organizers could control the event and overpower a "passive" and "innocent" public. If one insists that being involved in a performance implies consent and hence partial responsibility, the idea of "manipulation" can only partly explain the proceedings.

The Transience of Performances

Performances cannot be contained in or translated into material artifacts. They are ephemeral and transitory; they deplete themselves in a continual cycle of waning and becoming; they are acts of autopoiesis (that is, self-creation). Material objects employed in performances remain as traces of the performance. The performance itself is irretrievably lost when it finishes and lies beyond repetition. Whereas a production is designed to be repeated, a performance is a unique event. We need to ask: how can we define the *materiality* of performance? The following three sections describe how its materiality emerges through spatiality, corporeality, and tonality.

Spatiality

At first glance, the question of spatiality may not seem like an obvious one to ask. Performance spaces are pre-existing, whether they are theatre buildings, convention halls, or sports stadiums. Even though these spaces outlast the performance itself, we can speak of a particular spatiality that is created during the performance. Here we must differentiate between the architectural space in which a performance takes place and the performance space that is created by the performance and in turn influences the performance.

The architectural space where a performance takes place exists before the start of a performance and does not cease to exist after the performance ends. If we are talking about a building, we might think of it as a container whose defining characteristics (floor plan, height, width, length, volume, etc.) are not affected by what happens within it. Even if over time the floorboards become warped and filled with holes and the paint peels from the walls, the architectural space remains the same.

The layout of the architectural space and its division of space between the stage and audience opens particular possibilities for—and even organizes and structures—the movement of actors on stage as well as the perception of the spectators, affecting the relationship between actors and spectators. Whatever is made of these possibilities, how they are used, realized, avoided, or thwarted constitutes the performance space. Each movement of people, objects, light, and each sound can change it. It is constantly fluctuating. The spatiality of a performance is created in, through, and as the performance space and is perceived under the conditions set by the space.

Theatre spaces, regardless of whether they are permanent or temporary, are always spaces for performance. The history of theatre buildings and of stage technology, which up to now has usually been written as part of the history of architecture, can also be understood as the history of performance spaces. Changes in these architectural spaces bear witness to the changing relationship between actors and spectators. The arena stage (as in Ancient Greek theatre, the *theatrum anatomicum*, or in Max Reinhardt's Arena-theatre); the thrust stage (during the Elizabethan period, for example); the end stage (the proscenium theatres developed in the seventeenth century in Italy); the catwalk (as in Japanese Kabuki theatre as well as in many experimental productions by Max Reinhardt or Vsevolod Meyerhold, or in productions by Einar Schleef in the late 1980s and early 1990s)—they each make different demands on actors and audiences. Actors may be able to move in a spacious, circular dance area in front of the *thymele* (altar) of the Ancient Greek theatre, or in a narrow space between the wings of a seventeenth-century proscenium theatre at court. Audiences have a different range of perceptual experience depending on the performance space. The changing conditions of light and vista in an open-air performance space are radically different to a candle-lit interior designed to create a central perspective. The performance is shaped by the space: whether that involves sitting in a dark auditorium with the stage as the only lit area (as became common only after the invention of electric light in the last quarter of the nineteenth century) or finding oneself in a room that changes shape and realizes the possibilities of an arena, a thrust stage, and a proscenium theatre all in one, as with Erwin Piscator's Total Theater designed in 1927.

The ability of a performance space to organize and structure the relationship between actors and spectators, movement and perception, does not mean that it entirely determines these relationships. Performance spaces open up possibilities without mandating how they will be used or realized. Furthermore, the space can be used in ways that were neither planned nor predicted. In French theatre of the seventeenth century, aristocratic spectators often sat on the stage itself, conversing loudly. In doing so, these particular spectators changed the relationship between audience and actors as suggested by the architecture of the space, including the blocking of the actors and the perspective of the audience. The spectators presented themselves as performers within the performance space. Performance space can be characterized by its ability to be used in unintended ways, even if some participants might find these unintended uses inappropriate or infuriating.

Since the end of the 1960s, theatre artists have moved productions out of dedicated buildings into spaces previously used for other purposes. These new spaces did not come with designs that implied a specific relationship between audiences and actors. Hence, theatre productions in these new spaces emphasized the role of performance itself in defining the relationship between actors and audiences and in redefining new possibilities for movement and perception. In other words, they emphasized how performance itself creates spatiality.

Performance spaces are always also atmospheric spaces. Spatiality is created not only by a particular use of the space, but also by the atmosphere emanating from the space. Atmospheres are, as the German philosopher Gernot Böhme proposes, placeless but can fill a space. They belong neither to objects nor to people. Yet they are usually the first thing a spectator/visitor senses. The atmosphere enables a specific experience of the space and creates a particular spatiality. This experience cannot be explained conclusively with recourse to dimensions, objects, smells, sounds, or lighting. It is not the individual components that create atmosphere, but rather their interplay with each other. Böhme calls atmospheres "spaces, insofar as they are affected by the presence of things, people, or the environmental surroundings and their ecstasies. They are themselves spheres of presence of these things, of their reality in space" (Böhme 1995: 33).

The term "spheres of presence" refers to a specific mode of existence of things. Böhme calls this the "ecstasy of things," the way a thing presents itself to someone. It is not only colors, smells, and sounds that comprise this ecstasy, but also dimensions and form. The ecstasy of things has outward effects and captures the attention of the perceiver. Above all else, the atmosphere of a performance reveals the transience of spatiality. Different lighting, a shift in sound design, or a smell can abruptly and powerfully change the atmosphere. Atmospheres are transient *per se*. Every attempt to give them permanence is destined to fail.

Atmosphere has a special meaning for the perception of spatiality. It is in the atmosphere that seems to emanate from the space and the things—including smells and sounds—that the space becomes present to the subject in an emphatic way. The atmosphere even infiltrates the body of the perceiving subject, especially in the case of light, noise, and smell. The spectator is surrounded and absorbed by the atmosphere, dives into it, and is immersed in it. Ultimately, spectators become a part of the atmosphere, their reactions strengthen, weaken, or even disperse the atmosphere—and thus create a new and different spatiality. The fleeting character of spatiality is most pronounced in the atmosphere of a performance.

Corporeality

The fleetingness of corporeality is immediately apparent. Whatever actors do on stage does not last beyond the moment of enactment. This is true whether the actor makes a sudden movement across the stage, raises their hands, or furrows their brow. Unlike painters, sculptors, poets, or composers, actors, singers, and dancers do not create a permanent "work" separate from themselves. Whatever they create is fleeting and transitory, and is created out of a unique material: their own bodies, or, as the philosopher Helmuth Plessner expressed it, "the material of their own existence" (Plessner 1982: 407). How, we might ask, does this very special material create the specific materiality of performance? The human body is a unique aesthetic material; it is a living organism, always in a state of becoming; that is, in a continual process of transformation. With every breath and every movement, the body creates itself anew. Bodily being-in-the-world, not *being*, but *becoming*, contradicts the concept of the artwork as a product. A human body can only become an artwork as a corpse. At that point it reaches, at least temporarily, a condition of being (albeit one that only quick embalming can maintain). In this condition, it not only can be used as material in burial rituals, but also can be worked upon, prepared, and displayed, as Gunter von Hagen's controversial "Body-Worlds" exhibition has demonstrated. A living body rejects every attempt to turn it into an artwork. It is a "material" that always re-creates itself anew.

At the same time, the human body can only be understood as material to a certain extent. As Plessner showed, there exists a doubleness with regard to the body. On the one hand, people *have* a body they can manipulate similarly to other objects, instrumentalize, and use as a sign for something else. On the other hand, people *are* their bodies; people are embodied subjects. Plessner sees this particularity as the foundation of the *conditio humana*—the distancing of a person from themselves. When actors step outside themselves in order to portray a figure through the "material of their own existence," they emphasize this doubling and the distancing of people from themselves. There is a tension between the actors' phenomenal body, their bodily being-in-the-world, and the use of that body as a sign to portray a character. In Plessner's view, this tension infuses the actor's actions in the performance with deep anthropological meaning and dignity. We will describe this tension as occurring between the "phenomenal body" and the "semiotic body."

This tension has long been discussed in theories of the theatre, and particularly in theories of acting. In eighteenth-century France, participants in the contentious *Querelle de la moralité du théâtre* saw the split of the subject into semiotic and phenomenal body onstage as the cause of far-reaching and disastrous effects on the spectators. They argued that the portrayal of passionate actions would infect the audience by arousing their passions. While supporters of theatre argued for the healing effects of catharsis, opponents feared for the moral equilibrium of theatre audiences and saw the theatre as ultimately alienating audiences from themselves and from God. Critics considered the seductive potential of the actors onstage as a danger to spectators. Since actors' phenomenal bodies (i.e. their physical, erotically attractive bodies) and semiotic bodies (i.e. the passionate roles they were playing) always appeared together, the effects on the audience were considered to be potentially ruinous. Famously, Jean-Jacques Rousseau formulated his ardent critique of the theatre in his "Letter to M. D'Alembert on Spectacles" (1758).

The acting theories of the eighteenth century attempted to eradicate the possible dangers stemming from the tension between the phenomenal body of the actor and the actor's portrayal of a role. They privileged the semiotic portrayal of a role over the phenomenal body by emphasizing the dominance of the literary text over the art of acting. Actors were no longer supposed to foreground physical playfulness, improvisational talents, or virtuosity. Instead they were to use their skills to communicate poetic meaning provided by a text. The art of acting was designed to enable the actor to express these meanings—in particular the emotions, spiritual state, thought processes, and personal traits of dramatic figures—in and through the actor's body. Actors were supposed to extinguish their phenomenal body in order to transform themselves as completely as possible into a "text" made up of signs that described the actions and emotions of a character.

In his book *Acting* (*Mimik*; 1785/86), the philosopher and later artistic director of Berlin's Court and National Theatre Johann Jakob Engel criticized actors who drew the attention of audiences to their phenomenal bodies, and thus prevented their bodies from being perceived as the sign for a character:

> I do not know what bad-spirited demon controls our actors, especially
> those of the female sex, such that they attempt such great art in falling, or

should I say plummeting? One watches an *Ariadne*, when she learns her sad fate from the goddess of the rock, hit the ground with the whole length of her body: faster than if she had been struck by lightning, and with such force that it seems she wanted to smash her skull. If loud applause follows such unnatural, unpleasant acting, it is certainly only from the hands of the ignorant, who do not know what is in the best service of the play, who only buy tickets in order to gawk, and would rather go to a circus side-show or a bull fight. The connoisseur, if he claps along probably only does so out of sympathetic joy that the poor creature, who might be a nice girl even if she's a bad actor, was able to escape without injury. Neck-breaking arts do not even belong in a real pantomime, because even this portrays a narrative and strives to focus interest and attention on this narrative: these antics belong in an acrobatics show, where the whole interest is in the real people and their bodily agility, and grows when the daredevil puts himself in increasing danger.

(Engel 1785/86: 59f)

In the theatre the spectator was supposed to perceive and empathize with the character. The sensual body of the performer was to be made invisible because it would tear the audience out of its illusion. The sensual body destabilized the fictive world of the play for the audience.

In effect, the actor had to go through a sort of "disembodiment." Everything that hinted at the bodily being-in-the-world of the actor had to be eradicated until only the semiotic body remained. Theorists like Engel assumed that only a purely semiotic body was capable of making the meaning of the text perceptible to the senses, thereby communicating its meaning to the audience. However, this sort of acting did not necessarily add to the understanding of a play. After one performance of a new play by Friedrich Ludwig Schroeder, the critic for the Berlin *Literature and Theatre Journal* wrote, "after the third performance, I will be able to share with you the content and order of the scenes" (*Litteratur und Theaterzeitung*: 1784a). Almost three months later, the reviewer apologized that he could not keep his promise, explaining, "I am still not able to give you a precise account of the play. My attention is so drawn to the acting of some of the actors that I cannot think about the order of the scenes" (*Litteratur und Theaterzeitung*: 1784b). We can assume that the fascination with the acting skills of individual actors was due to the impression that the ultimately inseparable entity of semiotic and phenomenal bodies created.

The paradigm of realistic–psychological acting was developed in the eighteenth century, and theoretically renewed by Constantin S. Stanislavski (1863–1938) at the turn of the nineteenth to the twentieth century. Stanislavski's techniques made a significant impact on American theatre, particularly once his book *An Actor Prepares* was published in English in 1936. The director Lee Strasberg (1901–82) built on Stanislavski's ideas when working with his Group Theatre, which he founded in 1931 together with Harold Clurman and Cheryl Crawford. Strasberg taught his techniques of "Method Acting" to many later famous American actors of the twentieth century including Paul Newman, Marilyn Monroe, and Dustin Hoffman. Method acting is characterized by its attempt to dissolve the tension between the phenomenal body and the semiotic body by merging the two into a single unit; Strasberg asked his actors to draw on their own feelings and temperaments in order not just to *act* a role, but to *live* the role (Carlson 1993: 377).

The historical avant-garde movement's rejection of literary theatre and drama led to a reconceptualization of acting. It sounds like a direct rebuttal to Engel when Vsevolod E. Meyerhold (1874–1940) invokes fair booths—and like a weak echo of Engel when critics of Max Reinhardt's productions of *Oedipus Rex* and the *Oresteia* complained that the performances were "circus-like in the most vulgar sense," intended for the kind of spectators who "grew up seeing bull fights" (Jacobson 1912: 49).

With the development of new forms of acting, the material character of the human body came to the fore. This development led to varied reactions among theatre practitioners. The British actor, director, set designer, and theorist Edward Gordon Craig (1872–1966) found the tension between phenomenal body and semiotic body to be uncontrollable, and thus unsuitable as artistic material. In his essay "The Actor and the Über-Marionette," first published in the journal *The Mask* in 1908, Craig argues that:

> Art arrives only by design. Therefore in order to make any work of art it is clear we may only work with those materials with which we can calculate. Man is not one of these materials ... The actions of the actor's body, the expression of his face, the sounds of his voice, all are at the mercy of the winds of his emotions ... emotion *possesses* him; it seizes upon his limbs, moving them whither it will ... Art, as we have said, can admit of no accidents. That, then, which the actor gives us, is not a work of art; it is a series of accidental confessions.
>
> (Craig 1911: 57–58)

Meyerhold, on the contrary, saw the body as an infinitely malleable and controllable material that actors could creatively shape:

> In art our constant concern is the organization of raw material ... the art of the actor consists in organizing his material; that is, in his capacity to utilize correctly his body's means of expression. The actor embodies in himself both the organizer and that which is organized (i.e. the artist and his material). The formula for acting may be expressed as follows: $N = A1 + A2$ (where N = the actor; $A1$ = the artist who conceives the idea and issues the instructions necessary for its execution; $A2$ = the executant who executes the conception of $A1$). The actor must train his material (the

body), so that it is capable of executing instantaneously those tasks, which are dictated externally (by the actor, the director).

(Meyerhold 1969: 198)

In Meyerhold's theory, the actor is freed from any dependence on literature, and with it from the type of representation promoted by eighteenth-century theorists. Yet even Meyerhold is eager to remove the tension between *being a body* and *having a body*: the subject is no longer thought of as being a body so much as having complete power over that body. While the theorists of the eighteenth century strove to eliminate the sensuality of the body in the process of semiotization—even if some, such as Friedrich Schiller, had doubts—Meyerhold and other members of the avant-garde considered the human body an infinitely perfectible machine that could be optimized through cleverly calculated interventions. For the avant-garde, the sign-character of the body was less interesting than the body's objective materiality, which it conceived of as completely malleable. Their attention was directed at movement *per se*, its "reflexive excitability" that "grips the spectator" and excites the audience (Meyerhold 1969: 199). To Meyerhold, this was a process of stimulus and effect in which neither the phenomenal body nor the body-subject came into the foreground.

The actor can manipulate his or her body like a machine, drawing the audience's attention to the body's perfect functioning, and affecting the audience in specific ways. The actor's body can also become a semiotic body in the perception of the spectators because they can attribute completely new meanings to the presented body. Thus, the spectators become the "creators of new meaning" (Meyerhold 1974: 72).

Bertolt Brecht (1898–1956) was responding to these new theories of acting when writing his "Short Description of a New Technique of Acting which Produces an Estrangement Effect" (1935–41).[2] In Brecht's theory of acting, the actor simultaneously portrays a character and takes a stance *vis-à-vis* that character. In contrast to Stanislavski's theories, the actor does not disappear behind their role. Nevertheless, Brecht's primary interest lies with the semiotic body. The spectator is supposed not only to follow the narrative and behavior of the character but also has to grasp the contingency of the presented actions and behavior. Because the actor "doesn't identify himself with [the character he is portraying] he can pick a definite attitude toward a character whom he portrays, can show what he thinks of him and invite the spectator, who is likewise not asked to identify himself, to criticize the character portrayed" (Brecht 1964: 139). The spectator reads the semiotic body of the actor both as marking the actions and behavior of the figure portrayed and as an expression of the actor's stance toward the role. This creation of distance enables the spectator to generate new and socially critical meaning. Brecht does not discuss if and how the phenomenal body is involved in this process. Instead he focuses on a specific application of the semiotic body of the actor.

Since the 1960s, theatre has experimented with uses of the body that are centered on the doubling of *being a body* and *having a body*. The Polish director Jerzy Grotowski (1933–99) emphasized this tension by reversing the relationship between actor and role. In his understanding, the actor does not portray a figure. He sees the role given by the text as a tool for the actor to "learn to use his role as if it were a surgeon's scalpel, to dissect himself" (Grotowski 1968: 37). The role is no longer the goal and purpose of the actor's activities, but rather a means to an end. When training an actor, Grotowski avoids

> teaching him something; we attempt to eliminate his organism's resistance to this psychic process. The result is freedom from the time-lapse between inner impulse and outer reaction in such a way that the impulse is already an outer reaction. Impulse and action are concurrent: the body vanishes, burns, and the spectator sees only a series of visible impulses.
>
> (Grotowski 1968: 16)

For Grotowski, having a body cannot be separated from being a body. The body is not an instrument; it is neither a means for expression nor material for creating signs. Instead, this "material" is "burned" and changed into energy in the moment of action. Actors do not control their bodies, as Engel and Meyerhold had each proposed in different ways. Rather, agency is given to actors' bodies, so that the actors emerge as body-subjects, as embodied minds.

Some directors, such as Robert Wilson, emphasize the individuality of each performer's body in their productions and exhibit these bodies so that they might not disappear behind the portrayed figure. Instead, the unique physicality of the actor pulls away from the role that the actor portrays. As in Grotowski's theatre, the performer's primary task lies not in the portrayal of a character. The goal is to bring forth the physicality of each individual body in order to display it quasi as an artifact—enhanced by costumes and make-up. Any reference to character emerges as if by accident.

Other directors and ensembles use a variety of techniques to create a disjuncture or contradiction between the phenomenal bodies of the actors and the figures they portray. In a production of *Julius Caesar* (1998), the Italian group Societas Raffaello Sanzio employed actors who drew attention to their disabled, weak, fragile, and supposedly abnormal bodies. The casting highlighted the tension between phenomenal and semiotic bodies as the production undercut the audience's expectation of a given character with the reality of the actor's body onstage.

Equally, cross-gender casting (the casting of male roles with female actors or female roles with male actors) can draw audience attention to the tension between the phenomenal body and the semiotic body of the actor. Drag performance (men playing women or women playing men) has become a popular, and often politicized, form of performance in recent decades. Drag performers (or "drag queens" and "drag kings") usually perform exaggerated versions of characteristics that society considers feminine or masculine. This form of drag performance is primarily a Western phenomenon connected to the fundamental instability of any set notions of what constitutes the "masculine" or the "feminine." Drag performance has been closely connected with homosexuality and struggles for gay rights (Senelick 2000).

Quite a different case of cross-gender casting can be found in European theatre history as well as in some traditional theatre forms in Asia. In Ancient Greek theatre, all parts were played by men. Female characters were characterized as such by mask and costume. In Elizabethan theatre, boy-actors played female characters. Okuni founded Japanese Kabuki theatre as an all-female theatre in the sixteenth century. However, the female actors were first replaced by an all-boy cast to dispel suspicions of prostitution and ultimately—because these suspicions persisted—by a cast of adult men. The tradition of the *onnagata*, the male impersonator of female roles, still exists today. In China, the tradition of the *dan*, the male impersonator of female characters in Chinese opera, has been revived in recent years. Moreover, there is an opera form called *yue*, casting exclusively women. In eighteenth- and nineteenth-century Europe it was also not unusual that female stars played male roles, with Sarah Bernhardt's portrayal of Hamlet as the most famous example.

Cross-gender casting shares some concerns with the historically more recent cross-racial casting, although ultimately the two differ by as much as they share. In the United States, there has been a long—and often nefarious—tradition of performing across race. In the nineteenth century, blackface minstrelsy became a popular, working-class theatre form across the United States. In these performances, white performers would darken their faces with burnt cork and perform racial caricatures of African-Americans. As the form developed, African-Americans would also perform in these shows. In 1965 the Negro Ensemble Company explored and reversed this tradition in Douglas Turner Ward's play *A Day of Absence*. The play tells the story of a small Southern town, where one day all of the African-Americans disappear: left on their own, the Whites in this town realize how much they depend on the African-American members of the community. One reviewer for the *New York Times* wrote that the play was a "very clever, very funny, and pertinent play." Beyond the subject matter, it was Ward's casting decisions that made this play so effective: "what gives it an extra power is Ward's conception of it as a minstrel show in reverse. All the white roles are played by blacks in white-face ... and the results are both savage and touching" (Barnes 1970: 39). The performance's power came not only from the content of the play but also from the tension between the phenomenal bodies and semiotic bodies of the performers.

More recently Korean-American playwright Young Jean Lee addressed the tradition of the minstrel show in *The Shipment* (2008). Instead of inverting racial signifiers onstage with the help of black-face or white-face, Lee casts racial identity as entirely performative. As the audience follows the African-American cast through a medley of stand-up comedy, stylized farce, musical theatre and drawing-room comedy, the drug-dealing rapper turns into a yuppie at a cocktail party. And only the final punch line of the play reveals that the switch from the inner city street to the middle-class apartment is one from black to white. Black performers impersonate white characters in the final drawing-room sequence of the play, while race turns from a physical marker into a performative stance and is ultimately set up as a collection of stereotypes. Lee exports Judith Butler's argument about the performative nature of gender into the realm of racial identity and belonging, and asks about the limits of identity politics. Here the distinction between phenomenal and semiotic body itself is called into question.

In different institutional contexts, action and performance artists sought to overpower the tension between phenomenal and semiotic bodies by refusing to portray fictional characters in fictional worlds. Fluxus artist Tomas Schmit created *Cycle for Water Buckets* (1962), in which he kneeled in the middle of a circle of thirty buckets. One of these buckets was filled with water. Schmit took this bucket and poured it into the next bucket in a clockwise direction, and continued this until the water had spilled entirely or evaporated. He was not portraying a fictional figure performing a goal-oriented action in the context of a fictional world. Rather, he was the artist Tomas Schmit who was performing an action in a real place and time without the action meaning anything other than itself: moving water from one bucket into another.

When thirty years later the critically ill Bob Flanagan built an infirmary in a New York gallery and displayed his illness to visitors, Flanagan was not referring to any figure or symbolic order. Instead, he was unmistakably exhibiting himself and his sickness. His phenomenal body was the center of the performance, and every gesture, movement, or sound he made and word he spoke did not represent anything other than itself. Instead of representing a fictional world, his actions presented his real phenomenal body, marked by sickness and death. With each new action, he would present his phenomenal body anew.

Whereas eighteenth-century theorists of acting demanded that actors should make their phenomenal bodies disappear into their semiotic bodies and the characters they were portraying, action and performance artists since the 1960s have been enacting their phenomenal bodies without using these bodies to convey any particular semiotic meaning. They focus on the phenomenal body as such while also creating it anew with every action. The spectators may still ascribe meaning to the artist's phenomenal body and his actions. In Schmit's case the spectators could interpret his actions in a variety of ways: as preparation for cleaning, as washing the buckets, as filling a drinking trough, or as a symbolic narrative about wasteful uses of life-sustaining resources. Alternatively, it could be merely the portrayal of a person completely absorbed by a single activity.

In the case of Bob Flanagan, the spectator might have seen the dying body of the artist as a symbol of mortality or a "memento mori," or as a challenge to stop exiling death to hospitals and hospices and to return it into the public sphere and consciousness. Likewise, the performance could stand for the artist's will to live and the creativity of an artist who continues to present his ideas to the public even in the face of death.

Overall, the spectrum of theoretical and programmatic positions on acting and performance is wide-ranging. It spans from calling for a disappearance of the phenomenal body behind the semiotic body to the presentation of the phenomenal body itself, from demanding a "purely" semiotic body to insisting on a "purely" phenomenal body. Ultimately, the phenomenal and semiotic bodies are insolubly linked and one cannot appear without the other (even though the phenomenal body can be conceived of without the semiotic body, while the inverse is impossible).

The concept of *embodiment* can help us think about the relationship between the phenomenal and semiotic bodies in a productive way. In the eighteenth century, the term "embodiment" described how the imperceptible world of concepts and ideas became perceptible by being articulated through a body. This definition reflects a two-world theory: meanings were understood as mental entities that were comprehensible only insofar as there were signs to convey them. While language functioned as a quasi-ideal sign system through which meanings could be expressed in "pure" and unadulterated ways, the human body was seen as a far less dependable medium and material for acts of signification. The body could be employed to convey meaning once it had been purged of its organicity until only a "pure" semiotic body remained. Only a "pure" semiotic body was capable of relaying the meaning of a text to the audience in an unadulterated way. In other words, embodiment required simultaneous disembodiment. The act of embodiment implied a further set of tensions: the transmission of truth conflicted with the transience of performance. While the gestures, movements, and sounds of the actor might be transitory, the meanings they expressed were thought to be permanent.

In the 1990s, the anthropologist Thomas Csórdas completely redefined the term "embodiment." He defined embodiment as the "existential ground of culture and self" (Csórdas 1994: 6). In his concept of embodiment, he rejects the dualism of mind and body. For him, the mind does not exist outside of or opposed to the body but must be conceived of as embodied. The concept of embodiment thus refers to those fleeting bodily processes through which the phenomenal body constitutes itself in its particularity and creates specific meanings. Actors present their phenomenal bodies in a particular manner, so that they are experienced as *present* and simultaneously as a dramatic character like Hamlet or Medea. The actor creates both presence and the character through a special process of embodiment; neither presence nor dramatic character exists outside of the performance.

The term *presence* implies three distinct meanings. First, it refers to the simple being of the actor's phenomenal body. This can be termed the *weak concept of presence*. In addition, there is a form of presence that allows an actor to control the performance space and captivate the attention of spectators. The audience feels a power emanating from the actor, which focuses their attention completely on the actor and registers as a source of strength. The spectator experiences the actor as present in an unusually intense way. This can be termed the *strong concept of presence*. Such strategies of embodiment combined with the presence of the performer create a circulating energy that affects the spectators and ultimately produces an energetic response from them. In other words, the spectators will also feel present in the here and now in a special way. When actors bring forth their phenomenal body and its energy, they appear as *embodied minds*. In the presence of the actor, the spectators experience both self and other as *embodied mind*. The circulating energy is perceived as a transformative power, and in this sense as a life force. This can be termed the *radical concept of presence*. The energy brought forward by the actors and spectators circulates in the space and can be felt by everyone there. The energetic exchange between actors and spectators affects everyone present and thus creates the performance.

Tonality

Tonality epitomizes the transience of performance. What could be more fleeting than sound? Emerging from silence, sound expands and fills the space, only to drift away and disappear in the next moment. Nevertheless, its impact on the listeners is immediate and fundamental. Sound transmits a sense of the space (after all, our sense of balance is in our ears), it penetrates the body and has a physiological and affective impact. Tonality has a strong affective potential: listeners may tremble and breathe more quickly, their hearts may beat faster; they may fall into melancholy or, on the contrary, become euphoric; they may be seized by desire or haunted by their memories.

The performance space is never exclusively a space for watching (*theatron*), but always also a space for listening (*auditorium*). Speaking or singing voices, music, and noises all sound in this space. Even today, many theatre scholars believe that Western theatre differs from other world cultures in its tonality, which is virtually synonymous with spoken language. Because of its proximity to language, the tonality of a performance has often been considered only in terms of linguistics, i.e. as a medium through which language emerges. A glance at European theatre history shows how mistaken this assumption is. As far back as ancient Greece, theatre was not merely recited. In tragedies and comedies, flutists accompanied recitations while lyrical texts were sung, some alternating with the chorus, some as virtuoso solo arias. Spoken language was not dominant.

Likewise, the invention of opera at the end of the sixteenth century speaks to the wide range of tonality in performance. Opera developed from the efforts of a group called the Florentine Camerata that aimed at reviving Greek tragedy. Since then, music-theatre (that is, opera, ballet, operetta, and musicals) has attracted audiences primarily through its use of music rather than its use of language. Even in dramatic theatre, the dominance of speech has been frequently challenged. Until the end of the eighteenth century, performances comprised different numbers including musical pieces, often as accompaniment to a concluding ballet. Performances of plays were interspersed with musical interludes.

Up to the present, theatre is unimaginable without music or other sounds. Tonality in European theatre is not exclusively, or even predominantly, created through spoken language. The performance space becomes a listening space far more through music, various noises, and voices, whether they are speaking, singing, laughing, sobbing, or screaming. John Cage's silent piece *4'33"* (premiered 29 April 1952 at Maverick Hall in Woodstock, New York) revealed the noises created by the audience—whispering, snickering, fidgeting, etc.—as well as the howling of the wind and the pattering of rain on the roof as constitutive. Peter Stein's production of *The Oresteia* (at the Schaubühne am Halleschen Ufer in Berlin in 1980) highlighted the materiality of voice in the chorus of old men: they shifted from mumbling to whining whistles to the *ololygmos*—the joyous cheers, half cricket chirp, half bird song—that they called out in falsetto.

Sound creates spatiality. Likewise, vocality creates physicality. In the actor's voice, all three forms of materiality come into being: physicality, spatiality, and tonality. The voice is produced by the body and resonates through space so that it becomes audible for the singer/speaker as well as for the listeners. The close relationship between body and voice is especially evident in screams, sighs, moans, sobs, and laughter. These utterances are unmistakably created through a process that affects the whole body: the body doubles over, contorts, and enlarges. These non-verbal utterances also impress themselves physically onto the listener. Anyone who hears someone scream, sigh, moan, or laugh will perceive these as specific processes of embodiment created through a particular kind of physicality. The screaming, sobbing, or laughing voice penetrates the bodies of the listeners, echoes in and is absorbed by their bodies.

In operatic coloratura we also hear the voice become detached from language. Since the 1960s, performance art and theatre has often experimented with this detachment, as in the so-called autobiographical performances of Spalding Gray, Laurie Anderson, Rachel Rosenthal, and Karen Finley, and above all in the performances of Diamanda Galás and David Moss. These artists search for and create moments in which the speaking or singing voice stops articulating language understandably and devolves into screams, high tones, laughter, moans, and noise. Such moments are emphasized through special vocal techniques as well as the use of electronic media. Electronic media can amplify or duplicate the voice, can broadcast it, fragmented and distorted, without de-materializing it (as film recordings do with the filmed body). The voice seems polymorphic. It loses markings of gender, age, and ethnic belonging. The aural space created is experienced as an in-between space, as a space of constant crossings, passages, and metamorphoses.

Such a sense of liminality pervades the aesthetics of many contemporary artists. Even when voice is connected to language, it maintains a life of its own, drawing the attention of the listener to its own materiality. Artists such as Moss or Anderson do not use their voices only in the service of language or as a medium for verbal expression. Instead, the voice makes itself heard on its own terms. This does not necessarily imply a de-semanticization of verbal expression, as is often claimed. The polymorphism of the voice opens up an ambiguity in verbal utterance; words become ambiguous, while remaining comprehensible. The voice also draws the attention of the listeners to its own particularities. Through voice, the subject's bodily being-in-the-world discloses itself.

The tension between voice and language is analogous to the tension between phenomenal body and semiotic body. Both these tensions spring from the doubleness of being a body and having a body. On the one hand, the voice enunciates the speaker's bodily being-in-the-world. On the other hand, it can be understood as a sign that encapsulates the multiple meanings of speech as well as the individual markers of the speaker such as age, gender, ethnicity, and emotional state. The moment in which the voice detaches from language seems to be the final stage, or even the collapse of the tension between voice and language. In this moment, the tension is dissolved and the voice itself becomes "language." The voice no longer transmits language, but has *become* language in that it expresses a bodily being-in-the-world that addresses itself to the listener. Expression and address coincide.

The materiality of the performance as a whole emerges through the materiality of the voice. It emerges as tonality because the voice sounds, it gains physicality because the voice leaves the body through breath, and it creates spatiality because it spreads through the space and enters the ears of the listeners. Voice becomes language by virtue of its materiality prior to being perceived as a sign. The bodily being-in-the-world of the speaker expresses itself and addresses the listener in his or her bodily-being-in-the-world. It fills the space between them, brings them together, and creates a relationship between them. With his or her voice the speaker touches both the speaker and the listener. The fleetingness of the moment in which the voice sounds creates the intensity of performance.

Rhythm

The materiality of performance, manifest above all in the transience of sound, is not simply a given. It emerges and disappears in the process of a performance. Performances occur in time—whether they last for 4′33″ or several days. Certain techniques help to control the duration and organize the different materials that make up any given performance. *Rhythm* has special relevance for the organization of time in a performance. It is the rhythm that creates a relationship between spatiality, physicality, and tonality and regulates the appearance and disappearance of phenomena in space. It is almost impossible to imagine a performance in which rhythm does not organize time in some way. Even when the narrative events or the psychological development of dramatic characters are the central structuring principles, rhythm plays a large role in organizing the chronology of the scenes, speech, movement through the space, and spatial constellations—whether in dance, speech, or music theatre. In these cases, rhythm is subordinate to and supports the overall structure. In many performances since the 1960s (particularly in performance art but also in spoken theatre), rhythm is used as the dominant organizing principle for structuring time.

Rhythm in this sense does not mean musical meter, but rather denotes an organizing principle that does not aim at symmetry but regularity. While symmetry fails to allow for divergence, regularity is a dynamic principle that works through repetition *and* divergence. In rhythm, the foreseen and the unforeseen come together. In this sense, rhythm can be an organizing principle that presupposes and spurs permanent transformations.

When rhythm turns into the dominant organizing principle of performance, the relationship between spatiality, physicality, and tonality remains in continual flux, while the appearance and disappearance of phenomena are regulated by repetition and divergence. Important directors of the past forty years such as Robert Wilson, Jan Fabre, Elizabeth LeCompte, Einar Schleef, Frank Castorf, and Heiner Goebbels have used rhythm as the foundational principle for performance. Productions directed by Christoph Marthaler such as *Murx den Europaer! Murx ihn! Murx ihn! Murx ihn! Murx ihn ab!* ("Kill the European! Kill him! Kill him! Kill him! Kill him dead!," Volksbühne at Rosa-Luxemburg Platz, Berlin, 1993), *Die Stunde Null oder Die Kunst des Servierens* ("The Zero Hour or the Art of Serving," Deutsches Schauspielhaus, Hamburg, 1995) or *Die schoene Muellerin* ("The Pretty Miller," Zurich Schauspielhaus, 2002) are particularly vivid examples of this use of rhythm based almost entirely on repetition. An element is introduced and repeated in ever new variations. A second element is added and repeats in variation, then a third, and so forth. The variations range from minimal elevations to near complete reversals. One variation can also yield the next variation. In *Murx*, the actors sang sixteen strophes of the psalm "Thank You." Each time they began a strophe, they transposed it up a half tone, until during the final strophes the singers' voices threatened to break. The longer it was repeated, the more the repetition prompted convulsive, uncontrollable laughter from the audience.

One reason that rhythm is such a powerful organizing principle lies in its fundamental connection to the human body. Our pulse, blood circulation, and breathing follow their own rhythm; when we walk, write, speak, or laugh, we continuously produce rhythmic patterns. Even movements within our bodies that we are not conscious of are rhythmic. Indeed, the human body is a rhythmical instrument, particularly suited to perceive and be moved by rhythm. In performance, different "rhythmic systems" come into contact: the rhythms of production with those of the spectators. Here we should keep in mind that every spectator follows different rhythmic patterns, both internally and externally. It is decisive for the success of a performance to develop strategies to calibrate the spectators' internal rhythms to the rhythm of the staging. Autopoiesis emerges out of the interplay of actors and spectators; in other words, out of their rhythmic attunement to one another. When the rhythms of individual spectators match the rhythms of the performance, it can impact other spectators and give new impulses to the actors. However this process works on an individual level, it can be assumed that performance operates to a large extent through rhythmic divergences, changes, and shifts. Performance organizes itself through rhythmic calibration, manifest on a basic physical level. Its transience is reflected in rhythm's dynamism and propensity to change.

The Emergence of Meaning

Traditionally, performances were seen as a means to transmit specific, pre-existing meanings. The long-standing premise of scholarship was that the performance of a given play represented a specific interpretation; that a courtly festival of the seventeenth century conveyed a specific allegorical program; or that a political festival and other mass spectacle displayed the power of an individual (such as Augustus, Louis XIV, Napoleon, Stalin, or Hitler) or group (as in festivals of the French Revolution or the mass spectacles of the early Soviet Union). If we assume that the bodily co-presence of actors and spectators is constitutive of performance, and that performance is transient, the notion of a fixed meaning becomes unsustainable. Both bodily co-presence and transience suggest that a performance does not convey a stable and preexisting meaning. Instead, meanings only emerge over the course of the performance and are different for each of the participants. It is impossible to know in advance which meanings individual participants will generate. The interaction between actors and spectators can always take an unexpected turn and disturb the planned program. In addition, the spectators can be distracted by the presence of phenomenal bodies and atmospheres that counteract any purely semiotic interpretation of the performance. Think, for example, of the audience watching Sarah Siddons perform in *Tamerlane* in 1819: it was supposed to understand that the character Siddons was playing had died within the fictional world of the play. Instead it thought Siddons herself had died, and even after the stage manager assured the audience that she was alive, the audience refused to let the performance continue.

Perceiving bodies and objects on stage in their specific presence does not necessarily mean perceiving them as meaningless. Rather, it means perceiving all of these phenomena as *something*. They are not simply stimuli or sensory data, but rather the perception *of something as something*. In the perception of the spectator things appear in a performance in their particular phenomenality; their appearance *is* their meaning. In *Murx* the iron oven on the right-hand side of the stage initially signified nothing other than a very specific iron oven that drew the spectators' attention to its special material qualities; the clock without a hand, hanging over a door center-stage, signified nothing other than itself. These objects challenged the audience to immerse themselves entirely in their particularity. This sort of self-referentiality neither transmits nor strips the object of a pre-existing meaning. Instead, this self-referentiality is in itself a way of creating meaning. In other words, the process of perception is also a process of creating meaning, since these objects "mean" what they appear as. One does not first perceive something and then—in an act of interpretation—give it meaning. Rather, the perception of something as something *simultaneously* constitutes meaning as part of a process that manifests its specific phenomenal being.

Furthermore, the appearance of a phenomenon is the prerequisite for another mode of perception and a different way of constituting meaning. In the moment that spectators cease to focus their attention on the phenomenal being of the perceived, they begin to perceive it as a signifier; that is, as a sign-bearer that is linked with associations—fantasies, memories, feelings, thoughts—to what it signifies, i.e. possible meanings. The iron oven may recall memories of a spectator's own childhood or a vacation house, just as the hand-less clock may remind a spectator of the old professor's dream in Ingmar Bergman's film *Wild Strawberries*.

These few examples suffice to show that perception and the constitution of meaning are largely dependent on subjective factors connected to individual spectators. The associations conjured by an object, a gesture, a sound, or a light cue depend on their individual experiences, their knowledge, and their specific sensitivities. This includes factors such as age, gender, class, and cultural background, which impact how people perceive and understand performances. It would be naïve to believe that perception and the constitution of meaning depend only on what is presented and how it is presented. Instead, both are founded in the specific conditions that each participating subject brings to the performance. Both perception and the chain of associations produced by it differ for everyone. It is also doubtful that these sorts of associations follow specific rules and are predictable for every individual. Instead, they arise spontaneously, as in the famous first scene of Marcel Proust's novel *In Search of Lost Time*. The narrator takes a bite from a madeleine and its taste conjures up a wave of involuntary memories and associations that overpower him. We can compare Proust's narrator to the spectator of a performance: the immediate sensation and perception of phenomena in the performance can stir a wide range of associations that are often not consciously created. Instead, they occur without being called upon or searched for.

We can call the oscillation of perception between concentration on phenomena in their self-referentiality and on the associations that they give rise to
the *perceptual order of presence* as opposed to the *perceptual order of representation*.
Both the body of the actor as bodily being-in-the-world and objects in their
phenomenal being create the foundation of the order of presence. Perceiving
a body or object as a sign—as a dramatic character and the character's
environment—is the foundation of the *perceptual order of representation*. The
order of representation demands that everything that is perceived is perceived
in relation to a dramatic character, the character's fictive world, or another
symbolic order. While the first order of perception (i.e. presence) focuses on
meaning as tied to phenomenal being, the second order of perception (i.e.
representation) creates meaning that comprehensively constitutes the character
and fictive world.

These two perceptual orders generate meaning according to different
principles. When one of these two orders becomes the dominant order of
perception, it affects how spectators perceive a performance. In the order of
representation, the process of perception has the goal of allowing a dramatic
character, fictive world, or symbolic order to come into existence. Only elements of the performance with relevance to the fictive world are perceived; all
else the spectator preemptively shuts out of the process of perception. The
dramatic framework of the performance affects the process of perception and
allows for the perception of only those elements that make sense within the
framework. Ultimately, this process of perception is goal-oriented, even
though it often follows the principle of trial and error.

Although the order of representation is goal-oriented, it does not follow
that each spectator will generate the same meaning about dramatic characters
and their fictive world. Personal experiences, knowledge, beliefs, values, con-
victions, a person's whole habitus—i.e. factors that are informed by cultural
and social milieu—create the preconditions for perception and the constitution of meaning. Part of this knowledge and experience is a person's previous
experiences with theatre. Whether the spectator goes to the theatre frequently
or rarely, whether the spectator knows the piece that is being performed, and
whether the spectator has already seen the actors perform in different roles
impacts the spectator's process of perception. Even when the perceptual process and constitution of meaning follow the order of representation, the outcome will vary among spectators depending on the conditions each brings to
the performance and it is likely that spectators will not all agree on the
meanings created (Carlson 2001).

We can assume that theatre performances that involve a realistic-psychological style of acting invite the spectators to privilege the perceptual order of
representation, while experimental theatre and performance art draw the
spectator toward the perceptual order of presence. Nevertheless it is almost
impossible to imagine a performance that an audience would perceive exclusively through one of these orders. Even in a psychologically realistic staging,

spectators sense the presence of an actor or a specific atmosphere without asking themselves what it is supposed to mean. Likewise, spectators of a performance art event will give specific meanings to the actions of the performer and objects in the room.

This means that in every performance the perception of each spectator oscillates between different modes of perception. The more often these oscillations occur, the more spectators feel like wanderers between two worlds. This creates a state of instability that the spectators experience as an in-between, or liminal state. Spectators can and will constantly but unsuccessfully attempt to reset their perception—and become aware that the oscillation between the modes of perception is out of their control. They can and will constantly but unsuccessfully attempt to reset their perception—either on the order of representation or the order of presence. It soon becomes clear that the oscillation undermines spectatorial intent: in effect, spectators are caught between the two orders. They experience their own perception as emergent, wrested from their control, inaccessible but also conscious. The oscillation draws the attention of spectators to the dynamic process of perception itself. The creation of meaning becomes less and less predictable and dependent on the course of a performance.

Meaning created during the performance must be differentiated from meaning constituted after the performance is over, divorced from immediate perception and not part of the performance itself. We will therefore focus on the latter in Chapter 4 ("Performance Analysis").

The Event-ness of Performance as Experienced by the Spectator

Performances, as the discussion so far has indicated, are "events" and can be characterized by their "event-ness." The concept of the "event," as we use it here, is distinguished by five characteristics:

1) A performance can be seen as an event rather than an artwork because it is created through the interaction of actors and spectators (i.e. an autopoietic feedback loop). This autopoietic process is the process of the performance. When the autopoietic process ends, the performance is over and irretrievably lost. In other words, this autopoietic process and the performance are not results or artifacts, but events.
2) As an event, a performance—in contrast to a staging—is unique and unrepeatable. Any particular constellation of actors and spectators is singular. The reactions of the spectators and their effect on the actors and other spectators will differ from performance to performance—even if the actors are performing a staging in which all of their actions are pre-planned.
3) A performance is an event in so far as no individual participant controls it completely. This is true not only because of the bodily co-presence of

actors and spectators, but also because of the specific mode of presence through which phenomena emerge and how meaning is constituted from these phenomena. To the extent that phenomena appear present in especially intensive ways, they separate from their context and appear to exist in and for themselves. The phenomena occur for those who perceive them; we can say that their perception *happens to* a person. The perceiving subject is overcome by an oscillation between two different orders of perception, and is placed in a state of liminality.

4) The event-ness of performance opens up a very specific sort of experience for its participants, especially for the spectators. In performance, participants experience themselves as subjects who partially control, and are partially controlled by, the conditions—neither fully autonomous nor fully determined. They experience performance as an aesthetic and a social, even political, process in which relationships are negotiated, power struggles fought out, and communities emerge and vanish. Concepts and ideas that we traditionally see as dichotomous pairs in our culture—such as autonomy and determinism, aesthetics and politics, and presence and representation—are experienced not in the form of *either/or* but as *not only/but also*. Oppositions collapse.

5) The collapse of these dichotomies draws the spectator's attention to the threshold. The spectator experiences instability and the dissolution of boundaries as part of the event. This opens up the liminal space between poles such as presence and representation, and a feeling of in-betweenness dominates. Performances enable a threshold experience that can transform those who experience it. These threshold experiences might involve specific physiological, affective, and energetic states as in Bob Flanagan's *Visiting Hours* or Christoph Schlingensief's *Art and Vegetables*; the shift from spectator to actor roles as in *Commune*; or inversely, from actor to spectator roles as in the Batsheva Company's *Hora*. Liminality is bound up with the event-ness of the performance. As a concept it draws on anthropology and its treatment of ritual. Richard Schechner's collaborator, the anthropologist Victor Turner, developed the concept of liminality with recourse to the work of Arnold van Gennep. Van Gennep's study, *The Rites of Passage* (1960), presented a wealth of ethnographic material that traced ritual's connection to symbolically loaded threshold experiences and rites of passage.

According to van Gennep, rites of passage across a variety of cultures can be divided into three phases. First, in the separation phase, the individual to be transformed is separated from his or her everyday life and social milieu. During the subsequent threshold or transformation phase, the individual is brought into a state "between" all possible realms and has a completely new, partly unsettling, experience. In the final incorporation phase, the newly transformed individual reintegrates into the community, bearing a new status and identity.

Victor Turner built on van Gennep's theory and called the threshold phase a "liminal state" (from the Latin *limen*). He defined this state more precisely as an unstable existence "betwixt and between the positions assigned and arrayed by law, custom, convention, and ceremonial" (Turner 1969: 95). Turner elaborated on how the threshold phase opens cultural space for experiments and innovations: "in liminality, new ways of acting, new combinations of symbols, are tried out, to be discarded or accepted" (Turner 1977: 40). According to Turner, the threshold phase usually leads to changes in the social status and identity of the individual who undergoes the rituals, and also includes changes to the society or community as a whole.

The rest of this section will explore Turner's conception of liminality in detail, particularly in relation to the characteristics of performance. We will focus on what happens when categories that structure our social existence collapse and how that affects participants in a performance. Dichotomous concepts regulate our actions and behavior. Destabilizing these dichotomies therefore results in a reevaluation of the rules and norms that guide our behavior. These conceptual pairs also allow us to categorize events: "this is theatre" or "this is a social or political situation." Such categories imply certain parameters for suitable behavior in a given situation. When different or opposing frames collide in performances such as *Visiting Hours* or *Art and Vegetables*, participants are confronted with potentially conflicting models of appropriate behavior. In the case of *Visiting Hours*, the frames of the hospital visit and gallery visit collided; they occurred simultaneously and annulled each other. Spectators/visitors entered a state "between" the rules, norms, and orders that would accompany each of these frames—they entered a liminal situation.

The experience of a liminal situation destabilizes one's sense of self and other, and of the world at large. Such an experience often implies strong feelings and changes in a person's physiological, energetic, and affective state. The experience of liminality is articulated in both cognitive and somatic ways. A person experiences liminality first and foremost as a bodily transformation. Liminality might be experienced primarily through the body, or it might be a state triggered by sudden physical changes in a person. Such is the case if intense emotions accompany the process of perception, especially when confronting a taboo, as was the case when encountering the ailing body of Angela Jansen in *Art and Vegetables*. Intense emotions elicit an impulse to act and might lead a spectator to interfere in the proceedings, thus effectively turning into an actor and challenging the normative relationships of a given event.

During such a performance, spectators enter a state of alienation that is potentially disorienting and can be enjoyable as well as agonizing. Spectators may experience a wide range of transformations. This is especially true of temporary transformations that last for part of or the duration of the performance alone. These include changes in the physiological, affective, energetic, and motor states of the body; shifts in status of actors and spectators; or the creation of a community of actors and spectators (or solely of spectators).

These changes take place over the course of the performance, but often do not extend beyond its end. It is only possible to say in individual, well-documented cases whether the experience of the destabilization of self, other, and the world actually creates a permanent transformation, as is the case with rituals. Spectators might dismiss their temporary destabilization as meaningless. Alternately, spectators might remain in a state of disorientation for an extended period and only upon later reflection come to a new orientation or return to their previous values and patterns of behavior. Regardless of the outcome, spectators experience their participation in the performance as a liminal experience.

Any performance has the potential to create a liminal experience, whether it is a ritual, festival, theatre performance, political demonstration, or athletic competition. Threshold experiences differ depending on the various kinds of performance. A ritual involves a new identity and its recognition by the community; it is also irreversible. A youth who has gone through an initiation ritual to become a warrior will never be a youth again. In this case, the threshold experience is goal-oriented. In athletic competitions, the goal is to generate winners and losers, festivals create communities, and political gatherings legitimate power. In contrast, artistic performances involve threshold experiences that are ends in themselves. Such liminal experiences can be called aesthetic experiences. Aesthetic experiences focus on the crossing of boundaries and the process of transformation as such. Non-aesthetic threshold experiences are a passage *to* something, transformation *into* something or another.

Since the eighteenth century the concept of aesthetics has been defined in various ways. Understanding aesthetic experience as liminal experience allows us to reconceive of the term. Having an aesthetic experience is most common in the encounter with art but not limited to it. The difference between aesthetic and non-aesthetic threshold experiences is not a sufficient criterion to differentiate between artistic and non-artistic performance. Aesthetic and non-aesthetic threshold experiences can occur in the same performative event. It depends on the perception of each individual whether the participants concentrate on the liminality of their perception or see the performance as a means to an end. Likewise, the perceptual order may change throughout the performance, whether the performance is *Art and Vegetables* or the World Cup final.

In this chapter, we have explained the concept of performance through its four elements: mediality, materiality, semioticity, and aestheticity. These elements exist in *all* kinds of performance, even if they have been discussed primarily with reference to theatre and performance art, genres that have traditionally been privileged in Theatre Studies. Theatre Studies is the only field that studies all forms of performance. Its subject of study can be any sort of situation that would fall under the concept of performance as developed here.

Further Reading

On Performance and Performativity

Austin, J. L. (1962) *How to Do Things with Words*, Cambridge, MA: Harvard University Press.

Carlson, M. (1996) *Performance: A Critical Introduction*, London/New York: Routledge.

Lehmann, H.-T. (2002) *Postdramatic Theatre*, Karen Jürs-Munby (trans.), London/New York: Routledge.

McKenzie, J. (2001) *Perform or Else: From Discipline to Performance*, London/New York: Routledge.

Sedgwick, E. K. and A. Parker (1995) *Performativity and Performance*, London/New York: Routledge.

On Theories of Acting

Artaud, A. (1958) *The Theatre and Its Double*, Mary Caroline Richards (trans.), New York: Grove Press.

Brecht, B. (1964) *Brecht on Theatre: The Development of an Aesthetic*, J. Willet (ed. and trans.), New York: Hill and Wang.

Craig, E. G. (1911) *On the Art of the Theatre*, London: William Heinemann.

Grotowski, J. (1968) *Towards a Poor Theatre*, New York: Simon and Schuster.

Meyerhold, V. (1969) "The Actor of the Future and Biomechanics," in E. Braun (ed.) *Meyerhold on Theatre*, New York: Hill and Wang.

On Performance Spaces

Carlson, M. (1989) *Places of Performance: The Semiotics of Theatre Architecture*, Ithaca, NY/London: Cornell University Press.

Fischer-Lichte, E. and B. Wihstutz (2012) *Performance and the Politics of Space: Theatre and Topology*. London/New York: Routledge.

Wiles, D. (2003) *A Short History of Western Performance Space*, Cambridge: Cambridge University Press.

On Ritual and Liminality

Durkheim, E. (1912/2008) *The Elementary Forms of Religious Life*, C. Cosman (trans.), Oxford/New York: Oxford University Press.

Goffman, E. (1967) *Interaction Ritual: Essays on Face to Face Behavior*, Chicago: Aldine Publishing Company.

Köpping, K. (2008) *Shattering Frames: Transgressions and Transformations in Anthropological Discourse and Practice*, Berlin: Dietrich Reimer.

Turner, V. (1982) *From Ritual to Theatre: The Human Seriousness of Play*, New York: Performing Arts Journal Publications.

Notes

1 Rehearsals may be classed as particular kinds of performances. See also McAuley, G. (2012), *Not Magic but Work: An Ethnographic Account of a Rehearsal Process*, Manchester: Manchester University Press.
2 Early translations of Brecht into English often translated his conception of *Verfremdungs-Effekt* as *alienation effect*. This translation is misleading, because the German term *Verfremdung* does not connote the Marxist conception of alienation; *estrangement effect* is a more accurate translation.

Part II

Methodologies

The study of performances is a rich field. Researchers can explore a wide range of research questions about performance and employ a variety of theoretical and methodological tools to study it. Whenever we embark on a research project about performance we have to begin by choosing one of various possible approaches to the subject.

To return to one of our earlier examples, we could analyze the performance *Art and Vegetables* by focusing on the relationships the performance created between the events onstage and the messages Angela Jansen sent to the audience. In other words, our analysis could be based on specific aesthetic techniques and procedures that we could connect to changes in the audience's attitude over the course of the performance. This sort of analysis would be useful to investigate whether this performance led to a re-evaluation of dominant ideas about what is "pure" and "impure," what is taboo and permissible in public.

We could analyze *Visiting Hours* as a collision of experiential frames between a visit to an art event and a hospital. We could focus on the expectations and behaviors connected to each of these kinds of visits and compare them to how spectators actually behaved. An approach like this would open up a range of possible foci: the role of art in American society in the 1990s; the relationship of aesthetics and politics as well as private and public realms; discourses and politics concerning the body; the image of the suffering artist (which has a long tradition in Western cultures)—the list continues.

Since *Art and Vegetables* and *Visiting Hours* were both performed in the recent past, it is possible for people who saw them performed to write an analysis of their experiences. The other two performances from the beginning of the book—Sarah Siddons' performance in *Tamerlane* and the 1723 anatomical dissection in Frankfurt—are only accessible through secondary sources. In these cases, we cannot analyze the performance itself. In order to investigate the performance, we must depend on existing sources. This also allows for a plethora of questions. The description of Siddons' death scene might lead us to ask what effects the emerging form of psychologically realistic theatre had on spectators in the eighteenth and nineteenth centuries and what function this form of acting was designed to fulfill.

The invitation by the medical professor Ottomar Goelicke to a public dissection in an anatomical theatre raises a series of questions related to the genre of this performance, its timing, and the function of both the performance and the invited audience. Why were anatomical dissections public—what connected theatre and science in this case? Why were they, like comic performances, presented during Carnival? Why were not just medical students, but also the city's elite, invited? Answering such questions requires careful research.

While the study of the first two cases can be approached through performance analysis, the second two performances require historiographic methods. Performance analysis can be conducted only when the researchers participate in the relevant performances and are part of the autopoietic process created in performance. In all other cases, we are dealing with an analysis of sources and documents about a performance or the traces left behind by the audience. This second kind of approach can be termed theatre historiography. This method is useful for investigating performances from both the recent and distant past. Even if we use a video recording of a production performed the day before that we did not see live, we need to use historiographic methods. Even the best video recording is only a document of a performance, not the performance itself, and so we cannot do a performance analysis of it. Whenever we study a performance solely through reference to sources and documents, without personal experience of the performance, it is a historiographic project. We can therefore study performance of contemporary theatre either through performance analysis (if we were there) or theatre historiography (if we were not).

It is important to differentiate between performance analysis and theatre historiography as two separate fields of inquiry with different methodological approaches. The concept of performance that we discussed in the first part of the book is highly relevant for both of these methods. As we have seen in the examples above, both the formulation of research questions and the conclusions of an analysis are often connected to a broad range of theoretical assumptions, which might in turn be transformed by research. This leads to a third important field of inquiry that we will discuss in Part II: developing theories.

Chapter 4

Performance analysis

Performance analysis may appear similar to textual and visual analysis: depending on the aim of our analysis, we use various methodological approaches to answer a research question. Performance analysis also is fundamentally different due to the specific medial conditions of performance (the bodily co-presence of actors and spectators) and the special materiality of performance (its transience). These characteristics of performance differentiate its analysis from textual or visual analysis.

First, when analyzing a text or image, one is distanced from one's object of study. In performance analysis, one becomes a part of the performance processes one intends to analyze. One is immersed and ultimately helps create the performance by one's own behavior. It is impossible to take the position of an external observer: one's analysis has to be partial and subjective.

Second, when analyzing a text, one can reread or jump between different sections of a book without changing the materiality of the text. When analyzing an image, one can look at it from different positions—from up close in order to examine the details, or at a distance in order to perceive the image as a whole. In both cases one separates oneself from the object periodically and consults other material; for example, other versions of the text or image, other texts or images, or documents about the objects, their creation, reception, and so forth. One might then re-read the text, or look at the image again with this new knowledge. In performance analysis, that is impossible. If one tries to pause to contemplate a particularly fascinating moment or to begin to analyze it, one will miss what happens next—which may cast a new light on that very moment and have a big impact on the proceedings. Attempts to create a systematic analysis of a performance can only begin once the performance is over and thus removed from one's immediate sensual perception.

Perception

Performance analysis must be based on our own memories of what we perceived during the performance. Because everything that can be perceived over the course of a performance becomes part of the process of its autopoiesis, no perception is "meaningless"—regardless of whether it relates to the actions on stage, the conduct of the audience, or our own physiological, emotional, energetic, or motor conditions and the way they change during the performance. Everything that is perceived during a performance counts. The multitude of perceptible phenomena during a performance is usually so expansive that it is impossible, even with the greatest attention, to perceive everything. The longer a performance lasts, the harder it is to maintain a high level of attention throughout. But even when we are paying close attention, we miss details. The psychology of perception teaches us that in the process of perception, we always make choices. In other words, we perceive that which is meaningful in some way to us, whether emotionally, creatively, or cognitively. We cannot access what we have not perceived. An analysis, therefore, can only be about what has meaning for us as researchers and spectators. Ultimately, every analysis is subjective, based on the subjectivity of our perception. This subjectivity is a fundamental condition of every analysis.

Memory

We need to remember what we perceived during a performance if it is going to be the foundation of our analysis. Memory is the prerequisite for analysis. Two kinds of memory are relevant for performances: episodic and semantic memory. Episodic memory allows us to remember details of the performance: where an actor stood in the opening scene; the particular way the light hit the stage and washed everything blue; the sweetish smell of alcohol as a beer bottle broke and poured out, and our own feeling of disgust at that moment while our neighbor gasped at the breaking of the bottle. It is episodic memory that allows us to remember innumerable concrete events during a performance.

Semantic memory stores all verbal meanings—both the words that are spoken and our own thoughts and interpretations during the performance. These memories include the "translations" that take place in our mind—for example that we identify a particular color as red, a movement as abrupt, an atmosphere as uncanny. Episodic memory would remember the nuances of that red, the specific quality of the movement, and the sensation we had upon entering the space. Semantic and episodic memory interact with and support each other. Remembering a sub-plot might motivate our episodic memory to remember concrete actions and details connected to that sub-plot. In turn, the episodic memory of a specific detail might stir our semantic memory to remember an entire narrative connected to that detail.

Memory is unreliable in manifold ways. It does not function like a reservoir that preserves past events as they occurred. Instead, it reconstitutes the past in relation to new situations and contexts. It often fails to recall specific memories on demand. The unreliability of memory, like the subjectivity of perception, factors into the process of analysis.

It is possible to develop strategies that increase the reliability of our memories and help us recall what we experienced. However, each of these strategies has certain risks and unintended consequences that can be counterproductive to performance analysis. These strategies include multiple visits to a production, writing down memos directly after the performance, taking notes during the performance, and watching video recordings.

Visiting the same production multiple times is an especially promising strategy to bolster the reliability of our memory. This is particularly true when it comes to remembering concrete details of a performance. But it is also important to keep in mind that each time one watches the production under different conditions. One will probably perceive new elements that one had missed the first time, and that will then influence other memories. In addition, memories of the first performance will influence one's evaluation of the second performance; this is true for every following visit as well.

When we go to a production multiple times, several major elements can change in each performance. Firstly, the novelty of the first performance disappears, which has an influence on how we perceive the performance. Secondly, the switch in perception between actor and character might happen at different moments, or even be reversed. Thirdly, each new visit also changes the dynamics between spectators and actors as their moods and attitudes shift. It often happens that the director or individual actors change elements of a staging after the first run of the production. Attending a production multiple times can reveal the differences between individual performances and thus highlight the singularity of each performance.

In order to remember and analyze the changes between performances, it is useful to *write a memo* to oneself after each attended performance. Such memos are useful to track the affective potential of the performance(s), and to trace how one's perception and the interaction between audience and actors changed. This sort of performance memo is not a formal essay. Instead, it is a way to jot down all one's reactions to a performance. Only later, when one rereads this memo in relation to memos from different performances of the same staging, or other research materials, one begins to organize these recollections. Visiting a staging multiple times is without a doubt the best way to support one's memory. Unfortunately, this is not always a possibility. Especially during guest performances and festivals it may be impossible to see the same production twice.

Taking notes during the performance has the benefit of preserving impressions for later analysis. In the case of a production that one can visit multiple times, taking notes the first time is hardly useful. Constant pressure to come up with hypotheses about the performance that can help determine what is relevant and what should be written down (since of course one cannot write down everything one perceives) might change one's perception so much that it affects one's experience of the performance. That danger is much smaller if one is only taking notes while watching a production for the third or fourth time. In general, taking notes might affect one's neighbors or even the actors and thus impact the performance.

Generally speaking, *video recordings* have become the most important memory aid for analysis. They can be used very effectively to counter the inadequacies of memory, in particular after attending multiple performances and once one has gained a clear set of motivating questions for the analysis. They are useful not only to help recall specific details of a performance, but also to clear up specific questions. For example, a video recording could tell us whether in the beginning of Robert Wilson's production of *King Lear* (Frankfurt on Main, 1990), a piercing, whirring sound and drum roll began the very moment when a narrow upright rod of light passed from left to right in the frame of the proscenium arch, or whether the sound began before the light moved. A video recording also makes it possible to concentrate on individual details such as the timing, speed, and intensity of specific movements—for example, to focus closely on the different stylized actions of unbuttoning that all the characters except Lear (Marianne Hoppe) perform with their fingers at the start of the Prologue, before Marianne Hoppe begins to recite William Carlos Williams' poem "The Last Words of My English Grandmother." Minute analysis of such details is only possible by re-playing the sequence multiple times.

Semantic memory often stores meanings that were created *ad hoc* during a performance, without the episodic memory being able to retain all of the details that created this meaning. A video recording can give access to precisely these details, which might either reveal how one arrived at a particular understanding of a scene or show up one's ideas as unfounded hypotheses. A performance video helps trace exactly when Lear ceases to move regally and engages in a new vocabulary of movement that marks the moment of transition to a new social status.

As useful as a video recording might be to help us remember concrete details, it can be useless and even counterproductive in other respects. A video recording is rarely able to help one's spatial memory. On the contrary, a video might confuse and disorient further if one lacks a good memory of the spatial dimensions and constellations of a performance space. A recording might capture some of the observable reactions of the audience, such as laughter, expressions of disgust, or general agitation. However, a video recording does not give access to the lighting, noises, smells, and atmosphere of a given performance. The recording cannot convey the flow of energy among actors and spectators who share in the performance. In Einar Schleef's production of Elfriede Jelinek's *Sports Play* (Vienna Burgtheater, 1998), for example, the actors filled the entire stage, repeating the same demanding exercises for forty-five minutes with extreme energy (to the point of total bodily exhaustion) while simultaneously speaking as a chorus. Some of the spectators could not bear it and escaped the room only minutes after the performance began. Those who watched until the end, however, experienced a field of energy between actors and spectators that increased as the performance progressed. Whereas a video recording can reproduce the individual exercises and create an impression of the power of the actors' movements, it fails to record such shared energetic fields. This energy requires bodily co-presence. The memory of this field of energy can hardly be evoked by a video recording.

A video recording is also sometimes used less to support and stimulate the memory of the researcher than to substitute for it, leading the researcher to forget his or her experiences of the performance. This is especially true when the video portrays the performance from a perspective that was inaccessible to the audience, or if it cuts out details that were occurring in the background that the researcher had focused on during the performance. The video might also offer close-ups of actors' faces during dialogue in the form of shot/counter-shot, eradicating the physical positioning of the actors toward one another. The use of film techniques such as slow motion that seek to guide the viewer's focus are particularly problematic and superimpose themselves on the memory of the actual movement in the space, sometimes even destroying one's memory entirely.

To benefit from these memory aids and to reduce their drawbacks, one should use them in conjunction rather than depend on a single one. By strategizing one's use of these aids, one might use combinations that will check and balance each other. These aids can only help if one is aware of their positive and negative values and employs them accordingly. Performance analysis depends on the memory of the researcher, and while we can use these various aids, the powers of memory are never perfect.

If a performance analysis can use notes taken during a performance, post-performance memos, and video recordings, we might ask what separates this form of analysis from a historiographic approach that depends on theatre reviews, audience responses, and even video clips. The difference may seem small, but it is fundamental. Whereas in the first case, these aids are used to recall, confirm, or challenge the memories of the researcher's personal perceptions during the performance, historiographic research depends entirely on documents in lieu of personal experience. This can be enough for a range of research questions, but it is not a performance analysis, which bases itself on the personal experience of a performance.

Articulation

The third fundamental element of a performance analysis lies in adequately articulating one's performance experiences. Without providing precise descriptions of one's perceptions it is impossible to offer a coherent analysis. Often it is very difficult to translate non-verbal elements of the performance— such as fantasies, emotions, or physical sensations—into language. Language implies abstraction, even when it refers to concrete things such as bodies, noises, or smells. Even the most precise verbal description cannot do justice to phenomenal being. It can only approximate what the researcher perceived. Elements from one's episodic memory are often extremely difficult to access through verbal descriptions. Elements from semantic memory, on the contrary, are already *per se* verbal structures, and thus are much easier to express through language. And still, even here the limits of language might distort memory, as when semantic memory recalls concepts and descriptions that were the result of a process of translation during the performance.

Every good analysis works to overcome the limits of language, even if that is never entirely possible. Language as a medium has its own materiality; it is a sign system with specific rules. Because writing is constrained by these rules, the writing process takes on its own agency. It develops its own dynamic that can bring a written description closer to one's memories but that can also increase the distance to them. Every act of interpretation implies another act of textual production, which creates an apparent paradox that we must make allowances for in performance analysis.

The Practice of Analysis

Research Questions

As we have already emphasized, every analysis begins with a specific question. This question might be one that emerges from the performance itself or one that the researcher brings to the performance. Investigating a performance without having a specific question and simply trying to analyze the performance from every angle is not feasible. As the earlier examples indicate, the questions and research interests behind an analysis can be extremely varied. These interests might range from a focus on a single artistic technique to the broad political significance of a performance.

A performance analysis aims to answer specific questions that the researcher has going into a performance and/or that arise during the performance or with regard to its public reception. When we approach a performance with a specific question, the question itself organizes our perception and structures our memory to a certain degree. Even if we only develop the question during or after the performance, this question will determine our methodological approach. Performance analysis is a cognitive process that should lead to the constitution of meaning.

Methodologies

Based on the concept of performance developed in the first part of this book, we can deduce two important characteristics about how meaning is created in a performance. First, the meaning of a performance is closely connected to how we experience the phenomena physiologically, affectively, and energetically. Second, perception oscillates between phenomenal bodies and objects (the physical bodies and objects that are present in front of the spectator) and semiotic bodies and objects (the dramatic figures and objects that they represent). If we understand performance analysis as a process of creating meaning, it follows that the analysis must attend to the specific somatic effects the performance evokes and to how they help create meaning. The same is true for one's split perception of actor and character. That is to say, the performance analysis must take into account all three dimensions of a given performance: the somatic, the phenomenal, and the semiotic dimensions.

Phenomenological Approaches

A phenomenological approach concentrates first and foremost on the perceptual order of presence. When taking a phenomenological approach to a performance, we concentrate on the ways that people, spaces, things, and sounds appeared during a performance. We emphasize the specific characteristics and qualities that made a conscious impact on us and that may have led to observable reactions among other spectators. Such an approach might begin with phenomena that had a particularly strong effect and created especially clear reactions from the audience. In the performance of Shakespeare's *Julius Caesar* by the Italian Societas Raffaello Sanzio (Hebbel Theater, Berlin, 1998), discussed earlier, the voice of the actor playing Antonius was particularly striking because the actor's larynx had recently been removed in an operation and replaced by a microphone. The audience did not know this in advance and was disoriented when perceiving his tormented, breathless attempts at articulation. The voice sounded hollow and distorted, as though it came from another world. It sent a chill up the spine of spectators. At the same time, the appearance of the actor playing Cicero stirred feelings of disgust and revulsion in the audience: the actor was an enormous man with the proportions of a sumo wrestler. He seemed to drown in his own masses of flesh. He wore a stocking mask over his face, which gave him the appearance of a faceless monster. The unique physicality of the actors made such a direct and disturbing impression on the spectators that they focused entirely on the actors' phenomenal bodies and initially were unable to perceive them as characters, i.e. Antonius or Cicero.

A phenomenological analysis must also take account of the energetic field created between actors and spectators over the course of a performance (as described earlier in *Sports Play*), including the shared sense of belonging to a community, if only momentarily. The experience of rhythm is an important part of this process, because it works directly on the bodies of the spectators and draws them in. When we analyze performances, we must consider our own bodily sensations and experience of the atmosphere. We must also take account of the observable reactions of other spectators, such as the abrupt departure of some spectators during *Sports Play* and the force with which they slammed the doors as they left the theatre. The phenomenological approach incorporates all these aspects of experience.

The phenomenological approach focuses on the interplay of appearance, perception, and experience. How do people, things, sounds, and spaces appear, and what effect do they have on the audience? These are the questions a phenomenological approach seeks to answer. It focuses on the experiences that the performance enables for its audience. These experiences—unlike interpretations—cannot be correct or incorrect. They are an important part of the performance and the autopoietic feedback loop responsible for them. The goal of a phenomenological analysis is to comprehend a performance through personal and shared audience reactions.

A spectator does not enter a performance as a blank page. Spectators bring previous experiences, knowledge, and a so-called *universe of discourse* with them into a performance. The experiences they live through during a performance relate to other, earlier experiences. New experiences have meaning within a larger context: they connect to an already existing structure of experience. The meanings that spectators give to performances are interwoven with the spectators' biographical, social, and culturally conditioned life experiences, all of which are important preconditions for the possibility of experiencing a performance. Some of these experiences are physically conditioned—for example, a glaring light shining into the auditorium that forces spectators to close their eyes. This reaction is primarily physiological, but it might also be connected to earlier experiences that might furnish a mere reflex with a specific meaning. Other experiences of sounds, lights, words and so forth might already carry meanings for various spectators. It is precisely these prior meanings that enable a new experience. In the case of *Julius Caesar* the audience greeted the fragile, injured and obese bodies of the actors with discomfort and disgust, exposing the social marginalization of sickness, death, and disability in our society. Since every spectator brings a different set of experiences to the performance, any act of analysis has to be subjectively conditioned. This subjectivity does not render individual experience completely arbitrary. In principle, it is always possible for spectators to communicate with each other about what they perceive and how it affects them.

Semiotic Approaches

Whereas a phenomenological approach focuses on experience, a semiotic approach focuses on the creation of meaning and the perceptual order of representation. In this perceptual order, everything that is perceived is understood as a sign: the space and objects within it; the bodies of the actors including their costumes and movements; the way light, movement, and sounds alter the space; the actors' movements in the space (proxemic signs); their body posture and gestures (gestural signs); their facial expressions (mimetic signs); the space between the various actors (proxemic signs); their voices and the noises they make, such as laughing, crying, or sighing (paralinguistic signs); words (linguistic signs); other sounds, such as song or music. The various signs possible in theatre can be systematized as in Table 4.1.

Table 4.1 The theatrical code as a system. In Fischer-Lichte (1992), Vol. 2: 15

Sounds Music Linguistic signs Paralinguistic signs	Acoustic	Transient	
Mimic signs Gestural signs Proxemic signs Lighting Mask Hair Costume Stage conception Stage decoration Props	Visual	Long-lasting	Space- and Actor-related

These theatrical signs can be presented, combined, and contextualized in radically different ways. In principle there are endless possibilities for creating meaning in the theatre.

Theatrical signs are often signs that spectators are familiar with from their everyday lives. How these signs reappear in the theatre often differs from how they appear in everyday life. Their meanings from everyday life do not carry over directly into the theatre. It is important to recognize a table as a table, a bed as a bed, or a cylinder as a cylinder. But that does not necessarily mean that the table functions as a sign for a table, a bed as a sign for a bed, or a cylinder as a sign for a cylinder. Depending on the circumstances, a table could be interpreted as a mountain that a character must climb, or as a cave in which a character can hide from pursuers, or, if turned upside down, as a boat in which two lovers cross a lake. In all these cases, the ways that the actors use the table creates new meanings. In the production of Brecht's *Puntila* mentioned below, the spectators recognized the table that the actor climbed on as a table, but also acknowledged that the dramatic character Puntila believed the said table to be a mountain.

All the examples given in the section "Phenomenological approaches" above can also be used as examples for semiotic approaches. The physical and affective impact of the actors playing Antonius and Cicero on spectators might be a basis for generating meaning. The discrepancy between the appearance of the actor and the image spectators had of their character might be understood as a kind of commentary, demanding that spectators reflect on the origin of their expectations. As indicated at the end of the last section, the apparently aberrant bodies on stage could also be read as critique of the social marginalization of sick and disabled bodies in our society.

In the case of Schleef's production of Elfriede Jelinek's *Sports Play*, the experience of rhythm working on and transferring energy to the bodies of the spectators combined with the powerful movements of the actors (i.e. proxemic signs). In conjunction, Schleef's use of rhythm and movement evoked the potentially darker side of sports that Jelinek seeks to highlight. Sports turns into an act of disciplining individuals, a violation of their bodies that wipes out their individuality and turns them into machine-like monsters. The audience's somatic experience of rhythm and movement gestures toward a broader social critique of competitive sports.

As emphasized in the section on the "emergence of meaning" (Chapter 3) the spectator's perception may shift between the order of presence, to which phenomenological approaches refer, and the order of representation, relevant to semiotic approaches. In performance analysis, it is vital to account for both orders as well as their interplay. What happens in the moments of shift? What kind of meaning emerges from what kinds of experience? And which meanings influence the emergence and/or intensity of an experience? Any analysis has to work with both approaches.

Performance Analysis: A Case Study

On their own, the semiotic and phenomenological analyses remain one-sided; the two must be conjoined. As the brief analyses in the preceding section show, the starting point for an analysis might be any of a wide variety of moments, processes, and elements in a performance. Generally, the researcher would want to choose as a starting point a moment that spoke to her—be it because it was irritating, fascinating, terrifying, boring, or upsetting in some way—or a moment that in retrospect seems particularly relevant to the researcher's research question. It is impractical to make any hard and fast rules about the sequence or order in which to analyze particular elements.

To conclude this section, we will carry out a performance analysis that brings together phenomenological and semiotic approaches. As a case study, we will use the production of *King Lear* directed by Robert Wilson, already mentioned in the preceding section. This production premiered in May 1990 at the Bockenheimer Depot, a former streetcar depot in Frankfurt on Main. I attended several performances of the production and will use my personal experiences of the performances as a starting point for the analysis. Before developing the question that will guide the analysis, it might be helpful as a first step to place the production within Wilson's oeuvre. After producing a string of operas such as *Einstein on the Beach* (1976), *Death, Destruction and Detroit* (1979), and *the CIVIL warS* (1983/4), Robert Wilson had long nursed the idea of doing Shakespeare's *King Lear*. This came as quite a surprise, considering Wilson's notorious rejection of the idea that performing dramatic texts is a way of interpreting them.

> The literary text is important to me, but I find the way in which it is presented on stage utterly dreadful. At home, I can read a play such as *Hamlet*, for example, over and over again and the ever fresh array of

meanings and possibilities I find in it gives me great pleasure. In the theatre, on the other hand, I find none of these riches. The actors interpret the text, they enter the stage as if they know everything and comprehend everything, and that is a lie, a swindle, it offends me.

(Quoted in Karasek and Urs 1987)

Wilson's comment suggests that if he were to stage a classical text, he would avoid any kind of interpretation. However, he did not stage *King Lear*. For each serious attempt to convert his somewhat vague idea into a concrete project had floundered when it came to casting. No one fitted his vision of Lear. Instead he staged another classic text, namely Euripides' *Alcestis*, while simultaneously doing a production of Gluck's opera *Alceste* (both 1986 in Stuttgart). Then came 1988 when by chance he met the actress Marianne Hoppe, who had made a great career as a theatre and film star in the 1930s. Immediately after their meeting, Wilson began to speak of nobody but "Marianne." He seemed to have found the ideal lead in the 77 year-old actress: "Marianne Hoppe is King Lear. She is the right age, she has the right face, the right image. And she has the strength to speak Shakespeare's language without interpreting it, simply, full of emotion. And I believe this comes closest to the work itself" (from an interview cited in *Vorwort*, Schauspiel Frankfurt, 23 (1990): 22—translation by the author). Obviously, this instance of cross-gender casting had nothing to do with drag, nor was it similar to that of a Kabuki *onnagata*. I will suggest one possible way to understand this cross-gender casting over the course of this analysis. The question guiding the analysis arose right at the beginning of the performance and developed clearer contours over the course of the performance. So, let us start at the beginning.

The spectator who enters the Bockenheimer Depot is confronted with an open picture-frame set, enclosed on both sides by several rows of black wings and a white canvas at the back. Extending forward is an apron stage covered in black carpet and accessed by ramps to the right and left. A bolt of lightning is projected on the stage floor in the center, and downstage center, where the main stage joins the apron stage, stands a thin upright rod about one meter in height which throws a "shadow" of light on the floor downstage left. As the lights dim, the lightning and "shadow" disappear and a piercing, whispering sound and drum roll are heard (music by Hans Peter Kuhn). A narrow upright rod of light passes from left to right, dazzling the spectators.

Both the sounds and the light have a strong physical impact on me and on other spectators. The sounds resonate in my body; moreover, they create an uncanny atmosphere. The light blinds me. Both sound and light transfer me into a liminal state. I find myself on the threshold between two worlds, leaving my everyday life behind and ready to enter another one—one from which the glare in my eyes still separates me. As the glare subsides, I perceive twelve figures spread out across the whole stage, wearing floor-length royal-blue coats. Each slowly mimes a different stylized action of unbuttoning with her or his fingers. A spotlight focuses on the face of Marianne Hoppe as she stands upstage to the right of the group of figures. While the light on stage grows alternately brighter and dimmer and as the sounds and the music swell and subside, she recites, immobile, William Carlos Williams' poem "The Last Words of My English Grandmother." I feel disoriented. I am also struck by the sheer materiality of sound and light that has literally opened up my senses to experience the performance afresh.

The scene highlights elements that prefigure the course the performance will take. The gesture of unbuttoning evokes two central motifs in the Shakespearean text. When Lear encounters Edgar (as Tom) and comes to the recognition that man "is no more but such a poor, bare, forked animal," he continues with the quest, "Off, off, you lendings! Come unbutton here" (Act III, scene 3, 111–12). Likewise, when Lear comprehends that Cordelia is indeed dead ("Thoul't come no more/Never, never, never, never, never!" Act V, scene 3, 307–8), he begs those around him, "Pray you undo this button" and dies. The unbuttoning mime in the beginning calls up Lear's descent into madness and death and prefigures the arc of the play.

The poem spoken by Marianne Hoppe contains a multitude of motifs that are picked up over the course of the performance. To give a few examples: the "cry of food: 'Gimme something to eat'" corresponds to Lear's call for food "Dinner, ho! dinner!" (Act I, scene 4, 45). The triple "no, no, no" with which the grandmother objects to being carried off to the hospital is taken up again when Lear turns toward the blind Gloucester (Act IV, scene 6, 100–101). The "stretcher" is picked up on both visual and verbal levels: in the shape of Lear's bed (Act IV, scene 7) and in Kent's words on Lear's death: "O! let him pass! He hates him/That would upon the rack of this tough world/Stretch him out longer" (Act V, scene 3, 313–15).

The opening sequence with special effects, poetry, and mime suggests one possible starting point for our analysis. They all point to the experience and theme of *passage*—a passage into a liminal state, a passage into madness, a passage into death. So, let us draw our guiding questions for this analysis from the moments of passage within the performance: When do they occur? In which ways are they brought about? What do they do with the spectators? Obviously, initially these questions may arise only for spectators who know the play and are able to relate the mime of unbuttoning as well as the "Last Words of My English Grandmother" to motifs and elements of the tragedy. For less well versed spectators, they would slowly emerge over the course of the performance.

At the beginning of the performance, the sounds and the lights draw the spectators into a liminal state. After the intermission, the rod of light, stretching to the full height of the proscenium, makes the reverse passage from right to left accompanied by drum rolls. The use of light and sound are worth further examination especially with regard to moments of passage made by dramatic characters—such as Gloucester's passage into blindness, and Lear's passage into madness and death.

When Gloucester (Jürgen Holtz) is caught, Cornwall's servants tie him up, tear his clothes and shove him into a square of light at center stage while from above, a spindle-like cage descends over him. Cornwall (Hans-Jörg Assmann) strikes him three times with his long spear; each time a loud metal clang rings out, resounding painfully in the bodies of the spectators. Regan (Astrid Gorvin) stands next to him, and bending over, her left foot lifted graciously behind her, she plucks one hair from Gloucester's (non-existent) beard with a stylized movement, laughing shrilly. The shrillness of the laughter is extremely unpleasant. Before the blinding, there is a sudden silence. Cornwall raises his spear and thrusts it down at an angle toward Gloucester's eyes. He remains in this pose, motionless for a few moments. In the same moment, a glowing red light falls on the caged Gloucester. Immediately after that, a black cloth that had hidden the white canvas at the back falls down. The canvas is now so brightly lit that it forces the spectators, painfully blinded, to close their eyes.

Gloucester's torment and blinding are not acted out realistically, in a way that might arouse empathy in the spectators. Rather, they are performed through stylized movements, sounds and lighting effects that impress themselves physically and painfully on the spectator. Without necessarily feeling empathy with the dramatic character, the spectators' experiences mirror those of Gloucester. The intense reactions triggered by sound and light correspond

Figure 4.1 Gloucester (Jürgen Holtz) in the cage with Regan (Astrid Gorvin) in front, tearing the invisible hair off the beard. Photo: Abisag Tüllmann. Copyright Deutsches Theatermuseum München, Archiv Abisag Tüllmann.

to the dramatic character's painful passage into blindness. Phenomenal and semiotic levels intertwine.

The same applies to Lear's transition into madness. It is first indicated by a change in movement. While the sounds of the raging storm are filling the space, Lear adopts the dancing step typical of the Fool. Suddenly the storm breaks off. Silence reigns for a while. It is broken by the continuous sound of dripping water that eventually becomes unbearable to the audience. Here, sound marks Lear's passage into madness. Simultaneously, it works on the bodies and minds of the spectators, some of whom, being unable to bear it any longer, stop their ears with their fingers.

Lear's death is staged through sound and stylized movement. Lear lies on a long, narrow bed—the stretcher—while Cordelia kneels by his side. Slowly, and with obvious effort, Marianne Hoppe sits up and says smilingly: "Pray you now, forget and forgive; I am old and foolish" (Act 4, scene 7, 59–60). Once sitting, Cordelia moves behind her and holds her left arm as if it were a stick— evoking Charon at the rudder carrying the dead in his bark across the river Lethe to the underworld. She slowly guides Lear forward. At this very moment sounds of babble and clatter, previously barely audible, grow increasingly loud. Combined, the noises and the stretcher remind the spectator of some of "The Last Words of My English Grandmother": "Let me take you to the hospital, I said." The soundscape transports the spectators to this very place.

The image of Cordelia holding Lear in her arms appears one final time before Lear's death in a reversal characteristic of the production: Lear enters from upstage left holding the (dead) Cordelia in his arms in front of him. The upper part of Cordelia's body leans back against Lear, her arms dangling behind her, and over Hoppe's arms. The pair slowly advance to center stage, where they turn slightly and walk to the front in a straight line. This is a remarkable move, since here—as in all other Wilson productions—the pre-ferred movement runs parallel to the back horizon and the apron. Slowly, Cordelia slides to her knees while leaning against Hoppe; both are facing the audience. Hoppe remains in this position when Lear dies—a moment marked by an enormous flash of light while Hoppe simply ceases to speak or move. The spectators are left with the burst of light as the marker of death, appar-ently drawing on reports about near-death experiences.

At the end of the performance, after Edgar's final words, Cordelia rises slowly to stand quietly behind Lear. (The dead) Edmund also rises; the other characters enter the stage and together the dead and the living create a single tableau. Downstage center stands Lear, behind him Cordelia. Cornwall, Goneril, Edmund, Regan, and Albany are spread out on the right half of the stage, while on the left remain Kent, Edgar, Gloucester, the Fool, and, far upstage left, the King of France. The light grows ever dimmer; just before it fades entirely, they appear once more as shadows against the white screen. Only at the complete blackout does the music cease. The spectators—potentially transformed—have to make their passage back into everyday life.

Figure 4.2 Lear (Marianne Hoppe) with Cordelia (Alexandra von Schwerin) at the moment of Lear's death. Photo: Abisag Tüllmann. Copyright Deutsches Theatermuseum München, Archiv Abisag Tüllmann.

So far, we have identified the passages between various states (vision/ blindness, life/death) and analyzed how they operate on the senses of the spectators. Our examination of these moments suggests that the production was executed within the parameters of Wilson's long-established theatre aesthetic (see also Shevtsova 2007). The characteristic features of his aesthetic, however, gain a new quality in this production by focusing on the final passage of death. Wilson seeks to capture the *changing awareness* that occurs in the moment of death. With that in mind, let us take our analysis one step further to examine the production in the light of the process of dying.

Objects barely feature on Wilson's stage; the space appears as a universe of changing light in which the space of the "here and now," the space of memory, and the space of the (imagined) future are superimposed onto one another. Sounds derived from the surroundings penetrate the spectators' con- sciousness (as in the case of Gloucester's blinding); or rise softly, gradually swelling, as if from memory; alternately, they are heard for the first time and gradually grow louder. The awareness of the space changes according to the interweaving web of light and sound. This holds true for the dramatic char- acters, in particular Lear, as well as for the spectators.

The perception of time changes in similar ways. The performance as a whole is framed by the two instances of light rods crossing the stage (left to right in the opening scene, then right to left after the intermission); in other words, the event seems to take place in the blink of an eye. Wilson puts the action of *King Lear* into the moment when "the eyelid opens between blinks," as Heiner Müller wrote in "Bildbeschreibung" (Description of a Picture). It is a text Wilson used as Prologue to his *Alcestis*, another piece concerned with the subject of death. The time span of this "blink" is malleable: it can expand as long as a lifetime or contract into the measured real time of 3.5 hours of the performance.

The changing perception of space and time merely scratches the surface of reality. And this surface does not propose any meaningful cohesion but disintegrates into single elements: color, movement, words and sentences, tone, sound. These enter the consciousness of the dying—and the spectator—as isolated elements *per se* instead of fragments of a formerly cohesive unity.

The process of dying opens up new experiences to the spectators. Marianne Hoppe performs dying as a rite of passage. Death commences when Lear relinquishes his powers as king. The passage into madness marks the irreversibility of the descent toward death. On Wilson's stage, new models of movement and behavior are playfully experimented with and acted out until—the transformation almost complete—the new identity is accepted. The last stage of the transformation begins—the phase of incorporation. Guided by a leader of souls of the dead (Cordelia), Lear is admitted into the fellowship of shadows in the kingdom of the dead. Wilson's *King Lear* plays with the concept of the rite of passage that marks the entrance into a new realm of experience: here, death is both a new realm and the end of human experience.

While death dominates this production, the death of a specific individual such as Lear or Gloucester is not the actual focal point. Far more, death becomes a structuring principle played out in all its many variations. The Prologue engages with the ordinary death of a grandmother in the twentieth century complete with bed, ambulance, stretcher, and hospital. At the opposite end of the spectrum, certain choreographies of light, sound, and gesture allude to the mythical dimension of death associated with those who lead the souls of the dead into the underworld. Embedded between these extremes—and superimposed on them—are the deaths of Lear and Gloucester in the play, entrenched in verbal imagery of madness, violence, and destruction. The dying individual in a specific socio-historical situation is not at stake in Wilson's production. Rather, the performance regards death as the ritual transition at the end of a long life into a new condition, a new reality. Herein lies one motivation for the cross-gender casting of Lear: Marianne Hoppe's outward appearance and voice identify the death as that of an old lady, while the accompanying words qualify it as the death of an old man—Lear. It is the death of an old human being, beyond any particular identity.

The structure of the performance follows a basic anthropological pattern: the rite of passage. It controls the passage from one status or stage of life into another (as in birth, initiation, marriage, childbirth, professional or social advancement, death). As discussed in Chapter 3, the rite of passage is performed in three phases: separation from previous life; a liminal phase when the actual transformation takes place; and finally the incorporation or reintegration of the transformed person back into the community—or into a new community. This structure underlies Wilson's production of *Lear* in relation to both the protagonist, Lear, *and* the spectators. They are lured, seduced, even forced to enter the phase of liminality and undergo certain—even if only temporary—transformation. In Wilson's *Lear*, aesthetic experience is a liminal experience.

The analysis could end here. We have answered the questions about passage that we laid out at the beginning of our analysis and have used the answers to interpret the performance as a rite of passage that both the protagonist and the spectators undergo. However, since the analysis started by placing the production within Wilson's *oeuvre*, we might want to conclude by situating this performance within twentieth-century theatre history and, in particular, in relation to the historical avant-garde movements. Edward Gordon Craig, in his programmatic essay "The Actor and the Über-Marionette," claimed that the goal of theatre as an art form is "to recall beautiful things from the imaginary world" and to make this "ideal world" visible:

> that mysterious, joyous and superbly complete life which is called Death ... the life of shadows and of unknown shapes, where all cannot be blackness and fog as supposed, but vivid colour, vivid light, sharp cut form, and what one finds peopled with strange, fierce and solemn figures and calm figures, and those figures impelled to some wondrous harmony of movement.
>
> (Craig 1908: 9)

This might prompt us to ask whether Wilson's *Lear* can also be understood as a reflection on theatre as an art form (as suggested by Craig), and furthermore on the relationship between theatre and death. Heiner Müller, for instance—and many others before him—defined theatre as a dialogue with the dead. Here our analysis comes full circle and ties back to the examples with which the book opened, all dealing with death and dying. Such a discussion about theatre and death might be triggered by our performance analysis, but reaches far beyond it into advanced theoretical and philosophical debates. Ultimately, there is no final, definitive end of a performance analysis: from each finding new questions may emerge. In this sense, the conclusion of any analysis is also a starting point for engaging in another broader discussion.

Excursus: Performance and Drama

Having engaged in a performance analysis, let's revisit the relationship of drama and performance. Performance and drama are not necessarily "opposites," as Max Herrmann claimed, because most dramas were written to be performed. Nevertheless, performance and drama are two different phenomena and research subjects, whose relationship to each other remains unresolved. Even today, some literary scholars and theatre critics—and even some theatre makers—are of the opinion that the performance is a concretization, realization, or transposition of the dramatic text. The text is seen as an authority that controls and governs the process of staging. Even if today few would go so far as to claim that any given drama has a single fixed meaning, the staging is sometimes seen as merely conveying to the audience ideas, fantasies, and visions inherent in the text. As already discussed in the section "The Emergence of Meaning" (Chapter 3), such a position is untenable. The ideas, fantasies, and visions that emerge from reading the text may inspire the director, the set designer, the composer, and the actors but is bound to do so in a different way for each individual who takes part in the staging process. To see the text as controlling and governing the production process is absurd.

The text can, nevertheless, be seen as an important source of inspiration. We might think of the text as a contributing element similar to the performance space or the cast of actors chosen for the production. Whereas the space and the bodies of the actors appear in their particular materiality in the performance, the text does not. During a performance, one can no longer perceive the text in its written form.

In the semiotic sense, every structured combination of signs is defined as a text, regardless of what sort of signs they are. This means that we can differentiate between written texts and performance texts. From a semiotic perspective, written texts and performance texts employ different sign systems. Each of these systems has specific characteristics and limitations, which influence their means of expression. In a performance, the written signs of a text must be translated into theatrical signs, whose semantic field and potential for meaning will be different. The meanings that can be attached to written signs therefore cannot be identical to the meanings of signs (such as gestures) used in their theatrical "translation." Linguistic signs—above all in writing—have a high degree of abstraction and indeterminacy. Even the most precise description of space, costume, or action—to be found above all in naturalistic drama—will be received differently by different people. Theatrical signs, in contrast, lend themselves to concreteness. They are connected to a specific space, the unique physique of the actor, words spoken in a particular manner by a specific voice, and so forth. They open up completely different possibilities for creating meaning than the written signs of a text. The experience of the space's atmosphere, the presence of an actor, the sound of certain words all affect how meaning is constituted. For that reason, we cannot call this a direct "translation."

We can describe the role of the text in the process of staging as an appropriation and assimilation through the participating artists. This is particularly true for the actors. During rehearsals, the actors must internalize and then externalize the text so that something perceptible emerges. This is always true, regardless of whether the text is performed in full, with cuts and changes, or interspersed with additional material. The artists must appropriate and assimilate the text or texts in such a way that something other than the written text is created—the performance.

Some contemporary stage directors are known for creating productions that emphasize the fundamental difference between words as they appear in the text and words spoken by an actor in performance, or between the stage directions regarding the set, costumes, and noises and the actual set, costumes, and noises in performance. The German director Frank Castorf, for example, frequently confronts audiences with this difference during performances of his productions. In his staging of Brecht's play *Herr Puntila and His Man Matti* (Deutsches Schauspielhaus Hamburg, 1996), for example, the actor playing Puntila (Michael Wittenborn) abruptly left the stage in the middle of the performance without any apparent motivation. He roamed around the auditorium, and would stop in front of individual spectators. He would scrutinize them from head to foot and make rude comments about their appearances, like "I don't like your feet. You'd rather just be loafing around, huh?" or "That's good for the kitchen," or "It's astonishing how people behave these days!" The attention and stares of the other spectators were suddenly directed at these individuals. Without any action on their parts and against their wills, they were turned into actors. The other spectators were mostly amused at this, some apparently enjoying their discomfort. Others seemed concerned that Wittenborn would come to them next.

The audience assumed that the actor Wittenborn was stepping out of his role when picking on individual spectators and criticizing their appearance. Actually, his words were written by Brecht—they are Puntila's comments when inspecting prospective domestic servants at a hiring fair. Yet the scene that framed Puntila's insults at the market was cut and replaced by a direct encounter with the audience. The insults suddenly changed their meaning. The difference between written text and performance was so striking that the audience realized only much later that this scene was supposed to "portray" a market fair.

Castorf also emphasized the difference between text and performance in his production called *Endstation Amerika* (*Last Stop America*, Volksbühne am Rosa-Luxemburg-Platz, Berlin, 2000) by using supertitles. The production worked with textual material from Tennessee Williams' play *A Streetcar Named Desire*, but Castorf had to change the title shortly before the premiere because of copyright laws. During the performance, English supertitles from the original play were projected that failed to correspond to anything that was happening onstage. Clearly, the text did not control the staging. Rather, the missing connection between the supertitles and the actions onstage marked the fundamental difference between text and performance and simultaneously drew attention to the senselessness of prevailing copyright regulations.

The fundamental phenomenal and semiotic difference between the dramatic text and performance renders obsolete the idea that performance should be "true to the artwork." Phenomenologically, semiotically, and historically such faithfulness to the letter of the text is impossible. If the stage direction of an eighteenth-century drama reads "hits his head against the wall in despair," should the actor follow these directions without fail and abide by the acting style of the period? The meaning of the text remains unstable, varying from epoch to epoch, and from reader to reader.

The analysis of the dramatic text is not a part of performance analysis, nor can it replace it. The dramatic text does not offer sufficient criteria by which to critique and evaluate a performance. Criticisms such as "This is not Antony" or "This is not Lear" do not say anything about the performance, but rather suggest the critic's perception of the performance based on his own reading of the text. Previous knowledge about a play—whether on the basis of a quick reading or painstaking analysis—as well as one's own performance history of the play affect one's reception of any further productions.

Whoever has read *King Lear* may have responded with surprise to the casting of Marianne Hoppe in the title role or the rendition of the Prologue, in which she recited a poem by William Carlos Williams. In the various performances that I visited, I could sense this expression of surprise in several other spectators but nevertheless did not get the impression that this surprise strongly influenced the perception and reception of the subsequent parts of the performance. Knowledge of the Shakespearean text made those spectators also capable of connecting the poem and the choreographed act of unbuttoning with other elements of the production that only emerged later; it allowed them to read the performance on a different level.

Overall, the specific use of music, sound, and light shaped our perception of the performance more than familiarity with the text of *King Lear*. The stylized gestures of the actors playing Goneril, Regan, Edmund, and Albany were disjointed from the words they spoke. Goneril stretched out like a cat in front of a crown lying on the ground; with catlike movements, she climbed up the back of the chair and sat on top of it. She crouched in front of her handkerchief and played with it with her "paws" as though it were a mouse. She entered and exited both scenes making "meowing"-sounds. Regan consistently held her head stretched forward like a vulture and bent her fingers on at least one hand into a sort of talon. As she exited, she held her arms twisted behind her so that they looked like bird wings, and strutted with her upper body stretched forward, neck and throat out. She squawked like a bird of prey and had a screeching laugh. In the play text, Lear explicitly calls Goneril "kite," "serpent," "wolf," and "vulture," and Regan "serpent," and we might connect these names to their animal gestures. However, there is never any mention of a cat, and Lear uses the word "vulture" to insult Goneril, not Regan. The reference to the text, therefore, can hardly be understood as decisive. Instead, we can connect these relationships with animals to death cults in various cultures in which animals such as the cat and vulture fulfill important symbolic roles. As these examples show, an analysis of the drama is not necessarily a precondition or substitute for performance analysis; in fact the analysis of the written text is entirely separate from performance analysis.

This does not mean, however, that theatre scholars should not read and analyze drama. On the contrary, many questions and problems with which theatre scholars are confronted require a precise knowledge of the texts used in performance—whether we are talking about classical drama or texts written for performance that do not necessarily differentiate between the main text (the speeches of people) and paratext (stage directions), such as a series of texts by Gertrude Stein, Heiner Müller, or Elfriede Jelinek. A more precise knowledge of the drama, or text, is required if in analysis of a performance we want to ask about the specific uses of the text and the mode in which it is embodied.

Researchers must be intimately acquainted with the text if their project includes fieldwork in the rehearsal room to explore the role of the text in different phases of the rehearsal process, including the processes of internalization and externalization of the text. While we can no longer assume that the text controls the rehearsal process, a number of new questions arise about the text's function and role—textual knowledge is a prerequisite in this context. Yet the dramatic text is *deficient* when it comes to performance. It cannot control the process of staging; it can only refer to that which can be verbally expressed. At the beginning of the twentieth century, the sociologist Georg Simmel observed:

> The dramatic character given in a text is, in some sense, an incomplete human being; he does not represent a sensual being but the sum of all that can be known about a human being through literature. The poet cannot predetermine the voice or pitch, the *ritardando* or *accelerando* of his speech, his gestures or even the special aura of the living figure.
>
> (Simmel 1968: 75)

For this reason, Simmel rejected the idea of evaluating a performance

> as if the ideal way of playing a role was inherently obvious and necessarily given along with that role; as if for the sharp eye and logical mind the theatrical sensualization of Hamlet would simply reveal itself on the pages of the book; so that there is but one "correct" representation of every role which the empirical actor approaches. This is already contradicted by the fact that three famous actors will play the role in three very different manners, each one equal to the other and neither more "correct" than the next; Hamlet thus [cannot] ... simply be played based on the text because it legitimizes Moissi's interpretation as much as it does that of Kainz or Salviati [*sic*].
>
> (Simmel 1968: 78)

The text can excite, inspire, and conjure memories. But because of its indeterminacy and deficits with regard to the performance, it cannot direct or
control a staging. It therefore seems more sensible to understand the text as
material for the staging process. The text exists in an interplay with other
materials—the space, the actors, the noises, the music—all of which combined
make up the performance.

There are a number of performance genres that do not require a dramatic
text, such as dance performances, some rituals, games, festivals, or sports
competitions. They work without a text, even if some version of a script is
characteristic for some of them—whether in the form of rules of a game,
choreography, a liturgy or some other form of organization. The subject of
performance analysis is in all cases the performance itself. The script remains an
integral part of the analysis but is not its fundamental subject.

Further Reading

On Memory

Carlson, M. (2001) *The Haunted Stage: The Theatre as Memory Machine*, Ann Arbor:
University of Michigan Press.
Schachter, D. (1996) *Searching for Memory: The Brain, the Mind, and the Past*, New York:
Basic Books.
Yates, F. (1966/2001) *The Art of Memory*, Chicago: University of Chicago Press.

On Semiotics

De Marinis, M. (1993) *The Semiotics of Performance*, Bloomington: University of Indiana
Press.
Elam, K. (1980) *The Semiotics of Theatre and Drama*, London: Methuen.
Fischer-Lichte, E. (1992) *The Semiotics of Theatre*, Bloomington: University of Indiana Press.
Mukařovský, J. (1970) *Aesthetic Function, Norm and Value as Social Facts*, Ann Arbor:
Michigan University Press.
Pavis, P. (1982) *Languages of the Stage: Essays in the Semiology of the Theatre*, New York:
Performing Arts Journal Publications.

On Phenomenology

Garner, S. B. (1994) *Bodied Spaces: Phenomenology and Performance in Contemporary Drama*,
Ithaca, NY: Cornell University Press.
Merleau-Ponty, M. (1962) *Phenomenology of Perception*, London: Routledge and Kegan
Paul.
Moran, D. and T. Mooney (2002) *The Phenomenology Reader*, London/New York:
Routledge.
States, B. (1985) *Great Reckonings in Little Rooms: On the Phenomenology of Theatre*, Berkeley/
London/Los Angeles: University of California Press.

Chapter 5

Theatre historiography

Performance analysis became a part of Theatre Studies only in the 1970s in the wake of the so-called *semiotic turn*. Theatre historical research, in contrast, had been conducted since the last decades of the nineteenth century, and became the foundation of Theatre Studies as an independent university discipline. Theatre Studies was initially conducted as theatre historiography. Since it was founded, intended and propagated as the study of performances, Theatre Studies was confronted with a paradoxical situation. It saw itself as a historical discipline but the objects that it studied were no longer accessible. Performances of the past are lost to theatre historians. One cannot relate to them aesthetically but only theoretically (Steinbeck 1970: 167). Theatre history cannot be written with recourse to performances themselves; it works with documents, remnants, and other types of secondary sources that can provide information about the performance. A theatre historian's work is close to that of a general historian, who depends on sources and documents to shed light on events such as the Reformation or the Thirty Years' War. Theatre historians face a range of challenges that we will discuss in the following sections.

Theoretical Considerations

If we are going to understand and write theatre history as the history of performances, we must first address the following questions:

- Which genres of performance should be our research subjects?
- Which criteria should we employ to determine which genres should be researched?
- How should we conceptualize history?

Performance Genres and the Concept of Theatre

Max Herrmann wanted to restrict the research of Theatre Studies to institutional, artistic theatre. At the same time he himself dedicated a large part of his theatre research to the study of performances by the Meistersinger (master-singers) of

Nuremberg's St Martha Church, which can hardly be counted as an institutional theatre. Artur Kutscher and Carl Niessen expanded the topics of theatre historical research to include all forms of cultural performances—in all cultures and ages—although they themselves did not carry out research projects in these expanded fields. As the introductory chapter showed, the concept of theatre has been in flux since the sixteenth century, making it very difficult to draw clear boundaries for the field. The choice of research subject will depend on the motivating research questions as well as the selected sources and documents (see Chapter 2). For example, an investigation of how performance generates knowledge could use dissections in the anatomical theatre as one of its examples, including documents like the one printed at the beginning of the book. If one is interested in questions about the relationship between ideas and discourses on the body and the creation of a new art of acting, the study of tracts about the art of acting from the eighteenth century and descriptions of individual actors, as well as philosophical, legal, and medical manuscripts, might be useful.

We cannot assume that scholars can reach any consensus about the proper subjects for theatre histories. There is consensus neither about what the term "theatre" means nor about which genres of performances it comprises. Nevertheless, most of the theatre histories from the past fifty years focus almost exclusively on the more or less well-documented performances of institutionalized spoken theatre in European and North American metropolitan areas. Hence, the discipline needs to expand its reach into other cultures and other kinds of performances. It is essential that theatre historians choose research subjects that fall within their fields of expertise, select performance events that are productive for answering their research questions, and—using the documents and sources available to them—write a history as *one* possible history rather than *the* definitive history.

Conceptions of History

We are starting to touch on another problem: the question of an underlying concept of history. Today, we no longer have a universal conception of history. We no longer read history as Hegel's "World Spirit" returning to itself, and we do not interpret it as a one-directional move from a supposed ur-community through feudalism and capitalism toward a classless society. We no longer adhere to Enlightenment theories of modernization, according to which the path of history is leading toward human perfection. Every totalizing, teleological conception of history is obsolete. This has consequences for historical research. Historians have sought to renew established strategies of how meaning is historically constructed, returning for example to narrative historiography (Rüsen 1990). The task of the historian turns from bringing facts into a natural order to telling a story according to literary principles (White 1973).

Attempts to create new forms of historical narratives can be contrasted to so-called "transgressive conceptions" of history that emphasize and theorize individual perspectives of history (Rüsen et al. 1988). Such histories focus on the everyday; women and gender histories; historical anthropology; the histories of the body, media, or science. These approaches all concentrate on particular microhistories rather than grand narratives:

> In place of thinking about progress as a series of temporal transformations whose direction can inform the orientation of contemporary praxis, we must see unilinear ideas of progress in relation to multiple possibilities of human ways of life. Instead of macrohistory that offers a comprehensive history of the modern world, microhistories emerge, composed of many little histories, that each have their own meaning.
>
> (Rüsen 1990: 70)

The "re-subjectivization" of history (Rüsen 1990: 72) has led to research questions that were traditionally studied in disciplines outside of history proper, such as Literature, Art History, and Theatre and Performance Studies. They are connected to human feelings and thoughts, "forms of consciousness, patterns of thinking, world-views, ideologies, etc." (Schöttler 1989: 85) that—especially in Germany—were the subject of intellectual history and approached in new ways based on Foucault's discourse analysis (Foucault 1970, 1977).

This reorientation in the discipline led primarily to an acknowledgment of a fundamental pluralism of theories and methods. The partiality of any given approach has become the condition of possibility for historiography: every theory explains a different microhistory; every method approaches a different historical level. These changes in the discipline of history have also had consequences for theatre historiography. Many recent textbooks on theatre historiography go to great lengths to emphasize the plurality of possible approaches. Works such as *Theatre Historiography: Critical Interventions* explore the political stakes implicit in researching and writing theatre history (Bial and Magelssen 2010).

Theatre histories of the twentieth century began with varied conceptions of history and methodological approaches. They saw theatre history as, for example, cultural history (Kernodle 1989), social history (Craik 1975–80 and Kindermann 1957–74), or intellectual history (Nicoll 1923–59). Despite such proclamations, most of these studies ultimately fell prey to the same underlying positivism as theatre historiographies of the nineteenth century. They piled source upon source without offering sufficient transparency on how the given material was selected. Such projects simply recognized that theatre history can be described as cultural, intellectual, or social history without drawing any methodological consequences. Scholars did not develop questions that justified the choice of documents or the methods of their analysis. It is hard to escape the conclusion that the only criterion for choosing the material was its availability. In all these cases, partiality is not acknowledged as the condition of theatre historiography—instead, the historical ideal of universality continued to dominate the methodologies. The deceptive hope that it would be possible to reconstruct the theatre of an epoch *as it really was* if only one could collect enough material seemed all too alluring.

In contrast, we must emphasize partiality as the condition of writing theatre history. In order to avoid universalisms, theatre historiography requires specific acts of framing on a case-by-case basis, with regard to both the object of study and the line of questioning. This can work both ways: a particular object of study can call for a specific line of questioning; likewise a specific question may demand focus on a particular object of study. In other words, theatre historiography can only be carried out by way of a problem-oriented approach—a matter of consensus among theatre historians today. Various theatre historical monographs and theatre histories have operated within this problem-oriented approach and developed theoretical and methodological frameworks that go hand in hand with it.[1]

Periodization

It is not surprising that this problem-oriented approach is particularly common in individual research projects about a relatively limited time period (such as the second half of the eighteenth century). For theatre histories that comprise a substantially longer time span and that work diachronically (for example, Oscar Brockett and Franklin Hildy's *History of Theatre*, 1982), the central problem lies in how to subdivide and structure its history. As sociologist Niklas Luhmann remarked, it is not enough "to draw everything together through differentiating between before and after—along the lines of Europe before the potato and after the potato" (or, in reference to European theatre, before the invention of the Italian stage and after its invention), "because this difference could then only describe the grandiose event that divides the epochs itself, but not history as a process" (Luhmann 1985, 11). History is not a sequence of events but an endless process that does not follow pre-determined structuring principles. The organization into segments—usually defined as periods—has to be undertaken by historians, who explicate how they arrive at their temporal structure.

In writing histories of theatre that are broad in scope, one unavoidably has to confront the problem of periodization, investigate the transitions between periods, and understand the differentiation between periods. The problem cannot be ignored, or obscured, by merely presenting a chronology of facts. Simple chronology ignores the dynamic character of theatre history and fails to connect events to one another. In response scholars have tended to turn toward historical categories developed within other contexts and disciplines, such as the Middle Ages, the Renaissance, the Baroque, and so forth.

This strategy carries its own problems, particularly evident in the transition from Antiquity to the Middle Ages. Whereas the end of the Roman Empire around 500 CE generally marks the close of Antiquity, most researchers locate the theatre of the Middle Ages as beginning with the rise of liturgical drama in 1000 CE. At this moment, European theatre was created "a second time" out of the Easter tropes of the tenth century. This thesis, first formulated in 1886 by Léon Gautier in *Histoire de la poésie liturgique au Moyen Âge* (*History of Liturgical Poetry in the Middle Ages*), continues to haunt European theatre history. What, one might ask, happened to theatre between the fifth and the tenth centuries? These 500 years did, in fact, witness a wide range of performances of traveling players, Goliards, wandering minstrels, jokers, and jugglers, as documented in visual portrayals (such as an illuminated manuscript prepared in 1360 in Prague for Emperor Charles IV) and written documents (such as the ruling of the Synod of Prague in 1367). None of these performances were text-based, or at least no texts have been transmitted. Hence they did not fit the nineteenth-century idea of theatre and were consequently not relevant to theatre history.

Theatre history can have a regional, national, continental, transcontinental, and global scope (for example the theatre history of London, Paris, or Hamburg; Spanish, Japanese, or Indian theatre history; European, African, or Latin American theatre history; the theatre history of Western cultures, theatre histories of the world). In each of these different types of history, the boundaries and transitions between periods will differ. The editors of *Theatre Histories: An Introduction*, which discusses theatre from cultures of every continent, decided to create their periodization around modes of human communication. They base this approach on a specific understanding of humans on one hand, and a specific understanding of theatre on the other:

> One of the identifying characteristics of human awareness and consciousness is the development of the ability to reflect upon and communicate who we are. Theatre and performance are complex, culturally embedded, historically specific kinds of communal reflection and communication. Because major new developments in modes of human communication led to profound changes in the ways people thought about, related to, and organized their world, each of the four parts of this book are organized to mark such transformations and relate them to theatre and performance.
>
> (Zarrilli, McConachie, Williams, and Sorgenfrei 2006: xxviiif)

Periodization here follows upheavals in communication technologies and media, such as the invention of book printing or the new media. Three periods emerge: (1) theatre/performances in oral and written cultures before 1600, (2) theatre since the rise of print cultures (1500–1900), (3) theatre in the modern media culture (1850–1970), (4) theatre/performances in the age of globalization and virtual communication (1950 to today). While this particular periodization is persuasive and captivating, it must be emphasized that there is no general rule for the periodization of theatre histories.

Historiographic Praxis

The most important steps for writing theatre history are: (a) formulating a research question or hypothesis; (b) selecting relevant sources; (c) choosing one or several methodological approaches to interpret sources in the light of the guiding question.

Questions

There are various ways to develop research questions. Research questions are usually derived from a particular scholarly interest. The two most common approaches develop research questions from opposite ends. The first approach is to proceed from a particular theory that opens up a certain question and then to find sources that can help answer that question. The second approach is to start with the sources themselves and develop a research question from them. One might stumble upon a fascinating source that cannot be explained by existing studies (or that contradicts them), and decide to develop a research question based on that source.

Let's begin with an example of what the first approach might look like. Say we have read Norbert Elias's book *The Civilizing Process* and are fascinated by his theory that Europe since the sixteenth century has undergone a "civilizing process" in which people's bodies are controlled and disciplined to ever-greater degrees (Elias 2000). Since performances are created through the bodily co-presence of actors and spectators, such changes in behavior must have had an impact on performance. Based on this research interest, we can formulate a research question. A general question might be: are these changes in bodily discipline apparent in performances that took place between the sixteenth and twentieth centuries? In order to answer this question we would have to go back to accounts from professional theatres in the sixteenth century to find out how the behavior of actors and spectators changed in this period. We would investigate theories of acting as well as first-hand accounts about acting in specific performances and the behavior of spectators (sources as diverse as travelogues, police reports, or newspaper reviews might come into play here). Alternatively, one could investigate the development of new genres of performance between the sixteenth and twentieth centuries, such as the circus, and investigate what kind of behaviors and discipline these genres demanded from actors and participants. Another avenue might explore how the "civilizing process" was connected to the ethnographic exhibitions at World's Fairs in the last third of the nineteenth century. The initial question opens up a number of ways to proceed, and it is important to be able to explain why one decides to proceed in a particular way.

Of course, answering even a small number of these questions would be well out of the scope of a term paper or even a thesis project. Often the initial question that one begins with will need to be narrowed down once the research begins. An appropriate topic for a term paper that began with our general research question about the relationship between performance and the "civilizing process" might be, for example, a discussion of one particular staging that exemplifies changes in bodily discipline in the theatre.

Often it takes a certain amount of research to be able to narrow down one's general interests and formulate a pertinent research question. In our second example we begin with a very general interest in intellectual history. To explore the relationship between knowledge and theatre, we might focus on the dominant concept of theatre in the seventeenth century, which included every space in which something worth knowing was introduced or shown. Now that we have narrowed down our interest to a particular period, we can develop more specific research questions. We could focus, for example, on public dissections in the anatomical theatre or publicly performed experiments at the Royal Society in London in order to ask why science used performance to transmit its developments. From a general interest in intellectual history, we have narrowed our study to manageable size: an analysis of public experiments performed at the Royal Society in the seventeenth century. Attempting to study the relationship between knowledge and theatre in Western culture through the ages, in contrast, would require decades of scholarship and research. Obviously, there are many alternative research topics and compelling questions about seventeenth-century theatre; the point is to find the right scope for one's project and formulate a question that speaks to one's interests.

Another possible topic in seventeenth-century theatre would be the use of new technologies in both institutionalized theatre and spectacles. We might inquire about the introduction of one specific technology and its effect on audiences. We have quite a number of sources that discuss the impact of machines that created special effects in performance. In the monthly journal *Mercure Galant*, the use and effects of machines in the theatre and, in particular, the wonders they created are repeatedly emphasized. An account of a theatre of machines in performance created by the Marquis de Sourdiac—incidentally also one of the machinists in Molière's company—reads: "He has prepared to do things that are so beautiful, so new and so surprising with the machines, that they will be admired in the four corners of the world" (*Mercure Galant*, Tome III, Paris, 1673, 341–42). The machines that he built and used in the performance of *Pièce de machine Circé* are described in the *Gazette d'Amsterdam* as "so extraordinary they surpass the imagination" (February 14, 1675).

Gian Lorenzo Bernini's *Fontana di Trevi* caused a powerful upheaval, which we will discuss in greater detail in Chapter 8. The piece was written for and performed during the carnival season in Rome in 1638 and featured dramatic special effects showing the flooding of the Tiber which, in fact, had happened the previous year. The documents on the effects in this and other performances are printed as an appendix to the edition of the piece in 1963 (Gian Lorenzo Bernini, *Fontana di Trevi. Commedia inedita*, ed. Cesare d'Onofrio, Rome, 1963, Appendix of documents). In another production by Bernini, a carnival procession was crossing the stage, with each actor holding a torch in his hand. Suddenly one actor, as if by mistake, set the decor on fire. The flame licked up the decor and spread out into a fireball, "so that everybody believed the fire was an accident and had no other thought than to get out of danger" (Bernini 1963: 96). Bernini himself was forced to appear on stage in order to calm the spectators down, while the scene changed into a blossoming garden. As can be gathered from the descriptions of these events, the machines were used to excite emotions in the spectators—be they awe, wonder and amazement, or fear and trembling.

These examples could be analyzed in terms of Elias' theory of the civilizing process that demanded of seventeenth-century courtiers utmost control over their emotions—in which, obviously, they did not succeed in these cases of theatre performances. This raises the question of whether, and if so why, the rules for behavior in theatre and in everyday life at court differed from one another. Alternatively, these examples could serve as a point of departure for discussing the relationship between theatre history and the history of technology in the seventeenth century: what spurred these sorts of discoveries? What kind of causality was at play between ideas about theatre, knowledge, and newly developed technologies? These are complex questions that require research for a book-length study.

Sources

Sources are the foundation of every study in theatre history, regardless of the specific research question. Primary sources are materials that have come to us from the past, such as texts, artifacts, and monuments. Through these sources, we can investigate and date events, forms of behavior, beliefs, and so forth. Some sources are remnants of performances, such as a theatre building, a costume, or a cast list. Other sources are purposely preserved for posterity, such as theatre reviews or photographs. Our research question will determine the relevance of each of these sources. Each time we begin a project, we have to decide what can be used as a source, and where it can be found.

In 1970, the German scholar Dietrich Steinbeck attempted to systematically categorize the various sources used for theatre historical research. He differentiates between primary and secondary sources, defining primary sources as those that were used in the process of the staging and/or performance and that can give direct information about the staging or performance. Secondary sources are those that relate to the staging or performance in other ways. We can see how he differentiates between various sources in Table 5.1.

All of these sources are connected to institutional theatre performances; in Steinbeck's classification we do not find sources connected to festivals, religious or political rituals, sports competitions, games, performances of science, or other kinds of *cultural performance*. That is fully legitimate, since Steinbeck made it clear that his concept of theatre would not include such performances.

Table 5.1 Theatre artifacts and theatre tradition, according to Steinbeck (1970: 159f)

Theatre artifacts (remnants of the performance)	Theatre tradition (preserved for posterity)
Theatre buildings	Images of the stage
Stage	Films
Stage technology	Images of scenes
Parts of the set	Images of characters
Costumes	Images of sets
Props	Blueprints
Masks	Costume designs
Director's journal	Performance reports
Cast list	Descriptions of roles
Prompt books	Memos from rehearsals and meetings
Stage manager books	Annual reports
Stage models	Almanacs
Technical sketches	Critiques
Files, contracts, public records	Theatre periodicals
Programs	Letters and open letters
Director's notes	Diaries and memoirs
	Biographies
	Anecdotes
	Pamphlets
	Theoretical writings
	Posters
	Portrayals in visual art

In order to include other genres of performance, we must expand this list of possible sources accordingly. Furthermore, the list of useful sources depends not only on our concept of theatre, but also on our research question. Let's say we want to research the relationship between psychologically realistic styles of acting and new behavioral norms of the middle class in the eighteenth century. Such a project requires sources directly related to institutional theatre, such as a 1758 letter that was sent from a family in Zurich to the actresses of the Ackermann Troupe, asking that they teach their daughters how to comport themselves and how to dress. In addition, the etiquette books of the second half of the eighteenth century and books on fashion of the period are crucial source material.

As Steinbeck's classification of sources shows, sources can be transmitted in a wide variety of media, each of which requires a different approach. First, we have theatre buildings and other performance spaces that we can still find and visit, such as the Palladio's Teatro Olimpico in Vicenza that opened in 1585 with the first Early Modern production of a Greek tragedy, Sophocles' *Oedipus Rex*; St Martha's Church in Nuremberg, where the Meistersinger performances that Herrmann studied took place; the Bayreuth Festspielhaus with its annual festival of Wagner operas that still takes place; the Public Theatre in New York City founded by Joseph Papp in 1954 as one of the first nonprofit theatres in the US; or the square in front of the Winter Palace in

St Petersburg, where Nikolai Evreinov and others staged *The Storming of the Winter Palace* in 1920.

The theatre in Drottningholm, Sweden, is a particularly fascinating source for research work on stage technology and set pieces. It preserves the original eighteenth-century stage including machines and sets still used in performances. The Lauchstaedter Theatre, used by Goethe's Weimar Theatre as a summer venue, also still holds a number of theatre machines from the period. In every theatre museum it is possible to find costumes, props, and masks used in a variety of performances. These sources can be termed authentic insofar as they were used in and contributed to performances. Just like other sources, they must be made to speak to the research questions at hand and require a critical approach. Each artifact allows one to draw a variety of conclusions, yet none offer an unequivocal demonstration of past performance.

The same goes for textual and visual sources, notes, and sound recordings. Textual sources might include a script, a director's book, scenarios, reviews, letters or pamphlets (most of the sources Steinbeck lists fall into this category). If the author, the context, and the authorial intentions of such material cannot be determined, it is very difficult to draw conclusions from them.

Visual sources are often assumed to be true and authentic regardless of whether they appear on vases, in paintings, in photos, or in video recordings. Yet the stylization and painterly conventions of an era always influence painting, and so they can only give us limited information about past performances. We would have to decide whether a given painting portrays a *commedia dell'arte* performance of the turn of the sixteenth to seventeenth centuries, actors from the eighteenth century in costume, or a private portrait of people dressed up as *commedia* actors. In the case of photos, we must keep in mind that in the nineteenth and early twentieth centuries, these photos were taken in studios rather than during a performance. We have already discussed the challenges when video recording in connection to performance analysis. Regardless of its medium, any source must be approached critically and with caution.

Sources can be interpreted and used in a wide variety of ways. Often a new theory can help us read a source in new ways. For example, recent theories about performance and performativity can cast new light on sources related to seventeenth-century spectacles. These spectacles were composed of multiple performance genres and included, most prominently, fireworks. Scholars have long had access to a number of sources related to these fireworks, including descriptions of fireworks in letters and visual portrayals of the fireworks. For a long time, all of these different sources were interpreted through one primary source: a text that gave allegorical meaning to the fireworks. Before the start of a firework display such a text would be read to the assembled guests by protagonists of the spectacle. Researchers understood fireworks as the realization of these allegorical programs and interpreted the political meaning of the spectacle through these texts.

This approach assumes that the meaning of a spectacle can be found in a textual source. If we take a different approach and instead understand the fireworks primarily as a performance, we will draw a different conclusion. Analyzing firework displays as performances implies recourse to theories of performance and performativity. These theories suggest that firework displays—like all performances—create a unique atmosphere through the interplay of light and darkness, sounds, noises, and smells. Furthermore, these theories require that we consider the experience of spectators, the majority of whom did not understand how fireworks worked. For these spectators, the fireworks seemed mysterious and incomprehensible. Because of this, we can postulate that the performance would not be experienced only as a cognitive process of recognizing and decoding the allegorical program that had been read out before the fireworks began. The spectators also *felt* the performance. It led to bodily changes in their physiological, affective, energetic, and motor conditions and drew them into a liminal state. Above all, witnesses reported that they were filled with wonder. This wonder can be understood as part of a political calculation that used the strong physical effect of the display as evidence of the ruler's powers (Horn 2004). It becomes evident how new theories (in this case theories of performance) enable us to reinterpret old sources and draw new conclusions about historical performances.

Methodologies

Theatre histories can be written as histories of art, emotion, science, bodies, or society, to name a few. The possibilities are endless. Each of these types of micro-history has different theoretical foundations with differing methodologies. There is no single History of the Theatre.

One can divide methodologies for studying performances into two broad categories: deductive (applying a general premise to a specific case) and inductive (moving from a specific case to a general conclusion). In an inductive project, we would start with a source (such as a document about a performance) that raises questions about what we already know about a historical period. We would then seek to draw in additional sources as well as theoretical frameworks to address the questions the initial source had raised. Deductive methods in theatre historiography would begin with a specific interest directed toward one of the micro-histories listed above. Drawing on these histories, we can form specific questions about the theatre. We would then answer these questions through recourse to historical sources and documents. In the next two sections, we will go over two exemplary research projects, the first of which takes a deductive and the second an inductive approach. Most actual research projects fall between the poles of a purely deductive or inductive approach, and instead combine these two methods.

Case Study 1: Theatre History and the History of Emotions

Our first case study begins with the current interest of theatre historians in the history of emotions, otherwise described as the "emotional turn" (Plamper 2009) or "affective turn" (Clough and Halley 2007; Agnew 2007). The focus lies on one of the most thoroughly researched periods of European theatre history—the eighteenth century, understood as the century of sensibility in English, French, and German theatre history.

The eighteenth century saw the rise of new ideas about sensibility and emotions. Up until then, affect had been read as afflicting the subject from the outside. There also had been a limited number of affects, between eight and eleven. The music theorist Athanasius Kircher, for example, enumerates eight affects in his considerations of how music expresses and conjures affects in listeners. These affects are: (1) love; (2) sorrow or pain; (3) joy; (4) anger or outrage; (5) sympathy; (6) fear or dejection; (7) boldness; (8) wonder (Kircher 1650: 258). Kircher suggests that there is both a musical medium and a gesture suitable for portraying each affect to the audience and in turn conjuring that affect in them.

A tract published in 1727 by the Jesuit priest Franciscus Lang called *De Actione Scenica* summarizes the seventeenth-century rules concerning the affect of sorrow: "*Weeping and Melancholy*: Both hands joined in the middle of the chest, either high on the chest or lower about the belt. Also accomplished by extending the right hand gently and motioning towards the chest." Lang also describes the affects of fear and admiration: "*Fear*: The right hand reaching towards the breast with the four digits visible while the rest of the body is bent, relaxed and bowed ... *Admiration*: Both hands outstretched above the chest and palms towards the audience" (quoted in Engle 1968: 107). Every affect was accorded one gesture, or sometimes multiple gestures, so that changes in affect were clearly visible to the audience. This style of acting was dominant until the middle of the eighteenth century.

Yet especially after the 1750s, the idea gained ground that sentiments and feelings arise *within* people. Much physiological research during the eighteenth century centered on the relationship between body and soul. Leading physicians of the time such as Louis Lacaze, Claude-Nicolas Le Cat, and Albrecht von Haller all agreed—despite diverging in other aspects of their theories—that the body was directly influenced by mental states (Lacaze 1755; Le Cat 1767; Haller 1756–60 and 1774). They came to the conclusion that there was a "natural law of analogy," according to which people's bodies are naturally active and changeable. Bodies are suited to express inner states and processes, especially feelings, and make them perceptible.

Around the same time (c. 1750–80), a fierce debate about acting arose in England, France, and Germany. Central figures in this debate included theorists of the theatre and philosophers such as Aaron Hill, Raymond de Saint Albine, Francisco Riccoboni, John Hill, Denis Diderot, Gotthold Ephraim

Figura VII.

Figure 5.1 Weeping and Melancholia, in Franciscus Lang (1727), Abhandlung über die Schauspielkunst, Alexander Rudin (trans. and ed.), Berne/Munich 1975.

Lessing, and Georg Christoph Lichtenberg.[2] The question at stake was how the actor—who until then had used strictly codified rhetorical gestures to portray affects—could achieve a "natural" portrayal of feelings. Should the actor conjure feelings internally and then—according to the principle of analogy—automatically express them in "natural" gestures (Aaron Hill, Saint Albine, John Hill)? Or should the actor study feelings precisely and then, following the principle of analogy, present them without actually feeling them (Diderot)? Lessing offered a middle ground. To Lessing, the principle of analogy worked in two directions: "modifications of the soul that bring about certain changes in the body can in return be produced by those changes to the body" (Lessing 2012, Third Essay). Lessing assumes a psychosomatic interplay between the body and soul.

The historical parallel between physiological research and the debate of philosophers and theorists of theatre might suggest that the philosophers and theorists were responding to the physiologists. However, the debate about the appropriate portrayal of feelings began before the first publications by physiologists. It is more likely that the changes in the art of acting had already begun and were not simply stimulated by this scientific research.

The English actor David Garrick (1717–79) played a key role in the writings of English, French, and German theorists including Diderot and Lichtenberg. In fact, his acting style was used to prove either side of the debate. Diderot's accounts of Garrick's acting might clarify why the latter was used to argue either position. In his *Letter to Madame Riccoboni* (November 17, 1758), Diderot describes a dispute over pantomime that took place during Garrick's first visit to Paris in 1751. In this dispute, Garrick argued that a person could make a great impression without words, a position that no one had anticipated. When others contradicted him, Garrick became animated. He grabbed a pillow and said:

> Gentlemen, I am this child's father. Thereupon he opened a window, took his cushion, tossed it in the air, kissed it, caressed it, and imitated all the fooleries of a father playing with his child. But then came a moment when the cushion, or rather, the child slipped from his hand and fell through the window. Then Garrick began to mime the father's despair ... His audience was seized with such consternation and horror that most of them could not bear it and had to leave the room.
>
> (Quoted in Benedetti 2001: 188)

Garrick's facial expressions, gestures, and movements captured a father's despair and elicited strong feelings from the spectators. They perceived these expressions, gestures, and movements as the manifestation of a deep despair. Nothing in this passage contradicts the idea that the actor may actually have felt a flash of despair.

In *The Paradox of Acting*, Diderot refers to one of Garrick's drawing-room circles in Paris in order to argue that the actor does not need to feel strong emotions in order to trigger them in the spectators:

> Garrick will put his head between two folding doors, and in the course of five or six seconds his expression will change successively from wild delight to temperate pleasure, from this to tranquility, from tranquility to surprise, from surprise to blank astonishment, from that to sorrow, from sorrow to the air of one overwhelmed, from that to fright, from fright to

horror, from horror to despair, and then, he will go up again to the point from which he started.

(Diderot 1883: 63)

This sort of quick transition from one feeling to the next is only possible through the controlled and intentional portrayal of facial expressions, gestures, and movements that are perceived as the complete expression for each of the feelings. It would be impossible for the actor to actually experience such a range of emotion at will.

Garrick's art of acting does not prove or disprove whether the actor *must* feel or must *not* feel an emotion in order to portray it. Whatever his technique, Garrick had a strong effect on audiences. Since he inspired both theorists of theatre and everyday theatre-goers, his acting provides us with a suitable case study for exploring how the art of acting in the second half of the eighteenth century influenced the development of scientific knowledge about feelings.

Before delving into historical documents, we must begin by clarifying the major concepts in our project. In English, the terms "sentiments," "affections," "passions" were all used in the seventeenth century, but the word "emotion" was not used at all until the middle of the eighteenth century. The concept of emotion first appeared in David Hume's *Treatise of Human Nature* (1739–40). Subsequently, the term was primarily used by the school of Scottish empiricist philosophers and mental scientists. The new concept of emotion was popularized above all by Thomas Brown's *Lectures on the Philosophy of the Human Mind* (1820), in which the term "emotion" was used to mean "all those feelings that were neither sensations nor intellectual states" (Dixon 2003: 23). In contrast to earlier terms such as "affection" and "passion," the concept of "emotion" did not carry specifically Christian associations and values. It was a "secular psychological category".

Understanding how the concept of "emotion" developed can help us expand and clarify the initial topic of our research. We began with an interest in the effect that acting had on the development of scientific knowledge in the second half of the eighteenth century. We now know that this development is related to the emergence of the new "secular psychological category" of "emotion," which would later become the most important hermeneutical instrument in empirical psychology.

Now we turn to historical documents to understand Garrick's art of acting. Garrick is a good research subject because a comparatively large number of reports and descriptions of his portrayal of various roles exist. In addition, a number of images survive that portray Garrick in the roles of Lear, Hamlet, or Macbeth, including William Hogarth's famous painting of Garrick as Richard III. Garrick's acting debut in London took place prior to the intense preoccupation with the relationship between body and soul and debates about the art of acting. In other words, Garrick's innovations in acting were not a direct response to these debates.

Garrick debuted in the role of Richard III in Colley Cibber's 1700 version of Shakespeare's tragedy on October 19, 1741. His debut as an actor and Hume's *Treatise of Human Nature* (in which the term "emotion" was used for the first time) were exactly a year apart. From the beginning of the performance, Garrick's new way of acting astonished the audience, and put them in a state of wonder that quickly turned to rapture:

> Mr. Garrick's easy and familiar, yet forcible style in speaking and acting, at first threw the critics into some hesitation concerning the novelty as well as propriety of his manner. They had long been accustomed to an elevation of the voice, with a sudden mechanical depression of its tones, calculated to excite admiration, and to entrap applause. To the just modulation of the words, and concurring expression of the features from the genuine workings of nature, they had been strangers, at least for some time. But after he had gone through a variety of scenes, in which he gave proof of consummate art, and perfect knowledge of character, their doubts were turned into surprise and amazement, from which they relieved themselves by loud and reiterated applause ... Mr. Garrick shone forth like a theatrical Newton; he threw new light on elocution and action.
>
> (Davies 1780/1808: 40–44)

If the comparison to Newton seems far-fetched, a letter of the famous actor Charles Macklin to William Cooke supports this claim:

> It was amazing how without any example, but on the contrary with great prejudice against him, he could throw such spirit and novelty into the part as to convince every impartial person on the very first impression that he was right. In short, Sir, he at once decided the public taste; and though the players formed a cabal against him ... it was a puff to thunder.
>
> (Cooke 1804: 99)

Even Garrick's first appearances on stage were revolutionary, as the reference to Newton suggests. It is unclear, though, what exactly constituted this revolution. Expressions like "the genuine workings of nature" or "perfect knowledge of character" were also used in the first half of the eighteenth century in order to legitimate rhetorical gestures. The concepts of nature and the natural changed substantially over the course of the century. The above descriptions of Garrick do not give us a very clear sense of how his art differed so radically from that of his predecessors.

To determine what was "revolutionary" in Garrick's acting, we need a more precise description of what he did in these scenes, such as Diderot's account of Garrick's improvised pantomimes. These descriptions are not often found in reviews, which generally focus on Garrick's rendition of dramatic character and the impression he made on critics and other spectators. A somewhat more precise description of the mad scene in *King Lear* can be found in a review by John Hill, the translator of Sainte Albine's treatise, which he had published under his own name with the title *The Actor, a Treatise on the Art of Playing* (1750). Hill writes:

> 'Tis an odd Effect of a Laugh to produce Tears; but I believe there was hardly a dry Eye in the House on his executing that first absolute Act of Madness in the Character. While I admired the action, I was almost at a Loss to comprehend in what Manner it was performed: 'Twas not anything like the Laugh of Mirth or Pleasantry, the Triumph of a happy Imagination; but seemed merely the Exertion of the Organs of the body, without any Connection with the Soul; an involuntary Emotion of the Muscles, while the Mind was fixed on something else. Upon the whole, other Lears I have seen ... Must pardon me, if I declare that the frantic Part of the character seems never to have been rightly understood till this gentleman studied it.
>
> (Quoted in Gray 1931: 113)

Hill describes here how Garrick's laughter at the start of Lear's madness makes a particularly strong impression on him as much as the rest of the audience, rousing them to tears. Garrick's acting also sheds new light on madness for Hill. In other words, the acting teaches Hill about the dramatic character. Garrick's acting does not present madness as a single affect that can always be expressed in the same way. Instead he shows a particular madness related to the character of the dramatic figure. The madness played here is not madness *per se*, but rather Lear's specific madness. What is remarkable in Hill's review is the use of the word "emotion," which here is used in the sense of an uncontrollable muscle movement.

Of all the theatre theorists, Lichtenberg most strongly emphasizes that actors must individualize the mental states they portray. During his stay in London in 1775, he saw Garrick in various roles. Lichtenberg's *Letters from England* offer the most precise portraits we have of Garrick's acting. In these letters, Lichtenberg describes extensively and in great detail Garrick's portrayals of Hamlet, Abel Drugger (in Ben Jonson's *The Alchemist*), and Sir John Brute (from Vanbrugh's *The Provoked Wife*). Lichtenberg describes the scene in which Hamlet's father's ghost appears to him for the first time:

> Hamlet appears in a black dress, the only one in the whole court, alas! Still worn for his poor father ... Horatio and Marcellus in uniform are with him ... Hamlet has folded his arms under his cloak and pulled his hat down over his eyes; it is a cold night and just twelve o'clock; the theatre

Figure 5.2 David Garrick as King Lear. Engraving by J. McArdell, 1761, from a painting by
Benjamin Wilson, ca 1760. Laver, James: *Populäre Druckgraphik Europas*: England:
vom 15. bis zum 20. Jahrhundert, Munich: Callwey 1972 (out of print; please get
in touch if rights have unintentionally been violated).

is darkened, and … quiet … Suddenly, as Hamlet moves toward the back
of the stage slightly to the left and turns his back on the audience, Horatio
starts, and saying: "Look, My Lord, it comes," points to the right, where
the ghost has already appeared and stands motionless, before anyone is
aware of him. At these words Garrick turns sharply and at the same
moment staggers back two or three paces with his knees giving way under
him; his hat falls to the ground and both his arms, especially the left, are
stretched out nearly full length, with the hands as high as his head, the
right arm more bent and the hand lower, the fingers apart; his mouth is
open: thus he stands rooted to the spot, with legs apart, but no loss of
dignity, supported by his friends, who are better acquainted with the
apparition and fear lest he should collapse. His whole demeanor is so
expressive of terror that it made my flesh creep even before he began to
speak. The almost terror-struck silence of the audience, which preceded
this appearance and filled one with a sense of insecurity, probably did
much to enhance this effect. At last he speaks, not at the beginning, but at

the end of a breath, with a trembling voice, "Angels and ministers of Grace defend us!" words, which supply anything this scene may lack and make it one of the greatest and most terrible, which will ever be played on any stage. The ghost beckons him, I wish you could see him, with eyes fixed on the ghost, though he is speaking to his companions, freeing himself from their restraining hands … He stands with his sword on guard against the specter, saying: "Go on, I follow thee," and the ghost goes on off stage. Hamlet still remains motionless … and at length when the spectator can no longer see the ghost, he begins slowly to follow him, now standing still and then going on, with sword still upon guard, eyes fixed on the ghost, hair disordered, and out of breath, until he too is lost to sight … What an amazing triumph.

(Lichtenberg 1938, 9–11)

The expression of terror Lichtenberg recounts goes into such detail about elements and phases that it extends far beyond the codified expression that Lang had provided. It also goes beyond the descriptions in physiological textbooks and observations of actors in later tracts, such as Johann Jakob Engel's 1784/85 work *Acting*.[3] This account describes the gestures, movements, and articulations that express terror itself. It also focuses on Hamlet's character traits—his particular sensibility as well as his social standing ("no loss of dignity") and his specific situation (still in mourning).

Garrick's portrayal of Hamlet's reaction to the appearance of his father's ghost, as Lichtenberg describes it, allows processes of the human "soul" to appear in ways that are not accounted for in either the physiology or the philosophy of the time. Hence, the art of acting opened up new dimensions of gaining knowledge about people, their mental states, and their emotions. Garrick's art of acting was epoch-making from his very first appearances in 1741. Through Garrick, theatre became a "psychological institution," a laboratory for empirical psychology.

What Garrick achieved so early and so exceptionally inspired other actors of his time, though without the same "genius" and success as Garrick. In his *Letters from England*, Lichtenberg expressly refers to the German actor Conrad Ekhof (1720–78), who was not at the same level as Garrick, but who nevertheless left some of the other celebrated London actors far behind. Detailed descriptions of acting and actors, as we find in Lichtenberg's letters, became increasingly common in German discussions about performances. Critics and theorists were no longer satisfied with individual descriptions, and compared how different actors performed the same roles and scenes. From these accounts we know, for example, that in Lear's mad scene, Johann Franz Hieronymus Brockmann (1745–1812) climbed onto a tree stump as he proclaimed, "I will preach to thee: mark." In Friedrich Ludwig Schröder's (1744–1816) portrayal of Lear in the same scene, Lear attempted to climb the stump, but then collapsed. Contemporaries

Figure 5.3 David Garrick as Hamlet. Act I, Scene 4. Engraving by J. McArdell, 1754, from a painting by Benjamin Wilson. Uncatalogued Garrickiana Maggs no. 146. Copyright: Folger Shakespeare Library, Washington, DC.

considered these variations particular "refinements" because they revealed more about the "truth" of Lear.

In his description of Schröder's portrayal of Hamlet, the critic of the *Litteratur und Theaterzeitung* (1779) compared the details of Schröder's portrayal with Brockmann's portrayal of Hamlet, the first celebrated Hamlet on the German stage. He ended his report with a description of Act III, scene 4 between Hamlet and his mother:

When speaking the words, "How is it with you, lady?" Schröder avoided a mistake that Brockmann made. The latter looked at his mother as he spoke. The former spoke to his mother, whom he held with a shaking hand, without shifting his gaze away from the ghost.

(Quoted in Litzmann 1890/1894)

These "refinements" were not seen as expressing psychological "truth" simply because they agreed with scientific knowledge about physiology. Far more, the art of acting made possible scientific knowledge about emotions. To conclude: in the second half of the eighteenth century the art of acting played a significant role in the expansion of the concept of "emotion" as a secular concept and in the development of empirical psychology *per se*. It provided contemporaries with insights into the emotional states of the human soul, previously hidden and as yet undiscovered by either physiology or philosophy.

At the beginning of the 1780s, Karl Philipp Moritz announced his plan to publish a *Journal for Empirical Psychology* that would be devoted above all else to case studies; that is, to empirical material that could provide the basis for further research. The first part of the first volume appeared in 1783 under the title, *KNOW THYSELF or Journal of Empirical Psychology, a reader for the learned and unlearned* (Förstl et al. 1992). Between 1783 and 1793, ten volumes were published that favored reports about special mental states and "sick" or deviant behaviors. These reports were only possible through minute introspection, provoked and enhanced by the new art of acting. Knowledge of the human soul as promoted by the acting of Garrick and a number of others became one of the most important goals toward the end of the century. In this context, secular categories such as the concept of emotion became a fundamental aid.

Case Study 2: Theatre History as the History of Aesthetics

We will now turn to a second example of a research project; this time we will begin with a specific document and use this document to pose larger questions about theatre history. We now know a bit about the development of the new art of acting during the second half of the eighteenth century and the strong emotional effect it had on spectators. Now imagine we come across the following document:

The newest law of theatre that now reigns and becomes more shameless and impertinent day by day, considers dramatic art to be representation and declamation alone. The content of the play is either entirely subordinate or disregarded in relation to the spectators. We are supposed to sit in the audience like wooden puppets and watch and listen to the declamations of the wooden puppets onstage, until we leave feeling drab and empty.

(Herder 1861–62, Vol. 1: 301)

The comment is part of a letter from Maria Karoline Herder (1750–1809) to the poet Wilhelm Ludwig Gleim (1719–1867). She wrote it on March 1, 1802 having seen a performance of August Wilhelm Schlegel's version of Euripides' tragedy *Ion* at the Weimar Court Theatre (January 2, 1802, subsequent performances took place on January 4, July 27, and August 9, 1802).

Karoline Herder's complaints create the impression that if bad actors ("wooden puppets") sought to return to seventeenth-century principles of the acting ("representation and declamation"), they would be incapable of arousing any kind of emotional response in the spectators ("we leave feeling drab and empty"). Since the arousal of feelings had commonly been seen as the purpose and goal of theatre performances, this account suggests that the performance of *Ion* was a complete disaster. We can also see this in another letter Karoline Herder wrote a few days after the performance to Karl Ludwig von Knebel (1744–1834). In this letter she writes, "Jena was again ordered to attend and applaud. Fewer people attended the second performance. They did not want to attempt a third time because the house might have stayed completely empty" (quoted in Fambach 1958: 579).

One might draw the conclusion that *Ion* was a bad production not worth spending time on. Yet other contemporary publications about *Ion* suggest a different story. Goethe not only prevented the publication of a critical review of *Ion* by Karl August Böttiger, who sharply criticized the play but generally praised the performance: he went even further and ensured that another review published in the *Zeitung für die elegante Welt* (*Newspaper for an Elegant World*) came from among the close circle of Schlegel. The following issues published letters that praised both play and performance. Furthermore, Goethe himself entered the debate publicly with an essay called "The Weimar Court Theatre" that was published in the 1802 issue of the *Journal des Luxus und der Moden* (*Journal of Luxury and Fashions*). The subsequent performances in July and August took place after this campaign in the press. The effort and time spent on publicizing the production suggests that it was not simply a failure.

Ion was the first Greek tragedy to be performed in Weimar. As Goethe writes in his essay, "masks raised the figures of the two older men ... to the sphere of the Tragic." The facial expressions, so important to the new acting style of the eighteenth century, were missing. Goethe emphasizes the painterly principles underlying the performance when stressing that "the eye traveled as it pleased over the groups" that the play offered in the form of "living tableaux ... from this perspective one can flatter oneself to have offered an almost perfect presentation" (Goethe 1802: 77). Goethe clearly considered the production a success.

The actors of *Ion* did not seek to present the closest possible imitation of reality or invite the spectators to sympathize with the characters. Instead, the spectators were held at a distance. Goethe assumed that the spectator should learn to perceive that not every play is like a coat which must be tailored precisely according to his own current needs, shape and size. We should not think of satisfying our actual spiritual, emotional and sensual needs in the theatre, but we should far more often see ourselves as travelers who visit foreign places and lands, to which we travel for the sake of learning and delight, and where we do not find all those comforts which we have the time at home to shape to our own individual needs.

(Goethe 1802: 82)

The goal of keeping spectators at an aesthetic distance is central to the *Rules for Actors* that Goethe had devised since taking over the direction of the Weimar Court Theatre in 1791. In 1803, they were edited and published by Johann Peter Eckermann. They concern the presentation of roles, the communication between characters, and the relationship between stage and audience. They reflect the anti-illusionistic direction of the new theatre aesthetic. The relationship between actors and audience was defined as follows: "the actor must always remember that he is there for the sake of the spectators" (Goethe 1986: 218).

Goethe ignored Diderot's demand for a fourth wall. The communication between characters on stage should not follow the same rules as everyday social reality:

actors should not, from a sense of misunderstood realism, play to one another as if no third party were present. They should never act in complete profile or with their backs to the audience … The actor also ought to take particular care never to speak upstage but always toward the audience.

(Goethe 1986: 219)

The idea that the stage plays by its own rules also guides the principles for acting: "the actor must remember that he should not only imitate nature but also present it in an idealized way. In his presentation he must unite reality and beauty" (Goethe 1986: 218). Some specific stipulations follow from this general requirement: the language must be free of dialects; declamation should be a "kind of music in prose" in which speeches, gestures, and poses are programmatically artificial. Some of the fingers of the actor should "be half bent, the others kept straight, but they must never appear cramped. The two middle fingers should always be kept together, and the thumb, index and little finger should be slightly bent. In this way, the hand is in its proper position, one suitable for all movements" (Goethe 1986: 219–20).

Though reminiscent of Lang's seventeenth-century rules, Goethe's instructions are ultimately different. In the seventeenth century, artificial gestures and postures are signs representing affect or social order. In contrast, gestures and postures in Goethe's theatre do not carry such specific meaning. They mark the performance as a work of art that stands out from nature and from social reality. They only gain meaning in relation to other elements of the performance. Goethe makes this argument in the dialogue *On Realism in Art* (1798) when talking about opera: "if the opera is good it becomes its own micro-world in which everything follows certain laws—a world which must be experienced on its own terms" (Goethe 1986: 76). Performance creates a world unto itself governed by laws that include visual tableaux—as in *Ion*—and the musical basis of rhythmic recitation. As we saw in the last chapter, these principles are also central to Robert Wilson's staging of *King Lear*—and his work more generally—though for very different reasons.

If performance is conceived of as a "whole" that is only "complete" when its individual elements are "in tune," it implies the rise of a new figure in European theatre history: the director. The performance turns into a carefully devised production, an "artwork" created by the artist that is the director. In effect, Goethe was a director. He led rehearsals, and made sure that the blocking on stage was visually appealing, the movements of the actors were carefully choreographed, and the colors of the stage décor and the costumes complemented each other. According to the actor Pius Alexander Wolff, who thought of himself as Goethe's student, the purpose and goal of rehearsals was

> […]to practice together long enough so that all of the parts are com-
> fortably and securely interwoven, until every hole is filled, every actor is
> so familiar with his own role as well as with the part of his adversary
> that … he knows the speech of the others; until everything … moves just
> like in an opera according to tempos chosen for specific reasons and
> feelings, while all moments still appear unconstrained.
>
> (Quoted in Flemming 1949: 109)

The rehearsal process described here differs radically from the sort of preparatory work common around 1800. The actors usually only knew the text of their own roles and the cue for their entrances on stage, so they would not make their entrances on stage at random. Preparations were focused on avoiding inappropriate laughter, for instance, when an actor would point stage right while another was entering stage left. Given the minimal preparatory work common on European stages around 1800, the care Goethe took with his rehearsal process to unify the performance is astonishing. Clearly, the reason why the performance of *Ion* struck people as so unsatisfying lay not in a lack of preparation or sloppy performances by actors (at the Weimar Court Theatre, actors were fined for sloppy performances). In spite of Karoline Herder's complaints, the first Greek tragedy to be performed on this stage must have been coherently and forcefully realized.

Ultimately, audiences disliked the production because of its level of aesthetic innovation. Since the end of the sixteenth century, it had been believed that theatre performance should have a specific effect on spectators. These effects included catharsis (Aristotle), the adoption of a stoic attitude (Protestant school theatre of the seventeenth century), the acceptance of the Catholic Church as the only avenue of salvation (Jesuit drama), and the experience of pity and terror central to bourgeois humanism. Goethe very clearly did not attempt to arouse strong feelings, but instead sought a distanced, reflective reception from his spectators. He wanted his spectators to pass aesthetic judgment on the "completeness" of the work as a whole. This meant turning away from a tradition of aesthetic practice that was centrally concerned with the transformation of the audience (we will return to the subject of "transformative aesthetics" in Chapter 9). In place of transformative aesthetics, Goethe sought to establish a new aesthetic that focused on the work of art rather than audience transformation. Why did Goethe make this major shift? In order to answer this question, we should look for additional sources.

In the summer of 1803, a new theatre was opened in Lauchstädt that would serve as the summer stage of the Weimar Court Theatre. Goethe used the opening of this theatre to publicize his artistic program in a "prologue" called *What We Offer*. In this prologue, the god Mercury informs the audience that it should not understand the events on stage literally—and therefore morally—but rather symbolically. The goal of theatre can be reached only if "we all watch and act together/to approach the high *Bildung* directly" (Goethe 1901, vol. 13: 73). The German term *Bildung* has no direct English translation, but can best be understood as the development of human potential. This concept of *Bildung* becomes something of a leitmotif in Goethe's theatre work. Goethe uses the term to mean the path to and process of free personal development. In Goethe's *Wilhelm Meisters Lehrjahren* (*Wilhelm Meister's Apprenticeship*, 1795–96), Wilhelm Meister echoes Goethe's own ideas, to a large extent, in analyzing the real conditions of contemporary society:

> To speak it in a word; the cultivation of my individual self, here, as I am, has from my youth upwards been constantly though dimly my wish and my purpose … but in Germany, a universal and if I may say so, personal cultivation is beyond the reach of any one, except a nobleman. A burgher may acquire merit; by excessive efforts he may even educate his mind; but his personal qualities are lost, or worse than lost, let him struggle as he will …
>
> If the nobleman, merely by his personal carriage, offers all that can be asked of him, the burgher by his personal carriage offers nothing, and can offer nothing … The former does and makes, the latter but effects and

procures; he must cultivate some single gifts in order to be useful, and it is beforehand settled, that in his manner of existence there is no harmony, and can be none, since he is bound to make himself of use in one department, and so has to relinquish all the others.

(Goethe 1871: 243–44)

Goethe did not believe that the problem of personal cultivation could be solved by a revolution: the excesses of the French Revolution had recently shown this. Instead the educated middle class had to develop their own potential and "cultivat[e] one's own individual self." Theatre turned into a means of personal cultivation. For Goethe, the performance was an autonomous work of art that keeps the spectators at an aesthetic distance and challenges them to reflect and judge the "harmonious whole" of the artwork:

And does not *Bildung* gain from acting,
that fantastic Godhead with a hundred arms,
offering an unending myriad of rich means?   (Goethe 1901: 73)

This new theatre no longer aims to imitate nature or social reality, but abides by its own rules. In this respect, it is autonomous and can lead the spectators through the process of developing their potential. Goethe's new theatre aesthetic breaks with earlier traditions of theatre by demanding the autonomy of the performance as a work of art. At the same time, it continues the tradition in casting this autonomy as the necessary condition for the transformation of the audience. To Goethe the transformation of the spectators manifests in the unfolding of their individual potential. The autonomy of the performance as a work of art ultimately reveals itself as a prerequisite for another kind of transformative aesthetics. Theatre itself—and art in a more general sense—is supposed to be revolutionary. The new work aesthetic developed by Goethe turns into a new transformative aesthetic for the bourgeoisie. This new aesthetics would enable them to reach their full individual potential, even if in civic life they must focus primarily on earning a sustainable income. We will end our analysis at this point, although the investigation could easily continue. It should have become clear how different lines of research questions and investigations open up when proceeding from a single document that, for whatever reasons, puzzles us. The example shows that theatre histories require theoretical approaches. These approaches help us decide which methodologies and conceptual frameworks we might employ most effectively in a given project.

Further Reading

On Historiography

Elias, N. (2000) *The Civilizing Process*, Oxford: Blackwell.
Foucault, M. (1970) *The Order of Things: An Archaeology of the Human Sciences*, New York: Random House.
Koselleck, R. (2004) *Futures Past: On the Semantics of Historical Time*, trans. Keith Tribe, New York: Columbia University Press.
White, H. (1973) *Metahistory: The Historical Imagination in Nineteenth Century Europe*, Baltimore: Johns Hopkins University Press.

On Theatre History and Historiography

Brockett, O. and F. J. Hildy (1982) *History of Theatre*, 10th revised edition 2007, Boston: Allyn and Bacon.
Craik, T. W. (ed.) (1975–80) *The Revels History of Drama in English* (8 vols.), London: Methuen.
Fischer-Lichte, E. (2004) "Some Critical Remarks on Theatre Historiography" in S. E. Wilmer (ed.) *Writing and Rewriting Theatre Histories*, Iowa City: Iowa University Press.
Kernodle, G. R. (1989) *The Theatre in History*, Fayetteville: University of Arkansas Press.
Nicholl, A. (1923–59) *A History of English Drama* (6 vols.), Cambridge: Cambridge University Press.
Postlewait, T. (2009) *The Cambridge Introduction to Theatre Historiography*, Cambridge: Cambridge University Press.
Postlewait, T. and B. A. McConachi (eds.) (1989) *Interpreting the Theatrical Past*, Iowa City: Iowa University Press.
Roach, J. (1996) *Cities of the Dead: Circum-Atlantic Performance*, New York: Columbia University Press.
Wiles, D. and C. Dymkowski (eds.) (2013) *The Cambridge Companion to Theatre History*, Cambridge: Cambridge University Press.
Zarrilli, P. B., B. McConachie, G. J. Williams, and C. F. Sorgenfrei (2006) *Theatre Histories: An Introduction*, New York/London: Routledge.

On Affect

Agnew, V. (2007) "History's Affective Turn: Historical Reenactment and Its Work in the Present," *Rethinking History*, 11/3: 299–312.
Clough, P. and J. Halley (eds.) (2007) *The Affective Turn: Theorizing the Social*, Durham, NC: Duke University Press.
Plamper, J. (2009) "Emotional Turn? Feeling in Russian History and Culture," *Slavic Review* 68: 229–37.

Notes

1 Two such histories are Thomas Postlewait and Bruce A. McConachie (eds.), *Interpreting the Theatrical Past* and Joseph Roach, *Cities of the Dead: Circum-Atlantic Performance* (see "Further reading").

2 Important works in these debates include Aaron Hill, *The Prompter; A Theatrical Paper* (1734–36), Raymond de Saint Albine, *Le Comédien* (1747), François Riccoboni, *L'Art du Théâtre* (1750), Denis Diderot, *Paradoxe sur le Comédien* (1769–78), Gotthold Ephraim Lessing, *Hamburgische Dramaturgie* (1767/68), Georg Friedrich Lichtenberg, *Über Physiognomik, wider die Physignomen. Zur Beförderung der Menschenliebe und Menschenkenntnis* (1778) and John Caspar Lavater, *Physiognomische Fragmente zur Beförderung der Menschenkenntnis und Menschenliebe* (1775–78).

3 Engel's book was translated into English by Henry Siddons and appeared in 1815 with the title *Practical Illustrations of Rhetorical Gesture and Action: Adapted To The English Drama; From A Work On The Subject by M. Engel, Member of The Royal Academy of Berlin; Embellished with sixty-nine Engravings, Expressive Of The Various Passions, And Representing The Modern Costume Of The London Theatres*. A second improved edition appeared in 1822, printed for Sherwood, Neely, and Jons, Paternoster Row, London. Remarkably, in this translation, the gestures that accord to the physiological "law of analogy" are termed "rhetorical" and the emotions that express them are termed "passions."

Chapter 6

Theorizing theatre and performance

In the first chapter, we discussed how the concepts "theatre" and "theory" both developed from the Greek word *thea* (the show). Walter Burkert, a preeminent scholar of Ancient Greece, explains this etymological relationship by showing that the terms "theatre" and "theory" derive from Greek festival culture:

> Allied cities and sacred sites send envoys to one another to participate in the "shows": in Greek they are called "the protectors of the show," the-oroi, their job is *theoria*. Paradoxically, then, the word and concept of "theory" stems from the festival culture of antiquity. If Greek philosophy elevated this concept to the "theoretical" realm it was because the abstract "show" of thinking seemed to them to be something celebratory.
>
> (Burkert 1987, 29f.)

A close relationship between theatre and theory also exists in the discipline of Theatre and Performance Studies. In the preceding chapters we discussed various theories about theatre. In the sections on performance analysis and theatre historiography, we also emphasized that research on performances must be oriented toward a question or hypothesis developed in relationship to specific theories. This final chapter of Part II will explain how we understand the concept of theory and how we can create and test theories about theatre and performance.

What Do We Mean by "Theory"?

The Concept of Theory

There are a number of different schools of theory—ranging from psycho-analytic to postcolonial and feminist theory—which have come to play an important role in Theatre and Performance Studies. Before delving into the specifics of each school, it is essential to understand the basics: what do we consider theory to be? How do we apply and test theories? And how can they inform our practice of Theatre and Performance Studies?

Whenever we want to understand something beyond the here and now, we need some sort of theoretical knowledge. This is true of every sort of knowledge, whether or not it relates to scholarship, and whether it is empirical or speculative. We can say that knowledge is theoretical in form and content in so far as it moves beyond the immediately given. Scholarly knowledge is a special type of theoretical knowledge that reflects on knowledge creation and seeks to formulate and organize concepts. Yet there is no sharp division between scholarly and non-scholarly knowledge. Theories should be understood as informative, feasible, and hypothetical systems of assertions to describe and make sense of what we perceive, do, and come to know. They can be formally described as a deductive set of both general and specific propositions, consisting of complex clusters of concepts.

Concepts lie at the core of every theory and its application.

Concepts

A concept always aims at generalization based on a collection of individual phenomena or ideas. Concepts are always abstract. They make the objects to which they refer comprehensible. In order to do so, they have to be clearly defined.

Scholarly concepts always require a definition that clarifies what the concept means, and in which contexts it can be used. Concepts do not describe the essence of a given object. They can be better understood as heuristic instruments that are capable of grasping specific aspects of an object that are essential within the theoretical framework in question. In Chapter 3 we defined the concept of performance with recourse to specific medial conditions (bodily co-presence), a particular characteristic of materiality (its transience), a special mode of creating meaning (the emergence of meaning), and a specific type of aesthetic experience (the experience of liminality). All phenomena that fall under this definition can be understood as performances. The definition delineates aspects that are essential in a given theoretical context. The right formulation for defining a theoretical concept is not "A performance *is* x, y, and z" but rather "A performance *will be defined as* x, y, and z" or "In the following analysis, we will understand performance to mean x, y, and z." The definition of a concept always needs to keep in view how and why that concept is being used: ultimately, a concept is just a tool to enable theoretical investigation. When we study a theory we have to understand the concepts as the theory defines them, not as they might be used in other contexts. Since theoretical concepts are used as heuristic instruments to answer specific questions, we can change their definitions if their common usage is inadequate to the question at hand. The success of a theory in explaining hitherto unexplainable findings depends to a large extent on how the theory defines the concepts it uses. Without clear definitions of concepts, it is impossible to develop theories, and vice versa: a given theory can only be useful for solving a particular problem when the central concepts of the theory are clearly defined.

All researchers work with concepts and definitions, but different disciplines think about and use them in different ways. In the natural sciences, concepts are usually defined narrowly, whereas in the humanities, concepts are often more broadly defined. The difference becomes apparent in our use of concepts such as "atmosphere" and "energy" in comparison to how a physicist would understand these terms. Even though we defined these terms, they are still open: they cannot be expressed as part of a formula like energy could be in physics. This openness is not a deficiency. On the contrary, it implies that the concept has potential to be developed through further research. Although they have different standards of definition, it is no less important to define a concept in Theatre and Performance Studies than in physics.

Applying and Validating Theories

It is impossible to imagine a theoretical approach that would be valid for every case; there is no universal formula or theory. Any given theory is only productive and viable in a limited number of fields. Depending on the problem or research question, we may therefore need to combine multiple theories in order to answer a question adequately.

When we think about the role of theory in research, it is important to differentiate between working *with* theories and working *on* theories; that is, between applying theories to research and creating theories. In this section we focus on working with theories, while the next section—"Developing Theories"—deals with working on theories. In both of these sections we will discuss specific examples of research projects that we, as students and scholars of theatre, might undertake.

Say, for example, we are interested in the emergence of psychologically realistic styles of acting in the eighteenth century and the critique and rejection of those styles by the historical avant-garde at the beginning of the twentieth century (c. 1900–30). Our first step is to explore the central theories of acting from each period. For the eighteenth century, these are the acting theories by Diderot, Lessing, and Engels. For the historical avant-garde movement, these are the acting theories by Meyerhold, Brecht, and Artaud, among others. From the outset, we notice something peculiar: the first set of theories is written by philosophers, the second set by theatre artists.

First, we have to understand central concepts such as nature, truth, beauty (for the theorists of the eighteenth century); contagion (Engel and Artaud); organization of material (Meyerhold); and estrangement (Brecht). We then need to investigate how all of these concepts relate to one another. They can be organized into three categories: processes of creation (like the organization of materials), qualities of representation (truth, beauty, estrangement) and their effects on the audience (contagion). Strikingly, the concept of contagion occurs in both the eighteenth century and the historical avant-garde. Hence we will need to differentiate between the divergent meanings of the concept.

Once we have come up with some preliminary ways that relate the concepts to each other, we need to consider how they operate in the various theories of acting. Do the individual concepts form coherent conceptual frameworks? How does each concept contribute to the development of a new theory of acting? It is also important to explain the general principles that inform the various theories, such as the law of analogy that the theorists of the eighteenth century conceived, or the law of the maximum use of work time at the center of Meyerhold's biomechanics. In this manner we can investigate the basic principles that led to the development of new forms of acting.

For the theories of the eighteenth century, these principles could be summarized as follows:

- The human body is naturally capable of and suited for expressing the soul truthfully and completely (creation).
- The art of acting imitates nature. The objects that it imitates are psychic states and spiritual processes of the (bourgeois) individual made perceptible through outward signs (representation).
- When perceiving such outward signs, the soul of the spectators can be infected by the represented emotion, which they again express through outward signs, such as tears (effect).

There are much wider variations among the theories of the historical avant-garde. Nevertheless it is possible to formulate some general principles:

- The human body is a material that can be formed at will (creation).
- The art of acting should bring forward a new reality of its own. It uses gestures, movements, and forces (creation = presentation).
- The goal of acting is the transformation of the spectator into a "new human being," which is defined differently in each theory (effect).

Such a research process is helpful for sketching out the fundamental differences between the theories of the eighteenth century and those of the early twentieth century. Yet it is not sufficient to answer the question we set out to explore. It is only one of several crucial steps.

Now that we have begun our research, it is important to return to our original question and formulate it more precisely. There are two parts to our question: first, what prompted calls in the second half of the eighteenth century for a new, psychologically realistic style of acting? Second, why did members of the historical avant-garde criticize this mode of acting and want to replace it with forms of acting that were neither realistic nor psychological?

These are still very complex questions that can be tackled with a range of different theories. Our next task, therefore, is to decide which theories are most appropriate for our project and for our personal research interests. The theories we use will above all depend on whether we are primarily interested in researching performances as aesthetic events (i.e. understanding and practicing Theatre and Performance Studies as the study of art), as a specific cultural practice (Theatre and Performance Studies as Cultural Studies), or as providing special medial conditions (Theatre and Performance Studies as Media Studies).

If we focus on performances as aesthetic events, we will want to connect the introduction and critique of psychologically realistic acting with emerging aesthetic theories. As we saw in the section on Methodologies in Chapter 5, Goethe's critique of psychologically realistic acting was based on its fundamental conception of art as *imitatio naturae*, imitation of nature. Goethe countered this view with his notion of the autonomy of art governed by its own rules and reality. Underlying this idea about art was a shift in the concept of nature—from nature as an *a priori* order governed by reason (early eighteenth century) to nature as an empirical reality, present to the senses of the observer (late eighteenth century). Imitation of nature thus came to mean something entirely different. It was dependent on observation and examination according to such principles as the unity of truth and beauty. We could argue that the development of a new, psychologically realistic style of acting can be explained in the context of a new understanding of art. This new understanding continued to demand an imitation of nature while redefining the concept of nature. The changing concept of nature strongly suggests an intertwining of philosophy, science, and art in this context. As discussed in Chapter 5, the work in natural sciences and particularly physiological theories about the creation of emotions and the relationship between body and soul resulted in the formulation of a "natural law" of analogy, on which theorists of acting built. The new knowledge about "human nature" demanded new acting styles. The theorists of acting in the eighteenth century took their cue from developments in the natural sciences.

Members of the historical avant-garde polemicized not only against understanding art as an imitation of nature but also against the claim that art was autonomous (promulgated by Goethe and generally accepted in the nineteenth century). They demanded that art be incorporated into everyday life. Whereas the acting theorists of the eighteenth century were engaging with the natural sciences, the avant-garde's theories of acting at the beginning of the twentieth century oriented themselves toward technological sciences (Meyerhold) and ethnology (Artaud). In Meyerhold's conception of acting, which we discussed in Chapter 3, the engineer becomes a central metaphor for the actor:

> In art our constant concern is the organization of raw material ... the art of the actor consists in organizing his material; that is, in his capacity to utilize correctly his body's means of expression. The actor embodies in

himself both the organizer and that which is organized (i.e. the artist and his material). The formula for acting may be expressed as follows: $N = A1 + A2$ (where N = the actor; $A1$ = the artist who conceives the idea and issues the instructions necessary for its execution; $A2$ = the executant who executes the conception of $A1$).

(Meyerhold 1969: 198)

Early twentieth-century theorists such as Meyerhold formulated theories of art that equated art and production and saw art as a "tool for reorganizing life" and theatre as a "factory of qualified people and a qualified way of life" (Arvatov 1926; Günther and Hielscher 1972). Frederick Taylor (Taylor 1911) and Alexei Gastev in his "Catechism of Work Exercises" (Gastev 1966) were important sources of inspiration for them. Physiology was another important reference, in particular the study of human reflexes. Vladimir Bekhterev and Ivan Pavlov, the two leading researchers on reflexes in Imperial Russia and the early Soviet Union, wanted to trace human motivation and behavior to biological and sociological laws and argued for conditioning behavior in laboratory conditions. A further reference point for this new understanding of art was behaviorism, as developed by John B. Watson and John Dewey. All in all, the historical avant-garde at the beginning of the twentieth century formulated a new understanding of art (including theories of a new, non-psychological style of acting) that connected directly to other scientific developments.

To come to a preliminary conclusion: in both the eighteenth and twentieth centuries, new theories of acting were connected to new scientific theories (even though they cannot be fully explained by these theories). The connection between theories of art and scientific theories allows us to take another approach to our research project by focusing on how performances and acting styles can be understood as specific cultural practices.

In our discussion of aesthetics, we focused on scientific theories that developed simultaneously with changes in acting styles. We compared these contemporaneous scientific and acting theories in order to explain why the historical avant-garde broke with psychologically realistic acting styles. It is also possible to interpret these changes using theories that developed in different periods; that is, to study these changes in acting styles diachronically by studying how they changed over time. Since theories of acting focus on how to use the body, we could try to answer our questions through recourse to the theory of the civilizing process developed by Norbert Elias (which we discussed in Chapter 4). Seen in light of Elias' theory, the acting theories of the eighteenth century and of the theatre avant-garde at the beginning of the twentieth century are different phases in a civilizing process that began in sixteenth-century Europe. This civilizing process is characterized by an ever-increasing discipline of the body that aims to suppress sensual nature and subordinate it to rational principles.

The theories of the eighteenth century can be seen in light of this over-arching theory as attempts to subordinate the body, voice, gesture, and movement to the "laws of analogy." Actors needed to acquire perfect control over their bodies and to mold their psychological state in accordance with the characters they were playing. The phenomenal body was supposed to disappear fully behind an easily readable semiotic body. Only the "sensuous nature" of the character as designated by the text, and not that of the actor, was allowed to appear. The theories of the early twentieth century avant-garde left no room for such a "sensuous nature." They saw the human body as a machine that could be controlled and manipulated. The "engineers" nullified the phenomenal body in the process of performance.

Using Elias's theory of the civilizing process, we can interpret theories of acting in the eighteenth and twentieth centuries as evidence for a powerful shift spurred by this civilizing process. However, Elias' theory does not help us explain why the eighteenth-century theorists were so fascinated with the new study of psychology as an empirical science, or why some theorists of the twentieth century were drawn to the study of technology and industrial science while others, such as Stanislavski, promoted theatre based on psychology. Elias' theory, while helpful, leaves an array of questions unanswered.

A Media Studies approach would try to explain the criticism of psycho-logically realistic acting styles at the beginning of the twentieth century by looking at the development of the new media of photography and film. Film and photography apparently presented an image of reality with hitherto inconceivable precision that seemed to make the actor's imitation of nature redundant. Naturalism in theatre had dominated since the 1880s but had become technologically outdated in the face of these new media. Comparisons between the possibilities of theatre and film were central to theoretical media debates in the first decades of the twentieth century. Sergei Eisenstein developed his theory of montage in the framework of his theatre productions in Meyerhold's studio. His staging of Ostrovsky's *Enough Stupidity in Every Wise Man* (1922) was a seminal moment in the development of non-psychological acting styles. Eisenstein replaced psychologically realistic acting entirely with acrobatics and slapstick comedy. Every short scene was conceived as an "attraction" supposed to have a direct bodily impact on the spectators. The performance was a "Montage of Attractions," as Eisenstein titled the essay that he wrote following the production (Eisenstein 1923). While Eisenstein used theatre to develop a theory of montage that was influential in the development of the new medium of film, Erwin Piscator used film clips in his productions in the 1920s. Film created a completely new context for the work of the actor and demanded a new conception of his role. Seen from the perspective of Media Studies, the new acting theories of the early twentieth century—in particular the rejection of psychologically realistic acting—can be plausibly explained by the invention of new media and the changes that these media prompted in individual perception.

The examples of aesthetic, cultural, and media theory we have discussed each offered an explanation of at least *one* aspect of our research question. But each theory failed to explain other aspects. In order to answer our research question comprehensively, we had to combine various theories of art, culture, and media. Our example allows us to draw two important conclusions about theoretical work. First, we have to assume that the validity of any theory is always limited, even if some are more generally applicable than others. In order to discuss and answer questions raised by contemporary and historical performances we will often require a combination of different theories. The theoretical approach we decide upon will depend on both the question at hand and our broader field of interest. The examples have also shown that just as it is impossible to know exactly which sources we will use, we cannot determine in advance which theories might be relevant for Theatre and Performance Studies research. Our research operates on a case-by-case basis.

Developing Theories

Whenever there are changes in cultures—and more specifically in performances—new questions and problems arise that cannot be solved by recourse to existing theories. In such cases we have to develop new theories in order to tackle our questions. How do we do this and where do we start? Let's begin with the example of how we developed the theory of performance discussed in Chapter 3.

Transforming Existing Theories

Current theories of performance were prompted by developments in theatre starting in the 1960s that were not compatible with existing theories of theatre. Participatory forms of theatre (to an extent that would have been unthinkable in the 1950s) were particularly influential in transforming the scholarly theories about theatrical performance.

When we want to create a theory, we have to start with the antecedents of that theory: there is little to be gained from reinventing the wheel. New theories are generally not suddenly "discovered." Even if they follow a certain intuition, they do not come from nowhere. Usually they are developed from already existing theories and change these theories in decisive ways. The idea of spectators as active participants in theatrical performance has its antecedents in both the theories of the historical avant-garde movement and Max Herrmann's conviction that the audience participates in creating a performance. In Chapter 2 we made an attempt at reconstructing Herrmann's understanding of theatre and performance and were then able to expand on his theory. We developed three characteristics of performance: its specific medial conditions (bodily co-presence), its materiality (transience), and its event-ness (aesthetic experience). We then looked to additional existing theories, such as semiotics, in order to develop a theory about the constitution of meaning in a performance.

We expanded our ideas about each of the characteristics of performance with the help of existing theories and used these theories to explore the relationships between performance and intellectual history. To explain bodily co-presence, for example, we employed theories of performativity. We theorized the transience of performance in relation to theories of space and atmosphere, anthropological accounts of acting, acting theories from the seventeenth through twentieth centuries, theories regarding the production of presence, and so forth. To explain the emergence of meaning in performance, we used various theories of perception and naming. To explain the event-ness of performance, we turned to anthropology and sociology such as Turner's theory of liminality and Goffman's frame theory.

In order to arrive at a theory about performance we have to transform our existing theoretical knowledge in order to develop a new theoretical framework. In general, new theories always develop from some sort of interplay between intuition, observation, and theoretical reflection.

Testing Theories

Every new theory must be tested. Is the new theory capable of solving problems that have arisen from new artistic and scholarly developments? Which questions can the new theory answer and which questions remain? This can only be determined in the process of application. In the case of the theory we have developed in the previous pages, this would mean using it to solve problems that arise in specific performances of contemporary theatre, or that can be formulated based on sources about performances in the past. We might say that our analysis of *Art and Vegetables* can plausibly explain part of the relationship between actors and spectators. Phenomena and processes in contemporary theatre performance may illuminate contemporary theatre performance in new ways and thus open more complex responses to criticism that finds *Art and Vegetables* dysfunctional, incomprehensible, and superfluous.

This is also the case for performances that took place in the past. For example, mass spectacles in the early Soviet Union and the *Thingspiele* (outdoor folk performances) in the Third Reich were long seen as useful instruments to manipulate the masses and instill in them new ideological values. This theory of manipulation, however, does not explain why contemporary mass spectacles that used the same techniques were also popular in democratic societies such as the United States, France, and Switzerland. The centrality of bodily co-presence and of community-creation in performance can help us argue that mass political performances do not simply coerce participants. Instead we must take account of the shared responsibility of

every spectator who participates in and guides the course of the performance, and who is in turn guided by the performance. Understanding
performance in this active way gives us grounds for rejecting a theory of
manipulation, which sees the spectator as fundamentally passive. Our theory
of performance shows that both totalitarian and democratic societies shared a
need for community building in the interwar period, expressed in mass
spectacles. Furthermore, everyone who participated in the spectacles, whether as directors, actors, or spectators, bore responsibility for the community
that developed over the course of the performance and that—despite proclamations to the contrary—usually did not extend much beyond the performance.

Theory and Practice

There is another way to develop and test theories: artistic practice. This
approach is common in many Theatre Studies departments that offer practical courses in directing, acting, set design, playwriting, or dramaturgy. In
the best cases, this work can be compared to laboratories in the natural sciences, where experiments are performed in order to try out theories. Shifting between theoretical reflection and artistic practice can be understood as
a process of both developing and testing theories. Obviously, not every sort
of theory can be developed in this way. Theories that are directly related to
artistic practice, such as theories about acting, movement, or creativity—to
name just a few examples—benefit from such artistic "laboratories" and
appear in many respects to be particularly valid. Whereas the theorists of the
eighteenth century developed their theories of acting in relation to and by
transforming other theories, the theories of the historical avant-garde were
overwhelmingly developed through artistic practice. Under the motto
"Performance as Research," this sort of approach has become increasingly
common in Theatre Departments in English-speaking countries, with a
range of results. In German universities, theories about theatre are very
rarely developed as exchanges between theoretical reflection and artistic
practice, and creative and academic training usually take place in different
institutions.

Regardless of how a theoretical approach is developed, it will not remain
valid indefinitely. Just as there is no such thing as a universal theory, there is
no such thing as a theory that remains valid across history. We must always
test theories with new questions and seek to reformulate our theories as a
result of findings in performance analysis and theatre historiography. It is not
enough to simply understand a theory; the ability to productively use a theory
and then change the theory if necessary is the sign of real theoretical compe-
tence. Theories are not universal truths. They are instruments of problem
solving and need to change with every newly emerging problem. They call
for adaptation and transformation.

Further Reading

On the Concept of Theory

Burkert, W. (1991) *Greek Religion: Archaic and Classical*, J. Raffan (trans.), Oxford: Blackwell.

Carlson, M. (1993) *Theories of the Theatre: A Historical and Critical Survey from the Greeks to the Present*, Ithaca, NY: Cornell University Press.

Krasner, D. (ed.) (2008) *Theatre in Theory: An Anthology*, Oxford: Blackwell Publishing.

Performance as Research

Kershaw, B. and H. Nicholson (eds.) (2011) *Research Methods in Theatre and Performance*, Edinburgh: Edinburgh University Press.

Riley, R. and L. Hunter (eds.) (2009) *Mapping Landscapes for Performance as Research: Scholarly Acts and Creative Cartographies*, New York: Palgrave Macmillan.

Part III

Pushing boundaries

In the first two sections of this book, we introduced Theatre and Performance Studies as the study of performances. The three main fields discussed in Part II (Performance Analysis, Theatre Historiography, and Theoretical Frameworks) are applicable to any genre of performance. However, the examples used in this book thus far have been taken predominantly from institutionalized European and North American theatre. We only touched upon a few performances from non-Western cultures, performances of other arts, and other genres of cultural performances in passing.

Defining Theatre and Performance Studies so broadly while using only a limited scope of references seems self-contradictory, yet there are reasons for it. The study of other genres of cultural performance and theatre from non-Western cultures requires qualifications that go beyond familiarity with performance analysis, theatre historiography, and theory. Be it Japanese Nô or Kabuki theatre, Indian Kathakali or Ramlila, the Yoruba Traveling Theatre in Nigeria, or the Mexican Lucha Libre—all require expertise in the relevant culture. The same goes for research on art exhibitions or video installations as performance; expertise in Art History as well as Theatre and Performance Studies is a prerequisite. The study of performance is cross-disciplinary and demands academic training in multiple disciplines. This third and final part of the book interrogates three kinds of interrelated performances and discusses possibilities for interdisciplinary cooperation from the perspective of Theatre and Performance Studies.

Pushing boundaries

Chapter 7

Interweaving performance cultures

As discussed in Chapter 5, histories that claim to offer a comprehensive discussion of theatre around the world often follow a predictable pattern. They begin with the theatre of Greek and Roman antiquity, continue with the liturgical and secular dramas of the Middle Ages, and then, starting with the Early Modern period, focus on the so-called high points of various European and later also North American cultures: Elizabethan theatre in England, *commedia dell'arte* in Italy, the theatre of the *Siglo de Oro* (the Golden Age) in Spain, the "classical" period in France, and so forth. The history of non-European theatre is rarely touched upon.

In part, this neglect is connected to a specific conception of theatre: realistic, psychological, literary theatre on a proscenium stage is a European phenomenon that did not exist elsewhere prior to the nineteenth century, except as the theatre of a colonial power. One could also blame a particular understanding of history that conceives of European theatre as ever-changing. During the nineteenth century in particular, there was a widespread belief that theatre was constantly evolving toward greater perfection. In contrast, other forms of theatre that European travelers encountered in places such as India, China, or Japan seemed to have remained unchanged for centuries. Indian Kathakali, the various styles of Chinese opera, Japanese Nô or Kabuki Theatre seemed to them a fixed system of elements, signs, and rules known to both actors and audience. These theatres included music, dance, song, masks, stylized acting, and in some cases acrobatics, and were seen as a fusion of spoken theatre, opera, and dance. The performances often took place on nearly bare stages with few props. In their widely read essays and books, nineteenth-century European travelers documented their encounter with other cultures and found that such theatres had little in common with the European stage. To them it appeared questionable whether such performances could be termed "theatre." Insofar as the travel accounts recognized these other performances as theatre, they doubted that they possessed a history similar to that of European theatre. For nineteenth-century colonialism with its implied superiority of Europeans and their "civilizing mission," it was unthinkable that performance practices in other cultures would be presented alongside European theatre in a "history of world theatre."

While the racism and Eurocentrism of the nineteenth century might have precluded serious attempts to study the histories of theatre around the world, it is still astonishing that such an attempt was only made in earnest at the beginning of the twenty-first century. *Theatre Histories: An Introduction* (Zarilli et al. 2006), discussed in Chapter 5, was first published in 2001 (Richard Southern's book *The Seven Ages of the Theatre* from 1961 can be bracketed here because his conception of history would seem highly problematic today). In this volume, specialists of various theatre cultures researched similar questions within different historical and cultural contexts. The second chapter, "Religious and Civic Festivals: Early Drama and Theatre in Context," for example, discusses the connections between theatre and ritual across a broad range of sites: memorials in Abydos in ancient Egypt, performances of tragedies and comedies in Dionysian festivals in Athens in the fifth century BC, the sacrificial rituals of the Aztecs, the sung dance-dramas of the Mayans, Christian plays of the Middle Ages, and the Islamic Ta'zieh from Persia. Crucially, the book accorded each of these theatrical traditions equal importance. The fourth chapter, on "Theatre and the State, 1600–1900," focuses on England, France, and Japan. *Theatre Histories* begins with a specific question that it approaches from various theoretical angles and subsequently puts to the test in several case studies. This sort of integrated theatre history, which moves past the old dichotomy of "the West and the Rest," can only be a serious project if, as in this case, it involves a collaboration between experts who have specialized knowledge in the relevant languages and cultures. It cannot be assumed that many Theatre and Performance Studies students will double-major in Middle Eastern, African, Indian, Chinese, Japanese, or Latin American Studies, although these would be very productive combinations. For students who do not possess such an area studies focus, it is nevertheless extremely advisable to be well versed in works such as *Theatre Histories*, as well as in individual studies of non-Western theatre traditions.

Above all, an integrated history of theatre makes apparent that in most cultures theatre did not develop in isolation but rather through cultural exchange. In fact, developments within specific theatre traditions were often prompted by confrontations with other cultures. Any given culture would appropriate individual elements of the other tradition and weave them into its own theatrical fabric in order to expand its possibilities and means of expression. The interaction of theatrical cultures has been a perpetual instrument and vehicle of change and renewal. In Japan during the Nara Period (640–794 AD), for example, the elegant courtly dance *bugaku* and the didactic Buddhist dance-theatre *gigaku* developed from the models of Chinese and Korean dance- and music-theatre. Actors from these regions were invited to Nara's court to teach young Japanese performers their art, while Japanese performers traveled to the courts of Silla and Tang to learn from Korean and Chinese masters.

The history of European theatre is rich in similar examples. In France, Molière created a new form of comic theatre by combining the French tradition of farce with elements of *commedia dell'arte*. Beginning in the six-teenth century, professional theatre in German lands developed out of the encounter with traveling English acting and Italian commedia troupes and opera societies. In these examples, exchange is limited to neighboring cultures that share a number of commonalities. Some exceptions exist, including the introduction of Jesuit drama in Japan during the Jesuits' short period of mis-sionary work there. These dramas left their traces in Okuni's founding of Kabuki theatre (between 1600 and 1610). Another example is Voltaire's tra-gedy *L'Orphelin de la Chine*, which premiered in 1755 in the Comédie Fran-çaise, and was a reworking of the Chinese opera *Zaoshi gue'er* (*The Orphan of the House of Zhao*) by Ji Junxiang from the time of the Yuan Dynasty (1280–1367). In such cases, theatrical elements of a barely known culture are decontextualized and appropriated by a different culture and ultimately adjusted to fit its own goals.

Since the middle of the nineteenth century, the reports from European travelers about varied theatre forms, and above all Asian theatre, had become increasingly precise. At the beginning of the twentieth century, theatre troupes from Japan and China traveled to Europe and the United States for the first time. During their extensive tours, they presented their productions to a public that was accustomed to a completely different set of theatrical conventions. Theatre artists in Europe such as Max Reinhardt, Edward Gordon Craig, Vsevolod Meyerhold, Alexander Tairov, Bertolt Brecht, and Antonin Artaud were inspired by these tours and appropriated elements and techniques in their own productions. In doing so, they created wholly new forms of theatre for European audiences. The influence went both ways: Japanese theatre artists traveled to Europe to work with directors such as Stanislavski, Reinhardt, or Meyerhold. After returning to their native country, they had recourse to European psychological realism in order to create a new form of Japanese spoken theatre: *shingeki* (new drama). It was received enthusiastically by Chinese students in Tokyo, who went on to create a form of Chinese spoken theatre, *huaju*, in Shanghai shortly thereafter.

The beginning of the twentieth century saw a level of cultural exchange that went far beyond nineteenth-century practices. New technologies of transportation allowed individual artists and entire ensembles to tour inter-nationally. Audiences could experience the bodily presence of unfamiliar cultures. Performances emerged from the confrontations and interactions between artists and audiences, each seeking to make claims about their own cultural identity. We can use the term *interweaving* to describe this phenom-enon. The shift from the nineteenth to the twentieth century saw expanded possibilities for transportation and new forms of telecommunication in a move toward modernization and globalization. The concept of interweaving performance cultures is closely connected to these interrelated processes of modernization and globalization.

Processes of Interweaving Performance Cultures

Since processes of interweaving are connected to modernization and globalization, it is important to differentiate between such processes during the first decades of the twentieth century and those that emerged at the end of the 1960s and throughout the 1970s. As will become evident, the success of the independence movements of former colonies and the further expansion of communication technologies in the 1960s and 1970s marked a new stage in the processes of modernization and globalization.

Interweaving in the First Decades of the Twentieth Century

As discussed in Chapter 5, the members of the historical avant-garde in Europe were convinced that European theatre was developing in the wrong direction. Newspaper articles and books about Asian and in particular Japanese theatre gave readers who were weary of naturalism the impression that Japanese forms of theatre offered a fruitful alternative. The first tours by Japanese theatre troupes together with publications about non-Western theatre gave Europeans the opportunity to encounter this other theatrical model. In particular, Adolph Fischer's essay "Japan's Stage Art and Its Development," published in 1900/1901 in the popular *Westermann's Illustrated German Monthly*, proved influential and was read by many theatre artists including Meyerhold (Fischer 1900/1901: 449–514).

In the following, we will explore aspects of interweaving and its relationship to processes of modernization. The concept of interweaving does not apply to just any sort of cultural encounter in performance. Rather, it designates those exchanges between cultures that open up new possibilities for the artists involved, and/or those that enable audiences to enter a new realm of experience. We will discuss three examples of interweaving between Japanese and European theatre cultures. The first two examples explore how Japanese theatre impacted existing forms of European theatre. We will study the reactions of European audiences to performances by a Japanese troupe trying to reform Kabuki theatre. We will then focus on Max Reinhard's move to integrate architectural elements of Japanese theatre into his productions. Finally, the third example focuses on how Japanese theatre practitioners integrated European acting techniques into their productions to create a new form of theatre in Japan.

"Kabuki" on European Tour

Between 1900 and 1902, Otojirō Kawakami and Sada Yakko's theatre ensemble toured all of Europe from Paris, London, and Berlin to Warsaw, St Petersburg, and Budapest. Many artists and theorists interested in reforming European theatre attended their performances. The troupe was not traditional Kabuki; rather, it belonged to the so-called *shinpa* school, trying to reform Kabuki. For this tour, Kawakami chose traditional Kabuki plays but changed them significantly to suit his notion of European taste. He cut the dialogue to a minimum to address the language barrier. In its place, he added dance scenes so that the *danmari*, a pantomimed scene that was usually presented as an intermezzo between the most exciting episodes, turned into the main part of the production. Furthermore, Kawakami significantly reduced the music that accompanied the entire narrative. Women had been prohibited from appearing on stage in Japan since 1630, and even the troupes of the *shinpa* school did not go so far as to allow female actors. Kawakami's wife Sada Yakko, who was trained as a dancer and geisha, was only able to begin playing female protagonists on their international tours (starting in 1899 in San Francisco). She immediately became the star of the troupe.

Contemporary sources about the performances in London, Paris, and Berlin trace the processes of interweaving that occurred between Japanese and European culture in and through these performances. The reviewers of the London performance give the impression that the audience—or at least the critics—greeted the staging with a certain arrogance and sense of superiority. They remarked disparagingly on "the quaint primitiveness and the extravagant oddity of their proceedings" (Review of the Kawakami Troupe, *The Graphic*, 1901a), or complained about "a disconcerting employment of quaint gesture, naïve pantomime, grotesque realism, a baffling insertion of dance and farce into would-be romance" (Review of the Kawakami Troupe, *Illustrated London News*, 1901b). The critics emphasized that not only the troupe's language, but also "many of their gestures and facial movements are Japanese to us" (Review of the Kawakami Troupe, *The Sketch*, 1901d) and came to the conclusion that "the persistent habit of introducing violently grotesque antics into tragic situations necessarily deprives their little pieces of anything like serious interest—at least for Western audiences" (Review of the Kawakami Troupe, *The Graphic*, 1901a). If the majority of spectators experienced the performance similarly to the critics, interweaving in our sense of the term did not occur between Japanese and British culture. Critics saw the productions as the expression of an earlier phase in human history—one they had already surpassed. Seeing the Japanese production confirmed their sense of British cultural identity and superiority. The production failed to prompt any revaluation of the British tradition.

The majority of French and German critics conveyed a radically different response. The Japanese seemed to have captivated French and German audiences completely. In particular, the death scenes of Sada Yakko moved audiences deeply. Emile Verhaeren, reviewer for *Mercure de France*, did not even attempt to find an explanation for the unusually strong impact these scenes had on the French audience. Instead, he was satisfied with giving the closest possible description of his own perceptions:

Never has one acted such a grim scene in the theatre. This death of Sada Yakko stirred fear like an actual death. The impact is completely physical. The facial features are torn apart: the eyes become fixed; slowly the mouth, lips, and skin turn violet; the hair, straw-like, the entire horror becomes visible. One doesn't know how such a phenomenon is executed. It borders on a miracle. And nevertheless, there is nothing that cannot be observed or which would come from deeper intuition.

(Review of the Kawakami Troupe, *Mercure de France* 1900a: 480–85)

In a certain sense, this passage is reminiscent of Macready's description of Sarah Siddons' performance in *Tamerlane*, despite fundamental differences between the two styles of acting. In each case the actor's portrayal of dying strongly affected the audience, eliciting pity and fear. One Paris critic went so far as to elevate Sada Yakko's death scenes above those of Sarah Bernhardt, a national saint to French audiences at the time:

An incomparable spectacle. Without contortions, without grimaces, she gives us the impression of a death that is physically progressive. We see life slowly abandoning the little body, almost second by second ... Even our Sarah Bernhardt, who so excels in dying, has never given us a stronger feeling of artistic truth.

(Pronko 1967: 121)

The critics of the *Neue Rundschau* also emphasized the unusual impact that this "completely non-literary type of acting" stirred in spectators, adding, "For us the effect is powerful as well" (Review of the Kawakami Troupe, *Der Neue Rundschau* 1902: 112).

We can observe the extent to which interweaving occurred in this powerful scene in a rather sarcastic remark by Franz Blei:

Everyone in Paris went to be enraptured by the "death of Sada": the polite Japanese woman expanded this scene, which when I saw it in New York lasted a minute, into the entire play in Paris; in Berlin the dying almost didn't come to an end at all.

(Blei 1902: 66)

What Blei here ascribes to the "politeness" of the Japanese was really a result of the autopoietic feedback loop through which the performance was created. The acting of Sada Yakko affected the corporeality of the audience so strongly that it triggered observable physiological, affective, volitional, energetic, and motor reactions. The artist responded to these reactions by altering her performance.

Sada Yakko—an actor from an entirely different "foreign" culture—had a strong impact on audiences and astonished the critics. Such moments are not about understanding or explaining another culture, but about the interweaving of performance cultures between Japanese and French or German culture. An emotional community was created that connected Japanese actors and French or German spectators. Theatre in this performance became primarily an embodied art rather than a literary one. This particular corporeality enabled the emergence of a community and caught the notice of reviewers. The reviewer for *Le Théâtre* commented particularly on the acting of Sada Yakko and Otojirō Kawakami:

> Above all, they express passion through gestures; and not just simple emotions, but the most nuanced subtleties of feeling. In the same way as the singer's voice in Wagner's music sometimes serves only as a recitative to portray the dramatic situation, while the orchestra provides the nuance of feeling, gestures are the essence of Japanese actors. These gestures are wondrous. Madame Sada Yakko and Monsieur Kawakami ... are, as regards facial expressions, equal to our greatest actors, and perhaps even superior to them in variety of expression. Horror and charm are equally known to them ... Their superiority lies in the expression of gestures and facial expressions that can achieve both the most profound horror and the highest pleasure.
>
> (Review of the Kawakami Troupe, *Le Théâtre* 1900b)

The reference to Wagner here is not arbitrary: many avant-garde artists, Meyerhold in particular, were interested in Wagner. The critics were surprised by the acting style of the Japanese troupe because in it "all the impact is directed at the senses" and "only from here does the impression travel to the soul" (Review of the Kawakami Troupe, *Der Neue Rundschau* 1902: 112). Such descriptions evoke the qualities that European theatre reformers and members of the avant-garde were calling for in their theatre of the future. The corporeality of acting was central to all of the reformers, no matter how much they diverged in other regards. Central too was the break with psychological realism. Following the production, Adolphe Appia remarked:

> The simplest occurrence (for example: how an impassioned woman follows her rival in order to beat her) is precisely dissected and then fixed into a chronological sequence, which yields all of the stylization that so captivates our eyes.
>
> (Appia 1986: 331)

André Gide and Georg Fuchs both emphasized rhythm as central for the expression of emotions as much as for their transmission to the spectators. Fuchs would later identify rhythm as the foundation of acting and dance in his work *The Stage of the Future* (Fuchs 1905).

French and German critics, theatre artists, and spectators generally experienced precisely those qualities in the performances of the Japanese ensemble that they found lacking in naturalist theatre (up to that point, the "most modern" kind of theatre in Europe). The newspaper *Der Tag* described it as follows:

> We were able to see and grasp the outward appearance, the physicality ... This is anything but naïve, undeveloped, immature art; anything but the art of the past, which lies behind us, and that we ourselves have overtaken. It is ahead of us, beyond us, perhaps we are orienting ourselves toward it. This culture already knows more than ours. We are looking into something from the future ... We can learn an endless amount from it (this art), and a bit of a Japanese touch would certainly be as useful to our theatres as it has been for our painting. At any rate, here we find great models that should be studied and that require the highest absorption.
> (quoted in "Die Kawakami-Truppe (Sada Yakko) in Berlin," *Ost-Asien* 1902: 450)

The Kawakami ensemble performances brought about an interweaving of performance cultures between Japanese and French culture (in Paris) and between Japanese and German culture (in Berlin, Bremen, Hannover, Leipzig, and Wiesbaden)—in contrast to the London shows. The ensemble's success on the continent grew out of a particular demand on theatre culture in Europe. At the time, naturalistic theatre was seen as outdated and unproductive in Germany and France: a dead end that did not merely need small changes, but rather required a "revolution of theatre" (as Fuchs titled his 1909 expanded edition of *The Stage of the Future*). Such a revolution demanded a new space for theatre, a new type of acting, an end to dependence on literature, and a reintroduction of music and musical principles of composition. In short, theatre needed a "re-theatricalization" (Georg Fuchs). The tour occurred when this discussion about re-theatricalization had just begun. It proved that such a theatrical revolution was actually possible. The new re-theatricalized theatre emerged in part from the processes of interweaving that took place during the Kawakami ensemble's performances—at least it gave important impulses to theatrical reform in Europe. The interweaving of performance cultures appeared here as a productive, creative process that reshaped Europe's theatrical landscape.

The Hanamichi in Berlin

Directors such as Reinhardt, Meyerhold, Tairow, Piscator, and Brecht employed a totally different, though no less productive, process of interweaving in their use of elements from Japanese or Chinese theatre. Max Reinhardt used the *hanamichi* of Kabuki Theatre (which he called the "flower walk") in his production of the pantomime *Sumurun* (based on the work of Friedrich Freksa). In doing so, he combined the *hanamichi* with theatrical conventions he himself had developed over the previous decade. His production created new theatrical conventions and with them an entirely new sense of space, new modes of perception, and new conceptions of the body that would make a lasting impact.

Traditionally, the proscenium had separated stage and auditorium; the *hanamichi* brought these two spaces together. At times, the action happened in both areas simultaneously. Used to focusing on the stage and ignoring everything else as much as possible, spectators were now forced to change position depending on whether they wanted to follow the action onstage or on the *hanamichi*. They claimed space and created noise in a totally different way. They no longer sat in front of the action; they were right in the thick of it. The two different playing areas energized the entire space.

The new space and the particular way it was used forced the audience to break with its own conventions of perception. Where should they direct their attention? Toward the stage or the *hanamichi*? Should they attempt to constantly switch back and forth between the two? Spectators had to configure a new mode of perception in order to cope with their inability to see everything that was going on. They also had to deal with the knowledge that they might miss something that their neighbors saw and found especially interesting. The spectators learned that the performance was not communicating one particular message. They instead had to make meaning for themselves based on their unique perceptions of the event. Learning to cope with these conditions of perception implied learning to cope with the conditions that characterize life in the modern metropolis.

The *hanamichi* redefined the relationship between actors and audience. The audience was used to sitting in a darkened hall (that itself had become predominant only in the 1870s), perceiving the actors onstage from a distance—a distance they would try to overcome through empathy. The *hanamichi* brought the actors into the midst of the audience, close enough to be touched. This new physical proximity between actors and audience affected audience perception and also created a new idea of the body. The bodies of the actors were no longer a part of a picture or tableau but rather moved through a three-dimensional space. Different spectators saw the actors from different angles. Some came so close that they could smell their sweat, touch the seam of their costumes, or see their make-up. From close up, all of these elements emphasized the theatrical situation: the performance did not imitate reality. The semiotic bodies of the actor receded into the background and the phenomenal bodies turned into the focal point. It was through their phenomenal bodies that they affected the bodies of the spectators. The actors and spectators thus became conscious of their bodily co-presence.

The interweaving of a fundamental element of Japanese Kabuki theatre with the constitutive elements of Reinhardt's theatre enabled a reflection on the theatricality of performance by theatrical means; in other words, a reflection on the "re-theatricalization" of theatre. It also led to changes in spatiality, modes of perception, and conceptions of the body that proved to be of major cultural significance insofar as they became characteristic of modernism. Through cultural interweaving, Reinhardt established a thoroughly modern theatre.

The Productive Reception of European Theatre in Japan

The situation was inversed in Japan and China. While the historical avant-garde in Europe was using elements of Japanese and Chinese theatre for theatrical innovation, Japan and China built their theatrical reform on precisely those conventions criticized by the European avant-garde: psychological realism on a proscenium stage. Since the opening of Japan to the West in 1853, and in particular since the beginning of the Meiji Period (1868–1912), theatre practitioners had endeavored to introduce European drama, and later a realistic-psychological style of acting and realistic set design. This process of interweaving between Japanese and European cultures began with performances of European dramas. The first dramas, such as Shakespeare's *Merchant of Venice* and Schiller's *William Tell*, were presented as Kabuki adaptations. In 1906, Tsubouchi Shoyo founded the *Bungei Kyokai* (literary society), which in 1911 presented a *Hamlet* in the style of psychological realism. In 1909, Tsubouchi had founded an acting school in which Shakespeare, Ibsen, and Chekhov were part of the curriculum. A "literarization" of the theatre through the introduction of European drama was both the means and the end of the new form of spoken theatre, *shingeki* (new drama). While Europeans strove for a de-literarization and re-theatricalization of theatre (and found their model in the performances of the Kawakami troupe), the Japanese avant-garde strove for a new literary spoken theatre oriented toward psychological realism.

The proponents of *shingeki* found traditional theatre forms such as Nô and Kabuki aesthetically outdated and sterile. To them these traditional forms were unable to react to the changing conditions of Japanese society, in particular to the challenges of modernization. Through recourse to realistic theatre from Europe, they attempted to further the development of a modern Japanese society, and offered it by way of an aesthetic model. To this end, various sorts of interweaving were put to the test.

Osanai Kaoru and the famous Kabuki actor Ichikawa Sadanji II founded the *Jiyu Gekijo* (free stage) in 1909 based on the models of Antoine's *Théâtre libre* in Paris and Otto Brahm's *Freie Bühne* in Berlin. The first performance took place on November 27, 1909 in a theatre modeled on Max Reinhardt's *Kammerspiele* (erected in 1906 as an intimate "chamber stage" that allowed the audience to sit in close proximity to the actors). It opened with *John Gabriel*

Borkman, the first Ibsen play to be performed in Japan. In this production, elements of realistic theatre were intertwined with elements of classical Kabuki. The text was intoned melodically in the Kabuki style. In the performance, the audience observed familiar elements alongside foreign, unfamiliar ones. This sort of interweaving pointed above all to the interconnection of the new with the old—both in theatre and in society. The performance initiated the most significant reception period of Ibsen in Japanese theatre, important in terms of both theatre and social history.

The first high point of Ibsen's reception was the Japanese premiere of *A Doll's House*, produced by Shimamura Hogetsu in November 1911. Matsui Sumako, a young actress who had received her training at Tsubouchi's school, played the leading part. She was not the first actress to have performed on stage since 1630: that was Sada Yakko, who received permission to appear on the Japanese stage after the ensemble's return. Yet actresses were still an unusual phenomenon for Japanese audiences. Matsui Sumako was indeed the first to practice a completely new style of acting. Her psychologically realistic acting enabled the audience to observe how everyday people discussed problems that increasingly had meaning for their own lives. According to critics, her acting not only surprised audiences but also drew them into the performance.

As this example shows, the new form of spoken theatre was supposed to give theatre a social and political function that traditional forms of theatre did not seem capable of fulfilling. Accordingly, the production of *A Doll's House* must be situated in the context of discussions about the role of women in Japanese society that became particularly salient following the Russo-Japanese War in 1905. Despite the collapse of feudalism, the new social order (the Meiji Restoration) did not provide new rights for women. Their activities were traditionally restricted to domestic duties. In 1890—the year the constitution was proclaimed—women were forbidden to participate in any political activity. Nevertheless, starting in 1874, various high schools and colleges for women were founded, opening the possibility of higher, in part European, education.

After the Russo-Japanese War, Japanese intellectuals began to consider new possibilities for educating a "new woman." In 1910 Tsubouchi gave lectures in Tokyo, Osaka, Kyoto, and Kobe on the themes of "New Women" and "New Women in Modern Drama." As examples of "new women," he proposed Nora and Hedda (from *A Doll's House* and *Hedda Gabler*), Vivie (from Shaw's *Mrs Warren's Profession*), and Magda (from Sudermann's *Heimat*). In his lecture, Tsubouchi listed the following ways that "new women" could be defined:

> Some interpreted "new women" to be women who naturally are to emerge in the new age; others interpreted them to be ideal women who must emerge by any means from now on; others, to be unwomanly women; others, to be aggressive revolutionary women who were born of

the reaction to centuries-old conventionalism; still others, to be sort of distasteful, uncontrollable and selfish women who were born of the restless, confused society in transition to the age.

(quoted in Sato 1981: 272)

Encouraged by these lectures, some young women with European educations organized a feminist society. Under the leadership of Hiratsuka Raicho, they founded a literary journal for women on June 1, 1911, that they ironically named *Seito* (*Bluestockings*). The first issue appeared on September 1, 1911. Hiratsuka Raicho wrote in an op-ed:

In ancient times, woman was the sun. Woman was the genuine human being. Now she is the moon. She is a pale moon like a sick man. She lives through others; she shines by the light of others ... We must recover our sun, which has been hidden away.

(quoted in Sato 1981: 275)

The first issue contained a number of programmatic essays that protested against Japanese hierarchical structures and demanded that individual freedoms be extended to women. This first issue was a success: the Japanese women's movement had found its voice.

Two months later, *A Doll's House* premiered. On the occasion of this performance, the critic Kusuyama Masao wrote:

Without reservation or exaggeration, I believe that the Nora played by this actress Matsui Sumako, must be remembered as a monument which resolved for the first time problems of using actresses in Japan, and which on stage, emancipated women for the first time in Japan.

(quoted in Sato 1981: 278)

The discussion begun here was resumed in the January issue of the *Seito* journal (1912).

With *shingeki*, a modern theatre was created in Japan that allowed pressing social and political problems to be examined on stage. Moreover, it fed into public discourse. In the process of modernization, Japanese culture interwove with the literary, psychological-realistic tradition of European culture through *shingeki* performances. This interweaving of performance cultures, as is apparent in the example of *A Doll's House*, propelled Japanese society toward other elements of modernization, or at least toward a discussion about them.

These three examples of different types of interweaving between Japanese and European cultures in performance bring up two important questions. The first question concerns expertise and scholarship: how much does a European scholar need to know about Japanese theatre to discuss cases of interweaving between European and Japanese theatre cultures? Secondly, we need to clarify how we define the term "modern theatre," and how our concepts of modernity and modernization underpin our research.

The answer to the first question will vary from case to case depending on the focus of the researcher. If researchers are only claiming to make an argument about Japanese impact on European theatre (and not about Japanese theatre itself), they may not have to be specialists in Japanese theatre. It is more important that they know how Europeans at the time understood Japanese theatre. The analysis of Reinhardt's use of the *hanamichi* is a useful example in this context. Of course, one must know how the *hanamichi* functions in Kabuki theatre. But this knowledge can easily be garnered through European publications from the turn of the century, such as the previously discussed essays by Adolph Fischer, or Georg Fuchs' explanation of the *hanamichi* in *The Stage of the Future*. Publications such as these are actually more suitable than even the best handbooks on Kabuki theatre because they convey the ideas that European theatre practitioners connected with the *hanamichi* at the beginning of the twentieth century.

Similarly, if researchers want to focus on the impact of the Kawakami tour on the reform efforts of European theatre, it is not essential to explore the ensemble's role in Japan or their goals when touring the United States and Europe. The researchers would be centrally interested in the performances as a catalyst for new theatrical ideas (and less interested in the performers themselves). This topic could be explored through recourse to English, German, or French sources because the question only addresses the processes of inter-weaving and its effects on European theatre history.

Other research projects about the same tour might require expertise in Japanese theatre. Some such questions might be: how did Kawakami's encounter with Antoine's *Théâtre Libre* in Paris inspire the reform of his own troupe? How do these reforms relate to Japan's processes of modernization? What goals did the troupe pursue during their tours and how did the process of interweaving that they had experienced in the West affect the development of Japanese theatre? Finding satisfactory answers for these questions would require cooperation between experts of the two theatre cultures and awareness of how Japanese theatre historians have explored these questions from their own perspective in Japanese theatre history.

Research about the introduction of *shingeki* in Japan requires expertise in Japanese theatre and society. Like the reform of Kabuki in the *shinpa* school, the introduction of *shingeki* is connected to the specific processes of modernization that occurred in Japanese society during the Meiji Period. Without the ability to read Japanese texts, researchers would have to depend on sources such as travelogues in European languages and consult with experts to determine the reliability of such sources. For this reason I carefully discussed this example with the Japanese theatre scholar Mitsuya Mori, who is an Ibsen specialist and recently created a production of *A Doll's House* (2005) that interwove techniques from Nô and *shingeki*.

Since these examples of interweaving cultures in performance come from the first decades of the twentieth century, some of them are already discussed in comprehensive studies that used Japanese sources but were published in English, French, or German. In individual cases, one can resort to a substantial body of critical literature. Naturally, such possibilities do not exist for more current processes of interweaving that are taking place today.

In our discussion of interweaving performance cultures in the first decades of the twentieth century, we have referred to "modern theatre" and the concept of modernization. We used Reinhardt's *Sumurun* as an example of modern theatre in Germany prior to World War I, while Tsubouchi's roughly contemporaneous staging of *A Doll's House* functioned as the starting point of modern theatre in Japan. We also designated the reforms of the *shinpa* school a modernization of Kabuki theatre. Ultimately, it is impossible to speak of the interweaving processes since the start of the twentieth century without recourse to terms such as "modern," "modernity," and "modernization." In historical research, modernization is often equated with Westernization. When we consider the above examples, it becomes immediately clear why such equivalence is untenable. Just as it would be unjustified to accuse Max Reinhardt of stealing from Kabuki by introducing the *hanamichi*, it is unjustified to denounce Tsubouchi's *A Doll's House* as a copy of European theatre. It is not productive to speak of an "Asianization" of German theatre or a "Westernization" of Japanese theatre in these examples. In both cases, we can however speak of "modern" theatre, because in both contexts there are specific, if very different, processes of modernization at play. We are left with the fundamental question of which definition (or definitions) of "modernity" and "modernization" to use in our study of theatre and performance.

As normative, relational, and historical concepts, "modernity" and "modernization" are contentious terms. There has been a good deal of justified criticism of the reigning positivist, Euro-centric models of modernization. One influential critic, sociologist Shmuel N. Eisenstadt, developed the theory of "multiple modernities" (Eisenstadt 2003, 2006). According to this theory, there is no single modernity—namely, that of Western cultures—that is taken on by other cultures through processes of "Westernization." Rather, there is a multiplicity of modernities, and the definition of modernity lies within cultures themselves rather than in relation to a monolithic European model. Following this concept of multiple modernities, the task for Theatre and Performance Studies is to clarify which ideas, models, and concepts of modernity and modernization developed within a particular culture and its theatre.

In this context, one must bear in mind that social processes of change such as modernization take multidimensional and non-simultaneous courses, and depend on a complex interplay of artistic, social, technological, economic, and political factors. Processes of transformation of such magnitude never run precisely parallel, nor do they always relate causally to one another:

technological modernization does not necessarily lead to a modernization of the theatre. What these terms come to mean in different cultures and how they are used must be investigated anew in each analysis of processes of interweaving. Unlike various kinds of cultural exchange and performance in earlier centuries, these exchanges are bound up in the processes of modernization. For this reason, clarity about the foundational concepts of modernity and modernization is essential to studies of interweaving in the nineteenth and twentieth centuries.

Interweaving Performance Cultures since the 1970s

The 1960s and more so the 1970s witnessed an interweaving of performance cultures on a hitherto unprecedented scale. Two major factors lie at base of this development: first, the independence of former colonies, and second, the expansion of new communication technologies. Regardless of how "similar" or "different" cultures are, how distant they are from one another, there is always the possibility of various sorts of interweaving between them. This interweaving of performance cultures can—as in the first decades of the twentieth century—occur in the form of international tours and through the transfer of elements such as texts, acting styles, aesthetic principles, and artistic techniques from one theatre culture to another. But it can also come about through collaboration between artists of different cultural backgrounds. This sort of internationally composed ensemble has become the norm for some forms of theatre, such as opera. Some prominent examples of international theatre ensembles include Peter Brook's International Center for Theatre Research at the Théâtre des Bouffes du Nord in Paris, Ariane Mnouchkine's Théâtre du Soleil in Vinciennes, Eugenio Barba's Odin Teatret in Holstebro, Denmark, Sasha Waltz & Guests in Berlin, and Ong Keng Sen's Flying Circus in Singapore.

In the following section, we will discuss what is at stake in touring and international festivals, in the transfer of elements from one theatre culture to another, and in international collaborations.

Tours and International Festivals

Touring was certainly a feature of the first decades of the twentieth century: we have already discussed Sarah Bernhardt's tours (in the nineteenth century) and Max Reinhardt's tours in various European countries and the United States. British ensembles would also tour the British colonies. Yet this does not compare to the touring schedules of ensembles today. Partly touring has increased because there no longer are only a few famous ensembles with canonical productions circling the globe. International dance, theatre, and music festivals have sprung up like mushrooms around the world, all aiming to produce the "most prominent" productions in spoken theatre, dance, and opera. Productions created in a specific place for a local public are brought to entirely new audiences and enter different cultural contexts.

This situation poses new challenges for Theatre and Performance Studies. As discussed earlier, performances are created through the bodily co-presence of actors and spectators, and in their interactions with each other. Every performance is unique and unrepeatable. It follows that with guest performances and festival productions the degree of unpredictability increases; so much so that the same production renders strikingly different performances. The conditions of performance have a profound effect. A painting can "travel" to museums in different cultures without—hopefully—changing its specific materiality, even though the aesthetic experience that viewers have in different parts of the world might differ. Yet the reactions of audiences, and the audience's impact on the actor/performer/dancer, belong to the materiality of a performance, therefore each performance remains unique. In theory, this seems straightforward. But how can one empirically study guest performances or international festivals with these performance aspects in mind? A production such as Heiner Müller's production of Brecht's *Arturo Ui* (Berliner Ensemble, 1995) dealt with national questions about Hitler's rise to power and was unmistakably created for a German audience. Still, the touring production was celebrated in both Western and non-Western cultures, but with different audience reactions in different cultural contexts. We might also think of the American director Peter Sellars and his 1989 trilogy of Mozart operas. He staged each of these operas in a very specific American cultural milieu and dealt with current political discussions about race, drugs, and foreign policy in the US: *Don Giovanni* took place in the inner city, *The Marriage of Figaro* in the Trump Towers, and *Cosi fan tutte* in a suburban diner. These productions successfully toured the United States as well as Europe, where the questions of race and class are framed very differently.

To what extent can our methods of performance analysis explain these reactions, without also consulting experts in the various other cultures? The pressing question here is how the process of interweaving in performance proceeds, and what consequences it has for the relevant theatres or cultures (i.e. the same question we asked in regard to the European avant-garde and the tours of the Kawakami ensemble). This question can only be answered in discussion and cooperation with experts in multiple theatre traditions and cultures.

The Transfer of Elements between Performance Cultures

A separate problem arises from the appropriation of elements from one culture into productions intended for audiences from a different culture (or cultures). The term "intercultural theatre" has gained currency to refer to productions such as Peter Brook's *Orghast* (Persepolis, 1971) or *Mahabharata* (Avignon,

1985); Ariane Mnouchkine's Shakespeare cycle—*Richard II* (1981) and *Henry IV* (1984)—or her antiquity project *Les Atrides* (1990/1993); Tadashi Suzuki's antiquity project *The Trojan Women* (1974), *The Bacchae* (1978), and *Clytemnestra* (1983)—or his *Three Sisters* (1985); Robert Wilson's *Knee Plays* (Minneapolis, 1984) and Shakespeare productions in the style of traditional Chinese opera such as *Macbeth* (1984 as Kunqu opera) or *Much Ado About Nothing* (1986 as Huangmeixi opera). The concept has come to denote stagings that use theatrical conventions from other cultures. Although this concept may seem fairly straightforward, on closer examination we find that it is based on two contentious assumptions.

The concept of "intercultural theatre" assumes that it is possible to separate one's "own" theatre from "other" theatres: in other words, that French audiences would necessarily identify specific elements in Mnouchkine's *Henry IV* as "Japanese" and thus "foreign," while Japanese audiences would recognize the "Western" elements in Suzuki's production of *Three Sisters* as "foreign."

Ariane Mnouchkine's design of masks, music, and gestures of *Henry IV* might have been inspired by Nô and Kabuki Theatre; however, she made so many changes that Europeans who were versed in Japanese theatre only saw vague references to Japanese theatre, and Japanese theatre experts were unable to identify anything "Japanese" about it. French and European audiences—insofar as they had seen the films of Kurosawa and Mizoguchi—associated certain elements with the Japanese Middle Ages; for others, these elements were completely new. Some design elements for the production followed a different aesthetic than had previously been characteristic for Mnouchkine's theatre. King Henry, his advisor Westmoreland, and the schemer Worcester, Hotspur's uncle, wore (supposedly Japanese) wooden masks, whereas Hotspur's rebels and the Prince wore the white face-paint that had been used at the Théâtre du Soleil since *Les Clowns* (1969). Incidentally, this white make-up initially had also seemed "foreign." The old regime in the drama (eager to maintain their power at any price) was juxtaposed to the younger generation aspiring to power. The stiff wooden masks underscored the rigidness of the old, whereas the make-up, though similarly estranging, allowed for facial expressions that showed the flexibility of youth. Entry into the court was signified by "Japanese"-sounding music, the courtly ceremonies through a set of "Japanese" gestures, the mutiny of the nobles against Henry through a pantomime that seemed "Japanese" to many. Finally, extreme psychological states were denoted by gestures perceived as Japanese: for example a series of increasingly powerful pirouettes used to express the war-obsession of Hotspur and the enemies of the king. Such pirouettes cannot actually be found in any form of traditional Japanese theatre. Mnouchkine did not in fact use specific elements of Japanese theatre but rather elements that a French or European audience would stereotype as "Japanese." They were merely elements designed to appear "foreign."

Tadashi Suzuki's production of *Three Sisters* was celebrated in Japan as an even greater break with *shingeki* than his antiquities project. Suzuki belonged to the so-called "Underground" or "Small Theatre Movement" (*Angura*) that developed in the 1960s. This movement struggled against *shingeki* and sought to connect with Japanese traditions. At the same time, they preserved *shingeki*'s initial mission: to create theatre that would deal with contemporary societal change and its problems. When Suzuki decided to produce the *Three Sisters* with his Suzuki Company of Toga (SCOT) in 1985, it came as a surprise because the play was one of the favorites in the *shingeki* repertoire. Suzuki, however, staged it in a new style his company developed with recourse to Nô, Kabuki, and Shinto rituals. The stage was reminiscent of the old Nô stage, albeit not identical—the *hashigakari*, which connected the dressing rooms with the stage, was missing, for example. Likewise, sliding doors replaced the painted wooden wall at the rear of the stage. While the three sisters wore modern dress, Andrei, Natasha, and Anfisa wore traditional Japanese clothes. For Japanese audiences, this was a purely Japanese production. The piece was a classic of *shingeki* repertoire, the acting style and stage design were bound up in Japanese traditions, and the costumes included traditional and modern Japanese clothing. Yet on tour at the Festival Theater der Welt in Frankfurt on Main in 1985 (which also featured Peter Brook's *Mahabharata* and Wilson's *Knee Plays*), Suzuki's production of the *Three Sisters* was deemed "intercultural." The text was seen exclusively as part of Western cultural heritage, the contemporary clothes were perceived as Western, while the traditional clothes were perceived as Japanese. Both the play and the contemporary costumes, which had long been a constitutive part of Japanese culture, were seen as non-Japanese. Whereas the Japanese perceived the production as Japanese, European festival audiences saw it as intercultural.

The concept of "intercultural" theatre makes the false assumption that cultures are sealed entities—once Japanese, always Japanese; once European, always European. Instead cultures are immersed in a continuous process of change and exchange. It often is difficult to disentangle or distinguish what is "one's own" and what is "foreign". The differences between cultures are dynamic and continually shifting. The existing research on so-called intercultural theatre is inadequate to assess this situation. Even more recent studies that focus on hybridization ignore this central point. Ultimately, the idea of hybridization itself assumes that there are elements that do not "originally" or "naturally" belong together, but are arbitrarily merged. In research on "intercultural theatre," the appropriation of elements from non-Western theatre cultures into Western theatre is generally valued differently than the appropriation of Western theatrical forms by non-Western cultures. Whereas the former are celebrated as bold aesthetic experiments, the latter are seen as a result of a modernization that equals Westernization. As the concept of "multiple modernities" has shown, modernization is not the same as Westernization. The interweaving of Asian with non-Asian cultures—as in the productions of Suzuki, Terayama Shuji, Ninagawa Yukio, or Miyagi Satoshi—is aesthetically as experimental and bold as those of Brook, Mnouchkine, Barba, and Wilson.

French or European audiences identified elements of Mnouchkine's *Henry IV* as "Japanese" or simply "foreign," and identified elements of Suzuki's *Three Sisters* as European or Western. They perceived both productions as "intercultural." Yet, according to Japanese theatre experts with whom I consulted, Japanese audiences perceived *Henry IV* as "purely" French, and the *Three Sisters* as "purely" Japanese. There is obviously no "objective" way to determine what was perceived by each group as part of their own culture, and what was perceived as foreign. Perceptions are always determined by a pre-existing system of signification: they depend to a degree on one's affiliations and assumptions. It is as unreasonable to try to distinguish between "correct" and "false" perceptions as it is to speak of experience itself as "right" or "wrong." Binary categories are inadequate to understand the sorts of processes of interweaving that occur in contemporary productions. The concept "intercultural theatre" implies a sharp division between "our" culture and "other" cultures, and should therefore be avoided.

A very different sort of transfer between performance cultures occurs in innumerable theatre and performance workshops that take place around the world. Such workshops teach practices and bodily techniques; one group develops them for another. The workshop is a site of interweaving which offers impulses for later productions. Here, it is no longer possible to differentiate between cultures in the sense of a confrontation of opposites. Any dichotomy between "self" and "other" is overcome in the learning process. In the workshop situation new artistic identities can develop. Theatre and Performance Studies has only addressed such situations in a cursory fashion. These processes can only be studied through interdisciplinary research that combines expertise in Theatre and Performance Studies with ethnography. In the case of workshops that teach bodily practices, it becomes particularly clear that analyzing processes of interweaving in a globalized world requires intensive collaboration between theatre scholars and ethnographers or anthropologists.

Cooperation Between Artists with Different Cultural Backgrounds

With the emergence of the first international ensembles in the 1970s, Theatre and Performance Studies had to respond to the phenomenon of co-creations by artists from different cultures. Such work renders obsolete the central opposition that was so important to the processes of interweaving in the first decades of the twentieth century: the European and non-European, the "self" and the "other." Once we abandon this opposition, the problem of cultural identity is posed anew; often it is thematized by the artists themselves and becomes the object of artistic investigation.

The African-American dancer and choreographer Ralph Lemon, for example, cast dancers from the Ivory Coast, India, China, and Taiwan in his *Geography* Trilogy (*Africa/Race*, 1997; *Tree*, 2000; and *Come Home, Charley Patton*, 2004). Not only did these dancers bring music and dance elements of their cultural background to the choreography, but the ensemble also performed the trilogy within different cultural contexts to study the reactions of different audiences. The cultural differences between the artists were used to produce a new, harmonious way of coexistence, marked by reciprocal respect and understanding. The performances created were not attributable to any one theatre culture; they instead created a new culture of cooperation.

Lemon's project can be compared to Sasha Waltz's body trilogy—*Körper* (*Body*, 2000), *S* (2000), and *noBody* (2002)—which involved dancers from different cultures presenting to audiences from various cultural backgrounds. Waltz's choreography approached cultural identity in innovative ways: bodies became fragmented or dissolved, they fused into mythical forms and super-individual patterns. Her choreography contained great utopian potential. The processes of interweaving that take place in and through such choreography show how cultural difference stimulates collaborative work and creates a shared future. If this potential is to be tapped and incorporated into the social life of immigration societies, it will require particularly close cooperation with researchers of other disciplines, such as sociologists. So far, hardly any research exists about these dimensions of interweaving performance cultures.

Dance performances may seem particularly suited to this sort of utopian interweaving because of the absence of spoken language. Performances of spoken theatre have also directly addressed the problem of language and imagined new cultural identities through multilingualism. In her production of Shakespeare's *A Midsummer Night's Dream* (Düsseldorf, 1995), Karin Beier gathered fourteen actors from eight European countries who did not have any language in common. Every actor spoke in his or her own language throughout the production. The resulting misunderstandings and unexpected results of communication both among the actors and between actors and audience were not merely tolerated but made spectacularly fruitful. Such misunderstandings and incomprehension were far from obstacles to collaborative work. On the contrary, they offered a productive way to foster spontaneity. The production was not based just on light-hearted misunderstandings. It provided an opportunity to discuss European cultural identity in an entertaining manner. Shakespeare's play traces the misunderstandings experienced by young lovers in their "liminal phase" of adolescence—beyond childhood but not yet furnished with their new social identities as married couples. Similarly, it might be possible for Europeans to move from their previous national identity toward a new, shared cultural identity, assuming they are capable of making their cultural and linguistic plurality, and the inevitable misunderstandings that will result from it, productive. The confusion—and at times antagonism—of the various languages and styles created a new aesthetic with a political dimension.

While Karin Beier created her production of *A Midsummer Night's Dream* as a "European" project, the Singaporean director Ong Keng Sen used his staging of *Lear* (1997) to reflect on the possibility of an Asian cultural identity, in

which a multiplicity of languages and artistic traditions could cooperate productively. He took a very different approach from Karin Beier. His production
did not focus on the problems of misunderstanding and incomprehension but
on the condition of "in-betweenness," a condition into which Ong Keng Sen
drew all the participants, actors as well as spectators. Here, varied acting styles
and languages confronted each other. Lear was played by a famous Nô actor
from Japan, who spoke in the antiquated Japanese of Nô plays and acted in Nô
style. An actor from the National Beijing Opera played Goneril in its style,
and spoke Chinese (Regan's role was cut). A Thai dancer, who danced in the
style of the traditional masked dance Khon, performed the part of Cordelia.
Goneril's three warriors moved in the traditional Indonesian fighting art
Pencak Silat. The musicians also came from those four different theatrical traditions. However, they did not accompany the action of the performers from
their own cultures but rather those of a performer from another culture. A
young Japanese actress played the Fool. She spoke English and used a realistic
style of acting. Shakespeare's play was changed substantially in order to make it
compatible with the conventions of all of these traditions. The production was
first shown in Japan, then in Hong Kong, Singapore, Jakarta, Perth, and finally
went on tour through various European countries. Given the multiplicity of
languages employed, the staging used supertitles throughout.

As in the other previously discussed dance and theatre pieces—by Ralph
Lemon, Sasha Waltz, and Karin Beier—cultural differences were not effaced,
but emphasized. Although every performer followed a style that was clearly
differentiated from the others, they all performed together and created specific
relationships between characters and theatrical styles. The use of accompanying music in still different styles further emphasized the fluidity of cultural
identity. As a whole the performance was not simply an act of hybridization
(i.e. the fusing of elements that would not "actually," "naturally" occur
together). Far more, it was a reflection on the concept of hybridity itself, on
hybrid identities, and on the passage from one identity to another. The stage
on which the performers moved comprised two wide wooden walkways that
crossed each other. They functioned as passageways, on which the performers
acted out their specific stylized identity, accompanied by music from another
tradition, which changed—perhaps indeed estranged—that identity. In effect,
the characters enacted a process of losing and reconstituting their identity in a
new manner. The fusion of acting styles and music from two different traditions anticipated how such processes of interweaving might proceed.

Although the performance began with specific, clearly constructed local
traditions, it then transitioned from one tradition to another, from one culture
to another, from one identity to another, and simultaneously reflected on
these transitions. Something new was created that was neither one nor the
other, but both at the same time. The performance exposed the audience to a
state of liminality. This cultural interweaving created a "third space," to use
Homi Bhabha's term (Bhabha 1994). Irrespective of where the production was

shown, it never allowed a spectator to feel completely at home, to identify fully with one acting style or dramatic figure. The performance released a force—on which it also reflected—that enacted the processes of globalization. It challenged the audience to think about its position. The aesthetic experience of the performance can be described as a very particular sort of liminal experience, comprising fascination and estrangement, enchantment and reflection. Whereas this aesthetic experience had a decidedly political dimension by proposing a new sense of cultural identity for Asian audiences, audiences in European countries focused on the aesthetic variability. These audiences experienced breathtaking beauty and an interweaving of widely varied traditions and languages.

This brief performance analysis (based on multiple visits to the Berlin performances of *Lear*) reads the performance through the central concepts of postcolonialism and above all Homi Bhabha's notion of hybridity and the "third space." Were this discussion to include audience reception in Asia, it would require relevant field research in collaboration with anthropologists, sociologists, and other experts in the respective cultures and their theatres. Unfortunately, the opportunity for such a study did not present itself. If Theatre and Performance Studies seeks to research such processes of interweaving performance cultures in the future, collaborative research projects will be essential.

Local and Global Theatres

For Ong Keng Sen's production of *Lear*, extensive changes were made to the text in order to adapt it to the conventions of various Asian theatre traditions. Similarly, the 1980s saw a number of Shakespeare productions in different Chinese opera styles. *Macbeth* was performed in the Kunqu style with the new title *Bloody Hands*; the names of places and characters were changed to the Chinese. The text was rewritten and adapted to the theatrical conventions of Kunqu. At a first glance, such adaptations to local conditions might seem reminiscent of the treatment of texts common in European theatre up to the late nineteenth century. When Goethe proclaimed his goal to create a comprehensive European repertoire for his stage in Weimar, he assumed that texts from other cultures and eras would have to be rewritten prior to performance. While Goethe postulated that "the audience will learn to accept that not every play is like a dress that must be completely tailored to contemporary desires" (Goethe 1802/1901: 82), he did find it necessary for plays to be adapted to the dominant staging conventions and moral norms of the Weimar audience. For this reason the porter scene in *Macbeth* was excised in its Weimar staging—it was deemed too obscene—and replaced by a pious song, written by Schiller. For similar reasons, Goethe reworked *Romeo and Juliet* so drastically that an English Shakespeare scholar of the 1950s called his version an "amazing travesty" (Bruford 1950).

In a letter to Caroline von Wolzogen, Goethe explained his process of reworking:

> The maxim that I followed was to concentrate on the most interesting elements, and to bring those into harmony because Shakespeare—in line with his genius, his era, and his audience—could bring together a lot of disharmonious horseplay, indeed he had to, to make peace with the ruling spirit of theatre.
>
> (Quoted in Hinck 1982: 19)

Goethe's method was to mediate plays from other cultures to his public and to turn them into a living part of his contemporary theatre. Commenting on his production of *The Constant Prince* by Calderón, Goethe wrote to Sartorius:

> This time we presented a play that was written nearly 200 years ago, under a different sky, for a completely differently educated people, so freshly that it seemed to have come hot from the oven.
>
> (Quoted in Hinck 1982: 14)

While Goethe's adaptations preserved a hint of foreignness in order to maintain aesthetic distance, Johann Nestroy went much further in his adaptations of English and French comedies and farces. He "translated" the plays by substituting names, places, and references with those of his Viennese milieu. He managed a total assimilation. What had been imported from Paris or London now appeared to be genuinely Viennese. The same was true of Nestroy's own plays when they appeared on the Paris and London stages. The changes were the result of a European market for plays that constantly had to offer new goods to different local publics.

We have already discussed two examples of Shakespeare plays rewritten to suit specific conventions of traditional Asian theatre forms. There are also other ways of localizing plays. When the Nepalese director Sumil Pokharel staged Ibsen's *A Doll's House* (Aarohan Theatre, 2003) he did not adapt the play to the Nepalese theatrical conventions, but rather to the living conditions and habits of contemporary Nepal (Nilu 2008). He set the action of the play in a room that was reminiscent of a Hindu temple, which in the characters' speeches was described as a middle-class Nepalese household complete with washing machine and microwave. The Christmas celebration was replaced by *Tihar*, the Hindi light festival in honor of the goddess Lakshmi. The characters had Nepalese names. As is common in Nepal today, the women were dressed in saris and the men in modern suits. Nepalese audiences clearly recognized the action as being set in contemporary Nepal.

Wherein lies the difference between adapting *Macbeth* to Goethe's stage and to the Kunqu opera? Equally, why define the Nepalese production of *A Doll's House* as a "localization" in contrast to Thomas Ostermeier's production of the same play at the Berlin Schaubühne in 2002, which was classed as a "topicalization"? The question of distinction runs through a wide range of adaptations and rewritings of the later twentieth century, such as Heiner Müller rewritings of Sophocles' *Philoktet* (1962–64), *Oedipus* (1966), or Aeschylus' *Prometheus* (1967/8) versus Wole Soyinka's rewriting of Euripides' *The Bacchae* (1974) or Femi Osofisan's adaptation of Sophocles' *Antigone* as *Tegonni: An African Antigone* (1999), and Euripides' *The Trojan Women* as *The Women of Owu* (2004). In terms of technique, there is no fundamental difference between these acts of rewriting, and yet their political meaning shifts within a postcolonial framework. The appropriation of texts from the European tradition by theatre artists from non-Western cultures, and above all from former colonies, contains a different kind of political dimension to the updating or rewriting of plays from one's own tradition. Localization can be understood as a strategy of using Western cultural artifacts as raw material to create work that is embedded in a local culture. An adaptation, as in Aimé Césaire's *A Tempest* (adapted from Shakespeare's *Tempest*), may also reframe the source text as a way of critiquing how the Western literary canon supported and justified the colonial endeavor. Through localization, the parity of cultures is not merely postulated and proclaimed, but actualized. The act of rewriting becomes an eminently political phenomenon. Nevertheless, the ethics of appropriation and localization are still contentious issues for both scholars and theatre practitioners given the violent (and in some countries unresolved) history of colonialism and postcolonial struggle.

Localization is closely connected to globalization insofar as globalization creates the prerequisites for texts, theatrical elements, and even artists themselves to circulate between various cultures. In another sense, globalization turns into the opposite of localization—in particular in the case of encroachments into the theatre of non-Western cultures made possible by financing from the West. The United States' National Endowment for the Humanities made its largest financial investment to date for a production of Euripides' *The Bacchae* (1996) at the China National Beijing Opera Theatre. The production was directed by Chen Shi-Zhen, a long-time resident of the United States. It came about through the efforts of Peter Steadman, the artistic director of the New York Greek Drama Company. Steadman developed the concept for the production and also chose the director. Rather than adapting the text to the conventions of the Beijing Opera—i.e. localizing it—the operatic form was changed to suit the text. Steadman asked that twelve actors from his New York Greek Drama Company sing the unabridged chorus songs in ancient Greek, accompanied by his version of "ancient Greek music." In order to reconstruct the music, the Chinese instruments had to be altered—for example, by drilling two additional finger holes into the *suona* (a Chinese oboe). Three male performers from the China National Beijing Opera played all eight roles in masks—as was common practice in Euripides' time. The encroachments into the form of the Beijing Opera aimed for a precise "reconstruction" of ancient Greek theatre; in other words, they aimed to satisfy the interests of the American Steadman that were not shared by either the ensemble of the Peking Opera or the audiences in Beijing. Steadman portrayed the situation as follows:

> The collaboration between the China National Beijing Opera Theatre and the New York Greek Drama Company for the production of the *Bacchae* is a historical event. Our performance is the largest collaboration between American and Chinese Theatre. The United States Endowment for the Humanities has given this project the largest grant since its inception. This is the first time that both archaic theatre traditions—the theatre of classical antiquity and the Chinese Peking Opera—hold the same status and join as equal partners to create real artistic work.
>
> (Steadman 1996: 22)

The designation of the Peking Opera as an "archaic theatre tradition" alone suggests that this was far from an equal cooperation. It was also not a localization that adapted Euripides' *Bacchae* to the aesthetics of Peking Opera. Far more, the Peking Opera was subordinated to what Steadman believed were the demands of the Greek text. He was interested in neither the Peking Opera itself nor a possible localization of the *Bacchae* through it. His goal was a "reconstruction" of ancient Greek theatre, for which he saw the Peking Opera as a convenient medium. This cultural imperialist course of action was only possible for him because of the large financial support that the National Endowment for the Humanities contributed to the project. Chinese critics remarked with bitterness upon this fact. Tang Xiao-bai wrote in *Chinese Theatre* (1996):

> In this co-production, Xiqu [Chinese opera] was really just used as a medium to approximate Greek theatre. There are neither Xipi nor Erhuang (Peking opera song) nor gongs and drums, nor stylized portrayals. Xiqu could not preserve its own characteristics as an independent theatre form. This cannot be seen as an "equal cooperation" because it takes for granted that a theatre form from the periphery must orient itself toward the theatre form of the Center [the West] … In this process we are actually in a passive role the whole time, and do not have any agency. The West cooks its own soup, in which Xiqu is thrown as a suitable ingredient.
>
> (Lin 2009: 304)

As with localization, Steadman's globalized *Bacchae* project is not merely developing a new aesthetic or "renewing" an older aesthetic. Rather, the production is fundamentally entangled in questions of power and politics. If localization is the expression of self-determination that gives parity to all involved cultures, the American–Chinese *Bacchae* is a particularly blatant example of cultural imperialism, made possible through lavish financing.

It is not always so evident whether and to what extent imperialistic assumptions play a role in such collaborations: this is also a question of perspective (see Fischer-Lichte 2014). When money is involved, suspicions easily arise. Some Asian states also accused Ong Keng Sen's *Lear* of cultural imperialism because the production was financed by the Japan Foundation. When the Norwegian government celebrated the centennial of Ibsen's death with a production of *Peer Gynt* at the pyramids in Giza, some Egyptian spectators read it as a gesture of cultural imperialism. The production was financed completely by Norway; only Norwegian actors were involved, and the play was performed in Norwegian. Similar suspicions arose when the Norwegian government made funding available for an Ibsen Festival in New Delhi (see Fischer-Lichte 2011).

The rise of international theatre festivals raises additional questions about the relationship between local and global theatres. How, for example, do we approach a "localized" production of Greek tragedy, Shakespeare, or Ibsen that is commissioned from outside the local culture? The Chinese director Luo Jin-Lin staged productions of *Oedipus* (1986) and *Antigone* (1988) in *huaju* (spoken theatre) style, including some conventions of the Peking opera. Both productions were invited to the International Meeting of Ancient Greek Drama in Delphi and received international recognition. The Greek director Theodoros Terzopoulos, a member of the committee, suggested to Luo Jin-Lin that he direct another Greek tragedy in the style of a traditional Chinese opera. Luo Jin-Lin followed this suggestion and, in 1989, created a production of *Medea* in the style of *Hebei Bangzi*, which was invited to Delphi. This production was undoubtedly an example of localization. The text was changed to fit the conventions of the chosen opera style, and to accord with the previous knowledge of the audience: a "local" production made it to the "global" market in Delphi (Lin 2009).

We can compare Luo Jin-Lin's production of *Medea* to Guru Sadanam P. V. Balakrishnan's 1995 production of *The Bacchae*. The committee from Delphi asked Balakrishnan, the head of the International Kathakali Centre in New Delhi, to stage Euripides' tragedy in Kathakali style. After reading the text, Balakrishnan agreed, and shortened and reworked the text substantially in order to adapt it to his form of theatre (of course, he also changed Kathakali theatre to retain the Greek chorus). This was another case of localization, which was received with enthusiasm in both Delphi and New Delhi. Whereas Luo Jin-Lin's *Medea* was performed for a local audience on multiple occasions, the *Bacchae* in Kathakali style only received one performance in New Delhi.

How can we evaluate the political dimension of the two cases? Do we understand the invitation to participate in one of the most important international theatre festivals—and thus to participate in the global market—as a strategy of cultural imperialism? Does it imply the "universality" of Greek tragedy—and thus Western culture—and exploit the desire of Asian theatre artists to participate in the global market? Alternatively, is it an opportunity to present Chinese and Indian theatre traditions to an international audience by localizing Greek tragedy? There is no clear answer to these questions: it all depends on one's perspective. In order to explore the connection between localization and globalization, one must be sensitive to a whole set of political questions. In the case of the *Bacchae* in Kathakali style, the local public had only one opportunity to participate in the performance, which may raise suspicions that the primary concern throughout the six-month rehearsal period was success in the global (rather than the local) market.

There are indeed a number of productions that are produced exclusively for the global market without any local audience in mind. The recourse to the Western "canon"—above all the Greek tragedies, Shakespeare, Ibsen, Chekhov, Brecht (the worldwide hit list of the most performed plays in the past 30 years)—guarantees a theatre ensemble the interest of a Western audience. Interestingly, Western audiences expect productions of canonical works from non-Western countries to be essentially different than productions of the same plays within their own cultures. In this case, elements of other theatrical forms are brought in not to localize but to self-exoticize the production and heighten the interest of a Western public. A festival aesthetic develops that becomes increasingly alienated from a local audience. Here localization and globalization no longer go hand in hand; rather, the global market is all that counts—even when such productions are not a success. This shows once more the truth of Heiner Müller's statement that theatre must be local in order to become truly international.

This chapter has presented a glimpse of a broadening sub-field within Theatre and Performance Studies, which will become increasingly important as processes of globalization continue. As the examples in this chapter have shown, this field can only be properly investigated through interdisciplinary cooperation.

Further Reading

On Non-European Theatre Traditions

Africa and the Middle East

Amine, K. and M. Carlson (2012) *The Theatres of Morocco, Algeria, and Tunisia: Performance Traditions of the Maghreb*, New York: Palgrave Macmillan.
Banham, M. (ed.) (2004) *The History of Theatre in Africa*, Cambridge: Cambridge University Press.
Okagbue, O. (2007) *African Theatre and Performance*, London/New York: Routledge.

Asia

Hollander, J. (2007) *Indian Folk Theatre*, New York/London: Routledge.
Huang, A. (2009) *Chinese Shakespeares: Two Centuries of Cultural Exchange*, New York: Columbia University Press.

Inoura, Y. (1981) *The Traditional Theatre in Japan*, New York/Tokyo: Weatherhill.
Makkerras, C. (1983) *Chinese Theatre: From Its Origins to the Present Day*, Honolulu: University of Hawaii Press.
Ortolani, B. (1995) *The Japanese Theatre: From Shamanistic Ritual to Contemporary Pluralism*, Princeton, NJ: Princeton University Press.
Varapande, M. L. (1987) *History of Indian Theatre*, New Delhi: Abhinav Publications.
Zarrilli, P. B. (2000) *Kathakali Dance-Drama: Where Gods and Demons Come to Play*, New York: Routledge.

Latin America

Taylor, D. (1991) *Theatre of Crisis: Drama and Politics in Latin America*, Lexington, KY: University Press of Kentucky.

On Intercultural Theatre and Interweaving Performance Cultures

Barba, E. and N. Savarese (1991) *A Dictionary of Theatre Anthropology: The Secret Art of the Performer*, Abingdon/New York: Routledge.
Carlson, M. (2006) *Speaking in Tongues: Language at Play in the Theatre*, Ann Arbor: University of Michigan Press.
Fischer-Lichte, E. (2014) *Dionysus Resurrected: Performances of Euripides' The Bacchae in a Globalizing World*, Oxford: Wiley-Blackwell.
Fischer-Lichte, E., B. Gronau, and C. Weiler (eds.) (2011) *Global Ibsen: Performing Multiple Modernities*, New York: Routledge.
Fischer-Lichte, E., T. Jost, and S. Jain (eds.) (2014) *Beyond Postcolonialism*, New York: Routledge.
Fischer-Lichte, E., J. Riley, and M. Gissenwehrer (eds.) (1990) *The Dramatic Touch of Difference*, Tuebingen: Narr.
Marranca, B. and G. Dasgupta (eds.) (2001) *Interculturalism and Performance*, New York: PAJ Publications.
Pavis, P. (ed.) (1996) *The Intercultural Performance Reader*, Abingdon/New York: Routledge.
Pavis, P. and C. Shanty (eds.) (1998) "Cross–Cultural Theatre," in *Dictionary of the Theatre*, Toronto: University of Toronto Press.
Scholz-Cionca, S. and S. L. Leiter (eds.) (2001) *Japanese Theatre and the International Stage*, Leiden: Brill.
Tatinge Nascimento, C. (2009) *Crossing Cultural Borders through the Actor's Work*, New York/Abingdon: Routledge.

On Postcolonialism

Beck, U. (1999) *What is Globalization?*, Cambridge: Polity Press.
Bhabha, H. (1994) *The Location of Culture*, New York/Abingdon: Routledge.
Chow, B. and C. Banfield (1996) *An Introduction to Postcolonial Theatre*, Cambridge: Cambridge University Press.
Eisenstadt, S. N. (2003) *Comparative Civilizations and Multiple Modernities*, Leiden: Brill.
—(2006) *The Great Revolutions and Civilizations of Modernity*, Leiden: Brill.
Said, E. (1993) *Culture and Imperialism*, New York: Knopf.
Spivak, G. (1999) *A Critique of Postcolonial Reason: Toward a History of the Vanishing Present*, Cambridge, MA: Harvard University Press.

Chapter 8

Performing the arts

Theatre and the Other Arts

> In terms of ideals, theatre is elevated so high that almost nothing else that man can create through genius, intellect, talent, technique, or practice can come close. If poetry with all of its ground rules to organize and direct the power of imagination is honorable, rhetoric with its historical and dialectical demands is valuable and essential, and the same goes for oral presentation that would be impossible without according facial expressions, we can understand how theatre makes the highest demands of mankind. If one adds visual arts, which architecture, sculpture, and painting bring to the stage, if one adds the high ingredient of music, one can see what a mass of human splendors is directed to this one point.
>
> (Goethe 1815 vol. 36: 278f)

This list of "human splendors" contained in theatre is from Goethe's *Annals*, written in 1815 after his twenty-four-year tenure as head of the Weimar Theatre. Today we can add film, video, and digital arts to the list. Theatre is different from all other forms of art, in part because it is capable of using the other arts for its own aims. In this sense, Theatre Studies is an interdisciplinary field. It requires expertise in literature, music, film, and art history. At the same time, it is important to keep in mind that the other arts are only a part of a theatre performance, and its meaning and impact is constituted through the process of performance itself. In other words, the arts involved do not maintain their autonomy as individual arts.

The Relationship Between the Arts in Performance

Because theatre grows out of the combination of various other arts, it is possible to distinguish between performances according to the hierarchy they establish between the art forms they employ. From descriptions of operas performed at court festivals in the seventeenth century, we can conclude that visual art and music dominated, each of them competing to make the greatest impact on the audience. In contrast, the spoken word dominated in performances of Racine's drama in the court festivals of Louis XIV. Contemporary accounts of *commedia dell'arte* performances from the sixteenth through the eighteenth century indicate that they championed physical acting.

These few examples allow us to see how European theatre worked with and created hierarchies among the arts throughout its history. Yet these hierarchies only rarely involved the complete elimination of one of the arts. Until far into the nineteenth century, music was by no means reserved for opera and ballet alone: it was also part of spoken theatre performances. In the Weimar, Stuttgart, and New York Performing Arts Library archives one can find an extensive corpus of music for dramatic theatre that speaks to this.

The attempt to present all of the arts equally without any hierarchy leads either to a close collaboration between the various arts or to an almost completely unconnected presentation of the arts side by side. The first variation finds its expression in Wagner's concept of the *Gesamtkunstwerk*, or "total work of art"; the second in John Cage's aleatoric aesthetic. There are several variations that fall between these two extremes.

Richard Wagner's Total Work of Art

Wagner developed his concept of the *Gesamtkunstwerk* (total work of art) in reference to Greek tragedy. In both of his early theoretical writings—*The Artwork of the Future* (1849) and *Opera and Drama* (1850/1)—he described Greek tragedy as a total work of art *avant la lettre*. His conception of a *Gesamtkunstwerk* was that it

> must gather up each branch of art to use it as a mean, and in some sense to undo it for the common aim of *all*, for the unconditioned, absolute portrayal of perfected human nature,—this great United Art-work ... [appears not] as the arbitrary act of one human individual, but only ... as the instinctive and associate product of the Manhood of the Future.
>
> (Wagner 1895 vol. 1: 88; emphasis in original)

In the *Gesamtkunstwerk*, the individual arts must come together in such a way that they cease to be individually recognizable. The *Gesamtkunstwerk* seeks to extinguish the concept of individual arts altogether. For Wagner, the "unification of all arts" into a *Gesamtkunstwerk* must follow special principles and conditions. If "in a picture-gallery and amidst a row of statues a romance of Goethe's should be read aloud while a symphony of Beethoven's was being played" (Wagner 1895 vol. 2: 121), the event would not qualify as a *Gesamtkunstwerk*. Wagner also polemicizes against grand opera, the most popular form of opera in his time, as a simple compilation of arts.

Rather than compiling the arts, Wagner proclaims that the unification of the arts lies in their complete fusion, a melting-together. The idea of fusion has wide-ranging consequences for the theoretical understanding of the *Gesamtkunstwerk*. Since the various arts are no longer individually recognizable, they also cannot be seen as individual building blocks that are conjoined to create the *Gesamtkunstwerk*. Instead, the *Gesamtkunstwerk* comprises other units that are either components of the individual arts or created in the process of fusion. Wagner stipulates that the *Gesamtkunstwerk*

> both in content and in form, consists of a chain of such organic members, conditioning, supplementing and supporting one another: exactly as the organic members of the human body, – which then alone is a complete and living body, when it consists of all the members whose mutual conditioning and supplementing make up its whole; when none are lacking to it; but also, when none are too many.
>
> (Wagner 1895 vol. 1: 362)

The individual arts participate in creating these "organic members" and hence become indistinguishable from each other. Each one fulfills a specific function for the respective "organic member." Hence, "the first thing to which the Orchestra has to devote its own peculiar faculty of expression, is the Action's *dramatic gesture*" (emphasis in original). The singer is "the representative of a definite dramatic Personality, primarily expressed by Speech" and conveys "to the eye the gestures requisite for an understanding of the Action" (Wagner 1895 vol. 1: 364–65). Wagner's descriptions return to the smaller elements of the individual arts, such as melody, gesture, and verbal expression. These elements join together to create the "organic members" as complex entities. We can understand the action as one example of an "organic member" created by the orchestra together with the singer's voice and gestures. Another example would be the "dramatic personality," which the orchestra, singing, words, and gestures all have a part in creating. In this sense, the individual arts create complex elements such as action and character through their constitutive elements. During this process they lose their uniqueness as particular art forms and merge into the work as a whole.

   This fusion is also apparent in the influence that the individual arts have on one another. Combining music and gesture with words heightens their semantic dimension. They become laden with meaning. In turn, language loses some of its semantic meaning. Wagner describes how this works in the crucial scene between Alberich and Hagen in the *Ring of the Nibelungen*: "it will be like two strange animals talking to one another, you do not understand anything, and everything is interesting" (C. Wagner 1976/77: 770). The transformation of the participating arts in the *Gesamtkunstwerk* effects a change in perception: feeling dominates over rational understanding. The unification of the arts in the *Gesamtkunstwerk* aims at enabling the spectators to have an aesthetic experience that Wagner thought would instill the individual with the sense of being "whole." It unified "bodily-man" (gestures, dance), "emotional-man" (music) and "rational-man" (language), opening up a utopian potential reminiscent of Schiller's conception of aesthetic education.

John Cage's Aleatoric Aesthetic

In a Wagnerian *Gesamtkunstwerk*, the hierarchy between the arts is lifted: all the arts participate equally in the creation of "organic members" such as action or character and all are equally transformed. John Cage's aleatoric aesthetic also features a de-hierarchization of the arts, but achieves this equality by different means. Cage's de-hierarchization is based on the principle of coincidence. Cage's performances investigate if and how the conjoining of the arts transforms them. They also explore the possibilities such transformations occasion for the aesthetic experience of the audience.

John Cage's *Untitled Event* was meant as such an experiment. It was presented in 1952—almost exactly 100 years after Wagner conceived of the *Gesamtkunstwerk*—in the cafeteria of Black Mountain College. Cage collaborated with pianist David Tudor, composer Jay Watts, painter Robert Rauschenberg, dancer Merce Cunningham, and poets Charles Olsen and Mary Caroline Richards. Preparations for the event were minimal: each performer was given a score, in which only time brackets were specified. These brackets dictated the duration of actions, pauses, and silences that were supposed to be filled in by each participant. The score ensured that no causal relationship would exist between actions, or indeed any pre-arranged relationship between them, so that "anything that happened after that happened in the observer himself" (Goldberg 1988: 126). In a sense, *Untitled Event* was Wagner's worst nightmare of "a picture-gallery" where "amidst a row of statues a romance of Goethe's should be read aloud while a symphony of Beethoven's was being played." From each wall of the cafeteria, chairs for the college's summer school participants, employees of the college and their families, and locals were set up in the shape of a triangle, so that four triangles pointed toward the center of the room. The remaining central space was open and functioned more as a passage than a stage; only some of the actions took place here. Between the triangles, wide paths were left open to make two diagonal passages that crossed in the center of the room. A white cup was placed on each chair. The spectators were given no explanation as to the possible use of the cup; some used it as an ashtray. Robert Rauschenberg's "White Paintings" hung from the ceiling. Cage, in a black suit and tie, stood on a step ladder and read a text about the relationship between music and Zen Buddhism along with texts by Meister Eckhart, a thirteenth-century German mystic. Afterwards, he performed "Composition with a Radio." At the same time, Rauschenberg played old records on a manually operated gramophone while a dog sat nearby, evoking the iconic ad for "His Master's Voice." David Tudor worked on a "prepared piano"; later he began to pour water from one bucket to another. At the same time, Olsen and Richards read their own poetry, sometimes from amongst the audience, sometimes from a ladder that leaned against one of the narrow walls. Cunningham and other dancers danced along the paths that crossed through the space. They were followed by the dog, which became increasingly frantic, even crazed. On the ceiling, Rauschenberg projected abstract slides that were created by grinding colored gelatin between two glass plates. He also projected film excerpts beginning with showing the cook at the college. He projected images first against the ceiling, and later against the wall: as the projections moved from the ceiling to the wall, the film showed the setting sun. In one corner of the room, the composer Jay Watts played on a variety of instruments, some of which would have struck spectators as exotic. The performance ended with four boys dressed in white pouring coffee into the audience's cups—regardless of whether they had used them as ashtrays.

In this experiment, combining the various arts affected the mediality and semioticity of each of the arts. The works of visual art (the "White Paintings" and the slides) as well as the literature (the work of Meister Eckhart and the poetry of Olsen and Richards) were subjugated to the medial conditions of music and dance performance. They played an important role in co-constituting the materiality of the performance. The attention of the observer was drawn away from the artifacts and texts as such and directed instead at how they were being used: the accelerating speed of the slideshow; the manner in which the texts were read; and so forth. Instead of simply con-templating the paintings, the observer had to follow the colors and forms flitting over the ceiling and walls. Instead of immersing themselves in a text by reading silently, the readers listened to the ephemeral sounds of speech articulated by Cage, Olsen, and Richards. The materiality of both literature and visual art changed in their encounter. In this sense, *Untitled Event* transformed the participating arts, even though it was constituted radically differently from Wagner's *Gesamtkunstwerk*.

Cage's performance did not use the various arts to narrate a story. Instead, its dramaturgy was predicated on accidental encounters. The conditions for perceiving and understanding the performance differed fundamentally from theatre performances of the time (1952). A dramaturgical and directorial frame was missing that would have set out to guide audience perception in con-necting actions, actors and space. Thus observers had to make their own decisions about what to watch, and how to make connections that would engage their imagination, memory, and associative capabilities. The aleatoric structure determined the aesthetics of the performance: because each observer had to create his or her own performance, the aesthetic experience of each individual was unique.

Changes in Theatre Through Changes in its Constitutive Arts

Between the two extremes of Wagner's *Gesamtkunstwerk* and Cage's aleatoric aesthetic lies a range of possibilities for how theatre can bring together and hierarchically organize the arts. Changes in theatre often begin with changes in one or more of its constitutive artistic genres. In Europe, theatre showed a strong affinity for technological innovation: if at all feasible, new technologies were adapted to the stage. This affinity can be observed from antiquity to the present. Brunelleschi invented the central perspective in painting in 1435; by the sixteenth century this technique had been adopted in the theatre. The first accounts of perspectival set decorations date to 1508. They were created by the painter Pellegrino da Udine for a performance of Ludovico Ariosto's *Cassaria* in Ferrara and by Girolamo Genga for a performance in Urbino. It is possible that the first perspectival sets were actually created before 1508 by Balthasar Peruzzi (1481–1536). Donato Bramante, the teacher of Genga and Peruzzi, may also have created a perspectival set for the tragic stage around 1500. Such perspectival sets created completely new conditions and possibilities for audience perception.

Visual artists—architects and painters—also developed stage machinery that enabled extraordinary special effects, which aroused strong emotional responses in the audience. They saw collapsing houses, erupting volcanoes, floods, firestorms, and much more on the stage. With the implementation of this sort of machinery, Gian Lorenzo Bernini (1598–1680) left "the whole world awestruck" in a performance of his comedy *Fontana di Trevi* during the carnival season of 1638 in Rome. The performance took place one year after the Tiber River had flooded the streets and buildings of Rome. The backdrop for the set was unmistakably the Roman skyline. The houses onstage collapsed in front of the audience's eyes, and the victims were portrayed so convincingly that spectators felt "pleasing" horror while watching. Then the waters rose further, only held back by dams at the front of the stage. Suddenly, the dams broke, and the water seemed to rush at the spectators in the first row, who jumped up to save themselves. At the last minute, before the waves could wash over them, another dam was raised out of the stage floor, and "the water dissipated, without causing anyone harm." (Bernini 1963: appendix 96). This stage machinery opened completely new possibilities for stirring strong affects such as amazement, terror, and revulsion in the audience. Today, we would liken Bernini's ability to shock and awe to the affective powers of film. Indeed, film is one of the more recent technological inventions that also began to be used on stage—first by Meyerhold and Piscator—leading to a series of changes in the theatre. Similar changes have occurred with the introduction of video and computers in the theatre. These technological innovations continue to change our habits of perception and enable performances that previously would have been unimaginable.

Another extremely influential change for European theatre was brought about by developments in music. The so-called *Florentine Camerata*, a circle of composers and scholars who wanted to revive ancient tragedy, believed that the best compositional technique gave more weight to monody than to polyphony. This led to the development of the first opera, which was composed in *stile recitativo* (recitative). *La favola di Dafne,* a pastoral piece with a libretto by Ottavio Rinuccini and a score by Jacopo Peri and Jacopo Corsi, premiered in

Corsi's house in 1597. Today we consider this performance to be the first opera. The new theatrical form of Italian opera began to conquer Europe thanks to the works of Claudio Monteverdi (1568–1643), starting with *Orfeo* (1607) and *Arianna* (1608). Both of these operas premiered in Mantua. Monteverdi expanded on the *"stile recitativo,"* adding arias, strophic songs, and polyphonic madrigals, as well as purely instrumental music. In addition, he introduced overtures and leitmotifs to create clear dramaturgical structures.

Important impulses for changes in European theatre also came from dramatic literature. The Elizabethan theatre, Spanish theatre of the Siglo de Oro, and French classical theatre were molded by the writings of Shakespeare, Lope de Vega, Calderón, Corneille, Molière, and Racine. Nineteenth-century theatre was shaped fundamentally by the dramas of Ibsen, Hauptmann, Strindberg, Wilde, Gorky, and Chekhov. Later, Pirandello, Brecht, and Beckett set out to change theatre aesthetics once more; theatre is still being innovated by playwrights today.

Neither theatre history nor contemporary theatre can be understood without recourse to developments in the other arts, which can become part of theatrical performance. Without at least rudimentary knowledge about architecture (theatre construction, stage design), painting, music, literature, film, and new media one cannot seriously engage in Theatre and Performance Studies. At the same time, it makes a fundamental difference whether the subject of study is a painting or a stage set, a symphony or an opera performance, a dramatic text or a performance, a film or a video used within a performance. With their entrance into the theatre, the works of painters, sculptors, poets, composers, and film and video artists lose their autonomous characters and become constitutive elements of the performance, even if (as in Cage's *Untitled Event*) they appear without any connection to each other. In this sense, theatre is an "interart," and Theatre and Performance Studies an interdisciplinary field.

The Performative Turn in the Arts

The developments within the various arts since at least the 1960s have presented new challenges to aesthetics. In the first third of the twentieth century, the historical avant-garde began to perform events such as the Futurist *serate*, Dada-soirées, and surrealist tours that crossed and eventually dissolved aesthetic boundaries. The arts of the end of the twentieth century have pushed this process to its culmination. We are talking about a radical performatization of the arts, in which artists began to bring forth their "works" as "events" (and thus as performances).

In the visual arts, performativity began to dominate *action painting* and *body art*, and later informed light sculptures and video installations. Artists would present themselves in front of an audience—in the act of painting, or in the display of their bodies—or the observer was challenged to move around and interact with the exhibits while other visitors were watching. Visiting an exhibition turned into participating in a performance. Often, the primary point for the visitors was to sense the particular atmosphere of the various spaces they had entered. *BeuysBlock* at the Darmstadt Museum (constructed in 1970 and slightly modified consistently until 1986) and Robert Wilson's *Mr. Bojangle* (1991) in the Centre Pompidou in Paris are examples of this strategy.

Above all, visual artists such as Joseph Beuys, Wolf Vostell, the Fluxus-Group, and the Viennese Actionists who created a new form of Action and Performance Art in the 1960s. Since the early sixties, the Viennese Actionist Hermann Nitsch has been performing actions in which he tears a lamb apart. These happenings bring all the participants into contact with taboo objects and enable them to have a particularly sensual experience.

The Fluxus artists also began their happenings in the early 1960s. Their third event was called *Actions/Agit Prop/De-collage/Happening/Events/Antiart/ L'autrisme/Art total/Refluxus—Festival of New Art* and took place on July 20, 1964 (the twentieth anniversary of Stauffenberg's assassination attempt on Hitler) in the Auditorium Maximum of the Technical University in Aachen, Germany. The majority of Fluxus artists participated, including Joseph Beuys, Bazon Brock, Tomas Schmit, Ben Vautier, and Wolf Vorstell. In his action *Kukei, akopee—Nein! Braunkreuz, Fettecken, Modellfettecken (Kukei, akopee—No! Brown Cross, Fatty Corners, Model Fatty Corners)*, Beuys clashed with the audience. Perhaps his majestic gestures provoked the audience as he held a copper bar wrapped in felt vertically over his head; or perhaps they reacted to Beuys spilling acid (according to the public prosecutor's investigation in 1964/65). Students stormed the stage. One punched Beuys repeatedly in the face, so that his face and shirt were bloodied. Beuys, still bleeding, responded by taking out chocolate bars and throwing them into the audience. Surrounded by a tumultuous crowd and frenzied screams, Beuys held up a crucifix in his left hand and stretched his right hand in the air, as though trying to stem the tumult (Schneede 1994). The happening developed as an interaction between artist and spectators; their relationship to each other emerged as a process of contestation and negotiation. Beuys' happening presents a perfect fit for our definition of performance.

While concerts are always performances of music, John Cage's *Silent Pieces* from the 1950s emphasized their specifically performative character. In these pieces, the actions and noises that became the aural event were those created by the spectators themselves, while the musicians, such as pianist David Tudor in *4′33″* (Woodstock, New York, 1952), did not play a single note. This first "Silent Piece" comprised three movements. David Tudor walked on stage wearing a black tuxedo, and sat at the piano. He opened the piano's lid and sat immobile in front of the keyboard. Then he closed the lid. After 33 seconds he opened it again. A short time thereafter, he closed it again, and didn't open it for another two minutes and forty seconds. He closed the lid a third time, this time for a minute and twenty seconds. Then he opened it for a final time. The piece was over. The performance consisted of the noises the pianist made when entering and while opening and closing the piano, as well as the noises the audience made in reaction to his not playing (expressed as clearing their throats, coughing, fidgeting with their feet, whispering, leaving, slamming doors, etc.). Another layer of sound was added by the noises from outside of the concert hall, like the howling wind during the first movement or the patter of rain during the second movement (Kostelanetz 1989). It was a performance of sounds from a variety of sources—the performer, the audience, and nature—combined by chance. With 4′33″, the performative character of the concert was emphasized and presented as a subject for reflection.

Other composers attempted to emphasize the performative character of concerts in alternate ways. In the 1960s, some composers began to include directions in their scores instructing the musicians on how to move in front of the audience. New concepts such as "scenic music" (Karlheinz Stockhausen), "visible music" (Dieter Schnebel), and "instrumental theatre" (Mauricio Kagel) emphasized the performative character of concerts (Brüstle 2001).

In literature, the performative turn in the 1960s resulted in both performances of literary texts and changes in literature itself. Experiments with interactive fiction (such as the "Choose your own adventure" books) in print media have recently taken on a new life with the help of digital technology, leading to new literary types such as hypertext fiction, in which a reader is able to navigate the text by choosing between different possible links (and different possible storylines). The performative turn is also evident in an increase in performed readings of literary genres such as the short story and poetry. Events such as poetry or book readings have become a common way for authors to publicize their works, and at the same time, theatre ensembles have looked to non-dramatic literary texts as the basis for performance.

In 1986, the group Angelus Novus produced *Homer Lesen* (*Reading Homer*) at the Künstlerhaus in Vienna. Members of the group read the 18,000 verses of the *Iliad* without interruption for twenty-two hours. During the performance, the audience was able to wander into other rooms where they could find copies of the *Iliad*. *Homer Lesen* emphasized the difference between reading a text and listening to a text read aloud, between reading as a process of deciphering text and "a reading" as performance. The attention of the individual spectators was drawn to the specific materiality of the voices reading— their timbre, volume, tone, etc.—which became especially apparent when readers would switch. Here, literature was realized in and as performance. It was brought to life in the voice of a physically present reader and entered the imagination of the physically present listeners. The voice here was not only a medium for communicating the text. Instead, the alternations between readers meant that the particularity of each individual voice became apparent and influenced the listener. The performance also played with the element of time. The long span of twenty-two consecutive hours of waking time spent together not only changed the perception of the participants but also made them aware of these changes. Spectators said afterwards that the performance changed them (Steinweg 1986).

While *The Iliad* was originally part of an oral tradition, theatre groups have also performed literary texts that were specifically designed for print. In 2004, Elevator Repair Service, a New York-based theatre group led by director John Collins, created a performance of *The Great Gatsby*. It is certainly not uncommon for novels to be adapted for the stage, but Elevator Repair Service did not perform an adaptation: they performed every line of the novel itself. The production, called *Gatz*, lasted a full eight hours. Because they did not change the novel at all, much of the performance was dominated by narration and there were a number of features that marked the production as the performance of a novel rather than a conventional drama. In dialogue, performers would often finish with an attribution such as "… he said," thus pointing to the fact that they were narrating and not fully embodying a character. The set for the entire staging was designed to look like a run-down office from the 1990s. This created a discrepancy between the descriptions of the setting and actions the narrator read out and what actually was visible and took place on stage. These differences drew the audience's attention to the relationship between text and action onstage. The narration of the novel was not, and could not be, directly translated onto the stage. By showing the gap between text and performance, Elevator Repair Service also prompted its audience to consider the unique dynamics of the two art forms it brought together—theatre and the novel.

Gatz and *Homer Lesen* were productions that explored the relationship between literature and performance as one between different artistic media. The political dimension this relationship can entail is revealed by another example taken from the performance of spoken word poetry. Spoken word poetry has its roots in the poetry and blues of the Harlem Renaissance. Starting in the 1970s, this form of poetry—explicitly written to be performed, rather than read silently—became increasingly important in American culture. Cafés such as the Nuyorican Poets Café on New York's Lower East Side offered poets a space for performance. Emphasizing the heritage of oral tradition both in Africa and in African-American communities, spoken word poetry is closely connected to popular contemporary musical genres such as hip hop. It poses an implicit critique of the primacy of the Western written tradition over oral traditions. In addition to this formal critique, the content of spoken word poetry often explicitly discusses political issues such as racism and poverty. Starting in the 1980s, "poetry slams," competitions in which poets perform original poems, which are then judged by spectators or special judges, have become increasingly popular.

One of the most famous examples of spoken word poetry is "The Revolution Will Not Be Televised" by Gil Scott Heron. This poem, which Heron performed many times throughout his career, emphasizes the importance of liveness for African-American liberation struggles in the United States. In verse after verse, Heron criticizes and connects American politics and commercial culture:

> … The revolution will not be televised.
> The revolution will not be brought to you by Xerox
> In 4 parts without commercial interruptions.
> … The revolution will not go better with Coke.
> The revolution will not fight the germs that may cause bad breath.
> The revolution will put you in the driver's seat.
> The revolution will not be televised,
> will not be televised, will not be televised, will not be televised.
> The revolution will be no re-run brothers
> The revolution will be live.

The final line of the poem, "the revolution will be live," connects revolutionary politics to live, embodied performance.

From a happening at an art gallery to a poetic call for revolution, each of these examples falls under the category of performance. Attending one of these performances is fundamentally different from perusing the felt-wrapped copper bar in a museum, studying the score of $4'33''$, or reading *The Iliad*, *The Great Gatsby*, or "The Revolution Will Not be Televised." Whereas the individual arts lose their autonomous character in theatrical performance, we are dealing here with performances of different arts that cannot be regarded as theatre although they are, without a doubt, performances.

Nevertheless, because we are dealing with performances, Theatre and Performance Studies can help understand these performances from a different angle than Art History, Musicology, or Literary Criticism. Theatre and Performance Studies offers an essential perspective for describing and understanding what happens in these events. While Art History, Musicology, and Literary Criticism usually foreground an analysis of the "work" itself—the *Iliad*, the score of $4'33''$, or, in the case of the Happenings, remaining materials and documentation that stand in for the work—theatre historians would focus above all on the situation, conditions, and constitutive elements of the performance. Our object of study does not end with the study of artifacts, such as the preserved elements of an action and its documentation in an art museum. In our research, we uncover sources that go beyond the score or text and instead describe the fundamental interactions between artists and spectators. Our aim is to capture the specific materiality of the phenomena that emerged during the performance and describe the observable effects it had on the audience. This is not a question of a better or worse methodological approach but of a *different* one, one that is most interested in understanding the performative character of a given event. It is a way of understanding art as event.

Since at least the 1990s, a number of visual artists have become interested in producing performance pieces in which nothing exists outside of the performance and no material traces are left behind. The artist Tino Sehgal, for example, conceives of his works as "staged situations" that come into being through encounters between museum visitors and interpreters whom he trains. In 2010, he created a piece called "This Progress" for the Guggenheim Museum in New York City. Visitors to the museum began at the bottom of the curved ramp that winds up the middle of the museum. There a young child greeted small groups of spectators with the question "What is progress?" The visitors would discuss progress with the child as they walked up the ramp until they reached another interpreter. Each new interpreter would be older than the one before, and would introduce more complicated ideas into the discussion. Individual visitors had the ability to respond to, challenge, or even reject the questions and statements of the interpreters and thus to co-create the performance.

In such cases, we are interested in the visitors' individual experiences. The methods developed for performance analysis by Theatre and Performance Studies are much better suited to understand these experiences than art historical approaches, which focus on analyzing the work. Staged events such as Sehgal's "This Progress" are performances. At the same time, they must be situated in the context of the contemporary art market (of which Sehgal is a part insofar as he sells his "staged situations" to art museums and collectors). Still, Sehgal's interventions also do not simply fit under the umbrella of Performance Art. In Performance Art, the artist himself or herself is part of the performance. Sehgal, however, does not appear in the exhibition space. Instead, he hires "interpreters," who memorize specific sentences and actions and also are given space for improvisation within clear parameters. Whether these "interpreters" should be understood as performers depends on one's perspective. Either way, we are dealing with performances of art.

Performance Art has been mostly created by visual artists. These artists have tried to distance themselves from the commercial art market by creating art that cannot be sold because it fails to produce an artifact. At the same time, performance artists have turned against commercial illusionistic theatre with its focus on dramatic character and action. Although theatre of the 1960s still differed formally from Performance Art, these differences have since decreased. Story and representation were brought into Performance Art, while theatre has taken on characteristics of Performance Art by focusing on presence and the phenomenal body of the actor, and by having actors and spectators swap roles. By its very name, Performance Art defines itself as a genre of performance and is thus indisputably a research subject for Theatre and Performance Studies.

Intermediality and Hybridization

This chapter began with a discussion of the relationship between the various arts in theatrical performance. This discussion is part of a long tradition, stretching back to Aristotle's *Poetics*, which explores the relationship between the arts in the performance of tragedy. Equally, the question of how each of the arts involved transmits experience to a spectator—as discussed earlier in this chapter—has a tradition that reaches back to classical antiquity. In particular, these early thinkers focused on the relationship between poetry and painting. Simonides of Keos claimed that poetry and painting were interrelated in so far as painting was a form of "mute poetry" and poetry a kind of "speaking painting." Plutarch adopted these descriptions in his *Moralia*. At the core of these considerations lies the question of how the specific capabilities of each individual art can be distinguished and how it is possible to transfer the potential of one art to another.

The question of transmission was a fundamental problem for the theorists of the eighteenth century and debated all over Europe. Theorists and philosophers including Perault, Du Bos, Batteux, Harris, Hogarth, and Diderot took on the question and focused in particular on how the various arts transmitted meaning. Building on their work, Lessing wrote his *Laokoon* in 1766. Here, Lessing challenges the thesis of his predecessors, who followed the idea of *ut-pictura-poesis* (i.e. that poetry should proceed like painting). Instead, Lessing concentrates on the differences between poetry and painting. His famous juxtaposition of the two is as follows:

> If it is true that in its imitations painting uses completely different means or signs than does poetry, namely figures and colors in space rather than articulated sounds in time, and if these signs must indisputably bear a suitable relation to the thing signified, then signs existing in space can express only objects whose wholes or parts coexist, while signs that follow each other can express only objects whose wholes or parts are consecutive.
>
> (Lessing 1984: 78)

The first step Lessing takes in his differentiation between painting and poetry is based on the specific materiality of the arts: figures and colors in painting are contrasted to articulated sound in poetry. Poetry to Lessing does not mean the written text but rather denotes performed poetry, materialized in the articulation of a voice. From this difference in materiality Lessing moves to poetry and painting's respective relationship to space and time. Space is essential for the figures and colors of painting, whereas time is essential for the articulated sound of poetry. Painting and poetry, then, are defined as two fundamentally different media. One uses signs that present the eye with a spatial arrangement based on simultaneity; the other gives the ear a transitory sequence of sounds.

Lessing draws fundamental conclusions from this difference in the materiality and mediality of the two arts (of course, his conclusions would be very different if Lessing understood poetry as a written text). If poetry and painting are different media with distinct materialities, they necessarily differ in their subject matter (i.e. their semioticity), as well as in the modes of perception and aesthetic experiences they enable (i.e. their aestheticity). In Lessing's argumentation, semioticity and aestheticity are not only closely related to each other but actually determined by the material and medial conditions of the two arts.

Lessing speaks of a "suitable relation" that the signs must have to what they signify and concludes that the capabilities of painting and poetry are fundamentally different. That is to say that "signs existing in space can express only objects whose wholes or parts coexist, while signs that follow each other can express only objects whose wholes or parts are consecutive." He continues:

> Objects or parts of objects which exist in space are called bodies. Accordingly, bodies with their visible properties are the true subjects of painting. Objects or parts of objects which follow one another are called actions. Accordingly, actions are the true subjects of poetry.
>
> (Lessing 1984: 78)

He acknowledges that it is possible for poetry to describe bodies, and for painting to portray actions. But he insists that poetry can only describe bodies allusively through actions, and similarly that painting can only portray actions through bodies.

One might be tempted to relate Lessing's concept of a "suitable relation" to a mimesis-based aesthetic. To mimic bodies or actions, it is easiest to use the signs that share material and medial conditions with what you want to portray: signs that relate to each other in space for portraying bodies, and a temporal sequence of signs that describe actions. Yet for Lessing, mimesis is less significant than reception. Lessing uses theories of mimesis only insofar as they serve an aesthetic of reception. The concept of a suitable relationship is thus not directed primarily at mimesis but at the effect that the work in question should have on the recipient and the specific aesthetic experiences that it enables. In this context, the relationship of the medial conditions of each art to the various senses (sight and hearing) is important. Sight and hearing set different preconditions for perception. The eye aims to perceive an object as a whole:

> We first look at its parts singly, then the combination of parts, and finally the totality. Our senses perform these various operations with such astonishing rapidity that they seem to us to be but one single operation,

and this rapidity is absolutely necessary if we are to receive an impression of the whole, which is nothing more than the result of the conceptions of the parts and of their combinations.

(Lessing 1984: 85–86)

For hearing, there are very different conditions. Above all, this becomes apparent when the poet attempts to enumerate piece by piece everything the eye can glean all at once.

For the ear … the parts once heard are lost unless they remain in the memory. And even if they do remain there, what trouble and effort it costs to renew all their impressions in the same order and with the same vividness; to review them in the mind all at once with only moderate rapidity, to arrive at an approximate idea of the whole!

(Lessing 1984: 85–86)

The "suitable relation" of sign and signified is thus not primarily a problem of mimesis. Nor is it a question of the difference between natural and arbitrary signs, which Lessing correlates to painting and poetry respectively. Rather, it is related to the different medial conditions of the two arts as determined by the specific conditions of aural versus visual perception. The art of acting is privileged because, as Lessing put it in his *Hamburg Dramaturgy* (1766/67), it stands between "the visual arts and poetry." Acting is an art that takes place both in space and in time, speaking to both eye and ear.

It follows that each of the two arts—painting and poetry—involves different aesthetic experiences. Accordingly, each of the arts opens up specific possibilities for the work of the imagination: "only that which gives free rein to the imagination is effective" (Lessing 1984: 19). Painting is able to portray actions only when it manages to distill a moment that stirs the mind to imagine what happened before and after it. Similarly, poetry is capable of representing bodies when its words create a vivid idea of bodies in one's imagination. The transfer between the arts is possible when each employs its own means to stir the imagination. If we return to examples introduced previously (in "The Performative Turn in the Arts" above), we see that they allow for particular aesthetic experiences through a transfer of medial conditions.

Wagner's theory of the *Gesamtkunstwerk* and Lessing's theory of the specificity of the individual arts are somewhat opposing models applicable to different contexts. Whereas Wagner's theory about the relationship between various arts refers to theatre performance and postulates the possibility of their fusion, Lessing focuses on the means each art employs and how it can integrate techniques from other arts to enhance the aesthetic experience. Since the 1960s, discussions about intermediality have developed new theoretical approaches that integrate both possibilities. The concept of "intermediality" can refer to combinations of media, shifts between media, and intermedial references.

The theatre itself is not a medium. It is more precise to say that theatrical performance combines multiple media. A thorough discussion of the concept of a medium would be too much of an excursion in this context; instead, a relatively concise definition will have to suffice. The so-called weak concept of media refers to any means through which something else appears, such as writing, voice, movement, or—on the level of technical media—telephone, film, radio, television, and computers. In the weak concept of media, the medium disappears behind what it mediates. In contrast, the strong concept of media, as put forward by Marshall McLuhan in *Understanding Media*, insists that "the medium is the message." A middle position is articulated by Sybille Krämer, when she writes "the medium is not simply the message: rather the message retains a trace of the medium" (Krämer 1998: 81). Our discussion of intermediality focuses on McLuhan's strong concept of media as well as on the middle concept favored by Krämer. The weak concept of media, however, is antithetical to the concept of intermediality itself in that intermediality can only be perceived when the medium does not entirely disappear behind the message it conveys.

The concept of intermediality is very important in our case because it pertains to any performance, be it theatrical, cultural, or a performance of other arts. In each type of performance, various media appear in combination. Transfers occur between different types of media if, for example, a novel, a film, or a script is used as the material for a performance. Likewise the shift from a score to a concert, from a written text to a poetry reading, from a written liturgy to the enactment of a ritual also count as forms of media transfer. Recent productions that featured media transfers include Peter Stein's production of *The Demons* (based on the novel by Dostoyevsky, Lincoln Center Festival, 2010); Frank Castorf's production of *The Master and Margarita* (based on the novel by Bulgakov, at the Volksbühne am Rosa-Luxemburg-Platz, 2002); Robert Wilson and Rufus Wainwright's *Shakespeares Sonnette* (Berliner Ensemble, 2009) and Peter Brook's *Love Is My Sin* (Theatre for a New Audience, 2009), both based on Shakespeare's sonnets; Ivo van Hove's adaptation of Ingmar Bergman's film *Cries and Whispers* (Brooklyn Academy of Music, 2011); and Julie Taymor's Broadway musical based on Disney's animated film *The Lion King* (New Amsterdam Theatre, 1997). In such cases, the performance itself is not a medium, but rather an occasion for a transfer between media.

Intermedial references are particularly interesting. In order to study such references, the first step is to determine whether the reference is to the product of another medium or to its devices. Examples of references to the product of another medium are the Wooster Group's production of *Hamlet* in which a film of Richard Burton's 1964 *Hamlet* production is presented; or Michael Thalheimer's choice of the soundtrack from the film *In the Mood for Love* as the musical accompaniment for his production of *Emilia Galotti*. In these cases, the reference is to a specific product of another medium, in this case film. In contrast, Sergei

Eisenstein referenced a filmic device and with it the medium of film itself when he structured his production of Alexander Ostrovsky's *Enough Stupidity in Every Wise Man* (1922 in Meyerhold's studio, Moscow) as a montage. Such performances show that not only products but also devices, modes of perception, and the particular medial conditions of a medium can be cited, imitated, reflected, transformed, and commented on in the product of another medium. In these cases, it is vital to understand the differences between the media—as Lessing emphasized—while also acknowledging the potential for their interaction, transfer, and even fusion. Media theories reflecting on these processes are, as already emphasized, very important for analyzing both historical and contemporary performances of various genres. How do these kinds of intermedial references function, which modes of perception do they challenge, and what effects do they have? Do they create a condition of in-betweenness that strengthens a spectator's sense of liminality, or have intermedial references become so common that they barely stand out any more?

A similar situation characterizes the combination of multiple media. Whereas the use of television monitors on stage in Hansguenter Heymes' production of *Hamlet* (with Wolf Vostell in Cologne) in 1979 created a huge sensation, today the use of monitors and screens on stage has become so common that it does not surprise audiences any more than the use of central perspective in an opera performance would have surprised audiences of the late seventeenth century.

The term was originally borrowed from biology where it described plants and animals that were the outcome of a special breeding process that intermingled two different species. In this sense a hybrid unites what "naturally" does not belong together. In recent years, and especially since the 1990s, *hybridization* and *hybrids* have become commonplace terms for work integrating a variety of arts and media.

The concept of hybridity can be misleading in characterizing cultural processes because of its underlying assumption of what is and is not natural. Are the different arts to be regarded as different phenomena according to their "nature"? If so, a performance created by multiple arts should be seen as a hybrid. In contrast, does human expression by default imply the intertwining of the arts in rituals, festivals, and games? Then their differentiation from each other could be seen as an "artificial encroachment" on their "natural" bonds. If one assumes with McLuhan that media can be understood as extensions of the human body—be it writing or digital media—then the concept of hybridization does not suffice to describe how media operate.

The concept of hybridity may seem out of place in the field of culture. Nevertheless, it is often used—not just in the context of postcolonialism, where one speaks of hybrid identities, but also in the realm of arts and media. The concept of hybridization is used to designate processes that combine phenomena traditionally conceived of as dichotomous and thus mutually exclusive. The hybrid connects the organic with the mechanical (as in the performances of the artist Stelarc, who operates a third mechanical arm, or connects himself to computers) or links historically distinct forms. The term "hybridity" is used more as a metaphor than as a clearly defined concept. "Hybridization" and "hybrid" are used in theoretical discussions to mean the mixing of materials, concatenations of codes, and combinations of patterns. The concept becomes clearer when defined in juxtaposition to unity and homogeneity. "Hybrid" in this sense connotes plurality, heterogeneity, and relativity. The term is also used in contrast to hierarchy and hegemony. Hybridity in this context is understood as a formal structure that does not result in a mixture. In this sense of the term, Cage's *Untitled Event* could be called a hybrid.

It remains to be seen whether the term will be more clearly defined in the future, or if its strength lies in its current metaphorical usage that allows for a wide range of applications. If the semantics of the term extend any further, and begin to mean any connection between different elements that do not initially seem to belong together, then the term will cease to be productive (Ha 2005). Since performances always include varied materials, media, sign systems, and even different forms of art, they would fall under the term "hybridity" by definition. In this case, calling a performance a hybrid would be tautological. If, in contrast, hybridity is understood as the opposite of unity—for example, as the opposite of Wagner's *Gesamtkunstwerk*—then it makes sense to classify performances such as *Untitled Event* or Cage's *Europeras 1 & 2* (Frankfurt Opera, 1988) as hybrids. The use of the term "hybridity" is often in danger of being naturalized; in other words, of appearing so natural that it is taken for granted. To counteract this diffusion of the term, one must highlight the historicity of techniques used in various media. Two examples might help in this context.

Ariane Mnouchkine's production *Le dernier caravanserail* (*Odyssées*, 2003) and Stefan Pucher's production of Shakespeare's *The Tempest* (Munich Kammerspiele, 2007) both began with a storm on the high seas, and a ship fighting against the waves. *The Tempest* used a film by the video artist Chris Kondek. It showed the rough sea and a few people in a boat that was in danger of sinking. At the same time, the film made it clear that this was not a film of a "real" sinking ship but created in a studio: stage hands appeared throughout, soaking the "crew" with water from tin buckets. Here, contemporary technology was used self-referentially and refused to create an "illusion."

In contrast, Mnouchkine worked with "outdated" technology. She created the impression of a stormy sea through blue-green strips of fabric that moved up and down and tossed around a tiny boat manned by many people. For contemporary spectators, the impression—but not the illusion—of a violent sea was created in the same way it may have been for audiences in the seventeenth century. In fact, the old technique was used to heighten the theatricality of the scene. At the same time it was combined with the sound of a contemporary helicopter.

Both productions distinguished themselves by contextualizing their own theatrical means historically and thus reflecting on their use of media. Old and new media can be used in the theatre; one may have particular advantages depending on the specific strategies of a given performance. Theatre is rife with techniques that display the historicity of their own media.

New Digital Media

In 1995 John Reaves, a member of the Gertrude Stein Repertory Theatre, published a manifesto about his company in the online magazine *CyberStage*.

> Theater has always been an integrative, collaborative art which potentially (and sometimes actually) includes all art: music, dance, painting, sculpture, etc. Why not be aggressive in the tumultuous context of the Digital Revolution? Why not claim all interactive art in the name of theater?
>
> (Reaves 1995)

In this passage we can see how Goethe's idea about theatre is echoed centuries later in the context of new technological innovations. Theatre practitioners, critics, and art managers in the 1990s became fascinated by the possibilities of new forms of media for the performing arts. Some of the more utopian fantasies about new technology have subsided in more recent years. Yet new forms of digital media have had a significant impact on both performance practice and scholarly thinking about theatre. Innovations in digital media have raised, and continue to raise, questions about the central elements of performance: bodily co-presence, transience, spatiality, and physicality.

Starting in the 1990s, dance companies were particularly quick to embrace the possibilities of new media. One of the most important early productions that combined dance with computer software was Merce Cunningham's *BIPED*, a collaboration with the Riverbed company led by Paul Kaiser and Shelley Eshkar. Kaiser and Eshkar used motion-capture techniques and software called *Biped* to capture the movements of live dancers in a studio and render them as animations. During the performance, live dancers performed in front of a screen, onto which these animations were projected. As a result, the live dancers seemed to dance and interact with the projected images. Almost five decades after taking part in Cage's aleatoric performance *Untitled Event*, Cunningham presented a new performance that combined different artistic media. *BIPED*, which premiered in New York on July 21, 1999, has been seen as a turning point for moving digital performance from the margins toward the center of performance practices. It impressed its audience with the possibilities of combining digital media with bodily presence. In the performance, audiences were presented with both a phenomenal body and a digital rendition of that body. Although not live itself, this rendition had its own phenomenal presence onstage and encouraged the audience to think about bodily co-presence: who was present onstage, the phenomenal body of the dancer alone or also to some extent the projected body onscreen?

Other theatre and performance artists have experimented with events in which the participants only encounter one another through digital representation. In 1992, the artist Susan Kozel performed in Paul Sermon's installation *Telematic Dreaming*. During her "performances" Kozel lay in a bed. She was recorded live and projected onto another bed in a separate room. Spectators would lie down on that second bed next to Kozel's projected image, and their image in turn would be projected onto the bed on which she lay. Each bed thus contained two bodies, one real and one virtual. The unique spatiality of the event and the lack of physical co-presence distinguish this performance from other performances we have discussed up to now. Despite the lack of physical co-presence, Kozel described a pronounced physical interchange during the piece. When she began to interact with the virtual body of the spectator (who in this case took on the role of an actor as well), she described feeling "little electric shocks" in response to caresses; when another spectator/actor elbowed her in the (virtual) stomach, she doubled over "wondering why I didn't actually feel it. But I felt something" (quoted in Dixon 2007: 218).

One step further removed from the live co-presence of actors and spectators are Internet theatre projects, such as waitingforgodot.com (by Adriane Jenik and Lisa Brenneis, 1997), a "performance" of Samuel Beckett's *Waiting for Godot* in which spectators could control an avatar in an open chat room in order to wait together for Godot. The virtual world *Second Life* has groups such as the Avatar Repertory Theatre and the Second Life Shakespeare Company devoted entirely to performing within the virtual world of Second Life. The Second Life Shakespeare Company even performs in a virtual reproduction of the Early Modern Blackfriar's Theatre, thus claiming to perform in an "authentic"—if virtual—space.

These examples each feature a different constellation of spatiality, bodily co-presence, transience, and physicality. In BIPED, it is clear that audiences are co-present with live performers in a theatre space, which integrated digital technology. In the second case, visitors to the gallery enter a space that is marked as a performance space but they are never physically co-present with the performer. In the third case, there is no physical space of performance, but rather a virtual space, and none of the participants are physically present. The artists still see their performances as events that are created collaboratively and whose meaning is constituted by the interplay of all participants. The most crucial point about the example of the Second Life Shakespeare Company is not whether we embrace or reject it as a form of theatre; it is to grasp that the technology of the Internet opens aesthetic possibilities that are already redefining performance as we know it.

If one approach in new technology-based performances has been to play with the relationship between digital image and physical bodies, other performers and theatre groups have become interested in non-human (robot) performers, or cyborgs (performers that have both human and non-human components, such as the performer Stelarc or Angela Jansen who communicated with the audience at *Art and Vegetables* via a computer). It is clear that both robots and cyborgs have a particular phenomenal presence on stage; after all, in the first section we described the ways that all objects have a phenomenal presence in performance (even traditional props like a table or chair). It is less certain how exactly the interplay between spectators and actors emerges in such a case. Can one speak of an autopoietic feedback loop between robots and humans? Could a robot or cyborg performer actually be more capable of perceiving physiological changes in the audience? The expanding possibilities of technology open new possible topics of inquiry for Theatre and Performance Studies.

In addition to interrogating spatiality and co-presence (as with the Second Life Shakespeare Company) and exploring the importance of human bodiliness in performance (as with robot and cyborg performances), new technology can be used to reflect on older media. As part of its centennial celebrations, the New York Public Library commissioned a collaboration between Elevator Repair Service statistician Mark Hansen, and media artist Ben Rubin (2011). Hansen and Rubin created a series of algorithms that would blend and "shuffle" the texts of the three novels Elevator Repair Service had performed in the past (*The Great Gatsby, The Sun Also Rises*, and *The Sound and the Fury*) according to specific rules, for example compiling all of the phrases that started with the words "She said" in each of the novels. This new script was created during the performance itself—held in the periodical room of the library—and streamed onto IPods that the performers held in their hands. The performers would then perform the new texts in real time, as they were being created. This performance compelled spectators to think about the relationship between print and digital media. Strikingly, this performance can be compared to Mnouchkine's use of outmoded technology. Both highlight the historicity of their technological media. While Mnouchkine herself decided to use technology in a particular way, *Shuffle* foregrounded the agency of the new technology itself (i.e. the computer code) to change and even distort the older print technology.

Digital media have reshaped our lives fundamentally. Moreover, the art created by digital media challenges our definition of performance by reconfiguring the notion of bodily co-presence. While digital forms of theatre do not provide bodily co-presence in the strict sense, they still enable and demand the kind of interactivity between actors and spectators that is a prerequisite for our understanding of performance. The question of defining performance in the face of digital technology remains an open one. A redefinition of the term goes beyond the scope of this Introduction. It will remain a task at hand for the readers of this book, the coming generation of Theatre and Performance Studies scholars that are part of our increasingly technological future.

Further Reading

On Media

Auslander, P. (2008) *Liveness: Performance in a Mediatized Culture*, Abingdon/New York: Routledge.

Dixon, S. and B. Smith (2007) *Digital Performance: A History of New Media in Theatre, Dance, Performance Art, and Installation*, Cambridge, MA: MIT Press.

Higgins, D. (1980) *Horizons: The Poetics and Theory of Intermedia*, Carbondale/Edwardsville: Southern Illinois University Press.

Laurel, B. (1992) *Computers as Theatre*, New York: Addison Wesley.

Murray, J. H. (1997) *Hamlet on the Holodeck: The Future of Narrative in Cyberspace*, New York: The Free Press.

On Interart

Bürger, P. (1984) *Theory of the Avant-Garde*, Michael Shaw (trans.), Minneapolis: University of Minnesota Press.

Finger, A. and D. Follett (eds.) (2011) *The Aesthetics of the Total Artwork: On Border and Fragments*, Baltimore: Johns Hopkins University Press.

Goldberg, R. (1988) *Performance Art: From Futurism to the Present*, New York: H.N. Abrams.

Koss, J. (2010) *Modernism after Wagner*, Minneapolis/London: University of Minnesota Press.

Lagerroth, U., H. Lund, and E. Hedling (eds.) (1997) *Interart Poetics*, Amsterdam/Atlanta: Rodopoi.

Lessing, G. E. (1984) *Laocoön: An Essay on the Limits of Painting and Poetry*, E. A. McCormick (trans.), Baltimore: Johns Hopkins University Press.

Roberts, D. (2001) *The Total Work of Art in European Modernism*, Ithaca, NY: Cornell University Press.

Smith, M. W. (2007) *The Total Work of Art: From Bayreuth to Cyberspace*, London/New York: Routledge.

Von Hantelmann, D. (2010) *How to Do Things with Art*, K. Marta (ed.), Zurich: JRP/Ringier.

Wellberry, D. (1984) *Lessing's Laocoon: Semiotics and Aesthetics in the Age of Reason*, Cambridge: Cambridge University Press.

Chapter 9

Cultural performances

In every culture, there is a plethora of performance genres. These include festivals, rituals (such as rituals of initiation, healing, burial, and punishment), courtroom trials, political events (such as inaugurations, coronations, public gatherings, parliamentary debates, party congresses), sports championships, games, storytelling events, dances, and performances of the other arts. In the late 1950s, the anthropologist Milton Singer coined the term *cultural performance* as an umbrella term for all such performances. Singer used the term "cultural performance" to describe "particular instances of cultural organization, e.g. weddings, temple festivals, recitations, plays, dances, music concerts, etc." According to Singer, a culture formulates its self-understanding and self-image through cultural performances that it presents both to those within the culture and those outside it:

> For the outsider, these can conveniently be taken as the most concrete observable unity of the cultural structure, for each performance has a definitely limited time span, a beginning and an end, an organized programme of activities, a set of performers, an audience and a place and occasion of performance.
>
> (Singer 1959: xxii)

Until far into the 1950s there was a broad consensus among Western scholars that culture was created through artifacts and manifest in them—especially texts and monuments. Accordingly, artifacts became the sole object of study. Singer drew attention to the fact that culture is also created through and manifest in performances. A performance of institutional theatre, for example, can be understood as a specific genre of cultural performance. Theatre contains some of the traits Singer ascribes to other genres of cultural performance such as rituals, political ceremonies, games, lectures, poetry readings, concerts, and sports competitions. Insofar as all of them are types of performance, they all depend on the bodily co-presence of actors and spectators and they deplete themselves in their execution (i.e. they leave no product behind). We might ask how different genres of cultural performances can be distinguished from one another, and if and how it is possible to differentiate between artistic and non-artistic performances. Finding an adequate answer to this question has been and continues to be challenging.

The philosopher Richard Shusterman has consistently refused to offer an essentialist definition of art that would differentiate artistic works and events from non-artistic ones. Instead, he offered a heuristic definition that sought "to emphasize certain features of art that may not be receiving enough attention." (Shusterman 2001: 364). He proposes to understand and categorize art as "dramatization" and draws on two meanings of the term. First, dramatization means "to 'put something on stage,' to take some event or story and put it in the frame of a theatrical performance" (Shusterman 2001: 367). The second meaning, taken from *Chambers Dictionary*, is "to treat something as, or make it seem, more exciting or important" (Shusterman 2001: 368). However, these features are not exclusive to art; they are shared by all performances, regardless of whether they belong to the realm of art or not. Soccer games, parliamentary sessions, legal trials, religious services, weddings, funerals, etc., are all "dramatized" in this sense. They frame specific scenes and enable a greater vitality of experience and action. It is, as Singer recognized, precisely the "dramatization" that distances cultural performances from everyday life. It is extremely difficult to find distinctions that actually serve as criteria to differentiate artistic from non-artistic performances.

Even though it is nearly impossible to find such criteria, it is strangely easy to say that Beuys' Fluxus-Happening, Cage's *4′33″*, and the Wooster Group's *Hamlet* are artistic performances, whereas the Olympics, the Love Parade, and party congresses are not. Of course, many artists push the boundary into non-artistic actions in their performances, while many producers of non-artistic performances increasingly seek to aestheticize and theatricalize their events. Yet we have no trouble drawing boundaries insofar as performances take place within specific institutions. A performance is seen as artistic if it happens within the space of an art institution; it is seen as non-artistic if it takes place within the frame of political, athletic, legal, religious, etc. institutions. What is decisive for the differentiation between artistic and non-artistic performances, then, is neither their specific "event-ness" nor their particular staging strategies. The institutional frame decides whether or not a given performance is understood as art. Such frames, however, only exist in societies with differentiated institutions.

When characterizing the particular "event-ness" of performances, we differentiated between the possibility of liminality in aesthetic and non-aesthetic experience. Aesthetic experience makes the state of liminality its goal, while non-aesthetic liminal experience can be understood as a means to an end—be it to obtain a new social status or identity, to create or affirm communities, or to legitimate claims to power. There is no clear correlation between aesthetic experience and artistic performance, or non-aesthetic experience and non-artistic performance—both kinds of experiences mix in any given performance. In artistic performances, liminality can be experienced both as an end in itself and as a means to another end. The overpowering and artistically elaborate performances of Jesuit theatre did not aim at enabling solely an aesthetic experience. Instead, the Jesuits sought to use aesthetic experience to confirm the audience's adherence to the Catholic Church as the only legitimate church, and to draw back members of the congregation who were in danger of going astray.

Erwin Piscator's aesthetically complex theatre of the 1920s as well as the *Living Newspaper* productions by the Federal Theatre Project in the 1930s—much like the performances of the Jesuits before—sought to impact the spectators and influence them politically. Piscator hoped his spectators would join the Communist Party, while the *Living Newspaper* productions sought to galvanize progressive politics in the United States and promote the goals of organized labor and Franklin D. Roosevelt's New Deal.

These three examples—all performances at the highest artistic level (if we can believe eyewitness accounts)—show that even attention to different forms of liminal experience does not suffice to differentiate between artistic and non-artistic performances.

In the first part of this book on performance theory, we emphasized that artistic performances are always a social, even political, process. And vice versa: non-artistic performances, in which social, political, or religious effects are foregrounded still follow certain principles of staging and design, i.e. aesthetic techniques. Accordingly, we must pay attention to the varied emphases and goals of such performances. In this final chapter, we explore theatre forms that either—like Brecht's *Lehrstücke* (or, "learning plays")—aim to permanently change the actors or are direct interventions in the everyday lives of audience members. Augusto Boal's "Theatre of the Oppressed" and the "Theatre for Development," which evolved from it and claims a particularly active role in African health campaigns, fall under this theatrical category. Additionally, we will discuss examples of specific kinds of cultural performance such as festivals and rituals to address what Theatre and Performance Studies can contribute alongside Anthropology, Theology, and Sociology.

New Transformative Aesthetics or Applied Theatre?

Theatre has always taken aesthetic experience—regardless of how it is defined—as a means to a specific end. It is always about the transformation of the spectator. In his *Poetics*, Aristotle describes the effect of tragic theatre as the arousal of *eleos* and *phobos*, of pity and fear, and the purging of these passions. He uses the term *catharsis* to designate purification as the goal of tragic theatre. Catharsis has its roots in ritual; it comes from healing rituals. Like a healing ritual, tragic theatre should lead to purification, albeit not necessarily an enduring or permanent one. Since tragedies were performed every spring at the Great Dionysian festival, one can assume that at least an annual repetition of catharsis was deemed necessary.

The concept of catharsis had a huge influence on discussions about the impact of theatre performances on audiences up to the end of the eighteenth century. Lessing attributed a transformative power to theatre performances: "making us sensitive enough that the unfortunate from all eras, and in all likenesses move us to take up their cause." Participating in a performance of tragedy permanently changes and improves a person:

> *the most empathetic person is the best person.* Of all social virtues, of all sorts of generosity, it is the best. He who makes us empathetic, makes us better and more virtuous, and tragedy, which does the former, also does the latter—it does the former in order to do the latter.
>
> (Lessing 1973:163; emphasis in original)

Lessing attributes a lasting effect to performances of tragedy. They lead to a permanent change in the spectators—at least regular theatre-goers. The repetition of the experience is a prerequisite for its lasting effect.

In Germany, there is a rich tradition of aesthetic theories that focus specifically on how theatre and the other arts impact their recipients. The German word for this field of philosophy is *Wirkungsaesthetik*. In English literary criticism, we can think of "reader response" criticism—literary criticism that is primarily interested in a reader's response to a work rather than the work itself—as connected to the idea of *Wirkungsaesthetik*. There is no standard translation for this term, when it comes to other arts, and so we will refer to this field of aesthetics here as "transformative aesthetics."

Despite postulating art as autonomous from social concerns (and thus declaring war on the transformative aesthetics of the Enlightenment), Goethe and Schiller followed the idea that performances can have a lasting effect, and used this idea to develop a concept of theatre that would develop human potential. Among other writings, Schiller's *Letters on the Aesthetic Education of Man* (1795) emphasizes this transformative power of performance. Schiller wrote the letters to sketch out a future ideal state following his disappointments with the French Revolution and its aftermath. He suggests that the average individual experiences a constant struggle between their sensuous and rational natures. These two conflicting parts in the individual, however, can be reconciled through aesthetic beauty. This reconciliation only takes place in the realm of art. In his account, a lasting change requires the individual's continuous exposure to art.

The return of transformative aesthetics around the turn of the nineteenth to twentieth centuries, and especially among the historical avant-garde, brought a new wave of interest in and proclamations about how man could be changed in and by the theatre. Georg Fuchs and Meyerhold, Brecht and Artaud, all proclaimed the creation of a "new man," created by the theatre. Of course, their ideas about these "new men" diverged significantly. In some cases they were diametrically opposed to each other.

In this context, "applied theatre" made its first appearance. The British pageant movement (1905–17) and its equivalent in the United States (starting in 1908) can be seen as a predecessor of what we would term "community theatre" today. Pageants were created communally by local inhabitants and focused on the local history of the town or place in which the performance was held. In Britain, pageants served as a bulwark against modernization and industrialization. In contrast, the pageants in the United States were designed to help integrate new immigrant groups into established communities. The communist agitprop groups that traveled through the Soviet Union and Weimar Republic in the 1920s understood themselves—like Boal's group did fifty years later—as a "Theatre of the Oppressed" that sought to give agency to the powerless.

Brecht's learning plays also belonged to this latter group. These plays were not intended to be performed in front of an audience, although they could be, as was the case with the performance of *The Measures Taken* during the festival "New Music Berlin 1930." Instead, the learning plays focused on the actors themselves. "Through the completion of certain ways of acting, the adoption of certain stances, the recitation of various speeches, etc.," the actors engaged in a learning process: "the learning play teaches by being acted, not by being watched" (Brecht 1967b: 1024f). Brecht somewhat marginalizes the performance situation here, in contrast to troupes such as the Living Newspaper Units who were interested precisely in their effect on the audience.

Brecht's learning plays share an emphasis on enactments with Jacob Lecy Moreno's psychodrama, although they differ radically in other ways. Starting in Vienna in 1910, Moreno used improvised enactments and discussions with marginalized groups such as homeless children, prostitutes, and refugees to develop specific techniques of psychodrama and therapeutic role-play. He used these techniques in the United States after his immigration in the mid-1920s. Psychodrama—despite the name—did not require a dramatic text, and it eliminated the distance between actors and spectators. Instead it aimed to create a permanent change in participants. As with Brecht's learning plays, the therapeutic situation is more similar to a rehearsal than to a public performance. In contrast to a performance, in which the actors constantly have to deal with unpredictable "intrusions" by the spectators, psychodrama creates a protected space within which the unpredictable may emerge in and between the patients, thus aiding the healing process.

These examples should suffice to show that many of the theatrical forms since the late 1960s and 1970s that have attempted to permanently alter the lives of the audience and/or actors have predecessors in the transformative initiatives of the first half of the twentieth century, if not in even older forms of transformative aesthetics. Such forms undoubtedly include Protestant school theatre, which since the sixteenth century had the task of helping students improve their Latin and Greek and training them in public speaking. In the eighteenth century, the transmission and internalization of new familial values and virtues became a primary aim of educational theatre. Theatre and Performance Studies has thoroughly explored the theory and praxis of Brecht's learning plays and Boal's "Invisible Theatre," in which spectators in subways, cafés, or markets were unaware that the scenes they were witnessing had been staged. Insofar as reports exist about them, theatre scholars have even studied Jerzy Grotowski's "Special Projects," which went beyond performances in specific environments and sought to practice new modes of living with their participants. Theatre for Development, prison theatre, community theatre, the various forms of therapeutic theatre, theatre in war zones—all of these forms of theatre rest on the conviction that theatre can have long-lasting effects on its participants (whether actors or audience members). Whereas professional theatre performance prioritizes the aesthetic experience of liminality in and of itself, the theatre forms above see that experience as a means to an end. The final goal is conceived of as a change of consciousness and behavior that extends beyond the performance itself. This goal cannot be reached simply by conveying a specific content; it requires new kinds of transformative aesthetics. The aesthetic dimension should not be overlooked in the various forms of theatre from our list above. It is never just "content in and of itself" that creates an effect, but rather its specific aesthetic presentation. This applies just as much to theatrical forms that seek to affect the audience as to those that focus on changing its actors.

In 2002, the British choreographer Royston Maldoom created a particularly impressive project in cooperation with the conductor of the Berlin Philharmonic, Sir Simon Rattle. The project gained unusual fame through the documentary *Rhythm Is It!* (directed by Thomas Grube and Enrique Sánchez Lansch, 2004), screened around the world. In three months, Maldoom and Rattle created a performance of Stravinsky's *The Rite of Spring* with 250 students aged eleven to seventeen, hailing from Berlin schools and dance studios. One third of the youths came from immigrant families. All in all, the ensemble included youths from twenty-five different nations. The performance took place in January of the following year in the Treptow Arena, a venue with over two thousand seats. Rattle conducted the Berlin Philharmonic in the performance.

The performance was certainly a set goal that all participants were working towards. But the actual aim lay in exposing the young participants to the challenges of the demanding rehearsal process, designed to affect their attitude and behavior more permanently. The film describes the fear of the school teachers that the choreographer Maldoom might be too demanding of their students, thus leaving them frustrated. Yet the choreographer would not compromise. He required from the students what seemed artistically necessary to him. The film follows a select group of students, who actually do change over the course of the rehearsal process, thus confirming Maldoom's claim: "You can change your life in a dance class." It lay beyond the scope of the film to show whether such transformations were common or exceptional and whether they lasted beyond the rehearsal period and were decisive for the lives of the participants.

The difficulty of evaluating the transformative potential in a project such as *Rhythm Is It!* highlights some of the difficulties with research in the area of therapeutic theatre. In the analysis of performance art or institutional theatre, a researcher can use the reactions of individual spectators during the performance to draw conclusions about the affective potential of the performance. While the reactions of spectators during the performance support the idea of the transformative power of performance, and of performance as an autopoietic feedback loop, these reactions do not give the researcher insight into the more permanent effects of the performance. Performance analysis cannot draw any conclusions about permanent changes in consciousness and behavior. In order to draw such conclusions, it is necessary to cooperate with social scientists. Social science has methodological tools that allow one to draw empirically sound conclusions about such changes—whether by way of interviews prior to and after the performance (whether a month or a year later), or ethnographic field research before and after the performance.

Even if these methods allow us to draw reliable conclusions about the lasting effect of any given performances, they do not enable us to make prognoses. In other words, evidence that a specific performance under specific conditions created durable changes in an individual's behavior does not ensure that such success is repeatable. Performances of applied theatre remain unique and unrepeatable. No careful staging strategies can completely ensure a particular response in either actors or spectators. Insofar as we are dealing with changing and/or stabilizing individuals and communities, and not with the programming of robots, the ultimate outcome remains incalculable. Methodological certainty can only apply to past, not future, performance. Nevertheless, social science methods can be helpful when preparing a performance. For example, they can be used to explore which kind of theatre might be most successful in affecting specific target groups or situations: body-centered versus speech-centered theatre; theatre that speaks to the eyes more than the ears; theatre of laughter or shock, and so forth. But here, too, projections are made on the basis of experiential data; reliable prognoses remain impossible.

In the past decade, some Theatre and Performance Studies scholars have become interested in neuroscience and in the possibility that not only the social sciences, but indeed the natural sciences, might be able to help us understand how spectators perceive and are transformed by theatre performances. This interest has led to collaborations between theatre scholars and cognitive scientists to develop new approaches for studying the neurological processes behind spectatorship, acting, and the construction of meaning.

While this research has the potential to illuminate certain aspects of cognition (for example, exploring the cognitive effects of watching mimetic acting), it cannot account for all of the processes at play in any given performance or fully predict how an individual will experience and make meaning of a performance. Each performance is a unique event.

The careful reader may have noticed that the title of this section, "New Transformative Aesthetics or Applied Theatre" is followed by a question mark, which remains to be discussed. The difference in terminology implies a difference in focus. If we discuss prison theatre, community theatre, therapeutic theatre, and so forth, as modes of "new transformative aesthetics," it draws attention to a specific tradition and continuity; as discussed, aesthetics that focus on transformation have a history in Europe that stretches back to the tragic theatre of the Greeks and its theorization by Aristotle. One can also find comparable traditions in other cultures. The *Natyasastra*, the Indian "Handbook for Theatre" which was written between the second centuries BCE and CE, explains how *rasas* could be triggered in both the dancers/actors and the spectators. The term *rasa* has been translated into the English terms "sentiment," "aesthetic rapture," or "emotional consciousness." The tenet of *rasas* is still meaningful in contemporary performing arts in India.

Even though the historical avant-garde polemicized against Aristotle, they still agreed with his premise that performances contain a transformative potential and tried to use that potential in different ways, and to different ends. The transformative potential of performance is a common premise for all performance that has been discussed. In addition, the term "transformative" emphasizes the specific *aesthetic* material and devices that determine the impact of the performance. Whoever uses the term "new transformative aesthetics" understands this form of theatre as part of a long-standing tradition, which sees the aesthetic as inherently transformative. In contrast, the term "applied theatre" focuses on the aspect of application. Theatre turns into a productive instrument, with which one seeks to accomplish something outside of the theatre itself, possibly also achievable by other means. In other words, the term "applied theatre" ignores the powers of theatre's aesthetic form. The premise of the concept "applied theatre" implies that theatre's tools may easily be applied to different contexts. Ultimately, such a premise is misleading because it is simplistic. We should consider whether to abolish the use of the term entirely.

Cultural Performances

The previous sections discussed performances that explicitly link themselves to theatre by their name, such as therapeutic theatre, school theatre, or prison theatre. For many other genres of cultural performance, no such explicit link exists. In the first chapter we defined Theatre and Performance Studies very generally as the study of performances. Hence cultural performances such as festivals, rituals, games, sports competitions, political gatherings, and court proceedings can also be our objects of study. Yet performative events such as these are already the subject of other disciplines: festivals are studied in anthropology and sociology; rituals in theology, anthropology, and sociology; games in philosophy, psychology, sociology, and economics ... the list continues. Which unique contributions can Theatre and Performance Studies bring to the realm of cultural performance?

Staging and Performance

Despite all disciplinary differences that exist in the study of various genres of cultural performance, there is one striking similarity. Virtually all of the other disciplines fail to distinguish between the performance event and the concept of staging. When studying historical performances, scholars of other disciplines tend to use sources that provide information about how the organizers conceived of the production. They read any additional sources about the actual proceedings during the performance through the lens of these quasi-authorial intentions. This approach is questionable because it fails to acknowledge the co-dependence of actors and spectators and because it excessively simplifies the process of creating and transmitting meaning in performance.

Relationships Among Participants

Although many sociologists today focus on productions instead of performances, some of the earliest sociological works were centrally concerned with the transformative potential of performance and the relationships among the various groups of participants. Emile Durkheim, one of the founders of the discipline of sociology, developed the theory of collective effervescence in the early twentieth century in order to make sense of the function of performance and the experience of participants. Durkheim argues that societies are built around rituals that involve the bodily co-presence of groups of people. These rituals could range from a harvest ceremony of a Native American tribe to national Flag Day ceremonies. These public gatherings spark a certain kind of energy among the participants—Durkheim calls it collective effervescence. By participating in communal rituals, individual members of society come to feel that they are part of a group. Indeed, Durkheim argues that it is through these performances that society constitutes itself. Events such as Flag Day may commonly be seen as a way for the national government to use the symbol of the American flag to transmit values to passive citizens. To Durkheim the collective effervescence produced in public gatherings such as Flag Day invests the flag with its symbolic power. Durkheim's theory of collective effervescence is a useful starting point for exploring how communities are constituted in performance.

Despite Durkheim's discussion of collective effervescence, subsequent sociological studies of rallies and demonstrations have focused on their staging (i.e. the intentions of the organizers, the materials such as banners and symbols used) rather than their performance (i.e. the particular and unique constellation of bodily co-presence, spatiality, and interplay between actors and spectators). In particular during the Cold War, social scientists saw cultural performances primarily as sites of manipulation, especially when discussing public gatherings in totalitarian societies. These studies assumed the passivity of the audience and the ultimate control of the organizers over the progress of the performance—in other words, staging strategies would overpower a "passive" and thus "innocent" audience in completely predictable ways to cause a desired effect. As discussed earlier, this position is untenable because it ignores the unpredictable interactions between spectators and actors, which are part of the autopoietic feedback loop that constitutes performance.

More recent scholarship has revised the idea of passive participants in political rallies and demonstrations, and instead focuses on how participants co-create such events. This change in focus is in part connected to the rise of popular social movements—from Civil Rights struggles in the United States and anti-colonial struggles around the world, to anti-nuclear proliferation campaigns and the Occupy movement—in which everyone participating in a march or rally sees themselves as actor rather than a spectator. According to the sociologist Charles Tilly, social movements depend on a "variable ensemble of performances" (such as public marches, demonstrations, and rallies), which he calls the "social movement repertoire" (Tilly 2004: 3). While a social movement might have a central leader or organizer, the performances are co-created by the movement's participants, who contribute to the shape of the performance and to the meaning it generates. While this literature takes account of the ways that individual participants shape an event, it is primarily interested in looking at participants in terms of the semiotic meanings they create or fail to create. The signs participants carry, the slogans they shout, and the symbolic use of their bodies are at the center of these studies. Sociologists are not as interested, however, in what we have termed the phenomenal bodies of the participants or the particular somatic experience of a performance as an ephemeral and unique event.

In effect, the primary focus on the semiotic bodies of participants reaffirms the fundamental interest sociologists have in "staging" rather than performance proper. It points to a fundamental difference in defining performance in the social sciences. Social scientists usually think of performance in terms of individual identity. Scholars such as Erving Goffman see performance as a way of creating identity: for example, a person is "female" because that person acts out a number of gestures that we recognize as feminine. This conception of performance is similar to ours in that it focuses on embodiment and the constitution of meaning. But it differs from ours in failing to emphasize the eventness of performance, and a performance's unique spatiality, transience, and bodily co-presence.

Creating Meaning in and through Performance

To answer questions about the meaning produced in and by specific cultural performances, historians often look first at sources that supply information about the intentions of the organizers. Such sources might include an allegorical program for a fireworks display during a court festival in the seventeenth century, or the symbols employed and speeches held during a political rally. From the interpretation of these sources, researchers deduce certain meanings and assume their transmission to the public in performance.

The approach ignores that the performance is not exclusively constituted out of written signs (i.e. those that appear in sources such as programs or transcripts). However, everything that happens in the space for the duration of the event is part of the sign system of the performance. We also cannot speak of the transmission of meaning as direct and unmediated. Participants create meaning for themselves based on their own experiences and interpretations. In addition, each individual's perception might shift in different patterns between phenomenal appearance and its interpretation within a sign system. Spectators should not be understood as passive recipients of a message. They create meaning themselves. As long as participants differ from each other in their interpretive framework, their universes of discourse, and their experiences, they will each deduce a different meaning from the event.

For this reason it is reductive to link the effects of a given performance exclusively to the intentions of the organizers and the symbolic, allegorical, and programmatic systems they employed. Instead, the effects could equally have emerged from a different set of dynamics, produced by unforeseen twists of the autopoietic feedback loop itself.

All cultural performance involves staging. Performances that gather many people in the same place at the same time to take part in a "programme of activities" (Milton Singer) require preparation, sometimes even diligent and elaborate practice. Whether the performance is a folk festival, a football game, a mass, a legal trial, a political convention, or a shareholder's meeting, extensive planning and preparation is necessary. Whilst these preparations aim to achieve the goals of the organizers, none of them can completely control the behavior of all participants in the performance. The actual outcome of any given performance cannot be known in advance. Theatre and Performance Studies' fundamental distinction between staging and performance is thus relevant for the study of cultural performances in all disciplines.

Crossovers Between Different Genres

In the study of cultural performances, we need to do more than just consider the fundamental difference between staging and performance. Above all, we must consider the various crossovers between performances of different genres present in all cultures, albeit in different forms. These crossovers highlight that there are no stable criteria to differentiate between artistic and non-artistic performances. Instead, one differentiates between them by referring to the institution in which the performance takes place, and these institutions differ significantly from culture to culture. Such crossovers include both the combination of different genres and specific structural similarities across genres.

Combinations of Genres

Festivals are a type of cultural performance that has other genres of performance embedded within it. The Great Dionysian festival in ancient Athens included processions, acts of national self-presentation, the awarding of armor to youths whose fathers fell in war, performances of dithyrambs, comedies, and tragedies, as well as a final public gathering. Urban festivals in the Middle Ages usually began with a mass followed by a procession and the performance of an Easter, Passion, or Christmas play that would culminate in the communal performance of a hymn. Courtly festivals of the sixteenth through eighteenth centuries comprised extremely wide-ranging programs of ceremonies, rituals, theatre performances, role playing, musical performances, fireworks, ball games, dances, and so forth. These festivals lasted for days, sometimes even weeks. Though no longer in such grand dimensions, these kinds of combined performance still occur on national holidays—starting with the festivals of the French Revolution such as the *Fête de l'Unité* in 1793—workers' festivals, and sports festivals since the nineteenth century. The Olympic Games, "revived" by Baron Pierre de Coubertin in Athens in 1896, combined sports competitions with various forms of ritual and ceremony. Since the 1932 Olympics in Los Angeles, they have also been supplemented with the performance of so-called pageants, festivals, and dance, opera and theatre performances. A comparable combination of genres of cultural performances in a festival setting can also be found in non-Western cultures.

Festivals lend themselves to a curious, apparently paradoxical structure that characterizes their temporality and also the behavior of their participants. The temporal structure of festivals is determined by the juxtaposition of liminality and periodicity. On the one hand, festivals are embedded in a daily routine that repeats regularly; on the other hand, they enable a temporal transgression because they create their own exceptional time frame that breaks with the everyday. Another paradox concerns people's actions during a festival. While their actions are subject to a precise set of rules, the essence of a festival ultimately lies in breaking with otherwise habitual rules. The festival seeks to prevent the intrusion of the mundane.

We can deduce four dimensions that are characteristic for festivals. The first is a *liminal* dimension: the unique temporality that constitutes a festival is an in-between time, a time of transition, embedded in mundane and historical time. It requires the participants to break out of their daily lives. After the end of the festival they will return to their daily lives changed, with either a strengthened or a renewed sense of identity. The liminal dimension is the precondition of the *transformative* dimension. During the festival, new identities can be tried out or adopted, or an existing identity can be strengthened (for example, one's membership in a specific community such as a church, a court, or a sports team). The extent to which these changed or strengthened identities extend beyond the festival itself—unlike classic rites of passage, but similar to theatre performances—cannot be pre-determined or verified. We can, however, presume a strengthening of the feeling of *communitas* and sense of belonging among participants.

From the opposition between breaking and keeping rules, we can deduce a *conventional* dimension. It is the regularity that prescribes specific interaction rituals, as the sociologist Erving Goffman calls them (Goffman 1967). Transgressions expressed as forms of excess, such as violent acting out, or watching portrayals of violence, invoke the fourth, *cathartic* dimension.

These four dimensions detected in many studies of festivals (Haug and Warning 1989) also apply to performance, as I have argued earlier in this book (even if in certain performances, some of these dimensions take a very weak or incomplete form). The other genres of cultural performance at play in the festival tend to emphasize one or another of these four dimensions, or—if all four frames are equally present—the paradoxical structure of the festival as such. When it comes to performances that researchers themselves take a part in, the methods of performance analysis can be used to investigate how the liminal, transformative, conventional, and cathartic dimensions interact with a given genre of performance.

The close relation between festival and theatre in European history is striking. Festivals are almost inconceivable without theatre performances. Until the early modern period, theatre performance could only take place within the wider frame of a festival. Even after professional acting troupes emerged in Italy, England, and other European countries in the sixteenth century and began to present their performances at fairs, there remained a close connection between theatre and festivals because theatrical performances were usually limited to specified festival seasons. Like other forms of cultural performance, theatrical performances strengthen one or more of the four dimensions mentioned above; if all of the dimensions are equally present in a performance, theatre performance enhances the specific paradoxical structure of the festival. Theatre performances were—and still partly are—a fixed component of festivals, whether courtly or civic, sports-, school-, or office-based.

Structural Similarities of Genres

Since the mid-nineteenth century, one can observe a tendency to create a new sort of celebration out of theatre itself, reversing the previous relationship between theatre and festival. Theatre itself was to become a festival, as Richard Wagner never tired of proclaiming. According to Wagner, theatre had lost its affective potential during the nineteenth century. He conceived of a theatre festival that he believed would revive the power of the theatre. The building that housed the festival would be a liminal space *par excellence*. Initially, Wagner conceived of this liminal space as democratic and devised for spectators from all social classes. In his speech at the festival house's brick-laying ceremony in Bayreuth on May 22, 1872, Wagner described the liminal state that the festival house was designed to create in its audiences as an "ideal illusion, which wraps us as it were in twilight, in dreams of truth beyond our ken" (Wagner, vol. 5: 284). Such a state can only be reached if each spectator becomes a "co-creator of the artwork," i.e. an active participant in the performance. By the time of construction Wagner had re-conceived of the house as a temple of art, a shift that was completed with the performance of *Parsifal* in 1882.

Around the turn of the nineteenth to twentieth centuries, Georg Fuchs and Max Reinhardt went even further. Not only did they develop and realize festival programs; they also proclaimed that every individual theatre performance should be a celebration in itself: "the theatre will become a festive play once more, as it was designed to be," as Max Reinhardt formulated it in 1902 (Kahane 1928: 119).

We can see a continuation of these developments—albeit in a changed form—today in the designation of a series of theatre performances as a "festival". Fuchs and Reinhardt did not think of themselves as connecting two different genres of cultural performance. Instead, they focused on the structural similarities between festival and theatre, implicit in the four dimensions common to them both. At the turn of the nineteenth to the twentieth century the attempt to trace the structural similarities between ritual and theatre came from scholars of antiquity and the theatrical avant-garde alike. Scholars of ritual from Classics departments, and in particular the group known as the Cambridge Ritualists, read these structural similarities in terms of historical development. They argued for theatre's emergence out of ritual. The avant-gardists took this development for granted when they proclaimed (like Georg Fuchs and twenty years later Antonin Artaud) that theatre must become ritual "once more" to reclaim its presumably lost liminal, cathartic, and transformative dimensions.

Jane Ellen Harrison (1850–1928), the head of the Cambridge Ritualists, tried to prove in her book *Themis: A Study of the Social Origins of Greek Religion* (1912) that Greek theatre developed from a specific ritual, which she called the *eniautos daimon* (year-god) ritual. In *The Golden Bough* (1890), anthropologist James George Frazer used a plethora of ethnological material to claim that such a ritual was practically universal. Harrison traced the origin of Greek theatre back to one such "Dionysian" ritual. Since Aristotle had posited in his *Poetics* that theatre developed from the dithyramb, she tried to show that the dithyramb developed from a Dionysian ritual. Harrison analyzed the *Hymn of the Kouretes*, which had been discovered not long before in a temple of Zeus in Palaikastro on Crete, using comparative methods that took account of other Greek texts and archeological finds, as well as ethnological material from African, Australian, and American cultures. She reached the conclusion that

> the Dithyramb ... is a Birth-Song ... giving rise to the divine figures of Mother, Full-grown Son and Child; it is a spring-song of magical fertility for the new year; it is a group song ... later sung by a *thiasos*, a song of those who leap and dance rhythmically together.
> (Harrison 1912: 203)

Harrison believed she had traced the chorus of tragic theatre back to a year-god ritual. Her fellow traveler and colleague Gilbert Murray (1866–1957), who created a new translation of Sophocles' *Oedipus Rex* for Max Reinhardt's 1912 London production, contributed a chapter to Harrison's study: "Excursus on the Ritual Forms Preserved in Tragedy." In this chapter, Murray tried to bolster Harrison's thesis by providing evidence of important structural elements of the annual-deity ritual in Greek tragedy, focusing especially on the last (!) of the classical Greek tragedies, Euripides' *The Bacchae*. These elements include *agon* (competition), *pathos* (a sacrificial ritual and a message that announces the death of the victim), *threnos* (lament), *anagnorisis* (recognition), and *theophaniea* (the appearance of a god). Murray also emphasized the difference between the usual year-god and Dionysus, who never dies despite being torn to pieces:

> An outer shape dominated by tough and undying tradition, an inner life fiery with sincerity and spiritual freedom; the vessels of a very ancient religion overfilled and broken by the new wine of reasoning and rebellious humanity, and still, in their rejection, shedding abroad the old aroma, as of eternal and mysterious things: these are the fundamental paradoxes presented to us by Greek Tragedy.
> (Harrison 1912: 362)

While the Cambridge Ritualists traced the structural similarities between ritual and theatre to show theatre's birth out of ritual, anthropologists studying ritual since the 1960s have ceased to make historical arguments. The theses on the origins of theatre clearly belong to the nineteenth century and its obsession with origins and evolution. We can differentiate between two schools of thought. Most anthropological research in the 1960s and 1970s was more interested in differences than similarities between theatre and ritual. They compared ritual in mostly oral-based cultures with the psychological-realistic proscenium theatre and teased out the fundamental differences between them.

In contrast, theatre artists such as Jerzy Grotowski and Richard Schechner were developing a new form of so-called "ritual theatre." In June 1968,

Richard Schechner's version of *The Bacchae, Dionysus in '69* premiered in New York's Performance Garage. This performance combined Euripides' tragedy with the adoption rituals of the Asmat in New Guinea as well as auto-biographical material provided by the performers. During the performance, the usual division between actors and spectators was eliminated, and the participation of the audience was not just allowed, but requested. Here, theatre was to become ritual "once more."

Schechner later worked with the anthropologist Victor Turner (referred to in Chapter 2), who began writing about the relationship between ritual and theatre in the 1960s. Turner shared an interest in the similarities between theatre and ritual, a school of thought that became dominant only in the 1990s. In contrast to the majority of his colleagues in anthropology, he saw structural similarities between "social drama" and stage drama, and between dramatic ritual and ritualistic drama. Nevertheless he tried to differentiate between rituals as experienced in African tribal societies and those he termed the leisure genres in complex industrial societies, such as theatre, dance, song, or performances of "mass-, pop-, folk-, high-, counter-, underground-culture, etc." (Turner 1982). He reserved the concept of liminality for rituals in tribal societies that mandated participation and emphasized the collective, as in a rite of passage ceremony that every young man in the community must complete. For the "leisure genres" of modern society, in which participation is voluntary and the individual is at the center (such as a rock concert), he employs the term "liminoid." The conceptual pair "liminal" and "liminoid" are not to be understood as opposites but rather point to structural similarities that should not be mistaken for structural equivalence.

In an expansion and critique of Turner, the anthropologists Ursula Rao and Peter Köpping emphasize the affinity between ritual and theatre:

> Starting on the formal level, ritual and theatre share a large number of components that point to more than just analogical similarities between these two domains of the performative. Most attempts to list specific formal criteria as characteristics of performative frames, are contradicted by both ethnographic observations and actors' accounts of their experiences. Both genres have staging, script (if one can call myths a script), improvisation, rehearsal, memorization. In both, participants and spectators can change their roles, and both can either be aimed at entertainment, or at showing new forms of reality.
>
> (Köpping and Rao 2000: 11)

As our discussion shows, it is impossible to draw any clear, systematically justified borders between ritual and theatre. They are both performances that can (but do not necessarily) lead to a transformation of the participants. This is not to say that ritual and theatre are identical. Yet one can differentiate between them only in the context of distinct historical periods in a given culture, in which ritual and theatre are given markedly different functions and accordingly are part of two different institutions. A differentiation between the two on a universal, systematic level is impossible.

Just as ritual and theatre go hand in hand here, ritualist and/or theatrical elements can be found in all genres of cultural performances, whether in games, sports competitions, legal trials, or political events. These elements are bound up in the performative character of the event. Hence the concept of performance developed at the outset of this book is applicable to *all* genres of cultural performance. Each may be analyzed using the methods of theatre historiography or performance analysis.

Nevertheless, there are a range of questions related to cultural performances that Theatre and Performance Studies is unable to answer alone. As our discussion of festival and ritual suggests, we have to draw on research in which Theatre and Performance Studies was only marginally involved. Depending on the research question, a theatre scholar will have to decide if and to what extent he or she must fall back on research from other disciplines, or cooperate with other scholars from these disciplines. The first of these two alternatives is commonly adopted—it is hard to imagine a question in Theatre and Performance Studies that does not need to draw on at least preliminary research from other disciplines. The second approach should be used in addition when the research subject lies in the realm of contemporary cultural performance, where there are fewer sources about a given performance readily available. The scope of a performance analysis will be limited if it lacks input from other relevant disciplines. Reciprocally, other disciplines require cooperation with theatre scholars to adequately consider the performative character of the event. The study of cultural performance is thus a paradigmatic research field for interdisciplinary research.

Further Reading

Transformative Aesthetics

Aristotle (1982) *Poetics*, James Hutton (trans.), New York: W.W. Norton & Company.

Bharata (2003) *The Natyasastra*, K. Vatsyayan (trans.), Mumbai: Sahitya Academi.

Fischer-Lichte, E. (2008) *The Transformative Power of Performance*, S. I. Jain (trans.), London/New York: Routledge.

Schiller, F. (1795/2004) *On the Aesthetic Education of Man*, R. Snell (trans.), New York: Dover.

Cultural Performance

Diamond, E. (1996) *Performance and Cultural Politics*, London/New York: Routledge.

Fischer-Lichte, E. (2005) *Theatre, Sacrifice, Ritual: Exploring Forms of Political Theatre*, London/New York: Routledge.

Glassberg, D. (1990) *American Historical Pageantry: The Uses of Tradition in the Early Twentieth Century*, Chapel Hill: University of North Carolina Press.

Tilly, C. (2004) *Social Movements, 1768–2004*, Boulder, CO/London: Paradigm Publishers.

Withington, R. (1918) *English Pageantry: A Historical Outline*, Cambridge, MA: Harvard University Press.

Applied Theatre

Nicholson, H. (2005) *Applied Drama: The Gift of Theatre*, Basingstoke/New York: Palgrave Macmillan.

Prendergast, M. and J. Saxton (2009) *Applied Theatre, International Case Studies and Challenges for Practice*, Bristol: Intellect Publishers.

Prentki, T. and S. Preston (2008) *The Applied Theatre Reader*, London/New York: Routledge.

Thompson, J. (2003) *Applied Theatre: Bewilderment and Beyond*, Bern: Peter Lang.

Epilogue: Not everything is theatre

We have seen that all kinds of cultural performance can become a possible research subject for Theatre and Performance Studies, even though the research often requires interdisciplinary methods, or even active cooperation with other disciplines. So how about phenomena and processes that do not fall under the umbrella of cultural performance? Are performances by default cultural performances, or are there other kinds of performance that can serve as research subjects for Theatre and Performance Studies?

We discussed Boal's "invisible theatre," whose performances belong to a special genre of cultural performance (namely, theatre), even though one group of participants, the spectators, were not aware that they were watching a theatre performance. But what about scenes that are performed in everyday life, such as Brecht's street scene, in which neither the actors nor the spectators are participating in a cultural performance, but are still participating in a performance?

Brecht modeled his "epic theatre" on the following street scene:

> An eyewitness demonstrating to a collection of people how a traffic accident took place. The bystanders may not have observed what happened, or they may simply not agree with him, may "see things a different way"; the point is that the demonstrator acts the behavior of driver or victim or both in such a way that the bystanders are able to form an opinion about the accident.
>
> (Brecht 1964: 121)

This street scene takes place in public. It develops from the interaction between an actor—the eyewitness, who is demonstrating what he witnessed—and a crowd of spectators surrounding him. People who disagree with the witness, and saw the accident take place "differently" will express their disagreement, the others will listen, nod in agreement, take sides, and so forth. We are certainly dealing with a performance here. So would this scene—which was used as the model for a specific form of theatre—in itself be a research subject for Theatre and Performance Studies?

Brecht himself seems to have thought so. In a journal entry from December 6, 1940, he wrote:

> After the studies in the *Street Scene* other kinds of everyday theater ought to be described and other examples of theater in real life identified, in the erotic sphere, in business, in politics, in the law, in religion, etc. ... I have already done some work on the application of theatrical techniques to politics in fascism, but in addition to this the kind of everyday theater that individuals indulge in when no one is watching should be studied, secret "role-playing." This is how one must approach the elementary need for expression in our aesthetic.
>
> (Brecht 1993: 115)

This discussion is particularly insightful. When Brecht references the "theatre" that takes place in politics, in courtrooms, or in the church, he is especially interested in specific genres of cultural performances such as political conventions, festivals, and memorials—which were particularly important under fascism—as well as legal trials and all kinds of religious rituals. Brecht's concept of theatre therefore also includes scenes of daily life, in which communication and interaction take place between the participants, even when there are no other witnesses present.

There is a long tradition of research in sociology that aims to find out how we "perform" in such situations, how people communicate and interact in daily life. Erving Goffman, for example, sought to isolate and describe various "natural" interactions in his book *Interaction Ritual* (1967). Albert Scheflen researched how the mobility of individuals and groups within a social hierarchy can be determined by their behavior in such situations.

These kinds of communication and interaction rituals in everyday life are performances in so far as they are created through an autopoietic feedback loop. The participants "perform" for each other. In other words, they act in a specific way in order to be perceived and understood by other people and to achieve a certain goal. Sociologists such as Goffman and Scheflen explored how the body is used to transmit certain "signals" and create particular effects in order to investigate the performance-character of these interactions. Given their research interests, both Goffman and Schelfen were only concerned with the semiotic body apparent in interaction: they did not take account of the body in its pure phenomenality.

Theatre and Performance Studies scholars can certainly contribute to the study of such everyday interactions with our methods of performance analysis. Whether such interactions are ultimately important subjects that should be pursued depends on a researcher's interests. If the focus is on therapeutic or pedagogical theatre projects, it might be important to explore models of communication and interaction in everyday life. "Everyday theatre" should be studied in connection to research on new styles and aesthetics of acting that explicitly reference behavior and communication in everyday social life. One example of this is the demand for a "natural" style of acting in the eighteenth century: in this case the existing forms of middle-class behavior and the newly developed styles of acting influenced each other. Furthermore, knowledge of everyday behavior is important for every analysis of contemporary theatre. Regardless of whether there are parallels or sharp divergences between everyday behavior and the behavior that takes place in the theatre, an analysis of the performance requires knowledge of the many forms of enactment outside the theatre. The forms of enactment in theatre are always related to the various forms of enactment in a culture at large.

Brecht brings another useful concept into play: the concept of "theatricality." This raises the question of how it is possible to differentiate between an everyday situation and a theatrical one—a performance. What transforms a mundane communicative situation into a theatrical one?

In Boal's theatre the spectators did not know that actors were performing the scene they perceived. Imagine an experiment in which this situation is reversed. A couple is sitting together in a café. They converse, express their affection for each other, and then begin to fight. At the next table, a lonely patron is drinking an espresso and observing the couple. We might assume that this is also a case of "invisible theatre" since the actors are not aware that they are "acting" before the eyes of another person. Is a scene theatrical simply because it is observed? Then we could say that any act of voyeurism or surveillance is a theatrical situation. The problem with claiming that these forms of surveillance or unobserved observation are theatre is that neither the voyeur nor the unobserved observer is capable of theatricalizing the performance, i.e. of starting the autopoietic feedback loop. The situation can only turn theatrical once the people notice they are being observed and continue to communicate with the full awareness of their voyeur. Interplay between the actors and spectators is a necessary precondition for theatre to take place.

These sorts of incidents require, as Brecht already suggested, careful investigation, and this is a task for theatre and performance scholars. We must figure out under which conditions a situation can or cannot be deemed theatrical.

In his discussion of the street scene, Brecht references "role-playing." This is a fundamentally important phenomenon not only for all of the performing arts, but also for social life in general. Since antiquity, the human capacity to play roles has been continually referenced and designated with the metaphors of *theatrum mundi* or *theatrum vitae humanae*. According to Helmuth Plessner, the capacity to play a role is central to the human condition; it is an anthropological given. He argues that people create an image of themselves when they appear before others. They see themselves reflected in the eyes of others. In other words, they see themselves as they appear to others. This means that people are always positioning themselves in relation to others, and that people have the capacity to step outside of themselves and watch themselves acting and behaving from a quasi-external position.

Plessner's definition of the human condition is also the fundamental situation of theatre and performance. An actor appears to spectators as a sort of magical mirror that reflects their own image back to them, allowing them to see themselves as others. Through action and speech, actors simultaneously constitute themselves and are also perceived and understood by the spectators in relation to themselves. Through role play, theatrical situations always pose questions about human identity.

It makes sense, then, that Plessner understands and characterizes the actor as the epitome of the human condition, and that in the social sciences the concept of the "role" has become a key concept for discussing identity creation. In the 1930s, George H. Mead brought the concept of the role to the center of his research on identity. Mead describes identity as the product of communication and negotiation that attribute possible roles to individuals (Mead 1934). Erving Goffman developed this idea more systematically. According to Goffman, every individual is confronted with the necessity of portraying himself or herself: people have to control the impressions they give, model a self, and make this self perceptible to others by projecting it with their bodies (Goffman 1959). People can always be understood as actors—theatre actors just make the situation of playing a role explicit. The philosopher Judith Butler goes even further in her book *Gender Trouble* (1990). Here she argues that gender—like all forms of identity—is not based on pre-existing (e.g. ontological or biological) categories but brought forth by the continuous constitution of bodily acts.

If the human condition itself can be seen as theatrical, should we understand human life generally as theatre, as the metaphor *theatrum vitae humanae* suggests? Accordingly, shouldn't all human activity and creation be seen and studied from a theatrical perspective? In this case, we would have to expand Theatre and Performance Studies to encompass a much more general study of culture, communications, and interaction. Theatre and Performance Studies in this expanded sense could approach almost any topic, but at the same time it would forfeit its core field of research. Even if Theatre and Performance Studies departments expanded greatly in terms of resources and faculty, it would still be impossible for Theatre and Performance Studies alone to answer questions about culture at large. In order to answer such broad questions, we need the methods and theories of multiple disciplines; without serious interdisciplinary cooperation there is no possibility of serious and groundbreaking research.

Instead of claiming that Theatre and Performance Studies should cover *everything*, it is more useful to delineate the field: Theatre and Performance Studies is a discipline that studies performances (in contrast to texts). It develops theories of performance, performativity, and theatricality, theories of aesthetic experiences or of transformative aesthetics (to name a few examples), and engages myriad methodological approaches of performance analysis. By delineating the current purview of the field, we can show the expertise that Theatre and Performance Studies has to offer to other disciplines and sketch what Theatre and Performance Studies stands to gain in the future from interdisciplinary collaboration.

Bibliography

Agnew, V. (2007) "History's Affective Turn: Historical Reenactment and Its Work in the Present," *Rethinking History*, 11.3: 299–312.

Amine, K. and M. Carlson, (2012) *The Theatres of Morocco, Algeria, and Tunisia: Performance Traditions of the Maghreb*, New York: Palgrave Macmillan.

Appia, A. (1986) *Oeuvres Complète*, vol. 2, Marie-Louise Bablet-Hahn (ed.), Montreux: L'âge d'homme.

Aristotle (1982) *Poetics*, James Hutton (trans.), New York: W.W. Norton & Company.

Artaud, A. (1958) *The Theatre and Its Double*, Mary Caroline Richards (trans.), New York: Grove Press.

Arvatov, B. (1926) *Kunst und Produktion*, Munich: Hanser.

Auslander, P. (2008) *Liveness: Performance in a Mediatized Culture*, Abingdon/New York: Routledge.

Austin, J. L. (1963) *How to Do Things with Words*, Oxford: Clarendon Press.

Baker, G. P. (1970/1919) *Dramatic Technique*, New York: Da Capo.

Balme, C. (1995) *Theater im postkolonialen Zeitalter*, Tübingen: Niemeyer.

———. (2007) *Pacific Performances: Theatricality and Cross-Cultural Encounters in the South Seas*, Basingstoke/New York: Palgrave.

———. (2008) *The Cambridge Introduction to Theatre Studies*, Cambridge: Cambridge University Press.

Banham, M. (ed.) (2004) *The History of Theatre in Africa*, Cambridge: Cambridge University Press.

Barba, E. and N. Savarese (1991) *A Dictionary of Theatre Anthropology: The Secret Art of the Performer*, Abingdon/New York: Routledge.

Barnes, C. (1970) "Theatre: 2 Plays by Ward: They Show Racial Gap Opened in 5 Years," *The New York Times*, 18 March: 39.

Beck, U. (1999) *What is Globalization?*, Cambridge: Polity Press.

Benedetti, J. (2001) *David Garrick and the Birth of Modern Theatre*, London: Methuen.

Bergmann, A. (2004) *Der entseelte Patient. Die moderne Medizin und der Tod*, Berlin: Aufbau.

Bernini, G. L. (1963) *Fontana di Trevi. Commedia inedita*, Usare d'Onofrio (ed.), Rome: Staderini.

Bhabha, H. (1994) *The Location of Culture*, London/New York: Routledge.

———. (1996) "Culture's In-Between," in Stuart Hall and Paul du Gay (eds.), *Questions of Cultural Identity*, London: Seyl.

Bharata (2003) *The Natyasastra*, K. Vatsyayan (trans.), Mumbai: Sahitya Academi.

Bial, H. (ed.) (2004) *The Performance Studies Reader*, London/New York: Routledge.

Bial, H. and S. Magelssen (eds.) (2010) *Theatre Historiography: Critical Interventions*, Ann Arbor: University of Michigan Press.

Blatner, A. (2000) *Foundations of Psychodrama: History, Theory and Practice*, 4th ed., Berlin: Springer.

Blei, F. (1902) "Otojirô Kawakami," in: *Die Insel* 3.7/8, Leipzig: Inselverlag: 63–68.

Böhme, G. (1995) *Atmosphäre: Essays zur neuen Aesthetik*, Frankfurt am Main: Suhrkamp.

Boon, R. and J. Palstow (eds.) (2004) *Theatre and Empowerment: Community Drama on the World Stage*, Cambridge: Cambridge University Press.

Brandon, J. (1998) "Kabuki Performance: Its Value and Use in Western Theatre," in *Kabuki, International Symposium on the Conservation and Restoration of Cultural Property*, Tokyo: Tokyo National Research Institute of Cultural Properties: 1–20.

Brecht, B. (1964) *Brecht on Theatre: The Development of an Aesthetic*, J. Willet (ed. and trans.), New York: Hill and Wang.

——. (1967a) *Gesammelte Werke in 20 Bänden*, Frankfurt: Suhrkamp.

——. (1967b) *Gesammelte Werke in 8 Bänden*, Frankfurt: Suhrkamp.

——. (1993) *Brecht Journals*, J. Willet (ed.), London: Methuen.

Brockett, O. and F. Hildy (1982) *History of Theatre*, 10th revised edition, 2007, Boston: Allyn and Bacon.

Bruford, W. H. (1950) *Theatre, Drama, and Audience in Goethe's Germany*, London: Routledge.

Brüstle, C. (2001) "Performance/Performativität in der neuen Musik," in E. Fischer-Lichte and C. Wulf (eds.), *Theorien des Performativen*, Berlin: Akademie Verlag.

Brüstle, C., N. Ghattas, C. Risi, and S. Schouten (eds.) (2005) *Aus dem Takt: Rhythmus in Kunst, Kultur, und Natur*, Bielefeld: transcript.

Bürger, P. (1984) *Theory of the Avant-Garde*, M. Shaw (trans.), Minneapolis: University of Minnesota Press.

Burkert, W. (1987) "Die antike Stadt als Festgemeinschaft," in P. Hugger (ed.) in cooperation with W. Burkert and E. Lichtenhahn, *Stadt und Fest: Zur Geschichte und Gegenwart europäischer Stadtkultur*, Stuttgart: Metzler: 29–57.

——. (1991) *Greek Religion: Archaic and Classical*, J. Raffan (trans.), Oxford: Blackwell.

Butler, J. (1990) *Gender Trouble: Feminism and the Subversion of Identity*, New York: Routledge.

Carlson, M. (1989) *Places of Performance: The Semiotics of Theatre Architecture*, Ithaca, NY/London: Cornell University Press.

——. (1993) *Theories of the Theatre: A Historical and Critical Survey from the Greeks to the Present*, Ithaca, NY: Cornell University Press.

——. (1996) *Performance: A Critical Introduction*, London/New York: Routledge.

——. (2001) *The Haunted Stage: The Theatre as Memory Machine*, Ann Arbor: University of Michigan Press.

——. (2006) *Speaking in Tongues: Language at Play in the Theatre*, Ann Arbor: University of Michigan Press.

——. (2008) "Introduction," in *The Transformative Power of Performance* by E. Fischer-Lichte, London/New York: Routledge.

Chow, B. and C. Banfield (1996) *An Introduction to Postcolonial Theatre*, Cambridge: Cambridge University Press.

Clough, P. and J. Halley (eds.) (2007) *The Affective Turn: Theorizing the Social*, Durham, NC: Duke University Press.

Cooke, W. (1804) *Memoirs of Charles Macklin*, London: J. Asperne.

Craig, E. G. (1908) "The Actor and the Über-Marionette," *Mask* 2: 3–15.

——. (1911) *On the Art of the Theatre*, London: William Heinemann.

Craik, T. W. (ed.) (1975–80) *The Revels History of Drama in English*, 8 vols., London: Methuen.

Csórdas, T. (ed.) (1994) *Embodiment and Experience: The Existential Ground of Culture and Self*, Cambridge: Cambridge University Press.

Davies, T. (1780/1808) *Memoirs of the Life of David Garrick*, vol. 1, S. Jones (ed.), London.

Davis, T. C. and T. Postlewait (ed.) (2003) *Theatricality*, Cambridge: Cambridge University Press.

De Marinis, M. (1993) *The Semiotics of Performance*, Bloomington: University of Indiana Press.

Devrient, E. (1848) *Geschichte der deutschen Schauspielkunst*, 5 vols., reprinted 1929, Berlin/ Zürich: Eigenbrödler.

Diamond, C. (1999) "The Floating World of Nouveau Chinoiserie: Asian Orientalistic Productions of Greek Tragedy," in *New Theatre Quarterly* 15.58: 142–64.

Diamond, E. (1996) *Performance and Cultural Politics*, London/ New York: Routledge.

Diderot, D. (1883) *The Paradox of Acting*, W. H. Pollock (trans.), London: Chatto & Windus.

——. (1968) *Ästhetischen Schriften*, F. Bassenge (ed.), Frankfurt am Main: Europäische Verlagsanstalt.

Dixon, S. and B. Smith (2007) *Digital Performance: A History of New Media in Theatre, Dance, Performance Art, and Installation*, Cambridge, MA: MIT Press.

Dixon, T. (2003) *From Passions to Emotions: The Creation of a Secular Psychological Category*, Cambridge: Cambridge University Press.

Durkheim, E. (1912/2008) *The Elementary Forms of Religious Life*, C. Cosman (trans.), Oxford/New York: Oxford University Press.

Eggington, W. (2003) *How the World Became a Stage: Presence, Theatricality and the Question of Modernity*, Albany: State University of New York Press.

Eisenstein, S. M. (1988) *Selected Works*, Vol. 1, Richard Taylor (ed.), London: BFI Publishing.

Eisenstadt, S. N. (2003) *Comparative Civilizations and Multiple Modernities*, Leiden: Brill.

——. (2006) *The Great Revolutions and Civilizations of Modernity*, Leiden: Brill.

Elam, K. (1980) *The Semiotics of Theatre and Drama*, London: Methuen.

Elias, N. (2000) *The Civilizing Process*, Oxford: Blackwell.

Engel, J. J. (1785/86) "Ideen zu einer Mimik in Schriften," vol. 7/8, Berlin: Mylius, 1804. Reprinted 1971 Frankfurt am Main: Athenaeum.

——. (1815/1822) *Practical Illustrations of Rhetorical Gesture and Action*, H. Siddons (ed.), London: Sherwood, Neely, and Jones.

Engle, R.G. (1968) "Franz Lang and the Jesuit Stage" (University of Illinois), Ann Arbor, MI: University Microfilms.

Erven, E. van (2001) *Community Theatre—Global Perspectives*, London/New York: Routledge.

Fambach, O. (ed.) (1958) *Ein Jahrhundert deutscher Literaturkritik (1750–1850)*, Berlin: Akademie.

Féral, J. (ed.) (2002) *Theatricality*, Madison: University of Wisconsin Press.

Fiebach, J. (1986) *Die Toten als die Macht der Lebenden. Zur Theorie und Geschichte von Theater in Afrika*, Berlin: Henschel.

Finger, A. and D. Follett (eds.) (2011) *The Aesthetics of the Total Artwork: On Border and Fragments*, Baltimore: Johns Hopkins University Press.

Fischer, A. (1900/1901) "Japan's Stage Art and Its Development," in *Westermanns Illustrierte deutsche Monatshelfe*, 45: 449–514.

Fischer-Lichte, E. (1989) "Theatre and the Civilizing Process," in T. Postlewait and B. A. McConachie (eds.), *Interpreting the Theatrical Past*, Iowa City: Iowa University Press.

——. (1992) *The Semiotics of Theatre*, Bloomington: University of Indiana Press.

——. (1995) "Theatricality: A Key Concept in Theatre and Cultural Studies," *Theatre Research International*, 20/2: 85–118.

——. (1997) *The Show and the Gaze of Theatre*, Iowa City: University of Iowa Press.

——. (1999) "From Text to Performance: The Rise of Theatre Studies as an Academic Discipline in Germany," in *Theatre Research International*, 24.2: 168–78.

——. (2002) *History of European Drama and Theatre*, J. Riley (trans.) London/New York: Routledge.

——. (2004) "Some Critical Remarks on Theatre Historiography" in S. E. Wilmer (ed.) *Writing and Rewriting Theatre Histories*, Iowa City: Iowa University Press.

——. (2005) *Theatre, Sacrifice, Ritual: Exploring Forms of Political Theatre*, London/New York: Routledge.

——. (2008) *The Transformative Power of Performance*, S. I. Jain (trans.), London/New York: Routledge.

Fischer-Lichte, E., B. Gronau, and C. Weiler (eds.) (2011) *Global Ibsen: Performing Multiple Modernities*, New York: Routledge.

——. (2014) *Dionysus Resurrected: Performances of Euripides' The Bacchae in a Globalizing World*, Oxford: Wiley-Blackwell.

Fischer-Lichte, E., B. Gronau, and C. Weiler (eds.) (2011) *Global Ibsen: Performing Multiple Modernities*, New York: Routledge.

Fischer-Lichte, E., T. Jost, and S. Jain (eds.) (2014) *Beyond Postcolonialism: The Politics of Interweaving Performance Cultures*, New York: Routledge.

Fischer-Lichte, E., J. Riley, and M. Gissenwehrer (eds.) (1990) *The Dramatic Touch of Difference*, Tuebingen: Narr.

Fischer-Lichte, E., C. Risi, and J. Roselt (eds.) (1998) *Kunst der Aufführung—Aufführung der Kunst*, Berlin: Fannei & Walz.

Fischer-Lichte, E. and B. Wihstutz (2012) *Performance and the Politics of Space: Theatre and Topology*, New York/London: Routledge.

Fischer-Lichte, E. and C. Wolf (eds.) (2001) *Theorien des Performativen* (= *Paragrana* 10.1), Berlin: Akademie Verlag.

Flemming, W. (1949) *Goethes Gestaltung des klassischen Theaters*, Cologne: H. Schaffstein.

Förstl, H., B. Rattay-Förstl, and M. Winston (1992) "Karl Philipp Moritz and the *Journal of Empirical Psychology*: an introductory note and a series of psychiatric case reports," *History of Psychiatry* 3: 95–98.

Foucault, M. (1970) *The Order of Things: An Archaeology of the Human Sciences*, New York: Random House.

——. (1977) *Discipline and Punish: The Birth of the Prison*, trans. A. Sheridan, London: Penguin.

Fried, M. (1980) *Absorption and Theatricality: Painting and the Beholder in the Age of Diderot*, Berkeley: University of California Press.

Fuchs, G. (1905) *Die Schaubühne der Zukunft*, Berlin: Schuster and Loeffler.

Garner, S. B. (1994) *Bodied Spaces: Phenomenology and Performance in Contemporary Drama*, NY: Cornell University Press.

Gastev, A. (1966) *Kak nado rabotat (How One Must Work)*, Moscow: Izd. Ekonomika.

Geertz, C. (1990) "History and Anthropology" in *New Literary History* 21.2: 321–35.

Genast, E. (1862/1866) *Aus dem Leben eines alten Schauspielers*, Leipzig: Voigt & Günter.

van Gennep, A. (1960) *Rites of Passage*, M.B. Virdou and G. L. Coffee (trans.), Chicago: University of Chicago Press.

Glassberg, D. (1990) *American Historical Pageantry: The Uses of Tradition in the Early Twentieth Century*, Chapel Hill: University of North Carolina Press.

Goethe, J. W. (1871) *Wilhelm Meister's Apprenticeship*, T. Carlyle (trans.), London: Chapman and Hall.

——. (1901/1802) *Goethes Werke*, S. von Sachsen (ed.), vols 13, 36, and 40, Weimar: Böhlau.

——. (1986) *Essays on Art and Literature*, J. Gearey (ed.), E. von Nardroff and E. H. von Nardroff (trans.), New York: Suhrkamp.

Goffman, E. (1959) *The Presentation of the Self in Everyday Life*, New York: Doubleday.

——. (1967) *Interaction Ritual: Essays on Face to Face Behavior*, Chicago: Aldine.

——. (1974) *Frame Analysis: An Essay on the Order of Experience*, Cambridge, MA: Harvard University Press.

Goldberg, R. (1988) *Performance Art: From Futurism to the Present*, New York: H. N. Abrams.

Grainger, R. (1990) *Drama and Healing: The Roots of Dramatherapy*, London: Jessica Kingsley.

Gray, C. H. (1931) *Theatrical Criticism in London to 1795*, New York: Columbia University Press.

Grotowski, J. (1968) *Towards a Poor Theatre*, New York: Simon and Schuster.

Günther, H. and K. Hielscher (eds.) (1972) *B. Arvatov, Kunst und Produktion*, Munich: Hanser.

Ha, K. N. (2005) *Hype um Hybriditaet: Kultureller Differenzkonsum und postmoderne Verwertungstechnik im Spätkapitalismus*, Bielefeld: transcript.

Haller, A. von (1756–60) *Mémoire sur la nature sensible et irritable des parties du corps animal*, 4 vols., Lausanne: M. M. Bousquet.

——. (1774) *Kleine Physiologie, Bibliotheca anatomica*, 2 vols., Zurich.

Hantelmann, D. von (2010) *How to Do Things with Art*, K. Marta (ed.), Zurich: JRP/ Ringier.

Harrison, J. E. (1912) *Themis: A Study of the Social Origin of Greek Religion*, reprinted 1962, Cleveland/New York: Macmillan.

Haug, W. and R. Warning (eds.) (1989) *Das Fest*, Munich: Fink.

Huang, A. (2009) *Chinese Shakespeares: Two Centuries of Cultural Exchange*, New York: Columbia University Press.

Herder, J. G. (1861–62) *Von und an Herder. Ungedruckte Briefe aus Herders Nachlass*, 3 vols., H. Düntzer and F. G. Herder (eds.), Leipzig: Dyk.

Herrmann, M. (1914) *Forschungen zur deutschen Theatergeschichte des Mittelalters und der Renaissance*, Berlin: Weidmann.

——. (1918) "Bühne und Drama," in *Vossische Zeitung*, 30 July.

——. (1931) "Das theatralische Raumerlebnis," in *Bericht vom 4. Kongress für Ästhetik und Allgemeine Kunstwissenschaft*, Berlin: 162–63.

——. (1981) "Über die Aufgaben eines theaterwissenschaftlichen Instituts" (lecture from 27 June 1920) in H. Klier (ed.), *Theaterwissenschaft im deutschsprachigen Raum*, Darmstadt: Wissenschaftliche Buchgesellschaft: 15–24.

Herzog, R. and R. Koselleck (eds.) (1987) *Epochenschwelle und Epochenbewusstsein, Poetik und Hermeneutik*, vol. 12, Munich: Fink.

Higgins, D. (1980) *Horizons: The Poetics and Theory of Intermedia*, Carbondale/Edwardsville: Southern Illinois University Press.

Hill, A. (1734–36) *The Prompter; A Theatrical Paper*, eds. W. W. Appleton and K. A. Barnim (1966), New York: B. Blom.

Hinck, W. (1982) *Goethe—Mann des Theatres*, Göttingen: Vandenhoek.

Hollander, J. (2007) *Indian Folk Theatre*, New York/London: Routledge.

Horn, C. (2004) *Der aufgeführte Staat. Zur Theatralität höfischer Repräsentation unter Kurfürst Johann Georg II von Sachsen*, Tübingen/Basel: Francke.

Hornbrook, D. (1998) *Education and Dramatic Art*, 2nd edition, London: Routledge.

Inoura, Y. (1981) *The Traditional Theatre in Japan*, New York/Tokyo: Weatherhill.

Jackson, A. (1993) *Learning through Theatre: New Perspectives on Theatre in Education*, London/New York: Routledge.

——. (2007) *Theatre, Education, and the Making of Meanings: Art or Instrument?*, Manchester: Manchester University Press.

Jackson, S. (2004) *Professing Performance: Theatre in the Academy from Philology to Performativity*, Cambridge: Cambridge University Press.

Jacobson, S. (1910) *Max Reinhardt*, Berlin: Erich Reiss.

——. (1912) *Das Jahr der Bühne*, vol. 1, Berlin: Verlag der Weltbühne.

Jennings, S. (1990) *Dramatherapy with Families, Groups and Individuals*, London: Jessica Kingsley.

——. (ed.) (1997) *Dramatherapy—Theory and Practice*, London: Routledge.

Kahane, A. (1928) *Tagebuch der Dramaturgen*, Berlin: Cassirer.

"Die Kawakami-Truppe (Sada Yakko) in Berlin" (1902) in *Ost-Asien*, 4.46: 450.

Karasek, H. and J. Urs (1987) "Franz Kafka Meets Rudolf Hess: *Spiegel* Interview with Robert Wilson on *Listen, Look, Act*," *Der Spiegel* 10: 205–14.

Kernodle, G. R. (1989) *The Theatre in History*, Fayettevill, Ark: University of Arkansas Press.

Kershaw, B. and H. Nicholson (eds.) (2011) *Research Methods in Theatre and Performance*, Edinburgh: Edinburgh University Press.

Kindermann, H. (1957–74) *Theatergeschichte Europas* (10 vols.), Salzburg: Otto Müller.

Kircher, A. (1650) *Musurgia universalis sive ars magna consoni et dissoni*, Rome.

——. (1662) *Musurgia universalis*, trans. A. Hirsch, Schwäbisch: Hall.

Klaar, A. (1911) Review of Reinhardt's *Oresteia* in the *Vossische Zeitung*, 14 October.

——. (1918) "Bühne und Drama," in *Vossische Zeitung*, 30 July.

Klier, H. (ed.) (1981) *Theaterwissenschaft im deutschschprachigen Raum*, Darmstadt: Wissenschaftliche Buchgesellschaft.

Köpping, K. (2008) *Shattering Frames: Transgressions and Transformations in Anthropological Discourse and Practice*, Berlin: Dietrich Reimer.

Köpping, K.-P. and U. Rao (eds.) (2000) *Im Rausch des Rituals. Gestaltung und Transformation der Wirklichkeit in körperlicher Performanz*, Münster: LIT.

Koselleck, R. (2004) *Futures Past: On the Semantics of Historical Time*, trans. Keith Tribe, New York: Columbia University Press.

Koss, J. (2010) *Modernism after Wagner*, Minneapolis/London: University of Minnesota Press.

Kostelanetz, R. (1989) *Cage im Gespräch*, Cologne: DuMont.

Krämer, S. (1998) "Das Medium als Spur und Apparat" in Sybille Krämer (ed.), *Medien, Computer, Realität, Wirklichkeitsvorstellungen und neue Medien*, Frankfurt am Main: Suhrkamp.

Krasner, D. (ed.) (2008) *Theater in Theory: An Anthology*, Oxford: Blackwell Publishing.

Kuppers, P. and G. Robertson (eds.) (2007) *The Community Performance Reader: An Introduction*, London/New York: Routledge.

Kutscher, A. (1936) *Grundriss der Theaterwissenschaft*, Düsseldorf: Pflugschar.

Lacaze, L. (1755) *L'idée de l'homme physique et moral*, Paris: Guerin & Delatour.

Lagerroth, U., H. Lund, and E. Hedling (eds.) (1997) *Interart Poetics*, Amsterdam/Atlanta: Rodopoi.

Laurel, B (1992) *Computers as Theatre*, New York: Addison Wesley.

Lavater, Johann Caspar (1829) *Physiognomische Fragmente zur Beförderung der Menschenkenntnis und Menschenliebe* (1775–78), Wien.

Le Cat, C.-N. (1767) *Traité des sensations et des passions en général, et des sens en particulier*, 3 vols., Paris: Vallat-La-Chapelle.

Lee, S.-K. (1996) "Influence of Kabuki on European Theatre," in *Kabuki, International Symposium on the Conservation and Restoration of Cultural Property*, Tokyo: Tokyo National Research Institute of Cultural Properties: 73–82.

Lehmann, H.-T. (2002) *Postdramatic Theatre*, Karen Jürs-Munby (trans.), London/New York: Routledge.

Lessing, G. E. (1973) *Werke 4*, H. G. Goepfert (ed.), Munich: Hanser.

———. (1984) *Laocoön: An Essay on the Limits of Painting and Poetry*, E. A. McCormick (trans.), Baltimore: Johns Hopkins University Press.

———. (2012) *Hamburg Dramaturgy*, W. Arons and S. Figal (trans.), N. Baldyda and M. Chemers (eds.), Advanced publication on MediaCommons. Accessed April 21, 2013: http://mediacommons.futureofthebook.org/mcpress/hamburg

Lichtenberg, G. C. (1938) *Lichtenberg's Visits to England, as Described in His Letters and Diaries*, M. L. Mare and W. H. Quarrell (eds. and trans.), Oxford: Clarendon.

———. (1972) "Über Physiognomik; wider die Physiognomen. Zur Beförderung der Menschenliebe und Menschenkenntnis," in *Schriften und Briefen*, 3 vols., W. Promies (ed.), Munich: Hanser: 256–95.

Lin, K. (2009) *Westlicher Geist im östlicher Körper?—Medea im interkulturellen Theater Chinas und Taiwans: "Universalisierung" des griechischen Antike*, Bielefeld: transcript.

Litteratur- und Theaterzeitung (Berlin, May 22, 1784a).

Litteratur- und Theaterzeitung (Berlin, July 3, 1784b).

Litzmann, B. (1890 and 1894) *Friedrich Ludwig Schröder: Ein Beitrag zur deutschen Literatur- und Theatergeschichte*, 2 vols., Hamburg/Leipzig: Voss.

Löwen, J. F. (1766) *Geschichte des deutschen Theaters*, reprinted 1905, H. Stümke (ed.), Berlin.

Luhmann, N. (1985) "Das Problem der Epochenbildung und die Evolutionstheorie," in H.-U. Gumbrecht and U. Link-Heer (eds.) *Epochenschwelle und Epochenstruktur im Diskurs der Literatur- und Sprachtheorie*, Frankfurt: Suhrkamp.

Macready, W. C. (1875) *Macready's Reminiscences and Selections from his Diaries and Letters*, F. Pollock (ed.), New York: Harper and Brothers.

Makkerras, C. (1983) *Chinese Theatre: From Its Origins to the Present Day*, Honolulu: University of Hawaii Press.

Marranca, B. and G. Dasgupta (eds.) (2001) *Interculturalism and Performance*, New York: PAJ Publications.

Matthews, B. (1972/1903) *The Development of Drama*. Freeport, NY: Books for Libraries Press.

McCarthy, J. (2004) *Enacting Participatory Developments—Theatre-Based Technique*, London: Earthscan.

McGregor, L., M. Tate, and K. Robinson (1977) *Learning through Drama*, London/New York: Routledge.

McKenzie, J. (2001) *Perform or Else: From Discipline to Performance*, London/New York: Routledge.

Mda, Z. (1993) *When People Play People: Development Communication through Theatre*, London: Zed Books.

Mead, G. H. (1934) *Mind, Self, and Society: From the Point of View of a Social Behavioralist*, Chicago: University of Chicago Press.

Merleau-Ponty, M. (1962) *Phenomenology of Perception*, London: Routledge and Kegan Paul.

Meyerhold, V. (1969) "The Actor of the Future and Biomechanics," in E. Braun (ed.), *Meyerhold on Theatre*, New York: Hill and Wang.

——. (1974) "Rezension des Buches 'Aufzeichnungen eines Regisseurs' von A. Ja. Tairov (1921/22)," in R. Tietze (ed.), *Vsevolod Meyerhold: Theaterarbeit 1917–1930*, Munich: Hanser: 63–72.

Mouchart, I. D. (1792–1803) *Allgemeines Repertorium für empirische Psychologie und verwandte Wissenschaften*.

Mukařovský, J. (1970) *Aesthetic Function, Norm and Value as Social Facts*, Ann Arbor: Michigan University Press.

Münz, R. (1998a) "'Theater—eine Leistung des Publikums und seiner Diener': Zu Max Herrmanns Vorstellungen von Theater," in E. Fischer-Lichte, D. Kolesch, and C. Weiler (eds.), *Berliner Theater im 20. Jahrhundert*, Berlin: Fannei & Walz: 43–52.

——. (1998b) "Giullari nudi, Goliarden und 'Freiheiter'," in *Theatralität und Theater: Zur Historiographie von Theatralitätsgefügen*, Berliner: Schwarzkopf & Schwarzkopf: 104–40.

Murray, G. (1912) "Excursus on the Ritual Forms Preserved in Tragedy," in J. E. Harrison (ed.), *Themis: A Study of the Social Origin of Greek Religion*, Cleveland/New York: Macmillan, 1962: 341–63.

Murray, J. H. (1997) *Hamlet on the Holodeck: The Future of Narrative in Cyberspace*, New York: The Free Press.

Nelle, F. (2006) "Bernini und das Experiment der Katastrophe," in H. Schramm, L. Schwarte, and J. Lazardzig (eds.), *Spektakulaere Experimente: Praktiken der Evidenzproduktion im 17. Jahrhundert*, Berlin/New York: de Gruyter: 114–130.

Nicholson, H. (2005) *Applied Drama: The Gift of Theatre*, Basingstoke: Palgrave Macmillan.

Nicholl, A. (1923–59) *A History of English Drama*, 6 vols., Cambridge: Cambridge University Press.

Niessen, C. (1927) "Aufgaben der Theaterwissenschaft," in *Die Scene, Blätter für Bühnenkunst* 17: 44–49.

Nilu, K. (2008) "*A Doll's House* in Asia: Juxtaposition of Tradition and Modernity," in *Ibsen Studies* 8.2: 112–33.

Okagbue, O. (2007) *African Theatre and Performance*, London/New York: Routledge.

Ortolani, B. (1995) *The Japanese Theatre: From Shamanistic Ritual to Contemporary Pluralism*, Princeton, NJ: Princeton University Press.

Pantzer, P. (ed.) (2005) *Japanischer Theaterhimmel über Europas Bühnen: Kawakami Otojirô, Sadayakko und ihre Truppe auf Tournee durch Mittel-und Osteuropa 1901/1902*, Munich: Iudicium.

Pannewick, F. (2000) *Das Wagnis Tradition: arabische Wege der Theatralität*, Wiesbaden: Reichert.

Pavis, P. (ed.) (1982) *Languages of the Stage: Essays in the Semiology of the Theatre*, New York: Performing Arts Journal Publications.

——. (1996) *The Intercultural Performance Reader*, Abingdon/New York: Routledge.

——. and C. Shanty (eds.) (1998) "Cross-Cultural Theatre," in *Dictionary of the Theatre*, Toronto: University of Toronto Press.

Plamper, J. (2009) "Emotional Turn? Feeling in Russian History and Culture," *Slavic Review* 68: 229–37.

Plessner, H. (1970) *Laughing and Crying: A Study of the Limits of Human Behavior*, trans. J. S. Churchill and M. Grene, Evanston, IL: Northwestern University Press.

——. (1982) "Zur Anthropologie des Schauspielers," in G. Dux, O. Marquard, and E. Stroeker (eds.) *Gesammelte Schriften*, Frankfurt am Main: Suhrkamp: 399–418.

Pockel, K. F. (1788/89) *Beiträge zur Beförderung der Menschenkenntnis, besonders in Rücksicht unserer moralischen Natur*, Berlin: Vieweg.

Postlewait, T. (2009) *The Cambridge Introduction to Theatre Historiography*, Cambridge: Cambridge University Press.

Postlewait, T. and B. A. McConachi (eds.) (1989) *Interpreting the Theatrical Past*, Iowa City: Iowa University Press.

Prendergast, M. and J. Saxton (2009) *Applied Theatre, International Case Studies and Challenges for Practice*, Bristol: Intellect Publishers.

Prentki, T. and S. Preston (2008) *The Applied Theatre Reader*. London/ New York: Routledge.

Pronko, L. (1967) *Theatre East & West: Perspectives Towards a Total Theatre*, Berkeley: University of California Press.

Puchner, M. (2002) *Stage Fright: Modernism, Anti-Theatricality, and Drama*, Baltimore: Johns Hopkins University Press.

Reaves, J. (1995) "Theory and Practice: The Gertrude Stein Repertory Theatre," *CyberStage* 1.3. Accessed April 20, 2012: http://www.cyberstage.org/archive/cstage13/gsrt13.html

Reinelt, J. and J. Roach (2007) *Critical Theory and Performance: Revised and Enlarged Edition*, Ann Arbor: University of Michigan Press.

Review of the Kawakami Troupe (1900a) "Chronique de l'Exposition," in *Mercure de France*: 480–85.

Review of the Kawakami Troupe (1900b) in *Le Théâtre* 44, October.

Review of the Kawakami Troupe (1901a) in *The Graphic*, June 22.

Review of the Kawakami Troupe (1901b) in *ILN* June 22.

Review of the Kawakami Troupe (1901c) in *The Sketch*, June 22.

Review of the Kawakami Troupe (1901d) in *The Sketch*, June 26.

Review of the Kawakami Troupe (1902) in *Der Neue Rundschau* 13.1.

Riley, R. and L. Hunter (eds.) (2009) *Mapping Landscapes for Performance as Research: Scholarly Acts and Creative Cartographies*, New York: Palgrave Macmillan.

Roach, J. (1996) *Cities of the Dead: Circum-Atlantic Performance*, New York: Columbia University Press.

——. (1999) "Reconstructing Theatre/History," in *Theatre Topics* 9.1: 3–10.

Roberts, D. (2001) *The Total Work of Art in European Modernism*, Ithaca, NY: Cornell University Press.

Roselt, J. (ed.) (2005) *Seelen mit Methode: Schauspieltheorien vom Barock bis zum postdramatischen Theater*, Berlin: Alexander.

——. (2008) *Phänomenologie des Theaters, Übergänge*, vol. 56, Munich: Fink.

Rüsen, J. (1990) *Zeit und Sinn: Strategien historischen Denkens*, Frankfurt am Main: Fischer.

Rüsen, J., E. Lámmert, and P. Glotz (eds.) (1988) *Die Zukunft der Aufklärung*, Frankfurt am Main: Suhrkamp.

Said, E. (1993) *Culture and Imperialism*, New York: Knopf.

Sato, T. (1981) "Ibsen's Drama and the Japanese Bluestockings," in *Edda* 5: 265–93.

Sauter, W. (ed.) (1988) *New Directions in Audience Research*, Utrecht: Institut voor Theaterwetenschap.

Schachter, D. (1996) *Searching for Memory: The Brain, the Mind, and the Past*, New York: Basic Books.

Schechner, R. (1985) *Between Theatre and Anthropology*, Philadelphia: University of Pennsylvania Press.

——. (1988) *Performance Theory*, revised and expanded edition, London/New York: Routledge.

——. (1992) "A New Paradigm for Theatre in the Academy," *The Drama Review* 36.4: 7–10.

Scheflen, A. E. (1973) *Body Language and the Social Order*, New York: Prentice Hall.

——. (1974) *How Behavior Means*, New York: Anchor Press.

Schiller, F. (1795/2004) *On the Aesthetic Education of Man*, R. Snell (trans.), New York: Dover.

Schininà, G. (2004a) "Here We Are: Social Theatre and Some Open Questions about Its Developments," in *The Drama Review* 48.3: 17–31.

——. (2004b) "'Far Away, So Close': Psychological and Theatre Activities with Serbian Refugees," in *The Drama Review* 48.3: 32–49.

Schink, J. F. (1818) *Zeitgenossen*, Leipzig: Brockhaus.

Schmid, F. E. (1796–98) *Psychologisches Magazin*, 3 vols.

Schneede, U. M. (1994) *Joseph Beuys—Die Aktionen, Kommentiertes Werkverzeichnis mit fotografisher Dokumentation*, Ostfildern-Ruit: Cantz.

Scholz-Cionca, S. and S. L. Leiter (eds.) (2001) *Japanese Theatre and the International Stage*, Leiden: Brill.

Schramm, H. L., L. Schwarte, and J. Lazardzig (ed.) (2005) *Collection, Laboratory, Theatre: Scenes of Knowledge in the Seventeenth Century*, Berlin/New York: Walter de Gruyter.

Schütze, J. F. (1794) *Hamburgische Theatergeschichte*, Hamburg: Treder. Reprinted 1975, Leipzig: Zentralantiquariat der DDR.

Schutzman, M. and J. Cohen-Cruz (eds.) (1994) *Playing Boal: Theatre, Therapy, Activism*, London: Routledge.

Sedgwick, E. K. and A. Parker (1995) *Performativity and Performance*, London: Routledge.

Seltmann, F. (1986) *Schattenspiel in Kerala, sakrales Theater in Süd-Indien*, Stuttgart: Steiner.

Senelick, L. (2000) *The Changing Room: Sex, Drag and the Theatre*, London and New York: Routledge.

Sennett, R. (1977) *The Fall of Public Man*, New York: Knopf.

Shevtsova, M. (2007) *Robert Wilson*, London/New York: Routledge.

Shusterman, R. (2001) "Art as Dramatization," *Journal of Aesthetics and Art Criticism* 59.4: 361–72.

Simmel, G. (1968) "Zur Philosophe des Schauspielers," in G. Simmel, *Das individuelle Gesetz: Philosophische Exkurse*, Frankfurt am Main: Suhrkamp, 75–95.

Singer, M. (ed.) (1959) *Traditional India: Structure and Change*, Philadelphia: American Folklore Society.

Smith, M. W. (2007) *The Total Work of Art: From Bayreuth to Cyberspace*, London/New York: Routledge.

Spivak, G. (1999) *A Critique of Postcolonial Reason: Toward a History of the Vanishing Point*, Cambridge, MA: Harvard University Press.

States, B. (1985) *Great Reckonings in Little Rooms: On the Phenomenology of Theatre*, Berkeley/London/Los Angeles: University of California Press.

Steadman, P. (1996) "Bakai: yanchu de yiyi" (The Meaning of the Performance Bakai), trans. L. Yü-hua, in *China Peking Opera* 2.

Steinbeck, D. (1970) *Einleitung in die Theorie und Systematik der Theaterwissenschaft*, Berlin: de Gruyter.

Steinweg, Reiner (1986) "Ein 'Theater der Zukunft': Über die Arbeit von Angelus Novus am Beispiel von Brecht und Homer," in *Falter* 23: 20–29.

Stierle, K. (1984) "Das bequeme Verhältnis. Lessings *Laokoon* und die Entdeckung des ästhetischen Mediums," in *Das Laokoon-Projekt. Pläne einer semiotischen Ästhetik*, Gunter Gebauer (ed.), Stuttgart: Metzler: 23–58.

Szeemann, H. (ed.) (1983) *Der Hang zum Gesamtkunstwerk, Europäische Utopien seit 1800*, Aarau/Frankfurt am Main: Sauerländer.

Tatinge Nascimento, C. (2009) *Crossing Cultural Borders through the Actor's Work*, New York/London: Routledge.

Taylor, D (1991) *Theatre of Crisis: Drama and Politics in Latin America*, Lexington, KY: University Press of Kentucky.

Taylor, F. W. (1911) *The Principles of Scientific Management*, New York: Harper and Brothers.

Taylor, P. (2003) *Applied Theatre: Creating Transformative Encounter in the Community*, Portsmouth, NH: Heinemann.

Thirouin, L. (ed.) (1998) *Pierre Nicole, Traité de la comédie et autres pièces d'un process du theater*, Paris: Champion.

Thompson, J. (ed.) (1997) *Prison Theatre—Perspectives and Practices*, London/New York: Jessica Kingsley.

——. (2003) *Applied Theatre: Bewilderment and Beyond*, Berne: Peter Lang.

——. (2004) "Digging Up Stories: An Archaeology of Theatre in War," *The Drama Review* 48.3: 150–64.

Tilly, C. (2004) *Social Movements, 1768–2004*, Boulder, CO/London: Paradigm Publishers.

Tschudin, J.-J. (1998) "Early Meiji Kabuki and Western Theatre: A Rendez-vous Manque" in *Kabuki, International Symposium on the Conservation and Restoration of Cultural Property*, Tokyo: Tokyo National Research Institute of Cultural Properties: 183–93.

Turner, V. (1969) *The Ritual Process: Structure and Anti-Structure*, London: Routledge & Kegan Paul.

——. (1977) "Variations on a Theme of Liminality," in *Secular Rites*, S. F. Moore and B. C. Myerhoff (eds.), Assen: Van Gorcum: 36–57.

——. (1982) *From Ritual to Theatre: The Human Seriousness of Play*, New York: Performing Arts Journal Publications.

——. (1987) *The Anthropology of Performance*, New York: Performing Arts Journal Publications.

Umathum, S. (2011) *Kunst als Aufführungserfahrung*, Bielefeld: transcript.

Varapande, M. L. (1987) *History of Indian Theatre*, New Delhi: Abhinav Publications.

Wagner, C. (1976/1977) *Die Tagebücher, 1869–1883*, vol. 2, M. Gregor-Dellin and D. Mack (eds.), Munich: Piper.

Wagner, R. (1895) *Richard Wagner's Prose Works*, trans. W. A. Ellis, London: K. Paul, Trench, Trübner & Co.

Warstat, M. (2005) *Theatrale Gemeinschaften: Zur Festkultur der Arbeiterbewegung 1918–33*, Tübingen/Basel: Francke.

——. (2009) *Krise und Heilung: Wirkungsästhetiken des Theaters*, Munich: Fink.

Warstat, M., J. Lazardzig, and V. Tkaczyk (2012) *Theaterhistoriographie: Eine Einführung*, Tübingen/Basel: Francke.

Weber, S. (2004) *Theatricality as Medium*, New York: Fordham University Press.

Wellberry, D. (1984) *Lessing's Laocoon: Semiotics and Aesthetics in the Age of Reason*, Cambridge: Cambridge University Press.

White, H. (1973) *Metahistory: The Historical Imagination in Nineteenth Century Europe*, Baltimore: Johns Hopkins University Press.

Wiles, D. (2003) *A Short History of Western Performance Space*, Cambridge: Cambridge University Press.

Wiles, D. and C. Dymkowski (eds.) (2013), *The Cambridge Companion to Theatre History*, Cambridge: Cambridge University Press.

Williams, R. M. (2003) *Teaching the Arts Behind Bars*, Boston: Northeastern.

Withington, R. (1918) *English Pageantry: A Historical Outline*, Cambridge, MA: Harvard University Press.

Yates, F. (1966/2001) *The Art of Memory*. Chicago: Chicago University Press.

Zarrilli, P. B. (2000) *Kathakali Dance-Drama: Where Gods and Demons Come to Play*, New York: Routledge.

Zarrilli, P. B., B. McConachie, G. J. Williams, and C. F. Sorgenfrei (2006) *Theatre Histories: An Introduction*, New York/London: Routledge.

Index of names and performance groups

Subject index

Index of works